tOMORROW AND tOMORROW

LAUREN EMILY WHALEN
& LILLAH LAWSON

toMorrow
AND
toMorrow

LAUREN EMILY WHALEN
& LILLAH LAWSON

Sword and Silk Books
1353 West 48th St, 4th Flr PMB 382, New York, NY 10036
Visit our website at SwordandSilkBooks.com
To request permissions, contact the publisher at admin@swordandsilk-books.com.

First Edition: OCT 2023

LILLAH:

For Mom

the original Teresa-Jo(sephine), and the reason I love Joan Jett

LAUREN:

For Abby

May you always rock (but don't read this 'til you're in high school)

PROLOGUE

"A little water clears us of this deed." — *Macbeth*, Act II, Scene I
"In pop music, you say, 'you can do what you want to me.' Rock n' roll
says, 'I'm gonna do what I want to YOU.'" —Joan Jett

TWO young women stood at the edge of the cliff, the scuffed toes of
their heeled shoes hanging over, clinging to each other, eyes squinting
in the ever-darkening twilight. A light drizzle had begun to fall, and
the moon had disappeared. A moment before, the round moon hung
there in the sky like a full pitcher, spilling moonlight across the cool,
damp ground, illuminating the reddish cliff and the muted green grass
beneath their feet in an effervescent light. Now, the sky was murky and
gray, like dirty charcoal.

Below, the fine, cool raindrops—little more than a misting—
landed on the sharp, gray rocks and mingled with the blood that

pooled there, thinning it and turning it pink. As the girls watched soundlessly, the puddle turned into a thin stream, collecting on the largest rock—the one that held the body—until it spilled over, mixing with the dark ocean water, running and running off the rock until the rain had gently cleansed it all away.

The girls huddled inside their jackets for warmth, bracing themselves against the cold Scottish wind that whipped around their hair and prickled at their flesh. Beneath them, the thin, light-blue tartan was lifted by the breeze and began to flap, whipping around pale, motionless legs, one laying at an unnatural angle. The wind picked up the strands of reddish hair, hair that had been in want of a haircut only an hour before, but now had no need of such things. A ginger five o'clock shadow nestled against a cheek that would no longer break into a dimpled smile. The wind fluttered an eyelash which once framed a blue iris, but now lay at eternal rest. The hands, scratched and bleeding, piano-fine fingers clutched together as though in prayer, clasped beneath the neck, like those of a sleeping child. A body in repose, at peace.

He was dead. He was surely dead.

And yet... was that a twitch of a leg, or a figment of hope, of imagination?

A jerk, a groan.

Oh god, oh god, oh god.

A new pool of blood had formed, and again it trickled off the rocks to mingle its salt with the salt of the North Sea.

It was a trick of the light. It wasn't real. No body that broken could survive.

The girls simply stared, unable to move—staring at the flapping blue kilt that seemed to wave like a flag of surrender and the once proud, now sad body shrouded in it, the fine mist of rain dampening their hair, their jackets, and finally their bones, until at last they felt the cold and began to stir, to blink, to realize what must be done.

It would be full dark soon.

Slowly, as though themselves underwater, the girls turned to one another, in lockstep, their legs and feet moving in tandem as though they were one body, one soul.

The dark-haired girl looked at the blonde one with wide, scared eyes. A deer caught in the headlights. Her face pale, her lips even paler, she uttered the words so quietly it was almost as though she hadn't spoken at all.

"Help him...or leave him?"

The second girl reached up with trembling fingers to push a strand of light hair from her forehead, a rivulet running down her cheek that might have been a tear—might have, had the circumstances been different.

Her shoulders convulsed in a shudder, which she held off at the pass and managed to disguise as a shrug. She swallowed hard and took a deep breath, bringing the salt of the sea air deep into her lungs, and spoke, her voice full of resolve.

The rain ceased as suddenly as it had begun, the mist floating away on the cold wind, a wind that felt like a reckoning.

"Leave him."

A cloud parted, and the moon revealed herself once more, white and cold and full of possibility.

No more words were spoken. The girls turned on their heels in the wet grass and walked away from the cliff with no backward glances.

The stars, their fires extinguished in the dampened sky, were the only ones to bear them witness.

CHAPTER ONE:

DUFF

"We wanted to shock people because we knew it was gonna blow people's minds to see teenage girls play sweaty, hard, serious rock and roll. And it did." —Joan Jett

I was ripped from my mother's womb.

C-sections happen every day. But according to Granny Devereaux, who'd had one too many glasses of red wine one Christmas, the one that brought me into the world was different. Unplanned, because I wouldn't come out the regular way. Urgent, because I was in distress, meaning I'd gone to the bathroom while I was still inside and therefore was at risk of poisoning myself (I was *eight* when I heard this). And very, very painful.

They shaved my mom "down there," Granny recalled, oddly nostalgic considering she was recalling the bald junk of her progeny.

Many drugs, screams, and attempted kicks to the doctor's head later, the medical team cut my mother open. By that time, my newborn self was also screaming and various bodily fluids from my mother splattered the walls. Like a really disgusting Van Gogh painting is how I picture it, yellow and red and brown and vile bile.

Five years before, my sister Elizabeth was born all-natural and drug-free, an eight-hour labor. Four years after, my sister Michelle was also a C-section, nice and scheduled and vile bile-free. But my birth basically set the stage for me, feeling like the odd girl out in the smart, pretty, generally on top O'Brien family of Grosse Pointe, Michigan.

On the night I was ripped out, no one was allowed in the hospital room outside of my dad and various medical staff. Being the stubborn Southerner she was, Granny Devereaux didn't listen to reason and, certain her only child wasn't going to survive the labor, ran into the hospital room to deliver her final words.

Sticking her head in the doorway before anyone could oust her, she yelled in the direction of my mom's hairless vulva, "I just wanted to let you know I love you!"

And my mom screamed back, "Get the fuck *OUT!*"

Seventeen years later, I moved to North Georgia. Just me.

Just like Granny Devereaux's story, it started with a pregnancy. Only this time, it was mine.

"I wish she hadn't told you," I muttered to my mom as we sat in the clinic's waiting room after mandatory "counseling" (a video that wasn't that horrifying considering the alternative).

My mom put down her copy of the latest "lean in" businesswoman how-to and took my hand, threading her fingers through mine in a way she hadn't done since I was little. "Elizabeth was worried, sweetheart," she said gently. "I know she can be…"

"Bitchy?" I offered.

"*Harsh,*" Mom corrected, tamping down a smile. "But she has the GRE and school exams coming up, and she wanted to make sure we were there for you."

"Duffy O'Brien?" A heavyset male nurse in scrubs looked my way expectantly, his deep baritone drawing the attention of terrified girls, younger women, and types who strongly resembled my own mother, all of us awaiting our fate.

Just then, my phone lit up with a message from my friend Julia. *Christine, Brayden, Jordan. And Julia, of course!* With an emoji of a big-eyed baby. Potential baby names from the former friend and born-again Christian who was judging me like crazy.

Squeezing my hand, my mom let go so I could proceed.

Tell Mom or I will, read the text from my older sister Elizabeth. *I won't tell her how it happened, though. Promise.*

Months earlier, out of sheer boredom and on a dare from Julia, who was very much *not* a born-again Christian at that point, I'd signed up for Tinder and swiped right, lying about my age the whole way. Looking back, I wonder if he knew how old I was, if he was practiced in sussing out naïve suburban girls. And really, what do you say about someone who doesn't even ask a person's last name and has sex with her on three different occasions in a car before ghosting her? Nothing positive, that's for goddamn sure.

The sex happened in the spring. In the early summer after I finished my junior year, my period *didn't* happen. In late summer, frantic, I texted Elizabeth and told her everything. That's when she, in her obnoxious early twenty-something I-know-everything way, gave me the ultimatum. Figuring I had two options, and I was definitely not having a baby, I cornered my mom just after she told my twelve-year-old sister Michelle good night. But she already knew.

Liz was, at least, partly as good as her word; she was still the only person who knew the whole story.

Would I have told my parents if they *had* asked? Even now, years removed, I don't know. I don't regret my abortion, of course I don't. I was a literal child knocked up by a lowlife. This was my best option, and I took it. And my family supported me through and through. I know that's a lot more than most in that clinic waiting room could say.

I swallowed my pride and my residual anger at Liz, and swallowed the first pill in a small, sterile room while a heavyset male nurse and an older female gynecologist watched, their eyes full of pity I didn't want to acknowledge. "How was it?" my mother, who never even looked at another dude after she met my dad, let alone terminated a pregnancy, asked when I returned. I shrugged. What was there to say?

That night, Mom sat outside the bathroom as I stuck the second pill, to paraphrase Granny, up my down there. At least no one had to shave me. She was ready with everything from maxi pads to hot tea with honey to my favorite homemade chocolate chip cookies in the recovery days after. My dad and Michelle, who had barely put away her American Girl dolls, were informed of the circumstances and reminded that it absolutely wasn't my fault.

Right after I stuck the pill up myself, wincing as I withdrew my fingers, my phone buzzed. More baby names—*Samantha, Duke, Marie*—from Julia, who, despite ignoring me in school for my *terrible choice,* held out hope that I'd save my baby for Jesus and myself for marriage. She always did have shitty timing.

I was not prepared for the ensuing depression that came from being pumped full of feel-good early-pregnancy hormones and then... emptiness. I missed more of the first month of school than I attended—my mom would knock on the door gently and peek in, I'd turn away, she wouldn't push and would go to work, having my sister bring me homework I ignored. All while I lay in bed streaming the same three TV shows over and over. And in the meantime, I was craving banana pudding and thinking about simpler times: summers in North Georgia where I caught fireflies and sneaked bites of pie crust and hadn't even heard of Tinder.

Is it any wonder I went to my parents and said, "I need Granny"?

I still had to go to high school.

"But whyyyyyy?" I whined that Sunday night when I arrived in Hiawassee, autumn leaves blooming in the mountains and Granny's house—now my house too—smelling like it always did, of cinnamon and nutmeg and pure goodness. "I could get my GED and work for you full-time at the restaurant. We all win!"

"Your parents and I agreed, honey," Granny said, serving me a second helping of candied sweet potatoes I hadn't asked for but really, really wanted. She was intuitive like that—as the owner and operator of Devereaux BBQ, Hiawassee's go-to joint, she had to be. "You can wait tables on evenings and weekends, much as you want, but studies come first."

Like the rest of my family, Granny didn't judge my abortion—she was a God-fearing Southern woman who gave to Planned Parenthood regularly and even served as a clinic escort before she shattered a knee— and she welcomed me with open arms and a hell of a first dinner. But like any Southern woman of a certain age, she was sweet as pie *and* stubborn as a mule.

"Don't you roll your eyes at me, Duffy Kate," Granny said, using the special combination of my first and middle names like she had since I was born, squalling and bloody and freshly ripped away from Mom. Her gentle smile softened the harsh words. "We all talked about this, 'member?"

"Yes, ma'am," I muttered, scooping another mouthful of sweet potato. I swear, this side dish tasted like unicorns and angels and dreams.

Granny reached across the oak table she'd gotten for her wedding, squeezing my hand just like my mom had at the clinic. "I love that you're here, honey." The wrinkles around her eyes deepened as she smiled, and I could see the tears at the corners. Her youth, and subsequent marriage to my long-departed Papa, hadn't been easy either. "But we all want you to finish high school the regular way. You can do it. I have faith."

Sentimental moment over, Granny stood up and brushed off her hands, motioning for me to help clear the many dishes of fried chicken, sweet potatoes, and greens. We'd have homemade pie and tea in the living room after cleanup, as was tradition. She looked at me. "How 'bout we set three Hiawassee ground rules?" I opened my mouth to protest—the last thing I wanted was a curfew or something childish like that—and she held up a hand. "No, not like that. Go to school. Come to work. Make a friend. That's all you gotta do and Granny'll be happy."

I loved my granny, and I knew what a big deal it was, her welcoming me into her house full-time for at least the next several months. I could do those three things for her.

Go to school. Come to work. Make a friend.

Fat chance of that last one, I thought when I entered the high school's main hallway the next morning. It didn't look that different from my old school. Maybe a little rougher around the edges, but it had the same faintly carbolic odor and ugly linoleum that you only see in institutional hallways. The kids were dressed a little more casually than my former classmates, in worn jeans and hoodies rather than preppy put-together outfits, their voices drawlier, their eyes trying not to bore holes through me, the new girl. This was the type of place where everyone had been together since kindergarten.

Whatever. I accepted my fate as an outsider. I planned to keep my head down and get my diploma and then... I didn't know, but it would be big.

And then I saw her.

Petite but she looked strong, with broad shoulders and big hands for her size, what Granny would call "small but mighty." At five-ten, I felt like a gawky giant next to her. She had a funky, layered haircut I'd learn was called a "shag," most popular in the 1970s. A flannel shirt that looked like it belonged to a boyfriend or an older brother. Lace-up shitkicker boots and a barbell pierced in the middle of her nose. And in the middle of her delicate face, bright blue eyes that fixed right on me.

Turned out, her locker was right next to mine.

"I'm Marian," she said. "Marian Shepherd. You can call me Marian or Mac, I don't care." I didn't know this girl but I had the gut feeling, right then and there, I'd see her name in lights sooner rather than later.

"Can I call you both?" Look at me, brand new and already bantering.

Marian/Mac snorted. Like I was being funny, not like I was being stupid. I hoped. Those bright eyes looked at me expectantly. "'N yew arrrrrre…" I could tell she was exaggerating her Southern drawl for the Midwesterner, just like Granny did for out-of-town tourists. Still, a valid question.

I hesitated. I'd always been plain old Katie at school in Grosse Pointe, ever since pre-K when the other kids—including Julia, ugh—thought my real first name was weird. At home, my parents and sisters called me Duffy. Granny had always called me Duffy Kate, in true Southern fashion.

But now I had an opportunity to be someone else, a whole new version of Duffy Katherine Devereaux O'Brien. A fallen angel with a turbulent past, but in a sexy way. And a consistent human who used the same name everywhere. Much less messy.

"Duff," I said, extending my hand. I didn't know if kids in Hiawassee shook hands. Hell, *I* didn't shake hands in Grosse Pointe, but I guess Duff of North Georgia did.

Marian's face lit up, and she took my hand. "Miz Devereaux's girl?" I must have looked confused—it's not like Granny and I had the same last name. She shrugged. "Small town. Plus, my mama works there sometimes. What's your first class?"

"English."

"Mine too." She shouldered her backpack. "Let's go."

What followed over the next few months could easily be a movie montage: the two of us became inseparable. She was a vegetarian, but

Granny always had her famous mac and cheese on hand when Marian visited me at work, which was often. Turns out Granny knew Marian's mom, Annie, pretty well. Small towns, man. Speaking of Annie, she didn't mind if we drank and smoked—pot *or* cigarettes. Marian didn't give a shit about school but was smarter than I was and let me copy if I needed to pass a test or was especially hungover before a paper was due.

Marian helped me bleach my hair from its natural dishwater blonde so it almost glowed—something I'd *always* wanted to do, but as Katie/Duffy, never had the nerve. Pretty soon I even started dressing like her: putting away my bland clearance Gap and stocking up on skinny jeans and secondhand lace-up boots, layering vintage slips over fishnet stockings when I was feeling real fancy. I perfected my thick, black-winged eyeliner (thanks to Annie, actually), had several new holes punched in my left ear at the local tattoo parlor, but left the bright makeup and barbell to Marian.

Granny started calling us "two peas in a pod" and we rolled our eyes and giggled at the cliché, but from the way Marian, who wasn't normally a hugger, put her arm around me and squeezed hard the first time Granny said it, I could tell she was genuinely happy. I was too. As my eye makeup got darker, my mood got lighter and lighter.

But our life together wasn't all wardrobe and makeup. We donned leggings and boots and went hiking almost every weekend. She pointed out the best fall foliage, and we staged impromptu photo shoots, then tucked into Granny-catered picnics atop Brasstown Bald: North Georgia at its most stunning. I'd *never* hiked before and hadn't pictured cool, tough Marian chugging water as she dodged stray rocks, but she told me it was the most peaceful she felt sober, and then I started to feel it too.

When we weren't at school or working up a sweat and breathing in crisp mountain air on the weekends, we drove into Athens, flashing our fake IDs (hers procured when she was fourteen, mine bright and shiny and bought from a random UGA senior). We didn't drink much because we had to drive back, but the cute college boys and live music, the likes of it I'd never heard in Grosse Pointe, even the clumsiest guitar work like a pulsating heartbeat, made up for it. And the latter ended up changing the course of our lives.

I still remember pulling the bass guitar from a pile of random crap at our fave Athens vintage store on a Saturday. Late afternoon light danced on the smudged glass windows and the instrument seemed to glow. It was missing a string and was pretty banged up, but I swear that bass *winked* at me. Like a dare.

"You should get it," Marian said. I must have given her a "yeah, right" look, because she nodded really hard. "Yeah. I'll chip in if you need it and you can pay me back whenever."

"I literally almost failed recorder in fourth grade," I said. "*Recorder*, Mac."

She grinned. "So, why are you still holding it?"

I snorted, a twelve-year-old at heart when it came to humor.

"No, really," Marian said. "We can jam. I play guitar."

That was news to me, who currently spent all my time with her unless I was sleeping, and sometimes even then. "Since when?"

"Okay, it was my dad's, and it's in our storage room," Marian said, suddenly finding the toes of her Chucks very interesting. She didn't like talking about her "deddy," I learned real quick. "But he taught me a little bit. And I can learn more." Her bright blue eyes flashed as she looked back up at me. "Seriously. You're, like, fated to play that bass."

"What the hell are you talking about, Mac?"

"Duh," Marian said. I must have looked confused, because her face softened. "There's a famous bass player in Guns N' Roses and Velvet Revolver. McKagan." A dramatic pause. *"Duff* McKagan."

By now, I realized I was cradling the instrument like a Madonna in a painting cradling her sacred child. Marian was right. I didn't want to let it go.

And I didn't: not when we paid up front (I had just enough tip money scrounged away thanks to Devereaux BBQ's weekly after-church crowd), not when we indulged in Golden Bowls and Smelts and kept an eye out for famous musicians at The Grit, our favorite restaurant, not when Marian blew up the air mattress in my room and cracked, "You gonna have sex with that thing?"

"Fuck you," I said with love, stroking the neck of the bass suggestively before turning out the same lamp my mom used when she was in high school. "Tomorrow."

"Tomorrow," she replied, a laugh in her voice. Early on, Marian told me she didn't like the word "goodbye." I thought it was probably because of her dad, somehow, but the guarded set of her jaw suggested I'd get my ass kicked if I asked. Instead, I suggested an alternative, and it became our goodbye, our good morning, and our good night. A call and response. Tomorrow and tomorrow.

From then on, when I wasn't at the restaurant, at school, or with Marian, I was holed up in my room with my bass. Marian helped me find YouTube videos, and I taught myself how to read music. She dragged over her dad's guitar, and we rehearsed in Granny's garage, just like Dave Grohl, one of our heroes, and generations of musicians before him. And just like Grohl famously said, at first, we sucked. We really sucked. But as fall kicked into a slightly colder winter (and I horrified Mac with tales of snowdrifts three feet high and parkas that felt like wearing mattresses) we started to suck a little less.

Mac never learned to read music, but as she pointed out, "neither does Lindsey Buckingham," who we agreed was one of the greatest guitar players of all time.

"And neither does Taylor Swift," I pointed out, gently poking fun at her music snobbery. Me, I was listening to Taylor obsessively. Her songs weren't all my style, necessarily, but girl could write a song. And I wanted to learn.

In that garage, I started making what would be our first hit.

But we had miles to go before any of that.

I knew Quincy Banks. Everyone did. She was senior class president, a chipper morning announcer in first period over the crackly intercom system, singing the national anthem with a surprisingly deep and sultry voice at pep rallies. Mac and I usually cut those, but we stayed long enough to hear her.

Quincy was strikingly beautiful. Like Disney Princess-Barbie doll beautiful. Like HBO streaming series about angsty teens who are actually played by twenty-five-year-old models beautiful. We're talking tiny waist, big boobs, muscular legs, ocean-blue eyes, and waist-length blonde hair.

Quincy Banks didn't hang out with the likes of Mac and me at first. She wasn't a bitch; in fact, she always smiled and said hi to us in the hallways, even when some of the popular crowd called us freaks stuck in the '90s. When I bleached my hair, she told me she'd always wanted to do that too, but didn't have the guts. And I could tell she meant it.

Mac thought she secretly wanted to be like us. We were, Mac claimed, the cool kids who sneaked into clubs, cut class, and didn't give a shit what people thought. I scoffed and rolled my eyes. What the fuck could *Quincy Banks* want that the two of us had? I wasn't sure we were all that cool.

But after Thanksgiving midterms, Quincy Banks quit her post as senior class president, chopped her waist-length golden hair into a piecey bob, and one day, without explanation, sat down at our lunch table. Soon, she was the third member of our unofficial hiking club and a willing road trip buddy to Athens. It was easy to accept Quincy: she was so genuinely sweet, even cynical Mac was easily won over. She had the nicest car of any of us and soon kept it stocked with popcorn for Marian and Doritos and pretzels for us, with seltzer for all. And she sometimes let Mac and me dress her at the vintage stores we liked, our own life-size, laughing doll. Of course, Quincy Banks looked fabulous in everything.

She didn't speak of her about-face, but she didn't have to. Hiawassee wasn't that big and people loved to talk. Quincy Banks's aunt and uncle were addicts, the messy kind you see on TV specials about the opioid epidemic. When they couldn't get pills, they turned to heroin, and when they couldn't get heroin, they turned to meth. And that's what killed them; not an overdose, but an explosion at a makeshift lab just outside of town.

Quin *did* tell us about one thing. Until her aunt and uncle died, she'd been a casual party drinker, taken the occasional puff of whatever was being passed around, maybe popped an Adderall now and then for fun. After she got the phone call, she told us she promised herself she'd never indulge again. She wouldn't end up like them.

"So I can be the DD from now on," she said tentatively, fiddling with her bob with one hand while popping a Tater Tot in her mouth with the other. We'd only been hanging out a couple of weeks, and I could tell from the way she wouldn't look at Mac or me that she wanted to be our friend. She needed us.

"Welllllll," I drawled, sneaking a glance at Mac, who nodded. Suddenly, *we* were the ones with the power. At least, I knew that's what Mac was thinking. "We could use a double D." It was more juvenile than funny, but the three of us cracked up.

We were officially a trio. And soon, we were something else. Something bigger.

Mac and I knew from those pep rallies that Quincy could sing like Sheryl Crow and Halsey's love child. Turned out she'd also played percussion in the school band since fifth grade, before dropping that along with all of her other extracurricular activities. She had the skills, the raw talent, and now, the spare time. Not to mention she was even hotter with shorter hair. Edgy, with eyes that were haunted. Big frontwoman energy.

One weekend at Marian's, the three of us found an old VHS tape of Annie's. The movie, *Light of Day*, was about a brother and sister trying to make it in the 80's music scene. As it happened, the star, Joan Jett, was not only a musical legend, but the *reason* Marian had a shag haircut and played guitar.

"We should start a band," Marian said, passing me the bottle of crappy Chardonnay she and I were sharing while the three of us waited for our pizza delivery.

Mesmerized by the raggedy yet clear voice of Mac's idol, Joan Jett, I took a swig as Quincy and I nodded in unison, as if choreographed. "We should."

CHAPTER TWO:

MARIAN

"By the pricking of my thumbs, something wicked this way comes."
—*Macbeth,* Act IV, Scene I

"**WELL**, don't you just look like something wicked," Mama said, leaning up against the doorway of the little bathroom we shared, watching me as I pushed the last nub of eyeliner pencil into the sharpener, winding it round with my thumb and forefinger. "I'm pretty sure that eyeliner's gone, darlin'."

"You gonna buy me another one?" I asked, not bothering to look over at her as I carefully glided the sharpened pencil over my lower lids, back and forth, back and forth, until I had the thick, jet-black line I was going for. I moved to the top lids, outlining my entire eye, Joan Jett-style. We shared most of the makeup, because neither of us had the money to buy it regularly on our own. Mama wouldn't touch my bright, heavy eyeshadow palette, but I knew she used my eyeliner.

"I can run to the Dollar Store," Mama answered, coming up to stand behind me and peering into the mirror as though I were doing her makeup and not my own. I tensed, catching a whiff of her White Diamonds perfume, cloying and strong. "You like that Wet n' Wild brand, right?"

"No, I *like* the good stuff," I countered, reaching for the bright purple tube of mascara. "But I can't afford it. And neither can you. Do you even *have* two dollars and the fourteen-cent tax?"

"You act like I'm ready for the poorhouse," Mama snapped back, her tone and the flash of her eyes conveying that I was starting to piss her off. She had a part-time job as a receptionist at a local tire and lube place, Sonny's Automotive, and supplemented that with the occasional shift bussing tables at Devereaux's BBQ on game days and around the holidays, whenever it was busy. Neither paid enough, though. I pitched in where I could, making extra cash selling homemade jewelry on Etsy, but I hadn't sold too many pieces lately.

I was considering throwing in the towel and applying for a job at McDonald's or Walmart, just to have a little extra spending money, but I dreaded the thought. Standing up for long periods sucked sometimes, especially that time of the month, thanks to my untreated endometriosis (forget finding a job with health insurance benefits). Besides, any hour I spent at work would take away from practice time. Band time. *My* time.

We'd been struggling to make ends meet as long as I'd been alive, so I supposed I should be used to being perpetually broke. But the bitterness never quite went away. My father hadn't paid a dime of child support in years and my mother, still half in love with him for reasons

I couldn't understand, was too proud to go after him for it. I knew the state would catch up with him eventually, but what good would a future check do for me *now*?

I tilted my head back and flicked on the mascara, deciding it'd be in my best interests not to get into a fight with Mama right now. For the most part she let me do (and say) whatever I wanted—not that I asked most of the time—but occasionally I'd snap back with a little too much sass, and she might suddenly get the urge to parent and hit me with one of her rare, but devastating, punishments.

Like not letting me go to the party.

And there was no way in *hell* I was missing the party.

"I didn't mean it like that," I said, caking coral blush in a straight line down my cheek. Sometimes I got teased at school for my eighties-style makeup–never by Duff and Quin, who got me–but I liked the look and thought it suited my dark hair and eyes. Besides, I liked looking like something wild and unhinged, like I might be feral. "I just meant that there's still a little left, so there's no sense in driving all the way to the dollar store just for eyeliner. I'll get some tomorrow." I certainly *had* meant it like that, and we both knew it, but thankfully Mama left it alone. She, too, knew how to choose her battles.

Mama reached forward and smoothed the back of my dark hair, and I tried to disguise the automatic flinch that started in my shoulders. I didn't like being touched much—I'd been that way since I was a kid—and especially not by Mama. We did not hug. We didn't have that kind of mother-daughter relationship. Not since before Deddy left, and barely then. Once upon a time I'd thought my mother was like a princess—a crispy-banged, gum-smacking princess right out of some fine Southern kingdom where small-town cheerleaders ruled in tandem with their hair-metal playing boyfriends—but those days were long gone, and so was my hero worship of her. Along with any desire I'd ever had for affection.

If Mama noticed the flinch, she gave no sign. She was good at ignoring my disdain, my coldness. I'd give her that. I think her guilt made that possible. But she never stopped trying to bond with me. I think she hoped we'd end up as one of those cheesy mother-daughter bestie duos. No thanks.

I bit back a retort and focused instead on the mirror, making sure no hair was out of place, and that my winged eyeliner hadn't run. What was I forgetting?

"Your charm bracelet, honey," Mama said, her hand still on my hair. She gave it a little pat, as though I were a child. "Put it on before you go."

She was right, but I still frowned. It made me so uncomfortable when she got all maternal. What was I supposed to do with it? The third sarcastic retort in as many minutes bubbled up to my lips, but I forced a smile. The bracelet had been a Christmas gift from my grandmother years ago, but I'd made its last four charms by hand. For some reason, Mama was insanely proud of it and was always trying to show people when we were out in public. It was too embarrassing for words. Not to mention a clear hint that she wanted me to make *her* one. Fat chance of that happening. "You're right. Lemme go get it from my room, then I've really gotta go. Can I still take the truck?"

"As long as you promise you won't drink and drive."

Fourth retort swallowed down.

"Have fun, honey. Love you!"

I grabbed the keys and bolted out the door before a fifth showed up.

My friend Teresa-Jo Garcia always got annoyed when I called her house a mansion, but to me, it was. I grew up in a double-wide, and Mama and I moved to a slightly nicer triple-wide when I turned seventeen, but let's be honest, a trailer is still a trailer in the eyes of the privileged no matter how many cheap, plyboard bedrooms it has. They even make two-story mobile homes now, and "tiny homes" are all the rage on HGTV, but "modular" homes are still a signifier of the poor. Nobody in my life had ever made me feel bad about where I lived, but it didn't matter. I still felt like an outsider every time I passed through the doors of Teresa-Jo's stately home or Duff's perfectly quaint country cottage where she lived with her grandma.

Teresa-Jo's huge, stately brick house with evergreen shutters and a perfectly manicured lawn included a pool and an actual tennis court in the back. It was gated and everything, what old-timers around here would call a "new money house." For my part, I didn't care if it was new or old money; I just wished I had it. More than once I'd stared up at the huge, white pillars on the Garcias' front porch and said to myself, *one day, I'll have a home like this. One day, I'll be somebody.*

Teresa-Jo's dad was something of a bigwig in town, one of very few Cuban-Americans in this part of North Georgia, and one of Hiawassee's most successful (and wealthy) residents. He spared no expense on his kids, and my girl Teresa-Jo was his much-treasured baby and only girl. And thankfully, she liked me enough to share some of the wealth from time to time. Otherwise, who knows how I would have gotten half my clothes and all the pot I smoked. I tried not to treat my friend like an

ATM but when she was all, "Get in, bitch, lunch is on me," it was hard to say no.

For all my ribbing about her being a spoiled little rich girl, Teresa-Jo really *was* a great friend. Today was her birthday, and even though I knew she'd rather go to one of those fancy hibachi-style sit-down restaurants with Brian, her steady boyfriend since ninth grade, she'd decided to have one of her infamous house parties in the huge, completely finished basement, and had asked my band to play. I suspected she'd done all this for *me*, bless her heart, but I was glad she had. Teresa-Jo was just like that—always doing things for me, most of the time without me even having to ask. Her spoiled-girl upbringing certainly hadn't turned her sour. Teresa-Jo was sweet as pie. Despite being brought up the way she was, she never put on airs or acted like she was better than anyone. She shared and shared alike, and she was bubbly and adorable; everyone loved her. For some inexplicable reason, she loved *me* best. And without Teresa-Jo, the only gig we'd have under our belts was an outdoor spring festival we'd shared with some bluegrass band of retired octogenarian police officers at the Georgia Mountain Fairgrounds.

You can imagine how that had gone. Sharing a stage with a bunch of creaky old yokels playing their worst rendition of "God Bless the USA," one of which–a seventy-something, flannel-clad geezer named Bubba who had a *Duck Dynasty* beard and the look of a man just *dyin'* to pat our bottoms–kept burping onstage mid-song.

Cringe-inducing patriotic parade aside, our band wasn't established yet—we didn't even have a name. We were still looking for a fourth member, a rhythm guitarist, and we'd only had two rehearsals as a full-fledged trio. But Teresa-Jo was nothing if not supportive of my dreams.

Sometimes, in my more bitter moments, I felt like I might be her pet project, or that she was trying to buy my friendship, but hey. There were worse things. We'd known each other since elementary school and she was one of the few friends who met Deddy before he'd shoved off. She knew all I'd been through with Mama and still stuck around. And I was truly, genuinely excited to play this house party. Teresa-Jo had even teased that she might be able to get one of her dad's music-biz colleagues to attend and check us out.

Our first ever *real* show! I was on cloud nine as I parked Mama's dusty blue Ranger behind Teresa-Jo's black Ford Echo and exited, grabbing my trusty guitar bag from the backseat and glancing at the sky. It looked and smelled like rain.

Maybe I'll meet a guy tonight, I thought hopefully as I rounded the manicured path toward the door in back of the house. Teresa-Jo's room was really an entire finished basement, complete with its own entrance. So far today was lucky—it was my good friend's birthday, and I was playing my first show—so why not hope for a little more luck? But as I knocked on the door, I saw a familiar VW bus inching up Teresa-Jo's driveway and grimaced. The Hecks, really? Why had she invited them? I crinkled up my nose as Teresa-Jo opened the door, a huge smile on her full lips. If those were the guys in attendance, I'd just as soon go home alone.

Pete and his two best friends, Josh and Zak, made up The Hecks, a trio of outliers who were into all things weird and occult. They were self-proclaimed witches (I was pretty sure the term was warlock, but for some reason they didn't like that; the one time I'd used that word for them outside in the courtyard between classes, they'd angrily moved away from me, never dropping the hacky sack they were kicking back and forth as they turned their backs). The three of them enjoyed telling fortunes, making prophecies, and bragging about the spells they'd cast.

They were always hanging outside by the Coke machines at school, kicking around hacky sacks and rattling off random fortunes, each one goofier than the next. Rumor was that Pete had tried a love charm on Quincy back during freshman year, but it obviously hadn't worked because Quincy hadn't so much as looked in his direction. We girls liked to joke that The Hecks were basically the boy-version of the squad in *The Craft*, but I'd never say it to their faces.

The Hecks weren't exactly in the upper echelon of our high school, but I didn't want to cross them, either. Just in case.

You'd think we'd have gotten along better–they were freaks, I was a freak–but they were a close-knit unit of three, and I'd always felt that their vibe was very much *no girls allowed.* Besides, the thought of doing spells with a bunch of zit-faced, horny teenagers did not appeal to me.

But it was TJ's birthday, not mine. She was welcome to invite whomever she liked. *Stop being such a gatekeeper,* I reminded myself for the millionth time.

"The entertainment's here!" Teresa-Jo cried, pulling me into the house and throwing her arms around me. It didn't matter how many times you'd seen each other that day, or how many times you told her you weren't a hugger, TJ gave you a hug every time, and every hug was as warm and sweet as she was. "I thought you were going to come early!"

"I tried," I said, shaking my head. "Mama held me up with her bullshit." TJ nodded sympathetically, and I looked away. "Looks like everybody is here already!"

Teresa-Jo gestured over to the snacks table, where Duff and Quincy were standing. Quincy was shoving pizza-flavored Goldfish in her mouth, while Duff's eyes trailed back and forth between Quincy and The Hecks, a bemused expression on her face as she sipped at a glass of punch. I very much hoped that the punch was spiked. "Your friends are here already."

"They're your friends too, TJ," I said, and she brightened. I knew how badly Teresa-Jo wanted to be friends with Duff and Quincy. She'd dropped a few hints. I loved TJ, but I wasn't sure I wanted to bring her into our trio. I just knew she'd show up for our movie night with a fancy charcuterie board, with a full face of make-up, glowing like a lightbulb and changing the vibe. I found TJ's wholesome perfection embarrassing sometimes. It was weird, having your ride-or-die bestie you'd had since elementary school and your brand-new-band-member bestie. Anyway, TJ was busy enough as it was with the prom committee and cheerleading, and her stage-four clinger boyfriend Brian. Plus, she couldn't sing. At all.

The truth was, I liked that they weren't close. I liked that I had them both to myself, in a way.

I never gave the first shit about being a "cool kid" growing up, but it did kinda suck to always be the odd one out, the only freak in the courtyard not gossiping or kicking up a hacky sack. To be the only girl in Spanish II not passing notes. I was neither popular nor unpopular; everyone knew who I was, and everyone was *nice,* for the most part—save for the usual bullies—but I felt the underlying vibes that came off my peers. They thought I was kinda weird. A little intimidating.

I couldn't help that I had a serious case of resting bitch face and cared more about music than I did most people; growing up with an unpredictable, depressed mother will give you all kinds of trust issues.

The only friend who never seemed to mind, who walked right past my barriers, was Teresa-Jo, who was as good as they came. Until Duff came along.

Duff thought I was cool. And she immediately took to me, always down for hanging out, talking music and make-up, and going for long, sweaty hikes, which was more than I could say for the rest of the losers at Hiawassee High. She was so laid-back and chill. Once Duff was in my circle, I found myself doing little things to make her happy, like offering to overdraw my account to help her buy a bass, to seal the deal.

Maybe I *had* been lonely. Maybe it *was* nice to have a ride-or-die that was always game, the type you were just copacetic with. TJ thought I hung the moon, but she had always acted a little afraid of me, fluttering around like she was the moth and I was the lightbulb.

Then came Quincy. I resisted at first—she was your usual blonde, busty student council nightmare, and I didn't want to share Duff. But then, after a late-night movie marathon, I discovered my girls loved Joan Jett as much as I did, and we decided to have a jam session. And I was sold. Quincy Banks was a rockstar in the making.

And so our band—and our trio—was born.

"I've got a little makeshift stage set up over there," Teresa-Jo was saying. "My dad and brothers helped me build it over the weekend." She looked proud and happy, and I'd never loved her as much as I did at that moment. "You wanna go set up for the show?"

"Does a bear shit in the woods?" I grinned and clapped my friend on the shoulder. Good old tried-and-true TJ.

Sweaty but grinning from ear to ear, I stepped off the small stage and made my way to the bathroom in the back of Teresa-Jo's basement apartment to check my makeup and wipe my dripping face. Duff followed me, her grin every bit as big as mine, her chest heaving with exertion; she had played her ass off. We all had.

And damn, we sounded *good*.

For a moment, I'd allowed myself to drift away, to close my eyes, letting my fingers do the walking—or the talking, as it were—no longer on a tiny stage built with pallets and two-by-fours in my friend's basement but a huge stage at some massive venue or outdoor festival, playing for a crowd of hundreds or even thousands…the swell of bodies and the roar of voices singing along with our every word.

When we'd finished the set, the thirty or so people at the party screamed and clapped, and to me, it sounded like a sea of potential fans; like our future. Judging from the sweaty, exalted grins on Duff and Quincy's faces, they had felt the same.

It was coming together now. I could *feel* it.

I laid my guitar outside the door and Duff followed suit, the two of us cramming into the tiny but immaculate bathroom, standing side by side at the sink. I dabbed at my face with a tissue and peered at my eye makeup, which was thankfully staying put. Wet 'n Wild doing me a solid. My armpits were soaking wet, but luckily, my vintage *Bad Reputation* tour tee was solid black. "Duff, we sounded so fucking awesome."

Duff pulled a comb from her purse and ran it through her white-blonde hair, nodding in agreement. "Jesus, I know. How the fuck did we pull that off? After two rehearsals?"

"That cover of 'Cherry Bomb' was fire!"

"It really was!"

Just yesterday the three of us—me, Duff, and Quincy—had considered cutting the cover, because the song was so overdone and overplayed as it was. Thank goddess Joan Jett we'd decided to keep it in. We'd opened with "Trouble"—none of us were Elvis fans, but the song wasn't hard to play and nothing was sexier than a former class president crooning about how evil she now was. It was the right call; our classmates went apeshit. I ran my fingers through my black hair, pulling at the sweaty tangles, and grinned at my reflection. "I hope somebody recorded that. I want it all over Instagram! We killed!"

Duff handed me her comb. "Use that. I couldn't see who all was here; the lights were so dim. I wonder if Teresa-Jo was able to get that record exec guy to show up! Or is he a manager? Do you know the difference?"

"I think she said he's both… He manages bands, and he's part owner of a small studio," I answered. "Either way… She said he couldn't make it. Something about his kid." I wasn't all that surprised. What middle-aged, big time record executive and manager wanted to come to a teenage house party? "But he did tell her to pass on his business card, and that we could give him a call."

"Are you serious?" Duff shrieked. "Like, he'll actually take our call?"

"He said he would," I answered, running the comb through my shaggy bangs, which fell right back into the same cowlick they'd been in before. "If he's a colleague of Teresa-Jo's dad, I doubt he'd lie about it."

"Oh my god, Mac, what if we—" Duff's eyes were bright and full of wonder, but her words died on her lips as a commotion sounded outside. There was a yell, then a shriek, then a loud crash. "What the fuck?"

Duff ripped open the door, and we tumbled out of the bathroom just in time to see one of The Hecks, Pete, flying through the air, his long, chestnut-brown hair trailing behind him as he rammed into the wall with a loud *thud*. The person who had undoubtedly shoved him, an upperclassman I thought might be named Aiden, was standing in the middle of the room, red-faced and snarling, his meaty hands closed into fists.

"No fighting in my house!" Teresa-Jo shrieked, her perfectly manicured hands spread out in front of her in a gesture of surrender. "If you're going to do that, take it outside. Better yet, take it off my property! The last thing we need is somebody calling the cops. My dad'll kill me!"

"Don't sweat it, Teresa-Jo," Pete said, still on the ground, his telltale red cheeks putting him somewhere between rage and humiliation, and betraying his calm voice.

"If Brian was here, I'd have him throw you both out right now!" Teresa-Jo snarled, her own face red with anger. "I swear to god, y'all, it's my birthday. Can't you *not* be dicks, just for once?"

"He started it," the beefy upperclassman said, pointing a thick finger toward Pete, who was still struggling to stand up. Pete was a really tall dude, 6'7" at least, but he was skinny as a rail. Everybody in our grade joked behind his back that he looked more like a vampire than a witch, with his pale skin, gangly limbs and huge, dark eyes, but he was actually a pretty decent athlete and the star of our school's soccer team.

Zak, whose curly, dyed purple (for now) hair never seemed to lie flat, held out his arm to his friend, who accepted it gratefully. He glared at Aiden, the freckles on his cheeks standing out. "Pete didn't do anything but walk through the door. Everybody saw you shove him when he wasn't even looking. Fucking *jocks.*" He spat the last word, and I choked out a laugh. Did anybody outside of a John Hughes movie even use that term anymore?

"Look here, you motherfuckin' *freak*—" Aiden started to retort, but Teresa-Jo cut him off. She walked over to Aiden, all five-foot-one inch of her, and poked a glossy blue fingernail into his chest.

"I think you should leave," she said, rising up to her full, tiny height. "I don't remember inviting you, and you're just causing trouble."

Aiden glowered down at her, mumbling something that sounded suspiciously like *Pete slept with my girlfriend,* but his voice had lost all its bass, all its power. He had been cowed, like a child. Teresa-Jo was even shorter than me; and while she was usually easygoing and kind, when she got riled up—watch out. She fixed her eyes on Aiden one more time with a look that meant business, and then he was gone, the door slamming behind him. Someone raced over to the stereo, and before we knew it, the party was back in full swing, everyone doing Jell-O shots and listening to Eagles of Death Metal, the fight from before forgotten.

I peered at The Hecks. It wouldn't surprise me at all if Pete *had* slept with Aiden's girlfriend. Somehow, despite being a gangly string bean with a major attitude problem, he had pulled his share of girls at our high school. They all did. I'd heard so much locker room talk about The Hecks that I could probably pick their junk out of a lineup. Maybe it was the hair, or maybe it was a spell they had going...or maybe—and most likely—it was just that lots of people, especially teenagers, enjoy flirting a little with danger.

"Before I forget, here's this," Teresa-Jo said, handing me a crisp white business card. I traced the lettering with my fingers—*Ian Duncan, Manager. Crowe Record Studio, Athens, Georgia*—before sliding it into my back pocket, my smile so big it hurt. "Do a shot with me?"

I hesitated only for a split second before taking the bright blue Jell-O cup from her extended hand.

I nodded my head toward Duff, Quincy, and Teresa-Jo in a silent "cheers" and tipped my head back, the berry blue alcohol sliding down my throat, cold and delicious.

"A fortune for the birthday girl?" Zak asked. The freckles on his pale cheeks, combined with his bright hair, made him look twelve years old, and I laughed.

"No, no." Teresa-Jo shook her head. "I don't want to know my fortune. Knowing the future, what's going to happen before it does? That sounds like a nightmare!" Brian, who had returned from his beer run, put a beefy arm around her shoulder. Teresa-Jo's man was apparently the strong and silent type; I could count the number of times he'd spoken to me on one hand.

"Come on," Pete said, gesturing for those of us left at the party—only seven or so—to sit down in a circle on the floor. "You kicked that asshole out, so I owe you. If you don't want a fortune, how about a tarot reading? It doesn't even have to be for you specifically. We can just do a general reading. Look, I bought the really good deck, the Rider Waite." He had pulled his long, dark hair back into a messy ponytail, and his white neck gleamed under the cool fluorescent lights in the basement. I noticed with bemusement that he was wearing a choker, but when he moved, the light caught it and I realized the pendant was a piece of bone, pale against his already pale flesh, and I shivered.

Right at that moment, a huge clap of thunder shook the house, and we all jumped about a mile in the air. Pete smiled as though he'd planned it.

I reached for my denim jacket from the couch, the sudden chill raising goosebumps on my arms. Duff caught my glance and rolled her eyes, grinning. The Hecks always had to usurp whatever social event was taking place with their magic and spells. It was harmless, but it did get a little irritating from time to time, probably because none of us were willing to admit they were really good at creeping us out. That old cliche about the one guy with the acoustic guitar derailing every party could never be true for our group, because The Hecks always got there first with their trusty tarot deck, ready to scare the bejeebus out of the cooler-than-cool kids.

I tended to avoid fortune telling—even the jokey kind—as a rule. I had my reasons.

Even their name was a joke. We'd all heard how they'd named their coven after the goddess Hecate and the three meddling, witchy sisters who worship her in Shakespeare's *Macbeth*, then shortened it later to "The Hex" because it was easier to say and sounded pretty metal. But, being in Hiawassee, or "the butthole of the North Georgia Mountains" as Quincy called it, the kids at our school had bastardized it, calling them "The Hecks" instead. It sounded the same, thanks to our good ol' fashioned drawls, but the guys *hated* it. Hated it so much that, of course, it had totally stuck.

Pete was shuffling the cards on the floor, his face downcast. "It's okay if you don't want us to," he said with a theatrical sigh that implied it really wasn't. "I could read your cards?"

"No tarot," Teresa-Jo said, shuddering. "That's even worse. Those cards scare me." She glanced toward the basement window, the steady rain that had started to fall outside visible through the glass. "Fine. Since you've guilted me into it, let's do a fortune. Just something small, though, okay? Keep it vague. I don't need y'all creeping everybody out at my house." She laughed, but I could hear the nervousness in it.

We all begrudgingly sat down in a circle on the floor, Quincy dutifully pulling a notebook out of her drum bag and sitting with a pen poised, as if she were going to take notes. I caught her eye and snickered, and she stuck her tongue out at me. Duff, on the other side of Quincy, looked as sufficiently bored as the rest of us, but I noticed her eye wandering over to Josh, the quietest—and arguably the most attractive, with his dark hair and dark-brown eyes—of The Hecks, who was sitting behind Pete, his posture straight, his eyes closed, his hands placed ceremoniously on his knees.

I was tempted to sneak outside to roll a joint, but hey, fair was fair. The Hecks had sat through our show, had even clapped afterward. The least I could do was feign interest in their stupid magic. So I sat and tried my best not to look bored, hoping there were more shots. Maybe it was the Jell-O goggles talking, but I thought Zak, with his purple hair and freckles, was kinda cute.

My mind began to wander. I allowed myself to fantasize about calling the record executive, Ian Duncan, whose card was in my pocket, scheduling a meeting, the band auditioning for him... Would he get us shows? Not just local, but maybe in Athens, or even Atlanta? Would we cut a demo? Book a tour? Get paid to perform? My blood quickened with anticipation. This was *it*. I could feel it.

"...will bring you down." There was a gasp, and I snapped back to attention just in time to see both Duff and Quincy's faces change—Duff's fearful, and Quincy's pinched with anger.

"What?" I asked, before realizing everyone was looking at me. I tried to play it off. "I didn't hear; can you repeat it?" Another clap of thunder sounded, but this time I was the only one who jumped.

Pete's face was even paler than usual as he stared down at his outstretched hands as though he were seeing into them like a crystal ball. I watched as he looked up and exchanged the smallest and briefest of glances with Josh and Zak, who both seemed uncomfortable. Josh was a little green around the gills, which I supposed could be from the Jell-O shots. Pete clasped his hands together, raising them as though in prayer, and looked right at me. "I said..." He swallowed. "A man will bring you down." He tugged on his ponytail nervously and bit his lip as he met each of our eyes in turn—Duff's, Quincy's, then mine, where his gaze lingered.

"Who?" I asked incredulously, right as Quincy whispered, "The band?" Pete did not answer, only continued to stare at the three of us, his face darkening, his expression equal parts pensive and elated, as though he was terrified and loving every minute of it. TJ caught my eye and shook her head as though to say, *I knew this was a bad idea.* The room was silent for a moment, utterly silent, and almost devoid of air, as if nobody could breathe even if they wanted to. I felt my chest heave.

The silence seemed to drown us all until a peal of laughter finally burst forth from deep within me. "Okay! "Good fortune, Pete!" I stood up on wobbly legs. "Are there more Jell-O shots?"

Ten minutes later, I was spirited to my car in the rain. I wanted to stay and party some more and Teresa-Jo had a whole tray of lemon-lime shots that I hadn't tried, but Duff was holding onto my right arm, and Quincy clinging to my left. They both needed a ride home, and thankfully Quincy was DD as usual because I was druuuunk.

"You guys are being such pussies," I whined, hearing the slur in my voice. "It was just a stupid tarot reading. You know how The Hecks are." It came out *Hecksh*. My tongue was so dry. "Oh shit, wait, I forgot my guitar!"

"It's hanging from your shoulder." Duff's voice was quiet in my ear. "I know it's just stupid stuff, Mac, that they're just playacting or whatever. But like...for some reason, when he said that, I felt this chill go all the way up my back. Freaked me out!"

I had felt it too, but I shook my head. "Seriously, don't worry about it, Duff. Those guys are total jokes."

The rain had slowed to little more than a drizzle, but it was enough to completely ruin my hair. Oh well, at least I was only heading home, and wouldn't be running into any hot guys. But wait. There was a car—a sleek, vintage black Stingray—that was pulling to a stop beside my old, crappy truck. I tried to focus, but I was so deliriously drunk. TJ must've upended a whole bottle of vodka into that Jell-O.

"I felt it, too," Quincy said. She kept talking, but I paid her no attention. I was watching the occupant of the car get out, suddenly breathless for the second time that night. But this time, it was for all the *best* reasons.

He was tall. Very tall. He had mid-length, reddish-auburn hair that curled slightly under his ears, droplets of water running down into his collar. Lean, muscular, tattooed arms and legs, the latter of which were peeking out of a light-blue kilt, threaded through with jewel green, red and gold. Black combat boots. A thin white T-shirt that stretched over a muscular chest under a black leather jacket. An earring in one ear.

A smile that was brighter than the moon hanging over us. And *dimples.*

"Good god," I said in a whisper, staring, my vision suddenly coming into sharp focus, momentarily sober from sheer shock. I suddenly found myself wanting to do nothing more than kneel on the wet ground before the guy and start counting his tattoos…maybe reach out and touch one. He leaned on one leg, the knee visible just below his thick blue kilt, the tiniest pop of color evident above that knee, and I wondered just how far up his thigh the tattoo went.…

The kilted god who stood before us was holding a case of Mango White Claw, the big box like you get at Sam's Club: "party size." It would've been a comical sight any other day, but I was blissfully drunk and totally spent on sarcasm. All I could do was stare at the gorgeous man before me, and if you had told me there was a puddle of drool beneath my feet, I wouldn't have even apologized.

"How far up does that tat go?" I asked, and his eyebrows scrunched together.

"Pardon?" he asked, a slightly confused grin on his face, his dimples popping out adorably. He pushed his wet hair back with a hand.

"Shut *up,*" Duff hissed, elbowing me in the ribs.

"Sorry. Hi," the god said, his voice deep and silky. I wasn't sure why *he* was apologizing. "Not leaving the party, are you?"

"Yes," Duff answered before I had a chance. "We've got to go."

"Did I miss the band?" he asked, propping the case of seltzers on his shoulder like it weighed nothing. Oh, to be a case of seltzers right now.

"Ain't no laws with the Claws," I recited, and erupted into giggles.

"Pardon?" he said again, his brows furrowing even further.

"Yep, um, yes," I said, trying not to slur, winking at the auburn-haired Adonis. "We *are* the band."

"Well, shit," he said, but he grinned. "No kidding. I hate that I missed it."

"Nice to meet you, anyway," Quincy said primly, even though we hadn't exactly met him.

And then they were shuffling me onto the truck bench, laughing at the *squeak* my wet clothes made against the seat, ignoring my protests that it was my vehicle and therefore I shouldn't have to suffer to the indignity of being in the middle. Then Duff was backing out of Teresa-Jo's driveway and rolling the foggy windows all the way up so I couldn't even admire the tattooed calves and firm backside of the handsome redhead as he went into the party I'd just been forced to leave.

I had *technically* met a guy, though, which had been my secret wish, hadn't it?

Stupid Hecks and their stupid prophecies, ruining everything.

CHAPTER THREE:

DUFF

"If nothing else, music lets you know you're not alone." —Joan Jett

"**WELL**, don't that beat all, girl!" Granny said, helping me bus the last table even as I waved her off. "A real, live record man right here in lil' ol' Hiawassee! And he wants to meet my baby!" Times like these, she sounded so very Georgia and so very Southern. I was surprised she didn't get hit with the vapors. Whatever those were.

"Calm down, Blanche," I said, picking up a half-full plate of drooly pulled pork. I sneaked a glance at her and she grinned, dark pink lipstick on point even though today had been particularly hectic. Granny's real first name wasn't Blanche—it was Katherine, same as my middle name—but over the past year I'd introduced her to the magic of streaming and she'd introduced *me* to her all-time favorite show, *The Golden Girls*. I thought she looked a lot like the actress who played the slutty one, Blanche, and the two shared a last name. "He hasn't said he'll rep us yet," I explained, as much to myself as to her. I didn't want to get my *own* hopes even more sky-high than they already were.

"Listen to you," she said. "*Rep*. Sounding like a real pro already." Tossing the last of the silverware into the bin, she stood straight, all five feet two inches, and I could see her eyes misting up. "Seems like just yesterday you were..."

I grabbed the bin and hightailed it to the kitchen, singing *lalalalala* very loudly to cover up whatever she was about to say next. Whether it was *ripped clean from your mama's insides* or *barely able to get outta bed*, I didn't want to hear it. I just wanted to dream about the possibilities ahead, even though I knew I shouldn't—for all I knew, our musical future wouldn't progress beyond this one meeting.

But...

What if this was *it* for us, a trio of lost girls who'd decided to start this band on a whim and who'd barely had two gigs? The first day I met Mac, I could see her name in lights—what if that wasn't a silly fantasy, but rather a prophecy that could actually come true? (Oh god, I sounded like The Hecks, and I didn't want to think about *that* tarot reading.) What if, instead of a ragtag group with second-hand instruments, we could become the next Runaways?

"Duffy Kate!" Granny's voice broke me out of my reverie. "It's almost time."

"Thank you, by the way," I told her as we fitted two four-tops together so there'd be room to spare. It was a Sunday afternoon and Granny had closed down Devereaux BBQ early, even though that was prime after-church eating time, *and* was cooking up her best dishes to serve family-style. I then remembered I was still wearing my apron from the brunch rush and hurried to untie it before smoothing out my nicest long-sleeved shirt and making sure it was tucked into my good jeans. I didn't have to look into a silver serving dish to know *my* lip color wasn't flawless, and I dug into my pockets so I could reapply.

"You look beautiful, honey," Granny said, walking around the joined tables to give me a squeeze. "I'm just so glad you're here," she added for the millionth time since I'd arrived in Hiawassee last fall. "And it's my pleasure to host. Help me bring everything out once they arrive?" I nodded, and she bustled back to the kitchen, where I could smell all my favorites. Knowing Granny, they'd be done and perfect at the exact same time, ready to impress.

I also knew Granny had an ulterior motive. She wanted to keep an eye on me, on *us*. As of now, we were not only underage but relatively formless, with vague plans for our band that didn't go beyond "superstardom," and a band that didn't even have a real name yet. Even though this guy was a friend of Teresa-Jo's dad and had repped a lot of big groups in the past, there were bad people everywhere.

It had only been a few weeks since Teresa-Jo's birthday party, when The Hecks gave that weird prophecy that a man would ruin us all. Ugh. I was thinking about them *again*.

I shivered at the memory, the idea that we weren't an unstoppable force, but lying in wait for one person to destroy us. What if the music manager was that man? What if he wanted money (ha) or worse, our bodies? I knew the horror stories. Hell, I'd been the subject of one myself. Granny wasn't the only one with her eyes wide open today.

And I worried about Mac. I knew she wanted *everything* for our little group. And that she'd give everything in return.

"Hey!" Speaking of, my best friend was pushing open the heavy wooden doors of Devereaux BBQ. "I heard there's a party." She was in her tightest jeans and bluest eye shadow, wearing her best red Chuck Taylors. Quincy came in behind her, fresh pink streaks in her blonde hair and wearing a white babydoll dress that looked new, bouncing on the balls of her booted feet.

I squealed, nerves and excitement congealing into one, and rushed to my girls, the ones who'd made senior year in a new town bearable, even fun. Marian wasn't much of a hugger, but she let me pull her into a tight squeeze with Quincy. "Come on in. We've got the table ready and Granny's cookin' up a storm."

"You almost sounded Southern there," Quincy observed in her typical dry manner. I rolled my eyes and grinned. I knew it was different for them, having grown up in the "butthole," as Quin called it, but I loved Hiawassee, and my childhood crush on the town had only intensified last October, when the fall colors were almost blindingly vivid and the mountains bright and tall. Despite the fact that *everyone* felt the need to comment on my Midwestern accent (I maintained I didn't even have one), I was happy here in a way I never had been in Grosse Pointe. And most of that was due to my friends.

My band.

"Hello?" a deep voice echoed off the walls of the empty restaurant.

"Hel*lo*," Quincy drawled under her breath as two figures stepped into Devereaux BBQ.

That was how we met Ian Duncan.

I'll be the first to admit that our manager never did anything for me, physically. I had a certain type. (That "type" was perfectly embodied in Josh the Heck, despite the fact that he was extremely weird, and not in a good way.) But Ian was definitely handsome, with his shaved head, clear olive skin, high cheekbones, and graying beard and mustache. He wasn't tall, but he was muscular in a way that showed he worked out. Despite his casual T-shirt and jeans, he looked distinguished, like one of those older actors who always has a job on some prestigious TV series. And behind those twinkly brown eyes was a seriousness. I could tell right away he wasn't going to treat us like stupid kids.

"Call me Ian," he said, shaking each of our hands and looking everyone straight in the eye. "I hope it's alright, I brought Crowe Germaine, my child. They were supposed to fly out to spend time with their mother, but she had an academic conference this weekend. Worked out fine, though, because Crowe didn't have to miss the trapeze workshop in Athens this morning."

"Hi!" the kid standing next to him piped up. They looked about my younger sister's age, maybe twelve or thirteen, and had darker skin than their dad with short-cropped brown hair. They held a gaming device in one hand, and pinned on their Ramones T-shirt was a button with "THEY/HE" in proud capital letters. Crowe's smile was both confident and contagious, and I could tell by Ian's smile that the two were close.

"Hello there! Miz Katherine Devereaux, owner of this establishment," Granny offered after she materialized out of nowhere with her trademark warm smile that, along with her insanely delicious food, made this place such a hit. "Welcome."

"Thank you so much for having us." Ian clasped my grandmother's tiny hand in his large one. "I'm sorry I didn't call ahead of time. Crowe is vegetarian, but we have snacks in the car."

"Marian is as well, so we have a gracious plenty," Granny responded. "Also, I'm fire in the kitchen, as my granddaughter likes to tell me, and can make about anything you'd want." She directed that last part at Crowe, who grinned even wider. Granny looked at me. "Duffy Kate, shall we?" I nodded and followed her back to the kitchen. I could tell from the way she was carrying herself and her whipped-out "company manners" that Granny immediately liked Ian.

You know how certain folks can make you feel like you're the only person in the room? Ian Duncan was like that. Not creepy. Just… magnetic, from that day until the very last time we saw him.

As Granny popped in and out, making sure everyone had enough water and sweet tea (and listening to every word; I knew her well), Ian ate seconds of everything and praised it all. "I knew this would be worth a double workout," he said with a smile, dishing up more collard greens. I knew with my first bite that Granny had dug up what she called her "real" recipes, the ones she served to locals, and I made a mental note to thank her later for, as always, being so generous with her time and talent.

Between mains and dessert, Ian brought out the contract.

"Now, I know this has been on your mind," he said, as the three of us leaned forward eagerly. I'd thought Crowe would be gaming away by now, but they leaned in too, eyes wide. "Teresa-Jo emailed me the video of your performance at her party, and I was very impressed. *Very* impressed." He paused, and I looked over at Mac. I saw she was trying her best *not* to levitate straight out of her seat. "But you're also young and green, and I want to respect that and give you the right opportunities to grow."

Marian cast her eyes down, defeated, but I nudged her. I liked that he was being real with us. She looked at me and I tried my best to convey *listen now* without saying anything.

On my other side, Quincy had absolute stars in her eyes, trying not to drool on her plate of picked-clean chicken bones. Oh, lord. Someone had a crush.

"My dad's the *best*," Crowe offered, and the three of us smiled at them. This kid was adorable.

"I swear I didn't pay them to say that," Ian said, laughing. His face grew serious. "But I do ask a lot of my artists. Practice all the time. Don't get lazy. Ask questions. I'm transparent, so I'll answer anything. I'm not here to take advantage of you." He stopped to take a swig of sweet tea. "God, this is good. Anyway, I'm ready to take you on. I've become a one-stop shop in my old age—manager, producer, what have you—and I have lots of connections." I knew Marian would like *that*. Ian passed us each a piece of paper. "You can look over this, but it's more of a gentleman's agreement than anything. I'll email it to you as well."

A contract. Our very first. I felt like it was going to burst into flames in my hand.

"Success isn't going to come overnight, mind you," Ian said. "Nothing in this business does." I *really* hoped Marian was listening. "I know you're all about to graduate high school, and if you want to go to college as well, that's just fine."

"Not me," Marian broke in before Ian even finished his sentence. "I'm all in."

"Me too," I said. My parents were coming in for graduation and I'd have to break the news to them, but I knew Granny would be on my side. And frankly, they were just happy I'd made it through the year without killing myself. I'd kept my end of the bargain and was getting my diploma the traditional way.

"I—" Quincy hesitated. All eyes went to her. "I, uh, was thinking about community college. Maybe a class or two at UGA?" She raked her fingers through her pink hair, which meant she was nervous. And afraid of how Marian would react.

I was too, sometimes.

"Quin!" Marian admonished, but Quincy went on, her voice growing stronger at Ian's encouraging nod. "I'd like to get my degree eventually," she added. Her eyes went down to the napkin in her lap and she started fiddling with it, her ragged black nails a sharp contrast to the pure white. "It was something my aunt really wanted for me."

"Then that's great," I said. "*Isn't it*, Mac?" I widened my eyes at her, and she rolled hers at me, just slightly.

"Great," Mac mumbled.

She really couldn't argue. Quincy's aunt was the one who had given her the drum set, and they'd been incredibly close before addiction reared its ugly head. Quin didn't talk about the tragedy much, opting instead for a tough exterior, only whispering her sadness at three a.m. when we were half asleep. But I understood the tragedy, and the ensuing grief, was never far from her mind.

I reached for Quin's hand under the table. She squeezed it. With my other hand, I pushed the plate with one chicken wing left her way.

"A Renaissance woman! I like it," Ian said, smiling right at Quincy, who lit up like the fancy Christmas trees she was obsessed with year-round. "Now, some housekeeping," he continued as Granny started busing dishes. "Teresa-Jo said you were looking for a rhythm guitarist. There's a young woman in Athens, a student at UGA about to graduate. Rosalyn Smith, goes by Ross. We've been looking for the right project for her. I'll send you her demo."

We nodded excitedly. Shit was getting real.

"And last," Ian said. Just then, Granny came through with bowls of peach cobbler and banana pudding. She put a dish of the latter right in front of Quincy, with crushed up Nilla Wafers on top, her favorite. Granny was extra protective of Quin, knowing as well as any of us what she'd been through. Despite the fact that Marian had a messy home life as well and Granny employed Mac's mom whenever Annie needed extra cash, Granny wasn't the same with her. Ian continued, "You need a band name. Have y'all thought about—"

"The Scottish Play," Mac blurted. "We read *Macbeth* this year and I thought the whole curse thing around saying the play's name was interesting."

We had never discussed The Scottish Play as a band name. In fact, any existing tensions in our tiny little band, more often than not, stemmed from Marian doing just this: deciding for the three of us without asking first. Quin and her Doc Martens had stomped out of Granny's garage over this at least twice.

But The Scottish Play. It was a perfect name. Especially after Teresa-Jo's party and that weird prophecy. What if we could respect that stupid curse while also turning it on its head?

I glanced at Quincy. We were still holding hands under the table, and she squeezed mine again. Then I looked at Marian, my best friend, the one who'd saved me from what could have been a shitty year. The one who predicted, correctly, that I'd rock a bass guitar. My bandmate. I nodded, looked at Ian, and delivered the verdict.

"We're The Scottish Play."

CHAPTER FOUR:

MARIAN

There would have been a time for such a word. Tomorrow, and tomorrow, and tomorrow, Creeps in this petty pace from day to day."
— *Macbeth*, Act V, Scene V

I never *mean* to speak over anyone, to push my own agenda, especially not with my friends, my band. It just sort of...happens.

Growing up, I had to be the loudest person in the room or else I didn't get heard. I had to shout what I wanted—and often, what I needed—from the rooftops, or else my mother would slap forget I existed. It was like that even before Deddy left, when the two of them did nothing but fight over his gambling debts and all the running around he did, Mama following him around with moony eyes, trying to get him to throw a crumb of affection her way. Then, after he was gone, Mama retreated into a sadness that never left her, seeking occasional solace from whatever random chucklehead happened to be at the bar that evening. Her favorite song back then was John Anderson's "Straight Tequila Night," and that'll tell you all you need to know.

I was far from the only kid from a single-parent house, nor was I the only one who had grown up in poverty and neglect. I knew that I was lucky in some respects—better a mama who sleeps the day away in a stupor and cries herself to sleep over the father who left years ago than one who might beat me or shoot up or something. But it was hard not to judge Annie Shepherd—she was just so *pathetic,* the way she moped around, depressed and lamenting her loneliness unless she had some guy's attention.

I couldn't dredge up too much sympathy for her. Deddy treated her pretty bad when I was a kid, but she'd made him crazy with her nagging and her neediness, and eventually she'd driven him right out of the house. I would never forgive her for him leaving. I felt anger toward them both, but my feelings toward Mama were white hot and tangible; they would scald me if I thought about it too much.

So I tried *not* to think about it. Instead, I kept my nose to the grindstone, meticulously planning out my dreams, and if my friends faltered, well, I could always persuade them. I was good at making people do what I wanted. I'd learned that early. I had to.

Five years had passed since that infamous meeting with dear, sweet Ian Duncan, and honestly? I was still railroading everybody. I just couldn't seem to stop myself from nagging them about everything. Duff could spend more time practicing her bass, and Quincy didn't spend enough time writing songs for someone who supposedly wanted to be the singer. And *none* of us were trying hard enough to get gigs; we would have been lost without Ian's guidance. I was holding myself accountable, too, but my friends seemed to take it all so personally. And Ross, well—Ross was every bit as proactive as I was, but nobody seemed to notice *that*. Because she could pull out her stern teacher voice and get away with it.

My dreams of music and stardom were all I had now that high school was over and college was most *definitely* out of the question. Even if I'd wanted to go, which I didn't, Mama sure as hell couldn't afford it. And I'd die before I took out a student loan and saddled myself with a bunch of debt. Besides, the only career aspirations I had were the same ones I'd always had: to be a rockstar. Was it so hard to understand that this was my *life?* Of course I took it seriously.

Bills had to be paid, so I worked as a cashier at the local Kroger—I'd finally had to stop relying on my few-and-far-between Etsy sales and get a real job when I'd moved to Athens—thankful that it was only part-time so I could focus on songwriting and practicing my guitar. Part-time meant that I was often late on rent, and the other two temped—Duff at a local dentist's office and Quincy at a data entry place, or occasionally they'd get hired on somewhere together—which paid way better but I didn't have the patience for that type of job.

Thank god for Teresa-Jo, who randomly dropped money into my PayPal without a word every month or so. When I'd first moved to Athens, I'd accidentally let it slip that I was having some money struggles, and ever since, she'd been my guardian angel. I protested at first, but she'd just told me to shut up and take the cash. Bless her heart; she believed in our band, and she believed in *me*. TJ was such a good friend. So were Duff and Quincy, who put up with my round-the-clock playing, plucking the strings of the beat-up Fender that I'd bought at a pawnshop years ago, plugged into the tiny, crappy little Walmart amp that threatened to catch fire any second. Our entire house was covered in scribbles of song lyrics and guitar picks covered every surface.

I was a woman with a mission. By any means necessary.

The night of my twenty-second birthday, I sat with my bandmates at The Grit, the best vegan/vegetarian restaurant in Athens, and our long-time favorite. I smiled at Duff and Quin, pleased that they were willing to put up with me—not only had I suggested the place, I'd picked the time, and had basically just told them where to be. I was a control freak like that—better to plan my own birthday than let someone else do it and be disappointed, or worse, forgotten.

I still hadn't managed to forgive, or forget, the forgotten birthdays from my childhood. Some of those were because Mama had been broke; I knew Deddy had never sent her a dime, and I got that, but damn. Couldn't she have managed something? Anything? Rather than holing herself up in her room, crying about how we didn't have a pot to piss in, about how Deddy hadn't even called? Every birthday, every holiday, became about how he'd left *her*. I was only a kid. The only birthday party I could recall her ever throwing me was when I was seven, and it was a pitiful affair. Teresa-Jo was the only guest, my "cake" a clearance package of cinnamon rolls with one solitary candle poked in it—the type with the thick, fondant-like white frosting—past their sell-by date and therefore slightly stale, and grape Kool-Aid. My only present was from Teresa-Jo—a beautifully wrapped, elaborate pink and yellow tea set. It was a meager affair, but I was thrilled. Well, until TJ had put her foot in it, asking me if Deddy was going to come. Mama had burst into a flood of tears and ran into her bedroom, slamming the door. TJ had sung "Happy Birthday" to me in a whisper and I'd blown out the candle, closing my eyes so I wouldn't see the pity in her dark brown eyes.

After that, I always planned my own birthdays. Even if I ended up doing nothing at all, which was often the case, but at least it was *my* choice.

And my girls loved me enough that they showed up to this birthday, despite my bossiness. After a week of crabby rehearsals where we'd argued over every single song on the setlist for our upcoming show, in which I'd griped about how sloppy we sounded more than once, I was surprised they even wanted to celebrate with me. For her part, Ross had begged off with a sore throat that I suspected was bullshit.

Ross and I...butted heads. A lot. We were too much alike, probably—she was a control-freak perfectionist, too, and she had a stronger musical background than I did; she'd taken lessons for years and played multiple instruments. We both wanted to be the one calling the shots, but the way I saw it, it was *my* band. Well, our band—Duff's, Quincy's, and mine. I loved Ross's sound, but I would always see her as the new girl, no matter how much she tried to assert herself over me.

Duff *had* given me a little grief about bringing them to The Grit again. I'd been dragging them here twice a week since we'd moved to Athens, and we'd come here plenty in high school. It wasn't just the vegetarian fare, which attracted plenty of carnivores, or the aesthetics, though both were on point. It was hard to say what was the most gorgeous—the custom cakes, the local art on the walls, or the waitstaff. And there was the establishment's deeply entrenched cultural history, how firmly it fit into the foundation of Athens music and the arts scene...plus I knew that local musicians and the odd celeb were often seen there, and I'd do *anything* to get us noticed.

I wanted to make it so bad I could taste it. I figured The Grit was as good a place as any to make that happen, rubbing shoulders with the cool kids. And it didn't hurt that they had the best tofu in town.

"Is Ian coming?" I asked hopefully, ripping off a piece of pita bread from our shared Mid-E platter and dipping it into the hummus. I didn't have time for most people, especially dudes, who, the older I got and the longer I lived in Athens, seemed to do nothing but follow me around with their tongues hanging out. But Ian was different.

Ian Duncan had been repping us ever since that day at Devereaux's BBQ, and he had done so much for us in that time period that I didn't know how we'd ever repay him. In that short time frame, we'd played many clubs and bars in the North Georgia Mountains and countless shows in Athens. Ian had booked us in town so much that we'd eventually ended up just moving here, renting his spare house (I was still marveling that someone could have enough money for not one, but two houses!) on Boulevard.

Now, not only did we live in arguably the coolest arts-friendly district in Athens, with a living room we'd converted to a practice space, but we were closer to Ross, and to countless recording studios and other musicians for networking. Ian had managed to book us a show at the infamous 40 Watt later in the month—one of Athens' oldest clubs and a staple; everyone from Nirvana to Iggy Pop to Snoop Dogg had played there. He'd even shelled out for studio time so we could cut our first EP.

I didn't love too many people, but Ian Duncan was my absolute hero.

"He texted. Said he can't make it; Crowe has something after school. But he sends you his love and says he has a present waiting for you next time he sees you," Quincy said, taking a swig of her root beer. She was such a Girl Scout—The Grit had a number of cool IPAs and fancy local brews on tap, but she always got the same old boring IBC; a teetotaler to a fault. Well, at least it meant she was always DD, just like she promised in high school.

"Bet you wish that present was for *you,* dirty girl," I responded, enjoying watching her cheeks flush. It was shitty to tease her about Ian, but I couldn't seem to help myself. Her crush on our manager had only deepened over the years, and her unrequited love for Ian was so poignantly chaste and sweet that it gave me a toothache.

"Quit messing with her," Duff hissed at me, but she was smiling, too.

"Sorry. It's just so easy," I said, grabbing a falafel from the platter. "Not that I don't get it, Quin. Ian is fine as hell, even if he is old, and if I wasn't afraid to screw up the band, I'd totally cut the line and take him for myself."

"He's not that old," Quincy retorted, staring at the table.

"Ew," Duff protested, swigging her beer. "He's old enough. No, thank you."

"You can lie all you want, but you know he's hot," I countered, laughing at Quincy's still red cheeks. "As Mama used to say, 'I'd let him park his boots under my bed anytime.'"

Honestly? I'd thought more than once about how I'd like to throw down with Ian Duncan... I could think of plenty of ways to thank him for his generosity and hard work. *Plenty* of ways. After five years, though, I knew not to try it. Ian was simply not that type of man. He was a good guy—a real one, not to mention totally, blindingly hung up on his ex-wife. Even I knew enough to know you don't shit where you eat. It was still fun to tease Quincy about it, though.

Duff cackled. "Annie did *not* use to say that."

"Sure did," I said, still using my exaggerated Southern drawl. "Probably still does, for all I know."

"Have you talked to her lately?" Quincy asked. I shook my head, instantly wishing I'd never brought her up. Trust Quin to take the heat off herself by putting it on *me*.

"Nope," I said, in a tone that made it clear I wanted to move on from the subject.

"Is she seeing anyone, or…" Quin trailed off, the end of that sentence—*or is she still crying over your Deddy*—loomed in the air.

"Granny said she's doing good," Duff answered for me. Her Midwestern accent was becoming more and more Southern by the day, and I wondered if she realized it. "She said Annie was planning a garden; she's going to pot some tomatoes on the porch this spring."

I frowned. Duff's granny and my mama went way back, being from the same small town, and Mama had been picking up shifts at Devereaux's on and off for years, more so now that Duff wasn't there to work. Despite the differences in their ages and circumstances, Mama and Granny Devereaux got along like gangbusters—Southern women find friendship easy, unless they're fighting over a man—but it stuck in my craw. Granny Devereaux was nice enough to me, dishing up her delicious mac and cheese gratis whenever I came by, but she thought I was a bad influence on her precious granddaughter, and she didn't like the way I talked to my mother. She'd never said it to my face—old genteel Southern manners and all—but I could tell.

Well, Annie Shepherd might be a charmer at work—she had to

be, to get those sweet trucker tips—and she might've been sweet-as-pie back in high school, but Granny Devereaux hadn't been there to see all the times she'd stumbled to bed while it was light out, leaving eight-year-old me to cook her own dinner, or the times there were no presents under the Christmas tree from Santa, Mama too useless to even take advantage of the local toy drives and giveaways put on by the local churches. She'd never seen Mama slumped beside the radio, playing "Iris" by Goo Goo Dolls over and over again—her and Deddy's wedding song—practically sobbing into her ramen while telling me about all the times he'd pushed her or said something horrible, only to reiterate how she still loved him, anyway. Those things were hard to forget, no matter how much Mama tried to gloss over it now and play the doting mother. Teresa-Jo was the only friend I'd ever had who had seen the Shepherd's pitiful excuse for parenting firsthand, before Deddy left and I'd grown old and wise enough to stop inviting friends over. *She* understood. Granny Devereaux could cut her eyes at me all she wanted when I sassed Mama. She didn't have the first clue what it had been like at home.

I shook my head again, willing away the memories. I tried not to bring the Mama shit to Duff—it'd only make her feel awkward and besides, it wasn't her problem to worry about. She knew her grandmother didn't like me much, and it bothered her, but she tried to pretend she didn't notice it. And she was close to her own mom. I don't think she'd ever had to choose between people; that sort of conflict was foreign to her. Lucky. Besides, I knew a version of Granny Devereaux's precious granddaughter she'd never know.

"Did Annie call for your birthday?" Quincy pressed, and I grimaced, not wanting to relay the short, awkward conversation my mother and

I'd had right before I'd gone into the restaurant. Just once, I'd love to meet someone who hated their parents, too. Just so I wouldn't feel like the only poor, lost soul out there in a family of butthole degenerates.

Serendipitously, the waiter showed up before I had to change the subject.

"You saved me," I said to him with a grin as he set a steaming Golden Bowl—the way I liked it, with melted white cheddar and a side of cornbread and gravy—in front of me. "They were about to make me talk about my drunk mother."

"God forbid," he said, placing Duff's Smelt—she always got hers without tomato—in front of her and handing Quincy her Mondo Burrito. "If your mother is anything like mine, I completely relate."

"A total fucking nightmare?" I joked, and he nodded. Dang, he was cute.

He was a birthday miracle, our waiter, and not just because he'd answered my silent plea. I'd clocked him the moment we'd walked in, noting his wavy auburn hair which curled slightly under his ears, and his vibrant blue eyes, straight white smile and pronounced dimples, noticeable even from the back of the restaurant. The sleeves of his white shirt were rolled up, revealing large, tattooed biceps and slightly freckled forearms, and beneath the black apron, he wore a pale blue kilt, ending just above muscular calves and worn combat boots. A man with a kilt, in the middle of a shift at The Grit. Could he *be* any hotter?

When the hostess had approached to seat us, Duff had cheekily spoken up and asked to be seated at one of his tables. "It's your birthday, after all," she'd said to me under her breath.

Bless my bestie.

"Can I get you ladies anything else?" the hot waiter asked as we dug into our food, and Duff smiled slyly, her eyes meeting mine. *Don't do it,* I mouthed, my eyes flashing a warning.

"A slice of the vegan peanut butter chocolate cake please, and three forks," she said in a cheerful voice, gesturing at me. "A big slice. It's her birthday." I shot her an eat-shit-and-die look, and she winked at me.

The waiter's eyes widened and his face broke into a grin that seemed to block out the sun for a moment. It was so bright and wide. And sexy. His dimples flashed, and I had a moment of déjà vu. Hadn't I seen this guy before somewhere? A flash of memory, of the beautiful blue kilt and that dimpled smile, pinged at my brain and then faded away. "Well, whaddaya know! The birthday girl! How old are we?"

"If I told you, I'd have to kill you," I joked, my face flushing to match Quincy's.

"Oh, come on. You can't be older than twenty-five," he said with a laugh.

"I'll tell you...but only if you give me your number," I said, gasping a little at my own gall, the sharp intake of breath causing me to cough and sputter. Quincy and Duff dissolved into laughter, and I wanted to crawl under the table. I couldn't even squeak out a line without choking on it. I was such a loser.

But the hot waiter didn't miss a beat. Nor did he break eye contact as he ripped a sheet off his notepad and scribbled out a phone number. "I'll do you one better," he said with a smooth smile as he handed it to me. "I'll give you my name, too." He extended his hand to shake mine, his skin warm and electric as I put my hand in his. "I'm Lawrence MacLaren."

"Marian Shepherd," I said, my voice husky. "I go by Mac sometimes. And I'm twenty-two."

"It's nice to meet you, Marian," he said, ignoring the nickname. "I hope you have the happiest of birthdays, and I hope you'll call that number sooner rather than later. Lemme get you that cake. On the house, of course, for your birthday." His smile was warm and flirtatious as he turned on his heel and headed toward the kitchen.

Holy shit.

"Is Teresa-Jo going to make it?" I heard Quincy asking me, but her voice sounded far away. I was too busy staring into the kitchen, hoping to get a glimpse of the handsome redhead as the doors swung to and fro. Suddenly my heart was pounding so hard I thought it might leap out of my chest.

"No," Duff answered for me, reaching over to grab a pita point from my plate. "She wanted to, but Brian had some military ball thing tonight. She was going on and on about her gown." I didn't tell them that TJ had texted me earlier, asking me to change the dinner to tomorrow night so she could join us. I'd already made our plans, and besides, *today* was my birthday. She'd understand.

"But what about the present?" Quincy asked.

"Teresa-Jo said to go ahead and give it to her," Duff replied. She gave me a nudge, and I waved her away with a hand, still craning my neck toward the kitchen, looking but trying not to make it obvious. Jesus, the guy was gorgeous, the most gorgeous man I'd ever seen. And he wanted me to call him! "Not that she'd give a shit right now."

"Clearly." Quincy giggled.

Duff nudged me again, this time harder. "Mac!"

"*What?*" I said in mock irritation, turning to her. "What could possibly be so important that you're taking my attention away from that absolute *piece* back there?"

"This," Duff said, and put a bundle in my arms.

It was very heavy, and wrapped awkwardly in thick brown paper, tied at the top with a silky black ribbon. I'd noticed it when we came in, but hadn't really paid it much attention, assuming it was some new vintage piece Duff had picked up from Habitat for Humanity. I felt the package with my hands, making a show of trying to figure out what it was, but the moment she put it in my lap, I knew.

You know a guitar when you feel one.

"You didn't," I whispered. "Guys."

"It's from us—me, Quincy, and Teresa-Jo," Duff said with a beaming smile.

"And Ian and Crowe," Quincy added. "Ian's the one who found it. And he chipped in a little."

I swallowed hard, a lump in my throat. *Found it* implied that it was something rare, or special. Maybe both. "Guys..."

"Just open it," Duff said, her smile widening even more. "Before we die of old age."

I took a deep breath and tore at the paper gingerly, prolonging the moment. Then I saw a flash of white and began to rip it open, letting the thick paper fall onto the floor around the table. I gasped.

I was holding a vintage Melody Maker, glossy black-and-white, an exact replica of the guitar Joan Jett played.

"Holy shit." I gulped. "You guys, this...this..."

"We thought you needed something nicer than that shitty Fender you've been lugging around," Quincy said, beaming. "It's like Joan's."

"I know," I said, my voice wavering. "I've been wanting one forever..."

"We know," Duff said. She put an arm around me and gave me a squeeze. "Happy birthday, Mac."

"Thank you, guys. So much," I managed to squeak before bursting into tears. For a moment, all I could do was bow my head and cry. It was the nicest gift anyone had ever given me. I made a mental note to text TJ and eat crow later.

"Glad you like it," Duff said, her own voice oddly husky. "Now wipe off your face. Hot boy alert."

I looked up, and through my happy tears, saw Lawrence MacLaren standing at the bar holding a slice of cake on a plate, watching our exchange with a huge grin on his face.

Quincy kept going off time. She wasn't doing it on purpose, but every time we ran through the song, right after the first verse, she'd start playing a beat too fast.

We'd just stopped mid-song for the fifth time. We'd already used up half an hour of our hour-long practice session in a place with actual acoustics, and so far, we hadn't been able to run through the entire song even once. And Historic Athens Porchfest was in *two days*.

Letting my Melody Maker dangle around my neck by the strap, I pulled my hair back into a messy ponytail and took a deep breath, exhaling extra long to try to keep my irritation in check. Quincy wasn't doing it on purpose, and she *had* just chipped in to buy me my new guitar, but she was costing us precious time. Time we simply did not have.

"We've got to try and get through this song at least once, guys," I said, keeping my voice as level as possible. As soon as the words came out of my mouth, Quincy grimaced and shot a look at Ross, who responded with a smirk. The burst of irritation I'd been trying so hard to suppress flared and I snapped, "Is there something y'all wanna say?"

"Marian—" Duff began, her voice calm and placating, but Ross cut her off.

"I think maybe you and I should step out for a bit, Mac. Let Duff and Quincy work out the bass and drums first. Once they've got it down, we can step back in and play the whole thing through."

"That would be great if we had the extra time," I said. "As it stands, we're already halfway through our practice session—well, *over* halfway through, now that we've sat here talking—and if we take even more time, we'll never get done!"

"It's okay," Duff said, plucking a string on her bass. "Mac, we'll cram in another practice session tomorrow afternoon. Maybe Quincy and I can come in early and I'll work through the song with her, then you and Ross can join us for the second half. Okay?"

"I have to work tomorrow," I said, annoyed. "I don't even get off until nine. I guess we could try to do a late-night session after my shift, but I hate playing after I've been working all day. I'm exhausted!"

"Aren't we all?" Ross muttered under her breath. I whipped my head toward her.

"What's your problem?"

"What's yours?" she answered back coolly.

"I'm just trying to figure this out," I answered her, staring her in the eye. "From what I can see, all you're trying to do is be a bitch."

"*I'm* the bitch? Are you high? I'm not the one sitting here browbeating my friend for something she's not doing on purpose!" Ross ran a hand through her curly hair. "You're being abusive as fuck, Marian. But what's new, huh?"

"Abusive? *Abusive?* How dare you use that fucking word when you know what I've—"

"Oh, here we go, our precious little victim is playing her sad song again." Ross sneered at me. "*Oh, you all have to do everything I say for the rest of my life because my mama was so mean to me.*"

Duff gasped. "Dude, Ross."

"You know what? That's fine." I laughed. "Little Miss Redcoat Nerd is just jealous." I rolled my eyes. "Ross, just because you went to UGA doesn't make you automatically smarter than the rest of us."

"When have I ever said that? You're just projecting."

"You guys," Quincy pleaded from behind the drum set, two bright pink spots on her cheeks. Her blonde hair was sweaty around her face and her mouth was pinched like she was trying not to cry. "Can we please not fight? Look, I'm so close to getting it. I'm not playing as fast as I was... I'll get there if I can just play through once or twice more. That's all I need, I promise."

"Sure thing, I'll just pull another hour of practice out of my ass," I said, shaking my head and staring at the setlist in front of me. Ten songs, and we'd only gotten through two before getting stuck on this piece of shit. And of course, it wasn't one of the ones I'd written. Of course, it was a Ross/Quincy piece that I didn't even like. "And I guess I'll come out of pocket for this phantom session, too, since nobody else has offered to pay."

"Come on, be fair, Mac. Teresa-Jo loaned us the money to rent the space, and we all know that," Duff said quietly, and Ross snorted. Duff set her bass aside and pulled her phone out of her pocket. "Shit, I forgot to Venmo her!"

"She doesn't care if you pay it back," I said, still irritated. Was this that Midwestern thing again, Duff's constant need to pay folks back? "As much money as her dad has, it's a drop in the bucket to her. She won't even notice."

"It's a matter of principle, Marian," Ross said, looking me in the eye. "It's about *not* taking advantage of a generous person. Not that you'd understand."

"You know what?" I pulled the guitar over my head and sat it on the guitar stand. "Why don't you all go fu—"

Before I could finish that spirited suggestion, Ian Duncan threw open the door and strode into the room. The look on his face made it clear that he'd heard every single word of our argument. "Ladies, I've purchased an extra hour of practice time for today. You're welcome." He winked, but his expression betrayed his annoyance. "Duff, Quincy, can you two stay and work out the bass and drum part on your own? I think Ross is right—you guys need to play it alone a few times so Quincy can pick out the bass line. You all can reconvene tomorrow if you have time."

Duff nodded. Quincy's face changed from forlorn to bright and peppy in the blink of an eye. "Of course, Ian!" She nodded enthusiastically, twirling her drum sticks, and I couldn't help but roll my eyes. God, she was so ridiculously horny for Ian.

A quick look in my direction from Ian stopped me in my tracks. His mouth was set in a hard line and his eyes flashed with what I could tell was controlled irritation. "Marian? Ross? I'd like a word with you both before you leave, please. Outside."

Shit.

I grabbed my stuff and followed him out, Ross fast on my heels. I'd really stepped in it this time. The band argued all the time; after all, we were practically sisters at this point, and we all had very clear ideas of how we wanted things to sound. We were all stubborn and butted heads a lot, especially me and Ross, who were like oil and water.

But it was rare that Ian witnessed our outbursts toward each other. This time, though, he'd heard it all, and I could tell by the tense set of his shoulders and how fast he was walking out of the studio toward the parking lot that, despite his charming wink, he was *pissed*.

When we were standing by his car, out of everyone else's earshot, Ian fished his keys out of his pocket and turned to face us. "I don't suppose I have to tell you two how unprofessional that was."

I cleared my throat. "Ian, I—"

He held up one hand to silence me, and that hand hurt my feelings more than if he'd cussed me on the spot. "Marian. Please. I heard what you two were saying to each other back there, and frankly, I'm shocked. It's no big deal for bands to argue. You want some creative differences, and with talented people you can expect some pushback from each other. But what I heard back there was straight-up *nasty*. I don't know what sort of issue the two of you have with each other, but the band isn't going to work if you two are going to be like this."

"I'm sorry, Ian. I was out of line. We're just frustrated because we can't get the song, and we're stressed about Porchfest," Ross said, and for a moment I was grateful to her.

"I can understand that's a lot of pressure, and I'm glad you're all taking it so seriously. But from what I've heard, this isn't the first time the band has dealt some low blows to each other, and furthermore, what I'm hearing is that you two are usually the ones making things difficult." His pointed stare said the unspoken part out loud: *And it's mainly you, Marian.*

"Who told you that?" I asked, but I already knew the answer. Quincy.

The little brown-noser. Fury flared up inside me and I forced myself to breathe through it.

"I'm sorry," Ross repeated. "We're just stressed. We didn't mean to let it get out of hand."

"The entire studio heard you two yelling at each other," Ian replied. "They won't let you guys come back if you make a habit out of this. Now, if we need to replace a member, we can do that if you can't find a way to get along. Do we need to do that?"

"No," I said automatically, horrified.

"No!" Ross repeated, looking equally terror-struck.

"Good," Ian said. To my relief, his face cracked into a smile. "I'm glad to hear that, because I love you both and you're so damn talented it gives me chills. And I'll do everything within my power to see you guys go all the way to the top. But I can't do that if you're fighting all the time. And I'll absolutely do what needs to be done if we can't see a way forward. So, are we all in understanding?"

"Yes," Ross and I said in unison, and Ian held out his arms.

"Get in here," he said, then added, "but only if you want to, Mac," and we both rushed in for a group hug. Relief flooded through me as I realized how close we'd come to really messing things up. I had to keep calm and stop being so pushy when it came to the band. I had to, or the whole thing was going to fail. Ian would can us and that would be the end of all my dreams.

Even as we were hugging, though, I had to suppress the urge to pinch the shit out of Ross, and from the way her arm sagged as she hugged me back, I knew she felt the exact same way about me.

CHAPTER FIVE:

DUFF

"As a kid, in the Runaways, I would see the interviewers start to ask about our personal lives and what we did—and I could see the look in their eyes. They were practically frothing at the mouth. So if I answered these questions, I knew they were never gonna talk about the music."

— Joan Jett

I didn't know my mouth was hanging open until Quincy reached over, placed two delicate gold-ringed fingers under my chin, and put my bottom lip back where it belonged.

"Yeah, I know," she said dryly from where she'd plopped down next to me. "What the fuck?"

"You okay?" I asked her. Quin had the occasional panic attack—sometimes triggered, sometimes random as hell—and we all tried to keep an eye on it. She nodded, eyes clear and focused, and I believed her. Besides, this wasn't anything new.

Look, I might've been what Mac occasionally referred to as "an irritating ray of sunshine," but I wasn't naïve. Bands mean drama. You get this many creatives in one tiny-ass room, we're all gonna have opinions and sometimes those opinions don't mesh.

I'm *sure* Cherie Currie or problematic AF Lita Ford stormed out of rehearsal at least once, as Sandy West or Jackie Fox or peacemaker Joanie looked on in shock.

I just didn't expect to be shocked when it happened to us.

"Ross and Mac have butted heads since day one," Quincy reminded me, as if she were reading my mind. Which she probably *was* by now. We spent most of our lives together, sometimes even at the same one-day temp gig where one of us kept watch while the other used the copier to run off show flyers.

"Day two," I corrected, looking over at my bandmate. "Day one was mostly us drinking Jack Daniels and fucking around with our instruments."

"What did Ian call it? Oh yeah. Bonding." Quincy chuckled. I loved the sound, deep and throaty, just like her singing voice. When Quincy laughed, she sounded like *home.* "I think he even bought the damn liquor."

I rested my chin on my palms. God only knew what was going on outside, how Ian was handling our two, uh, *least level-headed* Scottish Players. "Do you think this is it for the band?"

Quincy gave me a look that could only be described as incredulous. "Come on. No. Don't even say that."

"I dunno." I stood up and picked up my bass again. I'd scrimped and saved last year for something better than the one we found in the vintage shop as teens, though I still plucked around on my old girl sometimes, especially when Mac was around, since she'd bought it for me and I didn't want to hurt her feelings. But even with this newer instrument, holding her in my arms gave me hope. (Always her. The Scottish Play was all-female, after all.) "They've never fought like this."

"Well," Quincy replied, going back to her place behind the kit. "Marian can be a bitch."

I started absentmindedly plucking; it helped me think and gave me something to do with my hands. It also helped when I needed to ignore the pangs in my heart, like now. "Quin. That's not fair. You know she has trust issues, what with her parents being so messed up. *And* she's not great with expressing her emotions as a result." I was kinda liking this impromptu bass line. I kept going.

Picking up on the rhythm, Quin grabbed her sticks and patted a gentle undertone of a beat. She had such good instincts, honed sharper than the point of a dagger. Plus, as we'd learned from gigs, everyone loved a hot girl drummer. "*Yeeeeeah,*" she sang out, and I giggled in surprise. "*But so have yooooooooou.*" Beat. Beat. Pluck. "*And so have IIIIIIIIIII.*" On the "i" syllable, she cocked her head at me and we harmonized, dragging out the note. Didn't sound half bad. My voice was the weakest of all of ours, but it did its job.

We stopped singing to take a breath. Then Quin, still drumming, now incorporating the cymbals, started again. "*But you, Duff. You're the heart of the band. Out with your feelings and you play a mean bass. Our Midwest ray of sunshiiiiiiine*"—I harmonized on that vowel too, even as I blushed—"*and also I think you're pretty.*"

Wait.

Now we stopped in sync. Quin held her sticks in her lap, suddenly very interested in the wood grain pattern. "Um." She reached up with one hand and tucked a pink strand behind her ear. "I said the quiet part out loud." She murmured *fuck* under her breath.

And now that I wasn't plucking my bass; my hands were shaking.

Okay, here's the thing. Quin was stunning. Objectively so. I wasn't blind. And like me (and *unlike* Marian), she was also physically affectionate. At least two or three times a week, we'd snuggle and watch *Sex and the City* after a grueling band practice, or she'd come into my room without knocking when I had the door open and flop on my bed while asking what I was doing. Or she'd ask me to braid her hair like I used to for my younger sister, Michelle.

Back in Michigan a million years ago, Julia was weird about stuff like that. "We're not *gay*, Katie," she'd said when she thought I hugged her a little too long after eighth grade graduation. Like gay was a bad thing. (That should have been my first clue about Julia, come to think of it.)

Speaking of gay, I wasn't. Quin liked "hearts, not parts," one of many cute things about her. And clearly, that included *my* heart and maybe my parts.

But…the band.

Still, she was my friend. In a lot of ways, she got me better than Marian, though I shooed that thought out of my head as fast as it came in. And Quin was my housemate. And one of the best goddamn drummers *and* singers I'd ever heard, better than Karen Carpenter even, and way less messed up, thank goodness. I couldn't, *wouldn't*, fuck that all up for thirty seconds of my body singing.

"Hey, *hey*," I said, crossing to the kit in a few quick steps. "Please don't feel bad." Quincy was still gazing at her lap. "I say the quiet part out loud *all the time.* Remember last week when Ross said she should dye her hair black, and I made that face without realizing it and she got all pissed?"

Now Quin laughed. Just a little, but I was getting somewhere.

"I just think it would be a bad idea for the band," I said. "I mean, we've got enough drama as it is, right?"

She laughed again, finally meeting my eyes.

Oh crap. Those were *eyes.* Like a baby deer, but sexy?

Maybe…

Suddenly, we were leaning in toward each other. Now *she* was the one to tuck a strand of hair behind my ear. I was close enough to smell her strawberry Burt's Bees when…

The door opened.

We popped apart fast, like it never happened. Years later, I'd actually question if it did.

"Look," Ross said in her usual forthcoming manner. I couldn't look at Quin. "I know I can be a bitch. I get stressed, and sometimes that manifests in crossing the line with someone"—here she looked over her shoulder at Marian, who along with Ian was right behind her—"and my big mouth gets me in trouble." She looked down at her sneakers. "I'm sorry. I love our band, and I don't want to mess this up."

So Ross and I were on the same page there.

"Marian?" Ian prompted gently, like the dad he was.

"Yeah, you were bitchy," Marian said, and Ross rolled her eyes but she was smiling, "but I could have handled the whole thing better, too." She looked at me and Quincy. "Are we okay?"

"Totally!"

"Absolutely!" That was me and Quin, syllables spilling over one another. We still hadn't made eye contact. My fingers itched to pluck again.

Actually, that wasn't a bad idea.

"You know what," I said. "While you were gone, we kinda came up with something." I thought of Quin's gentle melody and started plucking a bass-y approximation of it, a little more mellow than our usual but still on The Scottish Play brand. Picking up my cue, Quin got right back in. She also started humming, leaving out the lyrics she'd improvised about who was mean and who was pretty. Thank goodness.

I looked back at her and winked. We'd be okay too.

Ross was already nodding along. "That's cool. I like it. I think…" She went to where she'd left her guitar. Strummed out a couple of chords. "This, maybe?"

I nodded. So did Quin. So did Ian.

We all looked at Marian. I could *tell* by the way her lower lip stuck out just the tiniest bit that she was bummed it wasn't *her* idea, that we weren't focusing on the songs already in the setlist. But she had this *it* factor, this star power. We just had to placate her sometimes, and I was the best at it.

"C'mon," I said, plucking away and looking right at her. "We need our Joan Jett."

That was all it took. Marian hopped over, grabbed her own guitar, and started on the melody.

That song, "Ray of Sunshine," eventually went viral.

But Quin and I never kissed.

CHAPTER SIX:

MARIAN

"My hands are of your color, but I shame to wear a heart so white." —
Macbeth, Act II, Scene II

I was already incredibly nervous about playing Historic Athens
Porchfest, especially after that doozy of a fight we'd had at the studio,
but when I saw *him* standing out in my front yard, leaning against his
sleek black vintage Stingray, I seriously thought I might throw up.

The hottie-hot-hot waiter from The Grit—otherwise known as
Lawrence MacLaren—had come to my show.

We'd played some cool venues already, and more than one festival,
but Porchfest was a huge opportunity. Historic Athens, a local nonprofit,
put on the show, which featured over a hundred bands spanning all
different genres. Homeowners in Athens' Historic District, where we
lived, "donated" their front porches for half a day, and bands played

gigs right out in the open, with the audience milling from house to house to hear the best in local music. Entire families came, with kids and fur friends in tow, but among the residents were often a lot of music journalists, photographers, and notables who could really make or break you in the local scene. Play a killer set with a big crowd, and you were *in*.

Nerves about this show were the main reason behind my and Ross' fight at the studio, but we were united in our goal to succeed. She and I might not have a ton in common, but we both desperately wanted this show to go perfectly. It *had* to.

Ian had readily agreed to donate the rental house's porch for the gig, which was ideal since we already lived there. Me, Duff, and Quincy had spent the better part of a month tidying up our yard, setting up our equipment, and making things perfect. To say nothing of the dozen or so band practices I'd scheduled. After all that work, I could confidently say we were ready. We looked and sounded awesome—one song aside—the house and yard looked great, and it was going to be killer.

Still, I couldn't believe the hot waiter had actually come.

After my birthday dinner two weeks before, when I'd finished mopping the happy tears off my face, Duff had settled the check and nudged me in the arm, hissing below her breath, "If you don't go invite cute guy to Porchfest, I will."

"He *said* to call him," I hissed back, my eyes wandering over to where Lawrence was dishing out chips and salsa to a couple in the corner. "He's busy. And I don't want to come on too strong."

"Look, bitch," Duff said in her I-mean-business voice. "It's your birthday, you're sexy as hell, you're about to play Historic Athens

Porchfest with your amazing-ass band, and if you don't invite that super-hot dude that was just *brazenly* flirting with you, I'm telling you *I will!*"

I looked down at my clothes. Hot as hell, really? I was just wearing my old, tattered White Stripes T-shirt and a pair of ripped jeans, and the pointy witch boots I'd stupidly spent a third of my share of the rent on (if Duff knew that, she probably wouldn't be so complimentary). I grabbed my phone and switched the camera angle, checking to see that my hot-pink-and-black eyeshadow was still in place, and wiggled my septum piercing. I only ever wore eye makeup and blush—no lip gloss or anything else, not even foundation, which felt disgusting on my skin—so it was as good as I was gonna get. I shrugged, touching my charm bracelet for comfort, then stood up. "Fuck it," I said. "I'll do it."

Both Duff and Quinn had whooped as I'd walked over to the bar, where Lawrence was pouring someone a beer. I couldn't remember what I'd said, or how I'd said it. I was too nervous. But at the end of our conversation, he had agreed, much to my excitement, to come to our show. I'd wandered back to our table half-drunk from nerves, half-convinced he wouldn't actually show.

But here he was, standing in my front yard, watching us play, among at least dozens of other music-lovers. Standing there in *my yard,* clad in that hot-ass leather jacket and the kilt that fit him so well; I could barely keep my tongue in my mouth. As I tried to focus on the notes I was playing, I couldn't help but wonder: was he bare beneath that kilt?

It was too much. I almost dropped my new guitar. Luckily, I only dropped a couple of notes. I recovered quickly, hoping nobody had noticed, especially after I'd made such a stink about Quincy's fuckup the other day. Thankfully, Ian wasn't present; he would have got me for sure. Duff cut me a sideways look and I smiled, brushing it off. I resumed playing, my heart pounding harder than Quincy's drums, which I had to admit, were absolutely on point.

I played the rest of the show without any further incidents, but my stomach was bubbling with nerves. Lawrence stood there, leaning against the car, watching me intently for the entire gig. At one point, he'd even raised his phone to take a picture or two.

After the show, he stood around, waiting while we put away all our gear, and eventually came out into the yard to mingle with the remaining crowd. I kept my eye on him the whole time I loaded out, unable to stop looking at him. The Scottish Play posed for a few photos for a photographer for *The Red & Black*, who promised we'd get a small write-up. Normally, that was the type of thing that would send me into happy hysterics, but I was too distracted by Lawrence, standing there by his vintage car, his large, folded arms encased in that black leather jacket, not unlike the one Joan Jett wore. Have mercy.

When I was finally off the clock and free to network, I approached Lawrence nervously, my heart in my throat. Luckily, he spoke first. "You wanna check out the show down the street with me?" he asked. I nodded, and he extended his leather-clad arm for me to take. "Can I leave my car parked here in your driveway?"

You can absolutely park your car in my driveway, I thought as I slid my arm through his, enjoying the way he had to look down at me; he was tall. He smelled good, too, like leather and cologne, gasoline, and some woodsy herb I couldn't identify. I nodded, and he smiled at me. I found myself smiling back, a smile that had to be bigger and brighter than any in recent memory. I'd put on my lucky black G-string before the show, which I'd bought at Frederick's of Hollywood the time Duff and I had taken a day trip to Mall of Georgia, just in case I might actually get lucky. Feeling the electricity between Lawrence and me as we walked along, our arms touching, I was pretty sure it might be doing the trick.

That afternoon, Lawrence MacLaren and I walked from house to house, show to show, checking out bluegrass bands, rap groups, and indie musicians. At one point, he let go of my arm and grabbed my hand instead, curling long, fine fingers through mine, sending electric shocks through me. We talked about our favorite local bands, about our hometowns, about what had brought us both to this small college town.

He was easy to talk to: funny and intelligent, peppering the conversation with anecdotes about the Athens music scene that I didn't know, but also asking me questions about myself and my band. He was genuinely interested, and I was touched.

Lawrence never let go of my hand the rest of the day, holding it into the night as the last bit of music trickled down the street. When he finally walked me home, we stood against his car, staring at each other, the moon illuminating Lawrence's handsome face as we said our goodbyes. Hours had passed, but I still wanted more.

"Thanks for inviting me," Lawrence said, his voice low in the dusky night. "I do Porchfest every year, but this is the first time I've enjoyed it with a pretty girl. And one that can play the hell out of a guitar—how lucky am I?"

"Oh, stop," I said, playfully pushing at his chest. He grabbed my hand and held it there, over his heart.

"It's true, though," he said, leaning down toward me. "You guys were easily the best band I saw today. You're all really, really good. Especially *you*."

"Really?" I asked. He was right—I knew how good we were—but hearing him say it filled my heart with glitter and rainbows.

"Really." His eyes were bright and wild as he stared back at me, his mouth inching closer and closer. "Maid Marian. I do believe you're trying to steal my heart."

I curled my fingers and made a grabby motion at his chest, mimicking ripping his heart out, making a goofy noise in my throat, along with some exaggerated smacking sounds. "Nom, nom, human hearts." I blushed to my hair. I'd ruined a perfectly romantic moment by being a dork.

But Lawrence only laughed. "Nom, nom," he repeated, leaning down, his lips millimeters from mine. "Devour me, I'm yours."

Then, just as the stars began to peek out from the dusky almost-night, he kissed me.

CHAPTER SEVEN:

DUFF

"Success isn't one straight line—it's a ladder, and there's always another rung above you to reach out for." —Joan Jett

"YOU'RE tense."

It was my turn to drive on our road trip back to Hiawassee for the holidays. Historic Athens Porchfest had gone off without a hitch, as had the Rumpus, the amazing Halloween event in Athens that we'd been a fixture at for the past three seasons. We'd even gotten an after-party this year, our first gig Ian didn't procure for us, and though I never drank before or during a show, it was a blur of smoke and brightly colored costumes and piercing screams begging us for more. A night to remember.

I wish I could forget what happened during our encore. I hadn't wanted to dress too sexy—no judgment on anyone else, I just wanted to be comfortable while I played—and I was happily plucking away on "Blood Orange" in my little black and white skeleton-print onesie when I heard a screech.

Thinking it was feedback from a speaker, I quickly glanced around. Marian and Ross were tearing it up and Quincy was pounding out like her life depended on it, wailing the bridge. Huh. I looked down to make sure my fingering was still on point…when a fly landed on my hand.

Even in Georgia, you didn't see a ton of those at this time of year, especially not in a packed-to-hell club. And this fly was now *crawling* on the back of my right hand. An itch spread through my body, but I couldn't scratch or even swat it away for fear of fucking up the bassline. It was a rare, almost-perfect set and I sure as hell wasn't going to be the one to mess it up when we were seconds away from (hopefully) raucous applause and cheers. Why did this damn thing itch so much, though?

And why was the fly now *looking* at me? Could flies stare with their tiny but bulgy eyes? I couldn't risk staring back.

I jerked my head up to face the crowd and saw…three ghostly images floating in the back of the club, looking almost disturbingly like The Hecks, who I hadn't seen since graduation. I didn't know if they were still in Georgia or off being bizarre someplace else, but I'd be able to spot Pete's gargantuan height anywhere.

But why were their heads hovering just above their bodies?

"THANK YOU and happy fuckin' Rumpus! We are The Scottish Play, GOOD NIGHT!" Quincy screamed into her mic as Mac got in one last riff. Oops, guess I'd been on autopilot.

When I looked back, The Ghost-Hecks were gone, heads and all.

The fly was still on my hand.

"I'm not tense." Marian's voice, from the backseat of the crappy roadster we shared, could have cut glass, and it jerked me back to the present. Right. Christmas.

"You are definitely tense," Quincy remarked from the front passenger seat, not even glancing up from her well-worn copy of *Flowers in the Attic*, V. C. Andrews at her trashy finest. Girl always had her nose in a book when she wasn't making music, if not one of her textbooks from whatever class she was taking at UGA that semester, then one of those historical romance novels, thick as a brick.

I looked over at our little bookworm in the rearview mirror and winked. She smirked back, green eyes glinting in the dusky light. Wearing a Santa hat, of all things, even though it was just us in the car, and humming along to the Bing Crosby holiday album she'd insisted we play. If there was one thing Quin loved more than reading and music, it was Christmas. She was like a little kid from November to January.

My phone rang, cutting off Bing mid-note, and Quincy lunged for it, hitting the speaker button. "Hey, Granny," she said happily, and Marian chimed in.

"Hello, girls!" my granny chirped. "You got an ETA? I'm getting your favorites ready."

"About an hour," I called. "And you didn't have to do that, Granny! Everyone's flying in tomorrow for Christmas Eve, and you know Deddy's gonna bug you for that special caramel apple pie." The other two girls snickered: I might have said *Deddy* like a dyed-in-the-wool Southern gal, but I couldn't let go of pronouncing it *car-mull*. Midwest to the end.

"I love yoooooou, see you soon!" Granny called, completely ignoring my admonishment as she usually did. "And Marian, your mama's coming too. Tomorrow!" she trilled, having adopted Mac's and my bespoke farewell. We hung up and Marian groaned.

"Tense!" Quincy and I chorused as I pointed at Marian in the backseat. The three of us burst out giggling, Marian included.

"It's so weird they're friends," she muttered for the millionth time.

"Oh, come on," Quincy said, picking her book back up and turning it to a page smack in the middle, even though she hadn't used a bookmark. "Hiawassee's a lil' bitty butthole." That set us off again.

"Stop making me laugh before I crash!" I protested, wiping a tear from my eye before putting my hand back on the wheel. "Quin's right, Mac. Besides…" I tried to find the right words. "Granny had a lot of… issues with Granddad before he passed. Like, issues that would have her at a shelter today, but people didn't talk about that stuff as much then. That and money were why she became a school lunch lady, before she opened the restaurant." We didn't talk much about my grandfather, who died when I was four, and there was a reason for that. He hadn't been great to my mom, either. "She and Annie might have a lot to talk about on that front—"

"Because my mama is a pathetic lush who loves toxic men. Got it." Shit. "You know, my deddy actually *wasn't* a piece of shit, though, right?" Aaaaand I'd officially stepped in it.

"Don't do that," Quincy said, looking back at Mac. I kept my eyes on the road. "Put words in her mouth," she clarified before Mac could say "what?" like the pissy teens we used to be.

Marian was quiet and guilt washed over me. She may have put

words in my mouth, but I was the one who'd put thoughts in her head. I loved Annie. I mean, when you're seventeen and your best friend's mom buys you alcohol, how could you not? I knew, though, she hadn't always been the best parent. Stumbling home smelling of whisky when there was nothing in the fridge for little Mac to eat. Locking herself in her room with bottles of god knows what when Mac needed permission slips signed, money for groceries, a hug. That kind of traumatic shit. I needed to make her feel better. Distract her from the trauma she was about to relive.

"Mac, you know we have plans for this break," I said in the most reassuring tone I could muster. I wished I could see her face, but now it was completely dark and we were getting into mountain territory. I had to fully concentrate on the road's hairpin curves, so I didn't kill us all. "Jogs, so we can increase our lung capacity for singing. Hikes, because we miss the mountains. Y'all are coming over for Boxing Day and leftovers, and you're free to swing by on Christmas if Annie's new boyfriend gets to be too much. We're gonna write at least one new song too, right, Quin?" I emphasized those last two words, which Quin recognized right away as one of my *tread lightly, young lady* mannerisms. I had a lot of those.

The bitch of being an easygoing Midwesterner in a band of bitter Southerners is that more often than not, I was the group mom. Not in the sense of making sure everyone was bundled up and ate right—we were all grown women, after all—but when I wasn't writing songs and perfecting my plucks, I had to break up arguments. I didn't mind, most of the time. I just wondered if, and when, I would get my own moment to be an asshole.

Quincy murmured her apology and assent as she closed her book and pulled out her phone—probably to watch one of those Hallmark Christmas movies she streamed nonstop during the winter holidays. I knew with her aunt and uncle gone, her parents still shadows of the selves they'd been before the accident, holidays weren't an easy time for her either. No one at Quin's home got into the Christmas spirit anymore.

I hoped Marian remembered she had a family who weren't traumatized shadows of their former selves. Her mama might not be perfect, but at least she was *present*.

As if reading my thoughts, which she was freaky good at more often than not, I saw the outline of Marian's hand reach from the backseat for Quincy's. They squeezed their joined hands before Mac brought Quin's hand to her mouth and kissed it.

"We love ya," I said, meaning all of us, every permutation of the three.

After five years of trying to make it, we were all tighter than ever before. Ross was a fantastic rhythm guitarist, who could also seriously jam on keyboards, not to mention a hell of a good time after shows. But she had a boyfriend, a real full-time job, and her own life outside of The Scottish Play. The three of us youngins shared Ian's spare house, scavenging the couch for quarters so we could buy ramen, sometimes begging a now-engaged Teresa-Jo, who had just moved to metro Atlanta after being accepted into Emory's pre-med program, to help us with rent (though I always paid her back, even when she returned my Venmo with "your money's no good here, bish"), so we wouldn't have to depend on our manager for *everything*. It was me, Mac, and Quin against the world, and I loved every second of it.

Sure, I worried sometimes that Ross would be *too* good of an influence and Quincy would leave us behind for campus life. Or that Marian would pull a coup d'état on Ian when she got extra impatient that he wasn't getting us bigger gigs. But when I stepped on stage and strapped on my bass, exchanging looks with the other girls before we started to fucking rock, I knew we'd be okay.

Prophecy *what*?

My phone buzzed. "Can you check that?" I asked Marian. I wasn't about to be a texting and driving fatality and give three-fourths of The Scottish Play the Big Bopper/Buddy Holly/Ritchie Valens treatment.

She did. "Holy shit, you guys, James proposed!"

A three-person squeal rang out through the car, diffusing any remaining tension. James was Ross's live-in guy, an English teacher at the same high school where she was ruling the STEM program with an iron fist. He was cute, quiet, and a little uptight, kind of a Jim-and-Dwight-from-*The-Office* hybrid, and they'd been together since sophomore year at UGA. They'd bought their house last year and we'd gone over for the housewarming party, standing out like flannel-clad sore thumbs among the teacher types, but Ross had opened Fireball just for us and gotten everyone to play a drinking game. Before now, though, Ross hadn't even mentioned looking at rings, and knowing Little Miss I Have a Plan for Everything, I wondered how much this proposal threw her.

"She said NO!" Mac yelled, and I had my answer.

"Awwww!" Quincy whined from the backseat. "He was nice!"

"He was fuckin' boring," Marian and I said in the same voice before cracking up. I kept my eyes on the road, but had to blink fast and hard not to cry. We used to do that all the time, but it had been…a while.

Truthfully, I'd felt more synced with Quincy for the past year or so, ever since we started our tradition of staying up late and bingeing *Sex and the City*. She was a light sleeper too, and that led to a lot of conversations about everything from how late we thought we'd be with rent this month to what kind of shoes we would wear if we were Carrie Bradshaw, to what we really wanted from our lives. We were uncertain about that last one, but I treasured those talks in the dark.

"Boring but stable! Secure!" Quin argued. Out of the corner of my eye, I could see her shake her head in emphasis, the pompom on the end of her Santa hat bobbing.

"Maybe that's it," Mac said. "I mean, yeah, she's this respectable teacher and stuff, but like, she's in a *band*. With a bunch of young ingrates. And like, she's wearing her hair curly now, did you notice? She told me she threw out her straightener." I chuckled, and Quin went *hmmmm*, chewing on that idea. "All I'm saying is, she's starting to rock out more. Y'know, she's gonna have to quit anyway when we make it big, which could be any day now. While James'll want, like, babies." Mac spat out that last word like it was dirty.

The three of us were silent, contemplating.

Then Marian's phone took its turn to buzz, and her energy changed.

"Larry M?" Quincy asked, and Mac giggled, a rare high-pitched sound from my usually gravelly friend.

"He told you not to call him that!" she protested, and Quincy laughed, now with a slight edge.

Larry M, I thought, a little rebellion firing in my brain. Our waiter at The Grit, now officially Marian's boyfriend.

I was still deciding how I felt about him.

"Look," I said, pulling into the parking lot of Devereaux BBQ, where Annie stood outside the door, waving. Her jeans were tight as ever, her hair long and luscious, and there was a brimming cocktail glass in one hand, a cigarette in the other (a sure sign Granny had kicked her outside). "We're home."

Behind me, I could feel Marian tense again.

"So this is where you hang out in bumblefuck," Elizabeth remarked dryly as I pushed open the door of my favorite Hiawassee coffee shop.

"Oh, shut up, Liz!" Michelle chirped. I could *hear* the roll in her eyes, and I could also hear the *ow!* when our older sister lightly socked her upper arm, like she'd been doing our entire childhoods.

I looked over my shoulder at my sisters and grinned. "Man, I missed you bitches."

Normally Granny and I went to Michigan for Christmas or the whole family took a trip together somewhere warm, but this year we'd convinced everyone to come to Georgia. The three of us had come here in the summers as young kids, but I loved showing Liz and Michelle around the places I'd haunted, both in high school and when I came back the odd weekend to hike, pick up a shift at the restaurant or just eat pie with Granny.

"Why couldn't you have played a show while we were here? I wanted to post a video!" Michelle whined, tucking a perfect strand of perfectly highlighted hair behind her perfectly pierced ear. The baby O'Brien had gone full-on sorority girl—guess a year and a half at Southern Methodist University even got to Michiganders. "I turned my whole house onto The Scottish Play and the queer girls all want a piece of Mac."

"There are queer girls at Smoo?" Elizabeth deadpanned, and now

Michelle socked *her* in the arm. "Kidding!" Elizabeth held up her hands, festooned with silver rings. Her leather leggings and dyed-red pixie screamed *Irish-ass dyke PhD student*, which was just the way she liked it.

"Ha!" I led them up to the counter while walking backward like a tour guide. "You got to meet them on Boxing Day, and we couldn't get a gig while y'all were in town. And don't tell Mac about the sorority crushes. Trust me, her ego doesn't need any more stroking."

Still facing them, I gestured at the menu above the counter. "This is my treat, but make up your minds quick. This place always got super busy when I was in high school." Finally, I turned around to give my usual order.

"Hi, I'll have—Josh!"

He grinned at me. "I mean, we haven't seen each other since high school, but twist my arm."

Behind me, Liz snorted. I could hear Michelle fussing with her sweater, straightening her skirt. Smacking her glossed lips.

Because the hottest Heck had only gotten hotter. Was his hair always this shiny? And holy muscles, Batgirl.

"Where are your boys?" were among the first words out of my mouth. Hey, at least it wasn't "have sex with me, you delicious weirdo."

Josh laughed. "Yeah, we're kind of a three-headed monster, huh? Pete's in Alabama with his family and Zak's at work."

Liz, always the manners queen, cleared her throat behind me. Right, Josh and I weren't the only people in the coffee shop. "Sorry! These are my sisters, Elizabeth and Michelle. We're having a Hiawassee holiday." I cocked my head. "Josh and I went to high school together once I moved here." *He and his pals made prophecies that freaked me out,*

I didn't add.

"Nice to meet y'all," Josh said. "I've seen your family pics up at Devereaux." Liz reached over and shook his hand, extra firm. Michelle giggled, and I rolled my eyes. Typical O'Brien sister reactions to, well, most things.

I noticed a line forming behind us. "Oh sorry, we better order," I said. Then I remembered the Rumpus. "Uh, weird question, but were you and your boys in Athens on Halloween?"

If Josh was weirded out, he didn't show it. He thought for a minute, then said, "Technically yeah, but I had a shift at the UGA library, so I had to miss Rumpus. And now that I think about it, both Zak and Pete had colds because they were blowing up my phone with chicken soup requests and I almost got written up."

The thought of The Hecks with man-colds made me smirk, and I internally breathed a sigh of relief. "Cool."

"Cool," Josh repeated. We just stood there for a second, nodding like assholes, until Michelle said, "Um, Duff? Coffee?"

We decided to get it to go—or rather, *I* decided. Part of me wanted to stay, ogle Josh, gossip with my sisters. A bigger part wanted to get the fuck out of that coffee shop, stat. Not because I felt threatened by Josh.

But…what *did* I see that night? Was Josh lying? And what about the disembodied *heads?*

"Duff O'Brien!" Josh called after we picked up our orders. I looked over. He smiled, innocent, with a hint of playboy. "I'll see you soon."

Before I could say anything back, a fly landed square on my nose.

I swatted it away.

"Hey, look who's here!"

Here's the thing: hiking was my happy place. Not something I could ever have predicted when I first moved here, a girl used to flat-flat-flatland with the occasional giant lake. But after Marian took me out my first month in Hiawassee—"I mean, Duff, there's not a hell of a lot to do here, y'know?"—I was hooked.

And here, in the midst of it all, was Larry M.

We'd all agreed this hike was just for the band and band-adjacent folks. New boyfriends were *not* band-adjacent. Especially when I didn't fully trust them.

I arranged my face in my best approximation of a smile and raised a hand in greeting next to our usual meeting spot. "Hi!" I called. It's an attitude we called *Midwestern nice*, and it would never, ever leave me. I could be plotting your murder and still worry I don't appear like I want to include you.

Lawrence MacLaren smiled back, just as Marian finished getting their stuff out of the trunk of his ridiculous Stingray, or whatever the fuck it was called. "Ian here yet?" Mac called.

"Texted. He's running behind a few, and he's bringing Crowe," I said. "Ross bailed because…you know. James didn't want to wait till the New Year to move out. Quin's on her way too."

Meaning I was temporarily stuck with the lovebirds, who made no qualms about making out *right in front of my face.*

Jesus.

It's not that I didn't want Marian to be happy. Of course I did. And I wasn't worried about the band. Until just a few days ago, Ross had a live-in boyfriend, and she still had a whole career, for Christ's sake. Plus, Marian was still obsessed with making it, whatever that meant, and her obsession seemed to grow bigger by the day, anthropomorphizing into something all its own. No one was going to distract her, no matter how cute.

And he *was* cute. It was why I'd egged her on only a couple of months ago. Vivid blue eyes, extremely touchable hair, tons of cool tats and a sartorial style that was unique even for Athens, which was saying something.

I just didn't expect him to be so...into her? Like every single bit of her. It was weird, seeing two grown-ass people in their twenties so clingy—making out in public, hands-in-each-other's-back-pockets like a couple of middle school kids. They were just trying so hard.

Maybe it was just new relationship energy. I hoped so. But something about Lawrence's interest, not just in Marian but in The Scottish Play, all aspects of it, wanting to know every minute detail of our songs and our style and even our rehearsal space—that very male energy in a space that was so sacredly *ours* and even Ian, our manager, understood and respected that—put me on edge.

And from the sidelong glances she always shot me when Marian wasn't looking, I knew Quin shared my suspicions.

"All right, Duffy Kate?" Larry said. Okay, this was a big part of it. First of all, the dude was from friggin' Tallulah Falls, not the UK. What's with "all right" used like that? *You're not on the BBC, Larry M,* I bit back. Plus, Duffy Kate was something only Granny was allowed to call me. Marian knew this, but from her giggling, I knew she wasn't going to correct him.

Fine.

My fake smile grew wider, but thankfully, I was saved by the honk of a very expensive SUV.

"Look who I picked up!" Ian cried, pulling up next to Marian's mom's car. Quincy hopped out of the back seat, her pretty face brighter than all three of Granny's Christmas trees. She rushed over and gave me a hug.

"Uggggh, Larry M," she groaned, so close to my ear it tickled, and I snickered.

"Duff!" Crowe was behind Quincy, shouldering what looked like a brand-new backpack, and I embraced them. They'd grown like three inches since Halloween, but I refrained from commenting, not wanting to sound like a middle-aged person who didn't know how to talk to teenagers.

"C'mere!" I said, grabbing them in a firm hug. Over Crowe's shoulder, did I see Larry side-eyeing our manager's lovely and amazing trans teenager? I *better* have been hallucinating or Marian and I were going to have a talk.

"Mac and I wrote a new song yesterday and I'm gonna need your feedback," I told Crowe. Kid had a phenomenal ear, just like their dad.

"Jeez, it's extra warm today," Ian said, flapping his T-shirt out of his shorts. I saw Quin's eyes widen at our manager's six-pack abs. "Do you need water, Ian?" she asked, beelining to his side.

"She is so in love with my dad," Crowe murmured to me, and I rolled my eyes and grinned.

I put my arm around them and kept my voice quiet. "You did *not* hear this from me, but he had to have a talk with her about that." A couple of weeks back, Ian had dropped in on band practice. After he gave us his trademark excellent notes, honed over decades in the industry, and we talked, gigging at a new venue, Quincy scooted...a bit *close* to him on the dingy couch we kept in the rehearsal room for breaks. Ian cleared his throat and the rest of us got busy with our instruments while he quietly asked her to step outside for a minute. (Yes, we were absolutely eavesdropping.)

Quincy came back ten minutes later. Ian was gone. She helped us pack up, eyes shining.

"He said he had to set some clear boundaries with me," she bubbled later in a way usually reserved for phrases like *he kissed me.* I took a swig of my post-practice beer and tried not to glance over at Marian.

Turns out Mac was just as befuddled. "Um, you're happy he rejected you?" she asked.

Quincy shrugged, sipping delicately on her co-cola. She could wail into a mic and bang out kickass rhythms *at the same time*, but I could still see the good girl class president in her every day. I hoped that never changed. "I am! You know why?"

She leaned forward, pushing a strand of newly blonde-and-pink hair behind her multiply pierced ear. A multitude of silver rings caught the low kitchen light and, for a moment, she looked like a Renaissance painting. "Older men...they take advantage of girls like us. All the time." I looked down, remembering the reason I'd come to Georgia in the first place all those years ago: an older man who'd indeed taken advantage of a girl like us. Me.

As if reading my mind, Quin took my hand, looked into my eyes. "Ian's different, though." Her cheeks flushed. "I love him even more now."

"Aw, Quin," I said, squeezing her hand. That *was* weirdly charming.

"Uggggggh," Marian groaned, rolling her eyes. "Someone needs to get laid." Her phone buzzed, and she raised an eyebrow. "Speaking of…"

"I hope you're ready, Lawrence!" Ian called, jerking me out of my memory. He took an enthusiastic swig of his water bottle. "These women can *hike*. It's like they were born on the trails." Crowe laughed, putting a hand on my shoulder so they could stretch their quads.

"I think I'll be all right," Larry M said, surveying Ian coolly. "And maybe while we hike, you and I can talk business? I think these girls have a big future ahead of them."

Another thing I wouldn't tell Marian: I haaaaated it when Larry called us "girls." And he did it a lot.

Ian cocked his head to the side. I could tell he wasn't expecting *that*. "Well, my friend, pleasure before business today, yeah?"

"Sure," Larry responded, nodding slowly, like Ian was this doddering old dude instead of someone who'd made some of the South's biggest bands what they were. "Pleasure." The way he enunciated that last word sent a chill running through me, even though the temp was sweat-inducing.

I looked to see if anyone else had witnessed this exchange. If anyone else was oddly put off. Or even a bit scared. Of what? I didn't know, but I wanted some validation.

Crowe's hand was still warm on my shoulder as they inspected their shoelaces, ensuring they were tied tight and wouldn't trip them up.

Quincy, as usual, only had eyes for Ian. I think she loved him more than her own dad.

And Marian was sliding her hand into the pocket of Larry's jean shorts, fitted and clearly expensive and completely inappropriate for a

Christmas season hike.

Just me, then.

"Ian's right!" I said, mustering the enthusiasm of my third-grade Girl Scout leader. "Let's hike!"

CHAPTER EIGHT:

MARIAN

"It will have blood, they say: blood will have blood." — *Macbeth,* Act III, Scene IV

LAWRENCE laced his fingers through mine as we traipsed down Broad Street, my other hand balancing a carrier of steaming red velvet lattes. "Are you sure he won't mind us dropping in on him like this?"

"Please, we do it to him all the time," I reassured him as we passed the square and turned onto College Avenue. It was sunny and warm, with the slightest sweet breeze in the air. I could have danced all the way to the end of Clayton, where Ian's office was, easily. I had a brand-new pair of mirrored sunglasses, my favorite coffee in my hand, a big show coming up, and a hot dude on my arm. Everything was coming up Mac.

"But you're in the band, and I'm not," Lawrence countered as we walked. "I don't want to overstep."

"Don't back out now. It was *your* idea," I reminded him with a grin as we passed by The Grill, the delicious smell of their infamous hand-cut fries hitting my nose. "Ian won't care. Besides, we brought him coffee."

After the hike in the mountains the day before, Lawrence had worried he'd made a bad impression—not only on the band, but on Ian. I couldn't see how he'd done anything wrong and honestly didn't care what any of them thought of him anyway—he was *my* boyfriend, not theirs—but it was endearing how much he wanted them to like him. How invested he already was in our band.

So when I'd told him I was dropping by Ian's office to bring him an updated bio for some promotional stuff and he asked to tag along, I acquiesced immediately. It would be fun to bring him downtown to Ian's office, where all the band magic happened. It made me feel proud, and a little important.

Ian's office was located in an old converted apartment on the second floor at the end of Clayton, just above an old bar that had recently gone out of business. Rumor was a froyo place was moving in, but for the moment, it was abandoned and empty. As we entered the building and headed toward the stairwell, Lawrence pulled me into a dark, dusty corner for a passionate kiss. His mouth was hungry and frenzied against mine, and my limbs melted as I leaned into him.

"If I wasn't holding three hot coffees, I'd rip your clothes off right now," I murmured against his mouth, pulling his bottom lip between my teeth and biting him none too gently.

"Set the coffee down, then," he groaned back, and I laughed softly.

"We have business to attend to, Mr. MacLaren."

"Tease."

"Always." I smirked. "But you love me." I reached down and fluffed his kilt with a chuckle, then grabbed his arm and led him up the stairwell to Ian's office, pushing open the door and ushering Lawrence into the small waiting area. It was decked out in Ian's familiar style, understated and classy: burnished wood, lush, live green plants, muted blues and grays.

Ian's secretary, Alyssa, looked up from her computer. "Good afternoon, Marian," she said. "Did you have an appointment today? Ian didn't mention…"

"No appointment," I said breezily, holding up the coffees. "I've got something to give Ian. We brought him nourishment, too." Lawrence held up the paper sack full of blueberry muffins with a smile. Alyssa gave us a wan nod, which was all any of us were ever able to get out of her.

"Mr. Duncan actually has a meeting at two—" she started, but I cut her off.

"We won't be long, Alyssa, I promise. He knew I was coming." I walked past the reception desk and into Ian's office, ignoring the look on her face.

Ian was sitting at his desk, tapping away at his keyboard, dressed in a white button-down shirt and red tie. "Working hard, or hardly working?" Lawrence asked him nervously as we entered, and I rolled my eyes. Ian looked up from his computer, irritation momentarily showing on his handsome face, but he smiled when he saw me.

"Afternoon, guys," he said. "You here with that bio, Marian?" When he'd asked the band to write out a one-page bio to use for local magazine articles, interviews, and the odd press piece for shows—now that we had played a few bigger gigs like Porchfest and 40 Watt, we had to think ahead to things like that—we were thrilled.

Nobody ever asked us for a bio before. In fact, the four of us argued a little over who should write it. In the end, Duff drafted most of it. We figured since she was the only one who hadn't *insisted* on doing it, she deserved the honor, with Ross, Quincy, and I adding our finishing touches.

"Yessir," I said happily, sitting the coffees down on the desk and fishing the paper out of my pocket. "Here you go," I said, handing it to him with a flourish. "And here's one red velvet latte from Jittery Joes, just for you."

"I told her those were a bit sugar-heavy for the likes of us menfolk, but I'm finding she doesn't listen," Lawrence cut in with a laugh.

"Ah, well, yes, thank you," Ian said. He took a dutiful sip of the coffee. "Thanks Marian, I'll get Alyssa to transcribe this for me and put it in the system. I told you Duff could have just emailed it to me and saved you a trip down here, though."

"But then, who would have brought you delicious coffee?"

"You're too much, Mac," Ian said with a laugh. "I do appreciate the caffeine boost. I have a big meeting in a few minutes, and I'm seriously dragging today."

"Hot date last night?"

Ian met Lawrence's eyes, smiling only slightly. "Unfortunately, no. Just a late night working."

"I know the feeling," Lawrence said sympathetically. "If you ever need a hand... Well, I'd like to throw my hat in the ring. I've got experience—I've worked at the record store here in town, and I interned for—"

"I can send you his resume," I cut in helpfully.

"Goodness. Coffee *and* a job interview?" Ian chuckled.

"I'm really passionate about Marian's band," Lawrence said, sitting down in the chair in front of Ian's desk. Ian's eyebrows raised slightly.

"Duff, Quincy, and Ross might take umbrage at you calling it that," Ian said with a laugh, and I jokingly pretended to pout. He smiled at me, taking another sip of coffee. Now that Lawrence had started, his nerves wouldn't allow him to stop.

"I know I don't have to tell you how good The Scottish Play is. And I know that's down to you and your management, Mr. Duncan. I've been working to get into the Athens music scene since I was fresh out of high school and the truth is, you're one of my heroes. I've always wanted to work for you. And now that I'm with Marian"—Lawrence smiled at me and I reached over to squeeze his shoulder—"well, I'd do anything to help her. And to assist you, in any way you need." He grinned at Ian. "I'd love the opportunity, and I believe I'm qualified for it."

"I'm not hiring at the moment, Mr. MacLaren." Ian sat the coffee down and started to rise from his chair. "But I'll keep you in mind if we have any openings in the future. Now, I hate to rush you two out, but I do have the meeting, so if you'll excuse—"

"Lawrence. Please, call me Lawrence."

"Of course." Ian sat back down. "Lawrence... Mac... Maybe we can talk shop another time, outside of business hours. I could put out some feelers around town and see if anyone is looking for staff. And in the meantime, I can share a few pointers if you're looking to start managing. Maybe we three can have dinner soon to discuss it more. Mac and I will get it set up." He looked at me. "My treat. As a thanks for the coffee."

"Sure," I said, a little stung. I knew Lawrence must be crushed; he'd thought he was a shoo-in. I hadn't even considered whether Ian might be hiring. I'd just assumed he'd take Lawrence on immediately. For *me,* if nothing else. Maybe he was trying not to play favorites? We'd convince him at the dinner, I was certain of that. Ian was just busy right now, that was all. I beamed at him. "We also brought you muffins. Blueberry. The big ones with the sugar on top. Crowe's favorite!"

"Aww, thank you, Mac. Crowe will be thrilled." Ian leaned back in his office chair and patted his stomach. "And so will my indigestion after I cave and eat a whole one of these things tonight in bed." This time he did stand up. "Guys, I've really got to get ready for that meeting." He held out a hand. "Lawrence, thanks for coming by. It was good to see you again. We'll talk soon, yeah?"

"Of course." Lawrence shook his hand. We walked out of the office, passing by Alyssa. I gave her a little wave. Lawrence, his face forlorn, said nothing.

As we walked back down the stairwell and onto Clayton Street, Lawrence turned to me, his face a little pinched. "Well, that was rude," he said.

"Ian?" I asked. "He wasn't rude. He's just really busy."

"He blew us off," Lawrence said. "I know a kiss off when I hear one. He doesn't like me."

"He doesn't *know* you. Anyway, Ian's not like that," I insisted. "I'm sure he'll be more open to your ideas when we go to dinner. I'll talk to him. He trusts me."

"I'm not going to fucking dinner with that guy, Marian," Lawrence said firmly. "Not after that." As we headed back toward College Avenue, me sipping my coffee and pretending to ignore Lawrence's deflated mood, I was beginning to have some indigestion of my own.

IAN DUNCAN

THE sun hung low in the sky as Ian Duncan poured himself another glass of port and stepped out onto his back porch. He settled in against his porch swing's cushions, sighing with contentment. The roast in the oven smelled heavenly (along with four different vegetables for Crowe, who refused to eat "anything with a face"), fresh-baked yeast rolls resting on the counter, and chocolate chess pie (he purchased those whenever he was in Hiawassee from Devereaux's so he'd have them on hand—they were that good) ready for dessert. Crowe was on their way home to have a quiet dinner in with dear old Dad. He had read Crowe's text at least half a dozen times: *Leaving now. See you soon, old man. Love ya.*

Ever since Gwendolyn had left, the two made it a tradition to have Sunday dinner. Well, Ian made it a tradition and Crowe, bless his heart, thankfully complied. With extremely busy schedules, Ian's constant traveling for work, and Crowe's rapidly maturing age (with all the dates, friend hangs and the rest that came with it), neither of them had that much to put toward "quality time," but Ian insisted that at least on Sunday evening, they take the time for each other. It was important to him that he spend time with Crowe, especially at this age, and forge the bonds that would hopefully last them the rest of their lives. Family was the most important thing in the world to Ian Duncan.

Ian took a sip of his wine and sat back in the swing, kicking his legs in front of him—they were a little sore after that last hike with the girls. He hated to admit it, but he was getting older and didn't have the stamina he once did, especially for Brasstown Bald, literally the highest point in Georgia. He grumbled a little, remembering that weasel Larry M (he'd gladly adopted the nickname that Quin and Duff slapped on the joker) and how he'd made it a point to *jog* the last part of the trail, right to the top. Showing off for Marian, of course, who had eaten it up with a spoon. Little shit. And then the way they'd ambushed him at the office, right before a huge meeting, taking him off guard with coffee-and-muffin bribes. There was no way in hell Ian was giving that kid a job, at least not until he sussed out his intentions better, and probably not even then. It was a total conflict of interest.

Ian's phone buzzed, and he picked it up, knowing before he looked at the screen who it would be. Like clockwork. "Hi, Gwen," he said to his ex-wife, smiling. "How goes it?"

Gwendolyn Duncan might've left for greener pastures—a tenured position as Indigenous Studies professor at the University of Arizona—but she knew that Sunday night was family dinner time, and always made it a point to call and say hello to "her babes," as she called them, even when she was knee-deep in term papers. Every time she said the words, Ian felt a pang in his chest. She still considered him "hers." The thought made him ache in a way that felt both good and bad.

It hadn't been his idea to separate. Gwen had always insisted she just needed freedom and space to follow her dreams. Dreams he certainly understood: he and Gwen were both Creek-Cherokee, in part, and having been raised among his Native family, Ian understood better than most why Gwen felt the history of her ancestors calling to her. Gwen swore there wasn't anybody else…but well, she was gorgeous, and Ian was no fool. Still, he nursed a secret hope she'd come home to them—he loved her and craved her so badly it hurt, but at the same time, he was so unbelievably proud. It was a bittersweet pill to swallow.

"How's my babes?" Gwen said, her voice warm and sweet like honey butter. After all those years out West, she still had her Southern drawl.

"Crowe hasn't pulled up yet," Ian explained. "They had a date; I just got the roast in the oven about an hour ago. Enjoying a glass of wine on the porch." After a pause, he added softly, "I wish you were having one with me."

There was a slight pause on Gwen's end, then she said, "A date, huh? Who with? Did you vet this person?"

Ian laughed, not failing to notice how she'd sideswiped him. "No, I didn't. What did you expect me to do, Gwen? Run a background check? They're dating, it's fine."

"I hope you speak to them about this school business," Gwen said.

"I'm thinking I should ease off for a bit on that," Ian replied, feeling his chest tighten. At last week's Sunday dinner, Crowe had announced that they were considering not going to college. Ian had let this momentary shock—Crowe had always been a stellar student and had been talking about college since they were knee high to a grasshopper—get the better of him. He'd expressed his displeasure a little too forcefully, and it had led to a pretty heated argument between the two of them. By the end, both were yelling. No compromise had been reached, and Crowe had stormed out of the house, slamming the door. "I don't know what caused this change, but suddenly he's having some real strong feelings and I think if I get pushy, it's just going to make things worse."

"I guess you're right," Gwen admitted. Ian closed his eyes as she talked. Her voice had never failed to calm him, the way it slipped over like cool water. "I just hope they come to their senses. All that prep, all those years saving for tuition…"

"Crowe is a good kid. Good head on their shoulders." Ian chuckled. "But is it really the *worst* thing if my kid follows in my footsteps?"

"Harrumph," said Gwen, and Ian's chuckle turned into a full-on laugh.

The two talked for another few moments before Ian hung up the phone, a mixture of nostalgia, sadness and, he had to admit, a little bit of good old-fashioned lust swirling low in his belly. He hadn't slept with anyone since Gwen. Oh, there had been moments, moments when he thought he might jump back into the dating game… He was an attractive man for his age; he had money, a nice house, a great job, he was fit and athletic, and could cook a mean Sunday roast, a skill he'd learned from his Scottish grandmother. Surely he'd be a fine catch for any red-blooded woman, even now, even just for a one-night stand, but he wasn't sure if he was ready for all that. If he ever would be.

It's funny, Ian thought as he drained the rest of his glass, the dusk deepening from the majestic shades of orange and pink to purple, *I'm so damned lonely these days that my best friends in the world are girls in their early twenties, and I'm their bloody manager.*

Ian would have been very lonely, were it not for The Scottish Play. If it weren't for those four coming into his life when they did, Ian wasn't sure what would've become of him. He'd signed them just after Gwen had left, and Marian, Duff, Quincy, and Ross filled a void he hadn't been able to acknowledge until then. Managing them as they developed from aspiring garage band to bona fide playing group had been a real joy, and had helped him come out of his funk and once again join the land of the living. Ian genuinely enjoyed their meetings and enjoyed their weekly hikes even more. Sometimes they even joined him and Crowe for Sunday dinner. He was so unbelievably proud of all of them. They worked so hard, were only occasionally behind on their rent, and they loved Crowe like a younger sibling.

Even dear Quincy had handled his gentle rejection with maturity and poise, surprising Ian and filling his heart with tender pride. She was a beautiful, talented girl with so much promise, and it had been such a hard few years for her. Oh, it was flattering for sure—and Ian knew that plenty of men his age would have jumped at the chance to bed a pretty, blonde young twenty-something—but Quin was barely older than his own kid, and she was simply too important to him. Ian would die before he ever did anything to cause Quincy pain. To cause *any* of them pain. He loved them—Duff, Marian, Quincy and Ross— like they were his own daughters.

Even if he did worry about Marian sometimes. More than sometimes.

She was immensely talented herself, and she had a good heart, but she was so angry. So singularly driven toward success. He could relate to that, and with his management, it could turn into something great. But there was something about the bitter, entitled way that she looked at things that made him uneasy.

Her childhood hadn't been a cakewalk either, he knew, and she was still in a lot of pain; pain that was rapidly turning into bitterness, the kind of bitterness that soured and turned ugly. She tried to hide it, to act brave. But Ian could see it there, beneath the surface, and it killed him. And now, on top of everything, she was dating that *guy.*

Larry Ms were a dime a dozen—just another young white boy in a college town trying to make a name for himself; harmless, but annoying in their dogged, over-confident persistence----—but something about Lawrence MacLaren niggled. Something about the gleam in his eye. How eager he was. That stunt at the office. He made Marian happy, and that should be all that mattered, but...

As if on cue, his phone dinged. Ian opened the text message and sighed. Marian. *What time is dinner tonight? Need us to bring anything?*

He specifically remembered telling Marian that they'd set a dinner up later. He hadn't invited them to *this* Sunday dinner with Crowe— had he? No, he was certain he hadn't. He'd had the band over before, but he didn't make a habit of bringing strangers like Larry into his Dad-and-Crowe time. He tapped back a message.

I think we got wires crossed, Marian... I'm having dinner tonight with Crowe, just the two of us. You and I can set up a dinner for us three later in the week, okay?

Three chat bubbles appeared, then disappeared. Marian didn't write back again. Oh well; Ian hoped she got the message. He loved Marian, but because of their professional relationship, boundaries had to be respected. He'd only just had to reiterate those boundaries with Quin. Now it was Marian's turn. He hoped she wouldn't take it too hard.

Ian loved those girls too much.

I think I've had enough booze, he thought to himself with a laugh, setting his glass down on the table beside him. The first star had appeared in the sky. *I'm waxing poetic again. But it's true—I'm a lucky man.*

Ian heard a crunch of gravel just before Crowe's car appeared in the winding driveway, heading toward the garage. Ian raised his hand in a happy wave to his only child, and headed back inside to check on dinner, his heart full to bursting.

Several hours later, Ian emerged from the shower in a cloud of steam, wrapping a fluffy black towel around his midsection. As he stepped out of the bathroom, he was surprised to hear the whirr of the dishwasher. *Damn kid*, he thought to himself with a smile as he headed to his bedroom. He'd told Crowe not to bother with the dishes, that he'd get to them later, but his sweet and ever-helpful child had done them anyway before heading out. Ian had not broached the topic of college, not wanting to ruin what had been a warm, cozy evening with Crowe. He'd get to it, eventually.

Ian dressed in his old blue flannel pajamas, a favorite pair that Gwen had bought him many Christmases ago, turning down the bed and grabbing the book he was reading. He'd had a fit of indigestion after dinner—he had overindulged in the too-rich food, eating several helpings, then dessert, to say nothing of the glasses of port he'd had beforehand. Now he was paying the price. "You might still be a hot, athletic piece, Dad," Crowe had admonished him with a laugh, "But your gut knows how old you are."

Ian had given a dutiful groan and a chuckle at that, and told Crowe he was going straight to bed after a shower. And he'd meant it. He climbed into bed and turned a few pages of the latest Stephen King before realizing he was actually reading the back of his eyelids. He put the book back on the nightstand and turned off the light, one hand clutched around his necklace's pendant—a gift from Crowe—as he often did, falling immediately to sleep.

Ian pushed himself forward, panting and out of breath as he managed the last few steep steps, finally standing at the top of Brasstown Bald. A little dome-shaped building that served as a visitor's center, museum, and restroom sat atop the mountain. Ian made his way to its door, still out of breath, hoping to get a momentary respite from the cold, whipping wind. It had picked up when he was halfway up the trail and was now a full-on bluster. Combined with the darkening sky, Ian could see a storm was about to break loose. The doors were all locked and Ian leaned against the outside wall, trying to catch his breath, an uneasy buzzing beginning in his chest. Where were Marian, Duff, and Quincy? He was supposed to meet them here, but they were nowhere to be found.

Since the door was locked, he had no choice but to climb the stairs to the viewing platform. He did this slowly, nursing a cramp that had started in his left calf. Reaching the top, he discovered that the wind was even stronger here, whipping the flagpole that bore the Georgia State flag to-and-fro so fiercely Ian was certain it would rip clean off and go flying down the mountain. The sky was dark and furious: a slate gray with tinges of blue that almost verged on purple. It was indeed going to storm, likely the kind that brought hail, or even tornadoes. Bad time to be on top of a mountain.

A very bad time.

The fog was so dense Ian could barely see a yard in front of him—the air was thick; the clouds settling around him, cold and imposing. A sudden sense of foreboding—actually, closer to outright fear—seized Ian, and he clutched at the railing, ready to turn and bound back down the steps, aching calf be damned.

But the thought of heading back down the ever-darkening trail, the one paved patch that cut through miles of wilderness, a wilderness traipsed by bears, foxes, coyotes and even spirits (Ian had lived in North Georgia long enough to feel the spirits in the mountains; no naysayer could tell him they didn't exist. They very much did) scared him almost as much as standing here at the literal top of the state, alone, in the path of an oncoming storm.

Where were they? Were they safe? The fear was palpable now. Ian could feel his armpits, soaked with sweat, dampening his jacket.

Then he saw them.

Ian could just make out their shapes as they stood in front of the railing, looking out over the mountains, as still as statues. Their backs were turned to him, shrouded in black jackets with the hoods pulled up over their ears and hair. The pair stood with their shoulders touching, making no sound or movement. They were utterly unremarkable, except for…

The flies.

If Ian craned his ear just so, he could hear them, the buzzing below the whipping of the wind, frenzied and fast. They were covered with flies on every surface

The buzzing got louder, and then louder still, finally overtaking the sound of the whipping wind, the buzzing so heavy it seemed to be inside Ian's ears. He clapped his hands over them, trying to drown out the sound, crying out in fear.

The figure on the right began to turn around. One pale hand raised up and grabbed the hood and began to pull it back. The flies buzzed louder and louder again.

Ian turned and ran.

Better a trail full of bears, foxes, and angry ghosts than this. He'd run down the entire mountain in the dark if he had to. He had to get away. He heard the furious buzzing behind him and rushed down the steps, tennis shoes slipping on the dampness, clearing the building and down toward the trail, pushing himself blindly into the woods, snapping twigs and brushing by foliage as he ran.

They were going to catch him. That cocky son-of-a-bitch was right, Ian thought wildly. I'm an old man now. I'm too slow.

He slipped and went sprawling onto the damp ground, his head making contact with a stump. It erupted in pain. Something seemed to give way. Ian clutched at a pile of leaves, moaning in pain, screaming, as the swarm of black flies descended upon him and—

Ian woke with a start, roused by the sound of a light switching on in the basement. It wouldn't have woken him, sleeping on the second floor, except the fluorescent light was old, ancient even, and made a distinctive, repetitive buzzing sound when it fired on. *Buzzing.* Ian clutched the covers, panting heavily in the dark, the last remnants of the nightmare fading.

"Fuck," he said aloud, gingerly touching his head, then his chest, making sure he was indeed okay. It felt so *real*. The buzzing of the basement light wasn't helping—it sounded so much like the flies that had followed him down the path, ready to devour... Ian lay there for a moment, listening, attempting to assure himself it was nothing. Perhaps he'd left the basement light on when he'd been down in the deep freeze getting the roast beef. Perhaps Crowe had gone down there...or perhaps it was only his imagination.

Thump. No; he had not imagined it. Ian lay there for another moment in the pitch black, perfectly still, his breath shallow, listening for more. His heart beat hard and fast. He would have to get up to check, if nothing else, to stop the buzzing in his ears, in his heart.

A faint *creak*. Footsteps on the stairs. Okay, now it was *really* time to get up. Someone was in the house. Ian got up quickly and soundlessly, reaching for the baseball bat he kept under the bed. As a second precaution, he groped on the nightstand until his fingers found the pocketknife he'd had since he was a child, passed down from his father—it was small, but serrated and very sharp.

Ian felt his blood pressure rise, fear replaced with anger as he stepped quietly toward the closed door. Who would dare to break into his house? A burglar? Well, Ian would teach them a lesson. He might not even need the baseball bat or the knife; he'd be happy to dole out some justice with his fists, if it came to it.

He reached the doorway. The room was as dark as ink, and the door was shut. Ian wasn't going to wait for the familiar rattle of someone opening it. He would let this intruder know he was here. Confront them head on.

In one quick movement, Ian flung the door wide open and flipped on the light, illuminating his bedroom and the hall in brightness.

Outlining the figure that stood there waiting on the other side.

Ian gasped. The knife fell from his hand and clattered to the floor.

"You…" he whispered, a sudden, sharp pain flooding through his chest. He stared at the figure before him, his mouth gaping in an expression of bewildered pain. They locked eyes, and Ian's other hand dropped the baseball bat as he clutched his chest, suddenly short of breath. "…why?" was all he managed to sputter before he fell to his knees.

Then Ian was on the ground, and the pain was so large it seemed to consume him whole. Ian clutched at his neck, to wrap his fingers around Crowe's pendant for comfort, but his fingers slipped against the cool of the white-gold chain, finding no purchase. "*Why?*" were the last words Ian Duncan spoke, and then his body was still, his eyes blank; the last thing Ian Duncan heard before he died, the buzzing of a housefly.

CHAPTER NINE:

DUFF

"Obviously, the music and lyrics are in me, but if I let myself get in my own way, I do. I empty out and let it come, and then the music spirits take over." —Joan Jett

HE was *just here*.

I couldn't stop thinking about it. Ian Duncan, our manager—the one who'd raised us up to where we were now, who was the closest thing to a dad I had within 700 miles, who, as far as I knew, was healthy as a fucking horse—was dead. I hadn't had a whole lot of experience with death, aside from elderly relatives I'd barely known, and this was a bitch of an introduction.

I couldn't begin to imagine how Crowe was feeling.

"I mean, what am I supposed to do?" they said from the couch in our makeshift rehearsal space where they'd been crashing when they weren't at their mom's. Of course we let them. After all, Ian owned the house, and naturally, they didn't want to go back to where their beloved father met his end. They'd also been going hard on trapeze workshops at Canopy, the local circus school, sweating out their grief, I guess. "Google, *what to do when your dad literally drops dead?*"

I exchanged a helpless glance with Marian and Quincy. We had a gig that night, but we were going to wing it, no question. Ross had to stay late at school so she'd come straight to the venue, and we were going to treat Crowe to after-show Grit as a surprise. Gwen was meeting us there.

As much as The Scottish Play mourned Ian, we ached for Crowe, our sweet younger proto-sibling, who we'd known since he stepped into Devereaux BBQ with his pronoun button (we soon learned Crowe used *he* and *they* interchangeably but slightly preferred *they*) and Ramones tee, still baby-faced and barely out of seventh grade. They deserved our full attention. They'd already offered to roadie for us tonight, showing us a fake ID we were willing to bet Ian hadn't known about.

Ian. I sucked on my lips, hard, so I wouldn't break down. I couldn't make it about me right now.

"Your mom's doing the funeral stuff, right?" Mac asked softly, reaching out to squeeze Crowe's shoulder. I thanked my lucky stars Larry M—*Lawrence.* I was trying my Midwestern best to call him the right name, even in my head—wasn't around, as he had been more and more lately, even sitting in on practice. I knew Quincy wasn't thrilled about that either, but our friend was in love and we wanted to be supportive.

In the meantime, we were just waiting for the explosive argument that usually precluded Marian's breakups. If her past relationships were any indication, Larry had already reached his sell-by date. Undoubtedly, that was a pattern she'd learned from Annie.

Still, it was nice to be Lawrence-less, even under these horrible circumstances.

Crowe nodded. "Yeah, she's been amazing. Devastated, but staying strong for me. Even staying at the house for moral support. She's handling the probate stuff too, like the will and where everything goes." He looked around at us. "We *do* know that this house is mine. So y'all are staying right where you are, because your new landlord says so." He managed a small smile.

I bit back a sigh of relief, because I *had* been worried about that—and felt guilty as hell about it. "You know we're here for you, right?" I told Crowe, moving from my place on the floor to perch next to them on the couch. "Whatever you need."

Marian nodded eagerly, and Quincy hopped up from the couch. "Who needs a Coke?" She bustled off to the kitchen. Next to Crowe, our drummer was taking Ian's death the hardest, and was doing her best not to show it. She didn't have the familial claim to Ian that Crowe did, of course, but I knew she was hurting. Panic attacks almost daily since we heard the news. She'd slept in my bed for several nights since it happened, not wanting to be by herself, ever. I was happy for the company.

"I'll go help her," Marian murmured, nodding at me. I smiled at her gratefully. We were taking the "divide and conquer" approach to the ones grieving the hardest.

As soon as Marian was out of the room, Crowe turned to me. "Duff, if I share something, will you not tell anyone?" Their eyes went wide, and they looked a lot younger. My mind rushed to the worst possible revelations.

I took a deep breath, making sure to measure my words carefully. This was a kid who had just lost a parent, after all. And I was barely above kid-age myself, but clearly, they trusted me and I had to do my absolute best. "That depends. If you're not safe, then I have to…"

"Oh, no, no, no!" Crowe said. "Not like *that*." They looked away. "It's just…"

"Just what?" Despite their reassurances, my mind was still racing. Crowe mumbled something. "Come again?"

"We had a fight," they said, now almost too loudly. "One of the last times I ever saw my dad, we had a fight and then he died, and it's all my fault."

"Oh." That was a *lot*. I racked my brain for the right response.

Apparently, the monosyllable was all Crowe needed to get going. "Dad wants me to go to college, at least for a couple of years. And I keep…" Crowe stopped, swallowed hard. I took their hand. "Um, I *kept* saying no, I want to start in the music business like *he* did after high school. I already lined up an internship with one of his friends I've known since I was a baby and I'm really excited. But Dad couldn't afford college at my age, and he wants me to have that experience, and Mom is being super pushy about it, and then we started yelling and we never yell…"

They trailed off, then inhaled noisily. "We made up later, but there was still some tension, and now I'm worried he was so stressed out about my future that… Why couldn't I have just said I'd go to college? Why did I have to be like this stupid rebel person?"

Suddenly, they grabbed me in a hug. I could smell dried sweat and Ian's preferred Old Spice scent. The shoulder of my T-shirt stayed dry, but I could feel Crowe's anguish in the force of their hug. Then they mumbled, "I feel like it's all my fault."

"Hey." I jostled them just the slightest bit, so they pulled back. "Look at me." It took a second, but Crowe's brown eyes met mine. "It's not your fault. Bodies are weird and your dad's broke down and there's *nothing* you could have done to change that."

Crowe shook their head. "But they say the body keeps the score and..."

"He loved you, Crowe." I was so confused about so much, but this I absolutely knew to be true. "More than anything in the world. You didn't see eye to eye on your future, but I guarantee you that wouldn't *kill* your dad. Okay?"

Crowe nodded. I wasn't entirely sure they believed me. I loved Ian, but I had my own dad. Who was still very much alive and probably golfing at the country club in Grosse Pointe at this very moment. We all looked on Ian as a father figure to some degree, but only Crowe could actually claim Ian as a *father.*

"There's one other thing that's bothering me," Crowe said, plucking at the strands of crushed green velveteen.

"What's that?"

"His necklace," Crowe said, looking up from the mess of threads. "Even when we argued, or I was on punishment, he never took it off. But now no one can find it, and he wasn't wearing it when he..." They trailed off, a tear trickling down their face. I pulled them close, not caring when the shoulder of my T-shirt got wet, my insides twisted up.

The necklace was a white gold chain with a symbol only Ian, Gwen, and Crowe understood. Crowe knew who they were early—it helped to have parents as open and loving as Gwen and Ian—and in sixth grade, when he officially came out as trans and queer, he'd made necklaces for both parents. Gwen kept hers in whatever purse or backpack she was carrying, a talisman of unbreakable familial bond. Ian always, *always* wore his.

So...the missing necklace was weird. Really weird.

I didn't know what to say, so I just let Crowe cry, holding silent space for them, while Quin and Marian fetched our sodas.

"Blood will have blood," Marian murmured.

Quincy's knees buckled, and she fell to the dirty ground. I worried for her knees, but I couldn't take my eyes away from our makeshift pyre.

We'd wanted to do *something* to commemorate Ian, just the three of us. We'd attended the memorial, of course, with Ross, who'd known him longer than we had, since she was a UGA freshman playing keyboard at coffeehouse open mics. The four of us played at the reception at Highwire, Ian's favorite Athens bar, a stripped-down acoustic set. I could hear the mourning in every chord, and it was cathartic, surrounded by his loved ones, a primal collective keen.

But we three, the original Scottish Play, wanted to honor him in our own way. Where would we be without Ian Duncan? Quincy would be fine, probably hurtling full time toward her degree, fulfilling her late aunt's wish. But what about me? On track to managerial roles at Devereaux BBQ? Granny wanted more for me. *I* wanted more for myself.

And Marian, as always, wanted the world.

The day after the funeral, the three of us drove down to hike

Brasstown Bald, the last place we'd been with Ian. We brought our own kindling. Matches. A letter each of us wrote.

"Just the band," I'd said to Marian when we came up with the plan. I'd expected a fight—*why don't you like Lawrence,* and so on—but to my surprise, she'd replied, "Of course, Duff. Just the band."

At the moment, her *Macbeth* quote could be considered bizarre. But it was a weird time. I didn't read too much into it then.

I wish I had.

As the small fire grew in size, not out of control but taller and more...powerful than we'd intended, Quincy got to her feet and straggled over to a nearby log. She'd been quiet the entire drive down, and yesterday, after the funeral and reception, she'd gone alone into the rehearsal space, banging the absolute shit out of her drums and wailing out what could only be called a funeral prayer. I was in the kitchen with Marian. The rehearsal space wasn't soundproof, so we heard every beautiful, painful note. I put my arms around Marian, right there in front of the oven we never used, and she squeezed me hard while I didn't bother brushing away the tears that ran down my face until I tasted salt.

An hour later, Quin came out with a new song, dummy lyrics and chords neatly outlined on a napkin. "Badass Funeral." I tweaked notes, wrote new lyrics straight from the heart. We played long into the night.

Now at Brasstown Bald, as Quincy started to sob, then wheeze, then hyperventilate, Marian gave me a look like, *I've got this.* She put her arms around Quin and turned her back to me, leaving me alone with my thoughts and the fragments of burning letters. I could see the word "want" in Marian's handwriting, curling in the orange of the flames. "Grateful" on my own, becoming ash. "You" in Quincy's, succumbing letter by letter. Could hear Marian whisper, "Breathe, honey, just breathe," as Quincy struggled to gulp in fresh mountain air.

Suddenly, I had to get out of there.

Twigs crunched under my hiking boots. I tried not to think of bones as I power-walked my way down the path, wandering this way and that, swatting flies. I knew I shouldn't do this, go deep in the woods alone without a plan or even water. We probably weren't supposed to start fires at Brasstown Bald, a state park, either. Then again, a healthy dad and stellar human being wasn't supposed to drop dead with no warning in his very own house. What the fuck made sense anymore?

"Duff O'Brien."

The deep, scratchy voice rang out through the trees. A sane person would have turned tail and run. I wasn't exactly having a sane day. I kept on.

"Duff O'Brien." Again, a different voice. Also masculine.

So I wasn't hearing things. Why were the woods calling to me?

My hiking boots took me through the trees, tall and imposing but infinitely more comforting than my friend's anguished cries. Until I heard the voices. My pack, containing only an empty water bottle and my wallet, suddenly felt like it was full of bricks. The day was cool. We were at a higher altitude, but all the same, sweat popped out on my forehead. I made a messy bun of my scraggly hair, using the tie from around my wrist, just to give my shaking hands something to do.

Yet what I *didn't* do was run away.

"Duff O'Brien!" Insistent this time. Like a teacher or an angry parent, with an implied *get over here!*

And then I saw them.

The fucking Hecks.

Zak's hair was now pink, long on top, curls sweeping across his forehead. He wore a Nine Inch Nails tee I recognized from high school, now even more threadbare. Pete's long brown hair was in a topknot, not unlike the one I'd just fashioned for myself, his formerly scrawny shoulders now sculpted and visible around the dirty pink tank top he was sporting. So he and Zak were coordinating, apparently. He'd filled out considerably since high school.

And Josh, in a light pink sweater that wouldn't have looked out of place on my sorority-girl sister. Coffee shop Josh. Josh of the shiny hair who'd charmed my sisters, even the one who hated most men. Josh who may have lied about the Rumpus. Or were they astral projecting? Or was I hallucinating that night?

What the fuck was even real anymore?

I tried to tear my eyes away from Josh Yang in his cutoff pants showcasing slender but powerful calves, the boy, now man, who'd popped into my thoughts since our holiday encounter. He was a Heck. He was fucking weird. He'd helped deliver that stupid prophecy at Teresa-Jo's party.

I couldn't.

"Duff O'Brien," Josh said again. His had been the first voice to call out to me. To summon me. I stood about twenty feet away from them, frozen in place. "It's been a minute."

"What the hell do you want?" Couldn't keep my voice from shaking, could I? Shit.

"Just to say hello." Zak smiled. He'd had braces at graduation, and now his teeth were block-straight, gleaming in the late afternoon light. Sinister. "We heard you're in mourning."

I squeezed my hands into fists. I wasn't scared of them. Not exactly.

I was a college town girl now, a musician, accustomed to grabby hands and drunk men at gigs. I could take all three of them if I needed to, and they weren't really threatening me. More...unsettling.

Now I wanted to run. And I couldn't.

"Y'all live here now?" Struggling to stay cool, I jutted my chin toward the pop-up tent, patched up in various places, the dirty sleeping bags, the half-full bags of chips. Wouldn't put it past them to haunt a national landmark. "Wearing pink? It's not Wednesday."

Pete laughed. They weren't moving any closer, giving me my space like gentlemen, but I still felt like they were closing in. "Nope. We don't live here. We felt *compelled*, though. To be out here this weekend. In pink." His smile grew wider until I could see his pointy canine teeth. Like a wolf's. "And once we heard you were here, we knew why."

How had they "heard" about our band's little road trip? We'd told no one, not even Larry. Forget about posting online, and it's not like reception was great out here, anyway. Was Quin's freakout that loud?

"We gotta give you a message!" Zak jumped in. He let out a high-pitched giggle, childlike. I took a shaky step back. It was getting dark. Where were my friends?

"Calm down, bud." Pete laughed a little. "Have some Doritos. You hungry, Duff?"

As if I'd take anything from them. "Just give me the message."

Zak looked at Josh, who'd stayed quiet, gaze fixed on me. "Can I tell her? Please? We have to tell her!" It was weird how keyed up he was. And tell me *what*?

"Go for it, Zacky," Pete said, picking up the bag of Doritos. He reached in, pulled out a chip, and chomped down hard, looking straight at me.

Zak gave me a big smile, but it seemed fake. "You're not done with death, Duff. Alliteration, huh? Just like English class."

Pete continued to chomp. Josh looked a little uneasy.

I wondered if anyone would hear me scream. How far was I off the beaten path?

Stay cool, Duff. "What's that mean, Zak?" My voice rang out clear and true. Steady for the first time since this bizarre encounter started.

"It means what it means, Duff O'Brien," Pete said through a mouthful of disgusting orange, smelly chips. I could never eat Doritos again; I knew that much already. He grabbed another, punctuating his next words with loud bites. "You're. Not. Done. With. Death." By now, he was spraying crumbs.

And suddenly, I found my footing.

Zak saw me starting to move away, and said in a low voice, "See you next time."

I turned and ran. Finally. Away from Zak's stupid Crayola hair and Pete's Doritos and that ragged blue tent and Josh's probing eyes. Away from the dumb excuse for a "prophecy" propagated by three freaks who were *still* hanging out when high school should have been a distant memory.

You're still hanging out with your high school friends, too, said a voice in my head that I promptly shushed as I concentrated on finding the trail, my way home.

"Duff!"

I turned, screaming like an animal.

It was Josh.

He held up a hand as he bent over, gulping in air. "Damn, girl! You run fast!"

"I…" I didn't know how to answer that. "What the fuck, Josh. Stop following me. Stop…calling to me. Go haunt someone else, or whatever you and your creepy little friends do."

I was finding my voice again, thank god. I wanted my friends, my band, my granny, very badly. My insides felt all sorts of raw from the loss I'd experienced, the fact that if The Hecks were right, I wasn't "done with death," whatever that meant. Nothing good, I'd reckon.

And yet, I was unable to tear my gaze away from Josh's.

"I'm so sorry we scared you. And they're right, you're not done with death. But you'll be okay, Duff. You will," he said. He was closer than he'd been a moment ago, but five feet away, a respectable distance. Not crowding me. Or smelling of Doritos. Just a fresh whiff of mountain air emanating from him.

Despite the rough ground, Josh was barefoot and his toes looked surprisingly clean. He almost had the look of a sprite, and there were a few leaves in his hair. I wanted to pick them out, one by one, run my fingers through the silky black strands. In fact, my hand went up of its own accord. I brought it down.

"You'll be okay, Duff O'Brien," Josh repeated, holding up his own hand. Like a blessing.

I turned my back. "Leave me alone, Josh."

Suddenly, nothing. No heavy breaths. No steps. I glanced over my shoulder.

Josh was gone. Not even a footprint left behind.

As if he'd never been there at all.

CHAPTER TEN:

MARIAN

"False face hide what the false heart doth know." — *Macbeth*, Act I, Scene VII

"YOU haven't finished that play yet?" Lawrence's voice came from behind me suddenly, startling me. I put down the worn, dog-eared copy of *Macbeth*—his—and hid my jitters, turning to him with a warm smile. The sight of his curling dark-red hair, bright blue eyes, and impossibly white smile with those dimples still undid me completely. He'd been pressing me to finish *Macbeth* for a couple of weeks now. It was on his bucket list, he'd said, because it was set at Glamis, one of the more infamous castles in Scotland, and dealt with the beginning of the House of Stuart line, of which he claimed to be a descendant.

While I found that interesting, I was also a little put off, though I'd never tell Lawrence. I couldn't trace my own family past Grandma

Ophelia, who'd had blue-rinsed hair and chain-smoked those super long cigarettes that needed their own zip code. She died when I was seven, and I barely remembered her, beyond a couple of family Christmases where she'd served us the tiered coconut cake that she'd been known for in three counties. Mama had that recipe somewhere, saved to give me when I ever got married; the only thing I was likely to inherit (unless you counted Mama's endometriosis).

She'd also given me my charm bracelet, which was as close as I'd ever gotten to a family heirloom of value. No culture, no heritage, no nothing. Just me and Mama. Hiawassee. Coconut cake. A cheap charm bracelet.

White Americans who claimed to be this or that—"Oh, I'm a quarter Italian," or, "Oh, I'm Irish on my father's side"—had always irrationally annoyed me. I knew it was unfair, but the only family history I had was that of being poor white trash, and I hated when people put on airs. Lawrence wasn't like that, though—he had a wide-eyed, childlike innocence when he talked about his ancestry, and I was trying my damndest not to be snide about it. Sometimes I worried if he knew how shriveled up and weathered my heart was—my true self—he'd run away screaming.

"I'm close to finished," I said in mock anger, but Lawrence could've asked me to do anything and I would've done it, shriveled heart or no. I'd already read *Macbeth* in high school—we'd named our band *The Scottish Play*, for Christ's sake—but Lawrence was just so *eager* to hand his copy to me, to see me reading it.

The things I do for love.

"It's very timely," he'd said, his eyes lighting up as he handed the red leather-bound book to me, and I nodded in agreement. Even if I did think it was slightly goofy, trying to compare some dusty old play written in the 1600s by a brown-nosing poet for a closeted gay king in balloon pants to our lives now. Though I did have to give old Willy Shakes credit for one thing: "Blood will have blood" was a pretty metal quote. I looked at Lawrence now and sighed. "I promise I'll finish. I've had a lot on my plate the last few days."

"Oh, honey," Lawrence responded, coming round to the couch and pulling me into his strong arms.

I just couldn't face being home right now. Both my housemates had posted quotes and pics about Ian's death on social media, which I found tacky. Quincy was trying to put on a brave face, but deep down, she was drowning in grief. She had been utterly, stupidly in love with Ian Duncan. After that post-memorial scene where she shut herself in with her drums and came out with a song, she'd carried on like she was Ian's classy, mature widow or something. Even that girl's *grief* was productive. It was totally irrational—I had no right to control others' emotions—but I found it so annoying. It wasn't easy, being an empath, picking up on things even when you didn't want to.

At least Duff, who could never hide her true feelings, was visibly falling apart. She'd run, practically in hysterics, from our campfire. Now *that* I could understand, even respect. Sometimes I envied Duff her easy emotions. She hugged, cried, and loved easily; everything was right there on the surface, accessible. Real. The only emotion I kept on the surface was anger.

But of course, Duff's volatility *had* caused us to get into a huge fight, which was one of the other reasons I was hiding out here at Lawrence's.

She'd finally straggled back to the campfire right as we were starting to put it all out and pack things up, dazed and red-faced, sweaty and her hair unkempt and full of leaves. She'd run into The Hecks, she'd said. They'd given her another prophecy. Then she'd sat down—right on the damp ground—and told us everything The Hecks had relayed to her.

When she finished, I'd asked, "Did they say anything else? Like about the band or —"

"I swear to god, Mac, I love you but if you start in on band shit right now when I've just had the bejesus scared out of me, when Ian *just died* and we're all grieving…" Her eyes met mine, full of angry fire.

"I'm sorry," I said in a cowed voice, but inside I was indignant. Who did she think she was, talking to me like that? Duff may have been emotional, but she *never* lost her cool. I bit down on the impulse to tell her off. *This isn't Ross*, I told myself. *This is your best friend, and she's hurting. Give her the benefit of the doubt.* "I just thought maybe they'd said more. I didn't mean to make you upset."

Duff stared off into the trees, her expression rattled and her limbs jumpy with nerves. "They had a tent set upright in the middle of the woods," she said, low and frightened. "Who camps on Brasstown Bald? There are bears everywhere!"

"Not to mention it's illegal," Quincy piped up in a small voice. "This is a state park."

"Um, I'm pretty sure the big fire we just set is also totally illegal," I said, going for a laugh, but the two of them glared at me.

"Whose side are you on these days, anyway, Mac?" Duff's laugh was dry, devoid of humor, and I bristled.

"Right. Well, if you guys are just going to bite my head off every time I speak, I'm going to head out," I'd said in a huff, packing up my backpack and taking special care to snuff out the fire. Both of them just sat there on the ground, watching me as I did everything, and I stalked off down the path toward the parking lot. I was shaking like a leaf by the time I got back to my car, shuddering at the thought of driving back down that steep-ass mountain by myself in a car whose transmission was getting faultier by the day. But Duff and Quincy had come separately from me anyway, so they wouldn't have come along for the ride even if they weren't mad at me.

Why *were* they mad at me? I honestly didn't know. I felt like some agreement had been breached, some line crossed, that I wasn't privy to. Something had happened between those two—maybe several somethings—and now it felt like the two of them against me. It drove me crazy.

I was *still* brooding about it as I lay on Larry's couch: warm and soft, covered with a blue corduroy fabric that was very masculine, but super comfy. I smiled as he lay back into the cushions and pulled a downy-soft, light-blue throw over us. It was the same tartan as the kilt he wore so often, which I'd learned was the MacLaren ancestral tartan. Today he was wearing it with my favorite White Stripes shirt, so faded and stretched out that it actually fit him. The fabric pulled against his muscular chest and arms and I had to admit, it looked better on him than it did on me. He leaned over and gave me a feather-light kiss on the cheek and I pressed into him, enjoying the way he smelled and how warm his skin felt against mine.

"Why do you wear that kilt so much?" I asked, nuzzling into his neck. "Not that I'm complaining. I'm just curious."

"It makes me feel closer to my heritage," he answered, wrapping an arm around me and pulling me in tighter. "I started doing it in high school, when my dad first went to jail… I guess it made me feel like I was carving out an identity for myself, something that was just mine, but also part of something bigger. And it just kinda became my thing, I guess."

"And here I was thinking you wore them because they make your legs look sexy." I giggled and trailed a finger up his thigh.

Lawrence was from the mountains like us—nearby Tallulah Falls—but had moved to Athens fresh out of high school (another thing we had in common) to pursue his dreams of a music career. He didn't play any instruments, so he'd fronted a couple of local bands as a singer before deciding that wasn't his wheelhouse and segueing into music production.

In Athens, there was no shortage of options for work *or* musical pursuits, and Lawrence had tried his hand at them all. He'd worked at a local recording studio, then moved on to a pressing plant, making brightly colored, limited-edition vinyl for local bands. He'd also interned at a management company, and done some PR for a few bands around town, acting as a promoter, booking shows at some of the bars in Athens, including my beloved Georgia Theater, all the while moonlighting as the hottest waiter at The Grit.

He and I were perfectly aligned. I wanted to be a star. He wanted to *make* a star.

But my bandmates weren't doing us any favors, the way they rolled their eyes at him and mocked him to his face. He hated being called Larry, because his father, Lawrence MacLaren Sr., who was serving a twenty-five-year sentence over at Arrendale Prison, had gone by Larry, making their choice to call him that shitty.

They're just jealous, I told myself. Jealous that I had someone now, and they didn't.

"Do you own any band tees that aren't Joan Jett or Jack White?" Lawrence teased.

"One," I confessed, feeling a familiar lump in my throat. "A Blue Oyster Cult T-shirt that was my dad's in high school. I wear it to sleep in." I'd never told anyone that, not even Duff or Teresa-Jo. Mama didn't even know I had it. I'd stolen it from one of her plastic storage bins when I was in eighth grade, never telling her even as she tore the house apart looking for it. I still wore it to bed sometimes when I was feeling lonely or sad. It made me feel closer to my father, like he was still in my life, however distant.

"I've never seen you wear that," Lawrence said, his hand grazing my hair. "You always sleep in underwear. Not that I'm complaining."

I laughed, but the pain in my chest was a chasm. "I keep it private. I grew up hearing how awful Deddy was, and it's like…if I even admit I miss him, I must be a horrible person. But I do. Miss him, I mean."

"Of course you do," Lawrence said tenderly. "That's normal."

I swallowed. "I don't like to talk about Deddy. People don't understand. I only told you because…well, because your dad is like my dad."

"A shitass."

I laughed again. "Yes. A shitass." I swallowed.

Lawrence tugged at the throw, making sure it was covering my legs. "I miss my dad, too, sometimes," he said after a moment. "Even though I hate him." His right hand, under the blanket, caressed my thigh and I felt my pulse quicken, welcoming any distraction that took away thoughts of Ian Duncan. Or my father, for that matter. Lawrence's voice was low and sensual in my ear. "Have you had a chance to talk to the girls?" he asked, and I tensed.

"No," I admitted. I turned to look into his bright blue eyes. "They're both out of their minds right now. I tried in the woods, but then Duff and I got into a snit." I sighed. "She's been in such a funk lately, moping around, eating her feelings. She ate a whole pecan pie from her granny by herself. There's no way I could have broached the topic without her clocking me." I smiled. "Not that I couldn't take her."

I frowned. Why had I said that? I didn't want to fight my best friend. And I knew she didn't want to fight me, either.

Lawrence didn't seem to notice. He was trailing kisses down my neck, toward my collarbone. I preened, not wanting him to ever stop. What he was doing felt a damn sight better than thinking about Ian, talking about my shitass father, or worrying over Duff and Quincy. So much better.

Lawrence's hand was trailing under my shirt, his fingers tickling my ribs and making their way up to my bra, the clasp popping open easily under his nimble fingers. He squeezed, laughing when I moaned with pleasure, his own voice rough and breathy. "Tomorrow?" he purred.

"Tomorrow," I agreed, fumbling with his waistband, needing to feel every inch of him, though it rankled a little that he'd taken to using mine and Duff's special phrase, a phrase that had always been ours. "I promise. I'll talk to them tomorrow."

Later, I lay in bed with my head on Lawrence's chest, listening to the steady thrum of his heartbeat as he napped. His breathing was slow and steady, too, lulling me into an almost-sleep. The only problem was, every time my eyes closed, I saw Ian Duncan's sad face staring back at me.

I got up, careful to be quiet, and grabbed my phone. I found myself scrolling through the pictures in my gallery, picking out ones of Ian. He had always smiled the same in photos, a big, wide, genuine smile that charmed everyone, from music producers and contacts to housewives and silly teenagers alike. I had yet to meet anyone as warm, easygoing, or as disarming as Ian Duncan.

I stopped swiping as I came to the picture I'd been looking for. It was a group of us, all crowded in front of the bar after our 40 Watt show, many of us holding drinks, a few people crouched down in front. We were all smiles; Ross and I even had our arms around each other.

The 40 Watt show had been even more nerve-inducing than the Porchfest gig, but somehow all four of us—with Ian's help—had managed to pull it off. We were all so excited and so proud to play the 40 Watt; most Athens bands had to pay serious dues and be on the scene for years before they got a venue like that, especially as headliners. Keeping the past pandemic in mind, when so many venues shut down or cut back on shows significantly, it was even harder, but here we were. Yeah, it was on a Tuesday night, but *still*. It was all because of Ian.

When I had walked into the venue early for load in, I found the bar empty save for the bartender and door guy. I took in the long, black bar, the threadbare but-still cool furniture in the middle of the floor, the posters adorning the walls, the merch table for our T-shirts, demos, and buttons… I felt a lump immediately begin to form in my throat. The stage was enormous, by far the biggest one we'd ever played on, and the iconic 40 Watt logo was lit up, huge, above it. Our band name was outside on the marquee as well.

It felt like my dreams were coming true.

The next person to walk in the door was a beaming Teresa-Jo, wearing a beautiful royal-blue sundress and beaming ear to ear. Brian, her fiancé, trailed behind her in pressed dark jeans and black cowboy boots. I ran to her, so excited and proud that I didn't even mind the bone-crushing hug she gave me, so strong she lifted me off the ground despite my being taller than her. "I'm so freaking proud of you, girl!" she exclaimed, and I felt tears rush to my eyes as I pulled away.

"I'm so glad you could make it!" I gushed. I hadn't seen TJ since she'd moved, and she was so busy at Emory that she didn't text as often now. Once upon a time I would've been annoyed at her for leaving me, for not telling me she was applying for med school, but with everything going on in the band and my personal life, I was in a good place. I was happy for TJ, truly.

"I know! I've been knee-deep in med-speak for days and I cannot wait to have a drink and hear y'all play!" TJ's happy tears matched my own. I wanted to stay and talk to her more, but I could see the rest of the band coming through the doors, dragging their equipment.

Brian gave me a quick nod and said, "Hey, break a leg, y'hear?" I'd never understand TJ's love for that good ol' boy, but I smiled and said a genuine thank you, anyway.

"I'll catch you two after, okay?" TJ nodded excitedly, and I cuffed her on the arm, heading toward Duff and Quincy.

I spent the next hour setting up my instruments and helping my bandmates, swallowing back tears the entire time. I don't know if the girls knew how emotional I was—I hoped not—but Ian certainly did. At one point backstage, he pulled me aside from where I was reading over the setlist, and whispered to me in a warm voice, "This means a lot to you, doesn't it?"

"Yes," I answered, and he pulled me in for a one-armed hug. His eyes were twinkling as he set me loose, and he gave me his signature wink.

"I'm glad," he said, and walked off to do manager things, as cool as ever.

We sat backstage, Quincy doing vocal runs, Ross going over lyrics with her then-boyfriend James, and Duff tuning her bass as we listened to the opening band, a cowpunk duo called Rope 'Em that hailed from Texas. After they played, they came backstage to introduce themselves and chat. The lead singer was especially cute—super tall with long, blond hair, wide green eyes, and a friendly, crooked smile.

About ten minutes before we were set to go on, the door opened and Ian sauntered in, followed by Lawrence, his hair freshly slicked back, dressed in a black blazer and black kilt with a silver chain hanging from the pocket. I jumped up and ran to him.

"You look good enough to eat," I said, throwing my arms around him. And boy, did he. His black kilt was freshly starched, crisp and fitted around his waist.

"What's *he* doing back here?" I heard Quincy mutter behind me, and I shot her a look over my shoulder. James was hanging out, and no one said shit.

I gave Lawrence a quick peck on the cheek as I pulled back and gestured around me. "Can you believe I'm backstage at the 40 Watt right now?"

"Pretty amazing," Lawrence agreed, his eyes cutting to the lead singer of the touring band, whose name I had learned was Jack. He was chatting with Ian and Quincy. "Who's the guy?"

"Oh, that's Jack. He's the lead singer for Rope 'Em."

Lawrence snorted, then tipped back his Boddington's to take a long swig. "That's the band name? For real?"

I punched him lightly on the arm. "They're really good. Come on, don't tell me you're jealous!"

"Definitely not." But his eyes flashed.

Duff came over, looping her arm through mine. In her other hand, she held a gin and tonic. She already had a good buzz on, but I wasn't concerned. Duff was one of those frustrating people who could play even better when she was inebriated, damn her. "Hey Larry!" she said, her red-lipped mouth curling into a big smile. "Are you excited for our show? We're gonna kick *all* the ass!"

"Looking forward to it, Duff," Lawrence replied, raising his beer in an invisible toast. "But would you mind not calling me Larry? Larry's my dad's name."

"Don't want people to think you're old?" she teased.

Lawrence frowned. "No. I just don't like it."

"Oh." Duff's face fell a little. "Sorry."

I became aware that everybody backstage—Quincy, Ross and her boyfriend James, Ian, even the guys from the touring band—were watching us. The room had gone completely silent, and suddenly everyone was incredibly aware of Lawrence's outward display of tension.

Thankfully, the sound guy popped his head into the room. "You guys go on in five," he said, and Quincy let out a whoop of excitement.

Ian whistled. "Alright, everyone who isn't Scottish Play, go find your seats. I need a huddle with my band." His eyes cut to Lawrence for the tiniest of seconds, and I felt myself bristle. Luckily, nobody else seemed to notice. Ross was busy giving James a passionate kiss, and Duff and Quincy were pressed together, taking a selfie. The guys from

Rope 'Em ventured to the door, and the cute one, Jack, turned to me and grinned.

"Go get 'em, tiger," he said as he exited, and I gave him finger guns, careful to smile without meeting his eyes, lest Lawrence think we were flirting.

"Wish me luck?" I asked, turning to give Lawrence a doe-eyed innocent look, and finally, his lips cracked into a grin. He took another long swig of his beer and handed it to me, his eyes working me over, then leaned over and roughly kissed me on the mouth. His voice was hoarse and sexy as he whispered, "Break a leg." I felt a thrill go through me as I caught his smoldering look.

As soon as the door shut, I shrugged, embarrassed. "Sorry, y'all. I think he was just excited to be backstage. I'm sure he didn't mean to be so weird about the Larry thing."

"He was clocking that guy, Jack," Duff said, downing the rest of her drink. "Don't tell me he's the jealous type."

"For real," Ross agreed, throwing her own empty can in the trash. "I have so totally been there myself, Mac. They don't get any easier."

"Oh stop," I said, irritated, remembering how Quincy had sneered about Lawrence being backstage even though Ross's boyfriend had been back here with us the whole time. "He isn't the jealous type. He was just nervous."

"Alright, y'all. Talk relationships on your own time; we've got business to discuss," Ian interrupted, raising his Terrapin in salute. We gathered around him. "Now, listen. I've got a story for you. It was in ye olde 1991—before you youngins were even a twinkle in your parents' eyes—that I was here, at this very venue, to see Nirvana. This was before they hit the big time, and in some ways, it wasn't even that memorable of a show… But the history…the legacy…that can't be measured. This place has seen so many amazing bands in the years since then, and a ton of them before that…and now you four are here, about to make your mark as The Scottish Play." His eyes were glistening. "I just want to say that I'm *very* proud of you guys. Now let's go get 'em!"

As soon as I stepped onstage, buoyed by Ian's speech, I spotted my mother sitting with Teresa-Jo and Granny Devereaux in the front row. But not even the sight of Mama, uninvited but clapping excitedly as she leaned in to whisper with Granny, could deflate my mood. Nor could my slight embarrassment from Lawrence's weird behavior backstage. I was standing onstage at the 40 Watt, Athens' most iconic bar. Playing a show with my girls. Making my mark. Nothing was gonna distract me. *Nothing* was gonna bring me down!

My grin was big enough to split my face wide open as I brought my arm down to launch into the opening chord of "Blood Orange," the first song I'd ever written. Now forever immortalized by my band. And that grin didn't leave my face the whole night.

After the show, we'd all gathered together to take a group photo in front of the bar. Me, Duff, Quincy, Ross, Ian, Granny Devereaux and Mama, Lawrence, Ross' boyfriend James, Teresa-Jo and Brian, and even Colton and Jack from Rope 'Em—who had kept trying to catch my eye all night, so maybe Lawrence hadn't been so paranoid after all—posed. Somewhere, Quincy had a framed copy of this photo.

Now I stared at mine on my phone, tears welling up in my eyes. So much had changed.

Lawrence's hand trailed up my hip and came to rest on the small of my back, tracing circles with a finger. I hadn't realized he'd woken up. "Penny for your thoughts?"

"I was just thinking about Ian," I said, holding my phone toward him so he could see the picture.

"I remember that," he said, sitting up in bed, the sheets falling down to reveal his muscular chest and the elaborate MacLaren crest tattoo above his left breast. "That guy Jack was trying to get into your pants."

"Of all the things that happened that night, *that's* what you remember?" I shook my head. "And anyway, you're wrong. He was just being friendly, networking. You know, what bands do." I swallowed, looking back at the picture. "Just look at Ian. How happy he is in this picture. He was so proud of us that night."

Lawrence squeezed my shoulder. "Marian, I know it's hard. But Ian led a good, long, successful life. He was happy in the end. That's all that matters."

I frowned.

But Lawrence was only trying to help. I knew that. I took his hand in mine, soft and warm. "Let's talk about the band," I said helpfully. "Tell me what you're cooking up for us!"

Lawrence's face lit up into a smile and he squeezed my hand back, excited. "You know me too well. I've got a bunch of stuff I'd like to run by you, actually. Have you thought much about recording? Because I had an idea…" He trailed off, then picked up a new thread, jumping out of bed and heading toward the doorway.

A flash of Ian's face, his sad brown eyes—I blinked it away.

Lawrence paused at the door, still talking, and I realized I'd tuned him out. "What are you thinking about?"

I smiled. "Nothing important. Just wondering if I should change up my look, now that we're getting more shows. Maybe something a little more sophisticated?"

"You could, sure. You thinking like a haircut, or…?"

"Yeah. And wardrobe, and maybe start doing some different makeup looks. I'm wondering if this whole heavy-eyeliner and bright eyeshadow thing is too much. You know, less eighties and more low-class hooker. What do you think?"

Lawrence grinned. "I think you always look hot. But you do have beautiful features, and there's nothing wrong with showing them off in a more natural way. Not that I don't love the grunge-meets-Joan-Jett aesthetic, but if you went a little less trailer rat and more like, sexy, sophisticated riot grrl…" He stood in the doorway, clapping his hands together like an excited kid.

I cocked an eyebrow. "'Trailer rat'? Did you seriously just say that to me?"

Lawrence rolled his eyes and gave me a look. "Oh, come on, Marian. I didn't mean anything by it. All I meant was you would look great with a classier look. Like, more of an Edward Norton-era Courtney Love aesthetic than a Kurt-era one. Know what I mean?"

"Uh-huh." I blinked. "Yeah, I get it."

"Are you mad at me?" Lawrence stared at me with puppy-dog eyes.

"No, I'm not mad."

He smiled. "Right, so shall we crack on, Marian?"

I sighed. I was going to have to grow a thicker skin if I was going to make it in this business. *Trailer rat*, huh? Well, that wouldn't do. Not if I wanted the world. I got out of bed, giggling at his prim-and-proper Britishisms, thinking ahead to the slinky black dresses I would need to buy. "Yes indeed, good sir, let's crack on."

CHAPTER ELEVEN:

"They say we're not ladylike." —Joan Jett, on The Runaways

"I hate him."

"Tell us how you really feel," I quipped, because I didn't know what else to say. Certainly not, "I'm starting to hate him too, Quincy." Because that would be disloyal to Marian.

Ross raised an eyebrow at me from her spot at the front of the chemistry lab. It was three-fifteen, and she wasn't quite out of teacher mode yet. Quin and I were slumped at a table like the students we used to be. Only instead of taking a test on the periodic table, we were possibly testing our friendship with Marian.

"Larry's a...problem," Ross agreed, gracefully stepping off the platform that allowed her to grade her students' papers without them seeing, not to mention keeping her out of the line of fire if an experiment went awry. "The question is," she continued, pulling up a chair, so it didn't *screeeech* against the linoleum floor, and sitting down across from us, "what are we going to do about it?"

"Shitcan him!" *That* opinion was courtesy of Ash, a teen with dreads sitting in the back of the room, who was supposed to be making up a quiz. Ross gave Ash a look that could have cut glass—not unlike looks she'd given Larry of late—and the kid quickly put their eyes back on their paper.

I smirked at the outburst, but Quin just sighed and said, "I don't disagree with Junior over there."

"Don't tell Ash, but they're the smartest kid in second period," Ross muttered. "Which is why"—she raised her voice, and Ash looked up—"I'm letting them make up this quiz and not sending them to detention for swearing." Ross and Ash exchanged a quick grin before Ash, chastened, bent down over their quiz once more.

"Anyway," Ross said, crossing one smartly trousered leg over the other. "Larry."

Quin threw up her hands. "I'm sorry, okay?" She glanced back at Ash before leaning in and lowering her voice. "He's just such a goddamn hypocrite. Trying to tell us how our riffs sound when we didn't even ask, and then saying *Marian* told him that, once she's out of the room. Pretty much haunting our practices, taking notes on his phone and then not showing us? Excuse you, you're in *our* space." Her pale face flushed. "Working the merch table last weekend—"

"I mean, that was pretty helpful," I cut in. And thanks to Larry's charm—which looked more like smarm to me, but I guess some people liked it—we'd sold out of T-shirts and buttons. He even did it for free, instead of Ross having to pay one of her students. But she *only* did that if it was an all-ages venue, otherwise we had to beg some rando and promise them free beer. Which we usually had to pay for, depending on which bartender was on shift.

Quin glanced at me sharply. "Whose side are you on, Duff?"

"Um, nobody's?" Now Ross was rolling her eyes. "Point taken," I conceded. "You know I hate stirring the pot, especially when Ian's barely…gone." Silence.

Hoping to further appeal to their compassion, I widened my eyes. "Come on, y'all. We need each other."

"What we *need* is Marian, and Marian's talent, and Marian's focus," Ross said. "Not her wannabe boyfriend trying to make decisions for us."

Seizing the opportunity, Quin perked up. "I know you're not a fan, Duff."

She had me there. I've never liked mansplaining, especially from someone who didn't know shit from apple butter when it came to the bass. Or rhythm guitar. Or drums. And yet, he'd tried to tell all of us how to play our own instruments.

It wasn't just that, either. Mansplaining, I could handle. I was a woman. I dealt with it every day.

I didn't like Larry because he was in Marian's head.

Sure, I was spending way more time with Quincy, and even Ross, these days. Quin and I had our *Sex and the City* nights, and after shows, the three of us would camp out at Waffle House and dissect every guitar riff and wrong note over coffee and hash browns until the sun came up. I was writing more lyrics, scribbling on napkins until one late night they presented me with a purple spiral notebook, both grinning as Ross pulled it with a flourish from the bottomless moss-green tote she carried everywhere. Only a drugstore cheapie, but the fact that they believed in my writing enough to invest their own money in it meant a lot to me. I carried that notebook everywhere. In fact, it rested under my hand now, just in case something about teen angst came to me.

But right now, my mind was blank of creative ideas. Instead, thoughts of Mac and Larry filled my head. The way she started every thought now with *Lawrence says*. When they fought, she always blamed herself—and I wasn't present for most of their conflicts, but I'd dated enough to know it usually takes two, unless someone's gaslighting. She'd even lightened up on her vibrant makeup, her trademark. If this were Mac's own idea, I'd fully support it, but I'd overheard her tell Quin that Lawrence had called her look "trashy."

"He was kidding, of course," she said with an uncharacteristic giggle. I could only see half of Quin's face from where I was standing, but I knew a horrified expression when I saw one.

"Duff? You there?" Ross snapped her fingers, jerking me out of my reverie.

"Sorry. But my point stands. He's her boyfriend. He makes her happy." And I would never say this out loud, but I knew Marian better than these two.

Mac and Quin had gone through school together longer, but I was Mac's friend first. She hadn't exactly had the most stable upbringing. Sure, I had trauma, and so did Quincy. But I also had a family who loved me so much they sent me away when I asked, trusting that I knew what was best for me, and whose group chat blew up my phone all hours of the day. Quin had lost her aunt and uncle, but before that she'd had a strong family unit, and more than anything, she was smart. I never worried about Quincy Banks.

Marian Shepherd, however? I worried about her all the time. She was so laser-focused on this band; it was all she had. Never mind that she'd made it that way herself. Now she had Larry, and yes, he was a dick, but he made her happier than I'd ever seen her. Why rock the boat?

"Because he's a controlling asshole!" Quincy said, and I realized I'd said that last part out loud.

"Toxic masculinity ruins the party!" Ash piped up, swiping pen across paper with a flourish like they were signing an autograph.

This time, Ross just laughed. "It's from a podcast we both like," she explained, holding out her hand as Ash skipped up to the front of the room and gave her the completed quiz. "Out, out, before your dads think I kidnapped you," Ross instructed her student, who didn't need to be told twice.

Quin sat back, folding her arms. "Larry M's ruining *our* party, that's for sure." Her brow furrowed. "It's not only that I don't like him, y'all. I could deal with a bad boyfriend. I… I don't trust him. He's angling hard to manage us, and he's not exactly being subtle about it. And Marian's—"

"Under his spell?" I volunteered right as Ross offered, "Brainwashed?"

The three of us chuckled, breaking some of the tension.

Quincy's expression softened. "I care about her. I care about our *band*." She looked at both of us with those Disney Princess eyes. "I'm really worried. Especially after our tiff at the Bald."

Ross sighed. "Okay, please don't hate me for saying this, but we *could* branch out on our own." She held up a hand at Quin's and my simultaneous protests. "Hear me out. I know Mac and I don't always see eye to eye, but I swear it's not about that. She's very talented and we get along when it counts. And I know I can be…a lot, too." Quin and I snorted. Ross grinned.

"And of course y'all are protective of her. You guys have a history, and I respect that," Ross continued, leaning on her elbows on the table space between us. "I still feel like the new gal sometimes, not because I'm unwelcome, but because you're all so tight. But here's the thing: with Ian gone, the dynamic is going to change. We're getting to the point where we *have* to have a manager, and both Marian and Larry are going to push for him. If it's three against two, it could get messy. And maybe become a deal-breaker.

"I'm gonna say this and then I'll shut up. You two,"—she pointed at me, then at Quin—"are so fucking talented it's sort of unreal. Quincy, I've never met a drummer who's an equally kickass singer, and you're hot to boot." Quincy rolled her eyes, but she was smiling.

Ross turned to me. "And you, Miss Optimist, are getting better and better as a lyricist. I don't think you give yourself enough credit. In fact, I *know* you don't. You're like…" She searched for the words. "You're our heart."

I sat back in my industrial school chair, stunned. I'd always thought of myself as the just-okay bass player and songwriter. The one who supported our three standouts. Yeah, they'd bought me a notebook, but I thought they were just being nice. Quin squeezed my shoulder. "She's right," she whispered.

"So yeah, the three of us are powerful. We could do this. We'd need another guitarist, but…" Ross trailed off. "It's an option," she finished.

For a second, I let myself imagine it: a power trio with a new guitarist. Athens was lousy with musicians—we wouldn't have a problem finding someone. Maybe even another person on keyboards—Ross did those sometimes, and was great, but this would take the pressure off her, and expand our sound. A new manager. A new look, a new name.

No Larry.

But also no Marian.

I knew the second I pictured it that I wasn't ready for Ross's option just yet.

"What say you?" That was Quin, looking at me intently, along with Ross.

So it was down to me. I'd really, *really* tried not to be in this position. I didn't like making waves; the wave-making I did as a teenager, pre-Hiawassee, had led to my first sexual experiences being awful ones—I was still shaking. Since then, I'd coasted, going along to get along, just in case the next big call I made was the wrong one.

And I had to look out for Marian. My bestie, my first real friend. The reason we were all together with our big talents. I couldn't cut her out simply because I didn't like her boyfriend.

I took a deep breath. "Here's what I'm thinking." The other two leaned in. We were still talking in hushed voices even though Ash was long gone. Like we were afraid to even speak our discord. Like it was some kind of curse.

I kept going, slowly measuring my words. Ross and Quin were my friends too, after all. My bandmates. I couldn't screw this up. "We don't want Larry as our manager. I agree with you there; he's too cocky, too green, and I don't quite trust him. But it's a delicate issue, because Marian's in love with him and we're *all* still feeling vulnerable, missing Ian. Emotions are high."

Quin grunted, then sniffled. I leaned my head on her shoulder briefly before pressing on. "With that in mind, I think Larry M's gonna be around for a while, whether we like it or not. We can't alienate Marian."

I looked at both of them. "We don't *want* to alienate Marian. So we talk to her. We're honest with her. Not brutally so—no 'we hate your boyfriend'—but we're reasonable and rational, in that we don't think he's the right fit for us. And she deals with that…however."

Please don't let her blow up. Please don't let her stop being my friend. I don't want to imagine a world without Mac Shepherd in it.

I kept my thoughts to myself, knotting my fingers together so they wouldn't shake.

Ross and Quin exchanged a glance, but I knew from their faces— Ross's resigned, Quin's slightly more hopeful—that I had them.

"Tonight?" Quincy offered. "When she gets home? I'll make popcorn the way she likes it." That was my girl.

"I'll hang out, too," Ross said. "All for one, one for all, right?" She smiled. As if choreographed, we all stood up, brushing invisible dust off our laps. Important meeting finished.

"Hey, is this a Bunsen burner?" Quin asked. She started fiddling around with it a little bit just as Ross said, "Yeah, but don't—"

A flame rose up, almost hitting the lab ceiling.

We three shrieked.

CHAPTER TWELVE:

MARIAN

"...I have bought golden opinions from all sorts of people,
Which would be worn now in their newest gloss." —*Macbeth*, Act I,
Scene VII

THE house was spotless when I came in the next day, and I felt guilty
even setting my duffel bag full of clothes on the floor. From the looks
of it, Duff and Quincy had channeled some of their grief through
obsessive cleaning. "Which one of you pulled a Monica Geller?" I
asked with a laugh, my shoulders letting go of a tension I didn't know
I'd held when they both rushed in from the kitchen to greet me.

"I'm so glad you're back!" Quincy said, giving my arm a squeeze.
"How we left things before... We were worried you wouldn't come
home."

"You're grieving too," Duff said, standing back and getting a good look at me. "We should have been more sensitive to you. Everyone handles these things differently. I know you weren't trying to be a jerk." She reached out and booped my nose, something she knew I hated, but I always let her do. "I'm sorry."

Guilt swirled in my belly. Neither of them had anything to be sorry for, not really. "No, I'm sorry," I said sincerely. "Sometimes my smart mouth gets ahead of me. I say things I shouldn't. I've got to learn some tact—I'm too old to be such a bitch."

"You're never too old for *that*," Quincy said with a laugh, and tugged on my arm. "Come into the kitchen. Ross is here. We just made your favorite."

The kitchen smelled buttery and spicy, and I waved at Ross and grinned as Duff pushed a bowl of my favorite snack—stove-popped popcorn, drizzled with vegan butter, sriracha, and nutritional yeast—in front of me. "Oh, yum," I said as I grabbed a handful, my mouth as happy as the rest of me.

The four of us munched and chatted, catching up as much as we could without bursting into tears. Duff mentioned that Crowe was upset about Ian's necklace going missing, and I frowned.

"It's probably just in his stuff, I said, grabbing another handful of popcorn. "Like a jewelry box or safe deposit box or something. Hanging in his bathroom, maybe."

"They've looked everywhere," Duff said. "It's gone. Like it never existed."

The popcorn was dry in my throat. I pushed the bowl away.

"He never took it off," Quincy said. "*Never.* Crowe gave him that, like, years ago? I never, ever saw Ian without it. Not on our hikes. Not even swimming at the lake." She shook her head. "Where *is* it?"

"Let's not talk about Ian right now," Ross said quickly, cutting off Quincy before she started to cry. "Marian's right. Let's talk about the band. Next steps, all of that. I know it's hard, but maybe it'll help."

Quincy pulled out her notepad—never far from her grasp—and we all smiled. She wiped at her eyes and took a deep breath, going into secretary mode. "Okay. Do we still want to play the show we've got booked at Flicker at the end of the month? Or cancel?"

"I'd like to keep it," Duff said, and I smiled at her, relieved. "Ian booked that show, and it's...well, it's the last one he'll ever book for us. Plus, it's a paying gig, and there's a band coming from out of town to open for us, and you know what he said..."

"Never say no to a networking gig, just say no to exposure gigs," we all chorused, and I smiled at the memory.

Duff continued, a catch in her voice, "It'll be weird, but I think we can do it."

"Oh yeah, we can," Ross agreed, and Quincy nodded in agreement. "We'll just be our own manager this time—chase up our own payment, drop off the flyers and merch ourselves, that sort of thing." We fell silent again, each of us thinking about just what that meant. No more manager. No more Ian.

"Or—" I cleared my throat. It was now or never. "I have another idea." Was that an instant wariness I saw on all their faces, a quick look at each other around the table, or was I imagining it? "But only if we all agree."

"What is it?" Duff asked, her voice oddly flat, as if she'd anticipated this. So I hadn't imagined it, then.

But it was too late to back out now. Besides, this was what *I* wanted. And it was a damn good idea. "I thought we'd ask Lawrence to be our manager. Temporarily, on a trial-run basis. If we like the job he does, we can talk about something more permanent."

The silence in the kitchen was deafening, so I went on. "He's got a lot of experience in the music industry. He worked at a recording studio, and as a promoter and PR agent. He loves our music, and he's passionate and hardworking. I think it makes perfect sense."

"Of course you do." Quincy's voice was tight. Her cheeks were bright red.

"What do you mean?"

"I mean, you're boning him, so of course you think the sun shines out of his ass." Ross cleared her throat, but Quin didn't look away from me.

"Wow." I stared back at her. "That's pretty fucking unfair, Quincy. He happens to be qualified. Do you think I'd do anything to compromise the band?"

"I don't know what the hell you'd do anymore," Quincy retorted, her voice wavering. "Or who."

"Quin…" Duff began, looking very uncomfortable, before mumbling something that sounded a lot like "we talked about this."

"Guys," Ross said, holding up a hand like we were the unruly teens she taught every day. She and Duff exchanged a worried glance. "Let's not get heated."

"I'm not sure it's a great idea, if I'm being honest," Duff cut in tentatively. "I know he's qualified, Mac, and it's not a judgment on him at all. It's just that…well, Larry M being our manager is kind of a conflict of interest, isn't it?"

"It's worked for Ozzy and Sharon for decades. Anyway, *Lawrence* asked you all to stop calling him that," I said crossly. "He hates it."

"Yeah, well, we all hate *Larry M* meddling in our fucking band," Quincy said, standing up and pushing her chair back with such force it fell over. "You're just stuck so far up his butt you haven't noticed! Or should I say *bum*—Mr. Talullah Falls loves to pretend he's from across the pond, doesn't he?"

"Quincy!" Duff admonished. Hot tears of anger prickled my eyelids. I was shocked at Quincy's gall—usually it was Ross who challenged me. Quincy had *never* spoken to me like that before.

At least Duff had the good sense to look contrite as she stared at the table and said, "I'm sorry, Mac. Force of habit. I meant to say Lawrence."

"You know, Mac, for someone who's obsessed with Joan Jett, you sure don't seem to have learned a damn thing from her," Quin remarked angrily. "She's been lifting up other women her whole career and she's so fucking independent. She does things her own way, and she'd never allow some man to swoop in and change her, or her music."

"Neither do I," I retorted, offended.

Quin shook her head. "You're not the same person anymore, Mac. I never thought you were the type to let a guy—or some dumb relationship—change you."

"Jeez, what has Lawrence done to any of you?" I demanded. "Not a damn thing other than show interest in our band! You guys are such little gatekeepers! God forbid an *outsider* try to join our ranks! Is that it?" I pushed away the popcorn bowl, my appetite gone. "Do y'all realize that one afternoon we let him sign into our Instagram and Twitter, and he gained us over a thousand followers in one day?"

"Organically?" Ross asked, her voice quiet. "Or paid for?"

"Jesus, nothing is good enough for y'all, I swear." I shook my head angrily.

Ross mumbled something under her breath that sounded suspiciously like "you're one to talk," but when I snapped my head toward her, she covered her mouth and coughed.

"So it's like that," I said, furious. "Three against one."

Ross leveled her gaze at me. "Isn't it always? You do love to play the victim."

"Oh, fuck you," I said, my voice low and full of fury.

"No way. Fuck *you*, Marian," Quincy yelled. She was working herself up into one of her panic attacks; I could tell by the sound of her breathing, shaky and gasping. Normally I was the one who comforted her through those, but today she was on her own. "You do *not* get to play victim here. Over my dead body will you replace Ian with that... that...sniveling little dickhead!"

She turned to Duff and Ross. "And you two, you're just sitting there letting it happen!" The girls stared at her in shock, Duff blinking back tears. "You *promised* we'd be a united front and you're both just folding!"

Ross snapped back, "We're not folding. Anyway, we *also* promised we'd talk to Marian calmly, and you popped off the moment she opened her mouth, Quincy."

Quincy spat, "I didn't know she was going to charge in and just tell us what was what. She didn't even *ask*, Ross!"

My brow furrowed. I *had* asked. Hadn't I?

A low hum of rage had begun low in my belly, traveling up through my chest into my extremities, making my hands tremble. Quincy was still sputtering and Duff was still staring down at the table, her face a deep shade of Joan Jett fuchsia. Ross just looked tired. I gripped the table, trying to fight the urge to throw popcorn all over the three of them.

They had been talking about me behind my back. They had been making plans without me. They were becoming a "united front" against me.

I tried to meet Duff's eye, but she wouldn't look at me. "Are y'all planning a coup or something? Trying to oust me from my own band?" I made it sound like I was joking, but I'd inadvertently made a fist with my right hand. I saw Ross look at it, then quickly look away. "Duff?"

She shook her head, her face sad. "No, Mac. Of course not. We just...we don't want you to push Lawrence on us as manager. Not right now. We need more time to grieve and to think. That's all."

"I'm not trying to *push* anything. I'm trying to—"

"All you do is push!" Quincy smacked her hands down on the table, making us all jump. "Ian's body is barely cold. He's the reason we're all here; we'd be nothing without him! You all make me sick!" And with that, Quincy ran out of the house, slamming the screen door behind her. We all sat there, stunned, listening to the sound of her tires peeling out of the driveway.

"You guys, we can't be like this," Duff said in a quiet voice, her eyes still brimming with tears. She had always been so protective of Quincy. I was furious with her, with all of them, but I felt bad for Duff. Likely, Quin and Ross had pulled her into their cattiness. This must be tearing her apart. "After the last time, we promised. And now that Ian's gone... The rest of us have to be on the same team. Or we lose a lot more than just the band."

I swallowed hard and nodded. Duff reached across and grabbed my hand.

"Good thing none of us are drummers," Ross said, looking at me with a halfway smile that didn't quite meet her eyes. "Our sense of timing is pretty bad."

She reached across the table and gave both Duff and me a nudge to indicate she was only teasing. But neither of us laughed.

QUINCY BANKS

I fucked up, and I knew it the second I slammed the door.

But I also knew I couldn't put the words back in my mouth. They were all true.

I'm not stupid. I could have been salutatorian in high school if I'd still given a shit (I finished fourth in my class. Still pretty smug about that). I knew it was weird, how I was acting like a "grieving widow," as I'd heard Marian say to Duff, about a guy old enough to be my dad, who I'd only known for five years. At this point, *Crowe* was handling it better, and they were Ian's kid!

I couldn't explain it, and at the same time I totally could. For me, it all came back to family.

We were all a little bit in love with Ian, even Duff, who vehemently denied it. How could we not be? Here's a guy who built a really successful career, who could have retired a decade ago, who absolutely did not need a ragtag group of teenage girls, who didn't even have a band name when we met him. And yet, his generosity was unparalleled. He let us live in one of his houses, covering new equipment and travel fees. Dude was a goddamn saint with a better body than any of the young guys we knew, well-maintained facial hair, and twinkling eyes to match.

But it was more than that for me. Deeper. Familial. I was the cliché lost soul looking for a daddy figure. No matter how much Marian bitched about Annie (and having gone through what I did with my own family, I *did* empathize with her—having a drunk for a mom wasn't easy) she had a mom who could still look her in the face. And Duff had Granny, who also doted on me, but I wasn't blood. So in that way, Ian was mine and mine alone.

I mean, I wanted to bang the guy senseless. But my love for Ian was more than that. His presence was steady, sweet, and most of all, validation that I was doing the right thing with my life.

Everyone thought they knew about my aunt and uncle, but they didn't.

One of the many, many shitty things about addiction is how people only remember the end result, whether that's a triumphant sobriety (never mind that most everyone relapses, or so I've read) or...worse. In the case of my aunt and uncle, it was the dictionary definition of "worse."

They'll always be the couple who blew up in the meth lab. Right after it happened, someone at school tried to start calling me "Breaking Bad," but I was tight with Marian by then and I'm pretty sure she let the air out of his tires. I always loved her for that.

See, I remember Jen and Rick as the ones who came to our house on random Saturday nights, bringing in gusts of chilly air and cigarette smoke. Jen and Rick who didn't finish college and wanted me to earn my degree. Jen and Rick, who were the first adults I told when I realized I liked boys and girls and everyone, who told me they loved me exactly how I was. Jen and Rick, who came to all my choir concerts from fourth grade on and whooped the loudest—"that's my girl!"—when I had a solo. Jen and Rick, who gave me my first drum set when I was ten, winking at me over my parents' *very* loud protests.

They loved music. A state-of-the-art sound system and a massive vinyl collection pretty much took over their house. They road-tripped to record stores whenever they could. Marian loved The Runaways and so did I—Jen taught me the lyrics to "Cherry Bomb" when I was five, to my parents' chagrin. When I got in trouble for teaching the song to my kindergarten classmates, Jen picked me up from school and took me out for ice cream. And when I wanted to learn how to play drums, and how to really *sing*, it was my aunt and uncle who paid for lessons. Not because my parents couldn't afford it, but because "we want to do this for her," Rick told my dad, squeezing my shoulder. I've never felt more special, before or since.

The only thing Jen and Rick loved more than music was a good time.

As I got older, I realized that meant drinking. A lot. Sometimes too much, but whatever, they were just fun. Never sloppy or mean or racist. More the type that sang a bunch of dumb old songs and encouraged me to harmonize and beat along, and maybe left them with a headache the next morning that only Waffle House breakfast could fix.

My sophomore year, Rick broke his leg, and it all went to shit.

Opioids. Looking so benign in their little orange bottle, but really the stuff of *Dateline* specials and pointed fingers at the supposedly stupid trash humans who don't know any better than to stop popping them. I guess at some point, Rick gave one to Jen, and that was all it took. That's when they discovered the dark web and started selling off their sound system, records, anything they could. When that got too hard, too expensive, they turned to the stuff that was way easier to get: heroin. And when they got really desperate, meth.

We found this out after they died.

Even in a butthole town like Hiawassee, secrets happen, as my family and I learned the hard way after we got the call on a Sunday night at dinnertime. I haven't looked at mashed potatoes the same way since. We knew about Rick's injury, of course, but by that time my mom was finally promoted off the mommy track and into partner of her firm and my dad was on this big civil engineering project in Atlanta. Friday night sleepovers at their house were a thing of the past, as I was a full-fledged high schooler with honors homework, choir practice, and popular-kid parties on weekends. Yeah, they looked a little haggard at Christmas and my dad had to bail Rick out of jail once, but when you're busy, it's easy to overlook red flags.

And then you get the really fun bonuses of survivor's guilt and perpetually beating yourself up for missing the signs. I did have *one* hint. Jen tracked me down at school once, begging for money. I never told my parents, but I gave her the twenty dollars in my wallet and went without lunch, pretending to giggle with my student council friends while doing my damnedest to forget her stringy hair, so greasy and gross, when she used to buy me the same special shampoo she used so we could be twins.

After we had a tiny and depressing memorial with just the three of us and a minister who didn't know shit, my parents couldn't deal. My mom threw herself into her law practice the next town over, was home less and less. She never said as much, but I know it was hard for her to see me, who looked so much like her younger sister as a teen. I'd seen pictures, and it hurt me too.

My dad, on the other hand, started working from home and never really left, perpetually on guard. He and Rick had been best friends. Now he didn't know who to trust, and he texted me constantly, wondering when I'd be home, if I was drinking, if I needed a ride. He got me a Lyft account, even though Hiawassee had maybe five drivers, just in case I was at a party and didn't have a safe ride home. When the three of us were in the same space, we bumped around, strangers.

The explosion, that's when everyone in town started talking and we learned the whole sordid story of Jen and Rick's descent to addict hell. Not before, when my parents and I could have possibly intervened. Or maybe we couldn't have.

There were still questions. We'd never know if they were using, buying, selling, or making meth, or if they were just in the wrong place at the wrong time. All we had left were rumors, a trashed-out house where I used to have Friday night sleepovers in grade school, and happy memories no one wanted to hear because they weren't salacious.

When my parents changed, blindsided by grief, so did I.

I had my first panic attack of many. I started spending less time on homework and more time in the basement, hitting my drums so hard I broke several pairs of sticks in the weeks after it happened. I didn't want to sing showtunes because they didn't have the rawness I now carried inside, so I left choir but kept my voice lessons, which my parents now paid for. I was crap at lyrics, but I had a great ear, so I started working out chords. Melodies. Beats. My first song was called "I Miss You." So goddamn corny in retrospect, but I cried every time I banged and yowled it out. Helped me breathe. Better than the therapy my parents made me undergo until the psychologist stared at my tits while mansplaining the five stages of grief and I left his office, never to return.

I found solace in music, and then I found a new family.

After I quit student council and cut my hair, I sat down next to the girl I'd known forever but wasn't a joiner, to put it mildly, and her pretty new friend with the weird accent and wide smile, whose bleached hair I'd complimented in the hall. Since Jen and Rick's deaths left me changed, I'd realized how *real* they were, Marian and Duff. They talked about things other than who was buying the vodka for this week's rager, who had sex in the bathroom at last week's, who'd gotten into Emory or Georgetown. They liked hiking and road trips—I immediately offered up my car for the latter, desperate for them to let me in their club of two—and when I told them I was a teetotaler because of what had happened, they didn't ask questions, just made sure to have Coke or LaCroix on hand when they indulged. Best of all, they didn't press me for details or gossip, just listened if I wanted to talk about it (which was almost never).

Marian and Duff were weird, and they embraced that. They embraced *me*, metaphorically and sometimes literally. We bared our souls in my car, in diners, and on the trails: Marian's frustrations with her drunk mom and her endometriosis pain, Duff's encounters with the lowlife who knocked her up, my desire to break free from our too-small town and a house suffocating me with unspoken sadness. We didn't judge. We *understood*. And when I found out they'd been jamming together in Duff's granny's garage, well, it was like fate.

Like family.

Which is why I shouldn't have yelled at Marian, should have talked to her before I plotted with the others to give her that ultimatum. I knew what that was like, to finally find a connection, the way she had with Larry. *Lawrence.* Granted, my connections were with an older man who was now dead and a band full of ladies I wasn't sleeping with, but whatever. So what if Duff and I thought he was a little pretentious, and Ross's hatred of the guy was becoming more obvious by the day? Lawrence *did* have connections and maybe he'd make a decent manager.

Either way, going off on a bandmate and best friend? Not okay. I was agreeing with Mac less and less, but that didn't matter. We could get through this without losing each other like I'd lost Rick and Jen and, in a lot of ways, my parents. With addicts in our past and present, Marian and I weathered storms together. She was my *family.*

Maybe that's what killed me, in the end. Because I knew better than anyone how family can stab you in the back, and yet I did nothing.

"Hey," I said the night after the blowup, plopping down at our usual table. I'd asked both Mac and Larry to meet me here and hash things out; after I finally came back late last night, she'd gone to Larry's. *Lawrence's.*

No live music tonight, just canned jukebox tunes. I made a mental note to see if they had any Joan Jett. Score—I found "I Love Rock 'n Roll," our favorite, and made that selection, hoping she'd get the message.

Marian said nothing when the first notes came on, just raised her eyebrows at me. She didn't have her usual '80s-esque makeup, more of a streamlined cat eye. Her septum ring was gone, her hair looked softer, less severe.

"You look pretty," I offered, because she did. Larry smirked, and I wondered if these changes were due to him. I'd bet our forthcoming bar tab I was right. But I had to try with him too. It was looking more and more like he'd be part of the family.

It looked like I'd have to straight-out apologize. No beating around the bush, as Granny Devereaux would proclaim before plunking down a big ol' dish of nanner pudding with Nilla Wafers crumbled on top just the way I liked it. I tried to summon some of her strength.

"Look, I'm sorry," I said. "Really. It's been a rough time for all of us, but that's not an excuse for me to just run off like that." Marian still didn't say anything, but she held out her hand, and I took it, lacing my fingers through hers. She was as straight as they came, whereas I liked hearts, not parts (and had harbored a crush on Duff since day one), but we'd done this since high school, squeezed hands for the hell of it. It was our version of a hug, since Marian wasn't much for those.

"It's okay," Larry said. I swallowed down my *I wasn't talking to you, asshole,* and gave him a tight smile. "We understand." Again with the *we,* huh?

"First round on me?" Marian offered. She squeezed my hand. We were okay.

"Deal." I grinned. "I'll be at the jukebox." My selections had run out, but there was more Joan Jett to be played and sung along to. Just like we did as teenagers.

Swiping my card and punching in the song numbers, I had a rush of happiness. We'd be okay, Marian and me. And Larry? We'd deal.

Maybe that euphoria was why I took a sip of her drink.

That was the other lasting, long-term effect of losing Jen and Rick. I became the biggest teetotaler on this side of the Mason-Dixon Line. And that extended to pot (yes, I took the whole "gateway drug" thing seriously even as I realized it was probably junk science), vaping, and even cigarettes.

You know what's not junk science? Addiction running in families. I never wanted to take that risk, put my mom and dad, estranged as we all were, through what we'd experienced with Jen and Rick. Somewhere, I'd like to think my dead aunt approved of my choices.

"You sure?" Marian asked when I reached my hand out for her Jack and Coke. "I thought you were still…" She nodded toward my empty Roy Rogers, ice melting and leaking onto the battered wood table.

"Oh, lighten up!" I said, laughing. "One sip. What's the worst that can happen?"

Turns out, the very worst of the worst is what can happen.

What followed was a blur. More rounds. The soundtrack going from Joanie to the Eagles to what I thought was Demi Lovato and back to Joanie. I tried to sing along until Larry and Marian pulled me down, laughing, from where I was standing on the table. Shared cigarettes outside, staggering in for more drinks before getting into a car. I wasn't sure whose, but Marian was with me. I knew she wouldn't let anything bad happen to me. Family, after all.

Then there was nothing.

Until I saw the needle come toward my arm. At this point I didn't know what was in it, and who exactly was pricking me like Sleeping Beauty. My hair used to look like hers, the Disney version, at least. Who was my evil witch? Someone else? Or my own hand?

Above me, a swarm of flies buzzed on the ceiling.

The last thing I remember was closing my eyes, opening them again to see myself, not crumpled on the concrete floor of a room I didn't recognize, but curled up on my side. Like I was just taking a nap. My lashes looked great.

"Come on." I heard the unmistakable rumble of the man I loved. Ian held out his hand, and I took it, feeling the rough texture envelop my skin, just like I'd always dreamed, only better.

Family. At last.

Even then, I wondered where my aunt Jen was.

CHAPTER THIRTEEN:

MARIAN

"Give sorrow words; the grief that does not speak knits up the o-er wrought heart and bids it break." —*Macbeth*, Act IV, Scene III

AFTER the seventh consecutive episode of *Queer Eye,* I padded in my threadbare Pepe Le Pew slippers into the kitchen, where I poured myself another cup of coffee. I dropped the spoon twice before it finally made its way into the cup. I stood there, stirring it over and over, staring into the swirling creamer, looking at the spiral pattern it made. My eyes were bleary and crusty and I let them go out of focus, willing myself to just disassociate and get it over with.

"What cup is that, Marian? Your fifth? Sixth?" I turned slowly to see Lawrence standing in the doorway, fresh from a shower, dressed in a pair of pressed black skinny jeans, his usual combat boots, and leather jacket over a starched white shirt. He looked equal parts metal and professional, and somehow it totally worked. I frowned, clutching my cup. Hadn't he *just* told me he was going out for a run? How had he already gone, gotten back, showered, and dressed? Evidently, I'd lost track of time.

"I don't know," I mumbled, turning back to my cup and taking a sip. I made a face. Even with the creamer, it was bitter. "However many, it isn't working."

"I'm just thinking of all the sugar in that stuff," Lawrence said, gesturing to the bottle of southern butter pecan coffee creamer on the counter. It was Duff's, and I owed her another bottle because I'd almost used it all. "It's not good for you."

"Oh, so now I'm getting fat, too?" I snapped, slamming the cup down on the counter. Milky coffee splashed all over the cabinets and the floor. "I've already changed my damn hair, okay?"

"That's not what I meant at all, honey," Lawrence said, walking over and pulling me into his arms. His voice was calm and steady. "I'm sorry. Look, you're distraught. And you have every right to be." A knowing silence passed between us before he spoke again. "I'm just trying to look after you, that's all. Maybe I'm doing a bad job."

"No, no, of course you aren't," I murmured, letting him hold me. "You're doing a great job." How had he managed to flip it around, so I was consoling him? Funny, that. But it felt so good, pressed up against his warm, strong chest, listening to his heartbeat thudding steadily in my ears, that I forgot it. I knew he meant well.

Lawrence pulled back, smiling tenderly and raising my chin up with a finger. "I love you, Marian Shepherd."

For a moment, I could only stare at him, totally overwhelmed, the emotions bubbling up inside me and swirling around my belly.

Nobody had ever said that to me before, at least not in a romantic way. This was it—the moment everyone dreamed about, the first "I love you..." and yet, he had chosen *now* to say it. Now—me standing in the kitchen with coffee breath, eyes puffy and crusted over from crying, wearing the same pajamas I'd been wearing for two days, with one of my best friends barely cold in the ground.

I beat back down the tears I felt coming. I had already shed so many. Lawrence was staring at me, his eyes bright and full of love. I was being a shit, as usual. I took in a shaking breath and, even though I wasn't ready, replied, "I love you, too."

"I'm so glad to hear that." He kissed me tenderly, softly, on the lips, as though I might break. "Right. Well, I've got to run. I'll be back later. Promise me you'll at least drink a glass of water?"

My brow furrowed. "Where are you going?"

He sighed. "I told you, Marian, remember? I'm going to run by Nuci's to see about renting you guys a space to rehearse, and then I'm going to meet with someone from Boulevard Records about possibly cutting some tracks. We talked about it."

I stared. "But..." We *had* talked about it, but that felt like light years ago. Before Quincy. Now with her gone, we had no drummer *or* singer. To say nothing of the fact that none of us exactly felt like recording or even jamming right now. "I mean... I just thought...I thought you'd wait. A little while, at least."

Lawrence sighed again. He brushed a strand of my hair out of my face. "I know. It seems impossible. But Marian...Quincy wouldn't want you to give up on your dreams. Nor would Ian. And when you guys are ready... Well, hopefully I'll have everything all set up for you to make a fresh start." He smiled, placing another kiss on my forehead. "I hate to leave you right now, but I promise I'll be back really soon. Okay?"

"No kilt today?"

He shook his head, noting my pitiful attempt at stalling. He gave me a crooked smile. "Missing my thigh tattoos, are you?"

I couldn't keep up my end of the playful banter today. All I could do was nod weakly and watch Lawrence walk out the door.

When it clicked shut, I grabbed a dishrag from the drawer and mopped up the coffee. *Quincy wouldn't want you to give up your dreams.* Well, Lawrence hadn't been there for that knock-down, drag-out fight we'd had around the kitchen table when Quincy, her eyes blazing and full of tears, had run from the apartment, saying we all made her sick for moving on too fast after Ian had died. After confessing that the three of them had been talking about me behind my back. I wasn't so sure Lawrence was right this time. There was grief, yes, but what we were getting into was dissent and bad blood territory. And that was *before* Quincy had...

But it didn't matter what Quincy thought anymore. Because she was dead. And life had to go on, didn't it?

I grabbed the too-bitter coffee and walked back into the living room, again taking up residence on the couch. My phone vibrated, and I looked at the screen, watching Duff's name light up, then hit silent. It rang again almost immediately, and when I hit silent again, a text came through. *Hey you. Call me.* I ignored it. Another text immediately following that: *Tomorrow.* Our usual sign off.

I knew Duff had been at Crowe's since yesterday, making sure they were okay. Quincy's death had taken a toll on everyone, but Crowe was just a kid—a kid who had just lost their dad. I was glad Duff was taking care of Crowe, but I didn't want to deal with her, or anyone, right now. I'd come around—I had no choice—but I just needed time to make sense of all that had happened. I'd been watching *Queer Eye* for so many hours I'd lost track at this point and I was almost out of episodes.

Lawrence was like those guys, in a way. He'd come out of nowhere and taken me—just like those loveable dolts from season one in Georgia—under his wing, hitting the ground running, taking meetings and making plans to blow The Scottish Play up into the next big thing. And if anyone could do it, it was Lawrence. He was just that type of person; when he wanted something, he made damn sure he got it. And he was doing it for *us*.

Only...well, he was doing all of this totally on his own, and he did not have the girls' blessing. Quincy and I had managed to mend fences, and she'd kinda sorta acquiesced on the Lawrence thing, but then she was gone. Nobody else heard that conversation, and even if they had, now that she was gone, the whole thing seemed moot. It wasn't likely that Ross and Duff would be on board now, after everything.

I guess when I really thought about it, Lawrence was just bulldozing over everyone's wishes and taking charge without even a verbal agreement. He had totally taken for granted that I'd just handled it, not thinking about the fact that we were all grieving or how awkward it would be. He meant well, but deep down, I could see why my friends were understandably pissed. I had mowed them all over and gotten exactly what I wanted, the same way I always did. I knew that eventually my reckoning would come if I didn't stop this.

I just didn't have the energy to fight it. Not now.

I could only hope my friends didn't have the energy, either.

Besides, Lawrence was doing all this for us.

For *me.*

Quincy was dancing on the bar, her arms raised up over her head, her shoes slipping on the slick wood. She laughed, her sweaty hair stuck to her beautiful face, now red with exertion. "I love this song!" Joan Jett and the Blackhearts "I Love Rock 'n Roll" was playing for the fifth time; Quin kept going back and playing it again and again. It was any wonder the barkeep hadn't banned her from the jukebox.

I somehow managed to get her down, hefting her off the bar and back onto solid ground so she didn't break her neck. She looked at Lawrence and me with a grin, her eyes a little dazed but very bright. "Don't you? Love this song? Like, we should cover it! We did 'Cherry Bomb' in high school, so it totally makes sense!"

Lawrence answered before I could speak up, his voice carrying over the loud chaos of the bar. "I think that's a great idea. Pick a classic that everyone loves. Let's talk more about that later."

"Yes, let's." Was that a hint of sarcasm in Quin's voice? Evidently, booze made her sassy.

Lawrence didn't seem to notice as he tipped back his beer. "Definitely the best song Joan's ever written!"

Quin smirked a little, grabbing my drink from my hand and sloshing it everywhere. I reached to grab it back from her, and she laughed. "Shows what you know, Larry M. Joan didn't write that song."

Lawrence frowned. "Lawrence. And it's her signature song. Everybody knows that."

"The Arrows," Quin slurred. She'd changed her mind about the drink. She sat it down on the table, then after a pause, plopped herself down,

hard, in the chair beside it. She slumped so quick she almost hit her head on the table, and I rushed to put my arm under her.

"Excuse me?" Lawrence looked irritated.

"It was by The Arrows," Quin said, looking up, her expression a mixture of triumph and drunken confusion. "Joan loves doing covers. So why don't we do another one? A cover of a cover of a cover..."

"She's drunk. She doesn't know what she's fucking talking about," Lawrence muttered, giving my arm a conciliatory squeeze, as if I needed to be consoled. Then he walked off toward the bathroom, his tense posture giving away his irritation.

I stared after him for a moment, then looked at Quin with a smile. She was right, of course. It was The Arrows who originally wrote and recorded that song, not Joan.

"You can do better, you know," Quin said, swatting a fly away from my drink before resting her head on her elbows and falling asleep right there at the table.

I awoke with a start, my head pounding, a sharp, stabbing pain in my temple like I had a hangover. But I hadn't had anything alcoholic to drink since two nights before at the bar. I was still sitting on the couch, my winter coat pulled over my legs like a blanket, coffee forgotten and cold on the coffee table. Netflix was asking me if I was still there.

Was I?

I winced, turning off the TV and putting my head in my hands. Quincy. Dancing to Joan Jett on the bar. Her beautiful blonde hair sweaty against her cheeks, flushed and full of life. How pretty she'd looked that night. How glowing and *alive*.

She would never look that way again.

"You can do better, you know." The last words Quin would ever say to me.

But she was wrong. I really couldn't. None of them, not even Duff, knew enough about me to know who—or what—I deserved.

My phone was vibrating again. With a groan, I turned it over, looking at the screen. Crowe. *Nope.* I hit silent again, unable to face them. I was being so awful. Doing the same thing, I'd just admonished Quincy for last week. I was a hypocrite and a bitch and a simp and everything else bad in the world.

But I just couldn't. I was still so hurt. They'd all been talking behind my back, uniting against me like I was the villain of the story. Might as well act like it.

A text came through from Crowe. *Duff's been trying to call. Quincy's parents have planned a memorial service for her this weekend, in the viewing room at the funeral home. Putting up a Christmas tree because she loved Christmas. They want you and Duff to speak. Afterward, Duff thought maybe the four of us—me, you, Duff, and Ross—could go hiking at Brasstown Bald to say a private goodbye. Let me know if you're coming. Love you.*

I read the text, then turned the phone back over. It had made no mention of Lawrence being invited, of course, but Crowe was? How unfair! A momentary impulse to write back and say no washed over me. I bit it off with a grimace. I could not do that. Not to Quin. Not to her parents. I'd just have to smile and make nice. Like I always did.

My phone rang again. This time, my mother. *Fat fucking chance.* I opened my music app and hit play on Joan's "Bad Reputation," turning it up loud enough that I wouldn't hear the vibrations if anyone called or texted again. Then I went back to sleep.

"You made it." Duff's eyes were every bit as puffy as mine had been as she pulled me into a brief hug, releasing me quickly. She was clad in a simple black dress and flats, her long hair pulled into a sleek, tight ponytail. She looked me up and down, her eyebrows raised in surprise. "You look...different," she said. "I mean, pretty. But I don't think Quin's folks would have minded you keeping your piercing."

"Oh, that." My hand flew to my nose. "That's not why I took it out. I just...I think I'm done with it for a while." I knew Duff was taking in my simple black slacks and gauzy black button-down, and my new haircut and understated makeup, too. I'd started watching makeup tutorials on YouTube, finally nailing a subtle cat-eye and contour. Lawrence had been right: all that flashy, neon-bright eyeshadow and heavy blush looked really cool, but I was trying to be a professional musician. Joan Jett pulled it off effortlessly, but she was a child of the late seventies and early eighties. If I wanted to find my audience, that meant no more Dollar Store eyeliner and orange blush.

Gone was my shaggy, messy half-mullet, replaced with a much sleeker, layered bob. It wasn't all that different, just easier to style, and far less chaotic. I'd spent years spiking up my hair and sporting a deliberate bedhead, trying to look like some riot grrl rebel—but I was beyond all that now. No more Jack White T-shirts and an endless array of Chuck Taylors in primary colors; it was sleek dresses and fitted pants now. It was time to be a woman, not a kid.

We all stood in the huge, ornately decorated viewing room inside the funeral home. The moment I'd walked in, I'd glanced over at the main wall, sighing with relief to see no casket or prepared body, just a podium that held a bright pink urn. I'd attended enough Southern wakes—everyone doing their best to hold polite, boring conversations without looking over at the deceased, and if they did, not to shed too many public tears—to last my lifetime. It was a quintessentially Southern thing, viewings…but I'd always hated them, preferring to remember people as they looked in life, rather than some made-up facsimile.

Someone had worked overtime to turn the normally understated, generic space into an homage to Christmas, even though it was March, and decorated in all things pink and purple. There were so many bright flowers, most of them pink, coming out of every corner and placed on every table; between that and the pollen outside, it was a wonder everybody wasn't sneezing. The funeral home had put rows of chairs near the back wall, and a huge Christmas tree was in the corner. I could see a little drum set ornament on one of the branches, and I wrenched my eyes away. I might be a grown woman, but being here, among Quincy's family in a funeral home, decorated to the nines in Christmas schtick, I felt like a five-year-old heartbroken orphan.

Duff reached out as if to tousle my head, and I stepped back on impulse. "Don't mess it up," I cautioned, patting it protectively. "It took me forever to style."

"I wasn't going to," she said with a laugh, ignoring my slight. It sounded good to hear her laugh, even if it was a little hollow.

So why didn't I smile back at her? I was still pissed that the invite to Brasstown Bald had not been extended to Lawrence, though he hadn't mentioned wanting to come. They certainly hadn't minded inviting Crowe. The truth was, I was just angry. In general. Mad at the world.

At anyone who dared try tapping into the careful, delicate shell I'd put up around myself.

Duff peered at me with wide blue eyes. "Will the real Mac Shepherd please stand up?" She was still smiling, but I grimaced.

"I'm the same fucking person, Duff," I hissed, and she put up her hands in mock surrender, her smile fading. I looked down at my feet.

"I'm sorry," I muttered, and she placed a hand on my shoulder.

"Me, too." Her voice was gentle. "It's okay." I exhaled deep through my nose, trying to will my blood pressure down. The nicer Duff was to me, the more on edge I felt. Part of me wanted to scream and yell, to have it out with her, just to get my feelings under control. To let off a little steam from the pressure cooker.

Ross stepped up to us, handing each of us memorial pamphlets. I tucked mine into my purse without looking; I couldn't bear to see Quincy's smiling face or read any of the undoubtedly heartbreaking verses of poetry or grieving overtures her parents had chosen to remember their daughter, at least not yet. I would do it later, when I was alone. I noticed that Duff did the same, putting the little booklet into her own purse with a swallowed sigh.

"Looks like they're about to start," she said, looking at Ross and me. "We should go sit. Are you coming to Brasstown Bald with us later? For the hike?"

"I didn't bring any other clothes," I said stupidly. I still didn't want to go, and hadn't allowed myself to even think of it, and yet... I hadn't bothered to think up an excuse, either.

Duff looked at me. "You can borrow from me. You know I've always got a change of clothes in the trunk. And you can ride with us if you don't want to drive up the mountain."

"I mean…" I paused for a moment. Honestly? I just *really* didn't want to go. But there was no way to convey that without looking like a total asshole. Ross and Duff stared at me, waiting for my answer, their eyes working me over, premature disappointment on both their faces. *Stop pressuring me!* I wanted to scream. Instead, I ripped the tissue in my hand into little shreds.

"Would it be easier if we waited to go tomorrow or the day after?" Duff asked, her voice taking on a note of pleading.

There was no getting out of it. I nodded. "Um, yeah. I think it would."

I scanned the sad faces, looking for Teresa-Jo, who I'd noticed coming in earlier. I hadn't had a chance to talk to her yet, to thank her for showing up. She'd always been cool to Quincy, even though they didn't know each other well. I thought I might extend the invite, see if she wanted to go on the memorial hike with us. The way I saw it, she had as much right to be there as Crowe did. Having her there would be a comfort, since she knew me so well. It would make having to go bearable.

I didn't see TJ anywhere, though. She must already be seated. I made a mental note to find her later.

And, to make matters worse, I could see the familiar profile of Annie Shepherd, dear old Mama, walking through the front door a few yards away, her hair teased into oblivion, the tear streaks through her foundation clear from yards away. Why the hell was she here? It wasn't like I'd had Quincy over for burgers and milkshakes any time in recent memory. They had barely known each other. I saw Granny Devereaux immediately rush to her, arms outstretched, and I bit my lip, hard.

"Of fucking course," I muttered under my breath.

"Mac," Duff said, her eyes staring straight through me. "*Please.*"

"Okay," I said, my shoulders slumping, wishing I could run out of the "Fine. I'll go on the hike. If we can go later."

"I can't believe she even had to ask you," Ross said, shaking her head. "Had to beg."

I said nothing, only walked over to a chair and sat. I had no argument. Because, for once, Ross was right.

CHAPTER FOURTEEN

DUFF

"Life is strong and fragile. It's a paradox... It's both things, like quantum physics: it's a particle and a wave at the same time. It all exists all together." —Joan Jett

QUIN'S "celebration of life"—the terminology used per her parents' wishes—was awful.

Not that we were expecting any different, but her parents wanted to make it a festive tribute. For all her punk sensibilities, Quincy Banks loved Christmas more than life itself. Every goddamn year I'd known her, she had the Hallmark Channel on 24/7 from the day after Thanksgiving till January second, blaring every possible configuration of boy meets girl over hot chocolate. She drove us all to Atlanta on Black Friday, made Marian and me stand outside of way too many stores as she agonized over the perfect gift.

She could never drag Marian to a production of *The Nutcracker*, but I was a somewhat softer touch, having taken ballet until fourth grade. I was even a Polichinelle one year in Grosse Pointe. Quin made me tell her stories of being backstage with the Sugar Plum Fairy way too many times.

This Yuletide obsession was a big ol' Quincy-quirk I took for granted, thinking we'd have all the Christmases together. Now that I knew we wouldn't, the memories rushing back over the short few years I'd known her overwhelmed me so much I could barely make it to my seat.

In theory, even though Christmas had come and gone, I could see why Mr. and Mrs. Banks wanted to go in this direction. But the evergreen trees and their glittery ornaments looked garish inside the funeral/memorial home, especially when most of us, even Quincy's parents, were wearing black. Guess no one thought about a dress code.

Instead of our own Scottish Play music—and I didn't judge, I could understand how Quin's parents might associate us with sex, drugs, and rock and roll—Tchaikovsky piped into the background. *The Nutcracker*'s sweet but haunting score mocked us mourners with its sweetness, then overwhelmingly sad as the final *pas de deux* played and I remembered (thank you, Quin) that he wrote it while mourning the death of his sister. I couldn't look at her mom and dad, who'd already lost two family members to drugs and now had to reckon with the fact that their own daughter was found in a dingy apartment that didn't belong to her, the needle still stuck in her arm that had previously contained enough heroin to kill a mule.

Gruesome.

And odd.

I couldn't shake that, the way Quin of all people had perished. She didn't even like bars when we weren't playing them. No, we didn't expect Ian to basically drop dead, but he was older—not *old*, but he had some years on him. And he was super healthy, but freaky things happened. He could have had a genetic thing even *he* didn't know about.

Quincy, on the other hand, was so vigilantly straight edge. She wouldn't so much as smoke a cigarette during what should have been her prime rebel years. How do you go from that to an overdose?

But grief did strange things to people. My abortion was the right call, and I *still* couldn't get out of bed for months. Who's to say that Quincy, who'd lost way too many loved ones for someone so young, couldn't have had one sip of Marian's drink and wanted more, now, again? And because she was a beacon of sobriety, untouched by the shit the rest of us poured into ourselves, did she not know when too much was, well, deadly? And wound up at a place where sober Quin never would have gone in a million years?

On one side of me, Marian and her brand-new hot-girl style that I would've loved if it had been all her idea, gave me the most subtle wink. At least one of my best friends was still here, not in an urn. Behind her, almost all of our graduation class and practically the whole population of Hiawassee were here to pay their final respects.

And Larry M. I resented the shit out of his presence, but I acknowledged he had a place here too. Our issues weren't important in this moment.

Ross leaned in from behind me, as if summoned. I shot her a grateful smile, and she smiled back. "You ready?" she whispered.

I shrugged. Who was ever ready to give a eulogy? As if understanding,

Ross leaned her head on my shoulder and I got a flashback of Quin doing the same thing. So many times.

Would it just be me and Ross at Waffle House from now on? We were going ahead with the band, no question. Quin would leap out of her urn fully formed and loudly protest if The Scottish Play disbanded because of her death. I used to hate it when people said "so-and-so would have wanted it that way," but now I understood. Sometimes we really did know what a person would want. Or not want.

Quin would *not* want Larry M here, for example. Or maybe she would. He and Mac were the last ones to see her alive, after all. Perhaps they'd made peace.

Though I didn't find that likely.

"Duff," Ross murmured. It was my turn. I made my way to the podium, and I saw them.

At the very back of the room, The Hecks stood. They *loomed*. My body physically jolted. I hadn't seen them since that day on the mountain. I looked away, looked down at my notes full of clichés, and looked back up.

Fuck it. I was gonna riff. I saw the hot pink urn out of the corner of my eye and willed all of Quincy's strength.

"Quin and I loved to watch *Sex and the City*," I said to the packed room. My voice was soft, so I leaned into the microphone. This posture I knew very well, but I wished I had my bass in my hands. Oh well.

"She and I sometimes had trouble sleeping, and one night I got out of bed to find her on the couch, watching this show that I thought was just for moms." The crowd laughed softly. Warming up, I went on. "I remember she turned to me and said, 'I think you're a Carrie with Samantha rising.' I had no idea what that meant, but it didn't take me long to figure out that she was absolutely right. Quin was right about most things."

More laughter. And sniffling.

"After that, whenever we couldn't sleep, which was a lot, we cued up *Sex and the City*. And Quincy had opinions on *all* of it. Strong ones. Big over Aidan. Steve over literally every other guy on the show. She secretly had a thing for Berger, despite the Post-It. How Samantha was the most underrated of the four, and the best overall friend, and how Carrie got a bum rap because people *hate* it when a female protagonist doesn't do every little thing perfectly, even though that is way more realistic."

I realized that I was shaking, but I pressed on. "She wanted me to have opinions too, ideally different from hers, so we could whisper-argue until the sun came up. When we finished the series, we'd start it again, and she'd always bug me to do my Samantha impression until I gave in." I took a deep breath and launched into it. "*If I worried what every bitch in New York was saying about me, I'd never leave the house.*"

Should I say *bitch* at a funeral? Well, it was out there and no one was running away screaming. In fact, there was more laughing, more sniffling.

And I felt her right then: Quin. Her essence. If I concentrated hard enough, I could smell her vanilla perfume.

"Anyway, I could say a million things about Quincy. If you didn't know she was obsessed with Christmas, you definitely do now." The crowd laughed again. "She had a gorgeous voice. She was completely gifted as a drummer, and really, what's more badass than a girl drummer?" Quin's dad put his arm around her mom, buried his face in her shoulder. I could see *his* shoulders shaking. I willed myself to keep it together for them.

"But what I'll remember the most is those late nights, watching an honestly pretty brilliant show about love and sex and friends and New York. Sharing a blanket with her, with the only sound Sarah Jessica Parker's narration, I finally understood the meaning of the word *comfort*. Because in the five years I knew her, Quincy Banks never failed to comfort me."

Some nights, cuddled with her on the couch, I wished I'd let her kiss me. I'd never felt cozier. But I didn't say that out loud, just held it in my heart, projected it out to the universe where Quin was hopefully at peace.

I'm sorry I couldn't save you.

People were full on sobbing. My knees shook, and I had to grip the podium as I stepped down so I wouldn't sprain my ankle or something stupid. I barely made my way back to Marian, who leaned her head on my shoulder and whispered, her lips touching my ear:

"Tomorrow."

CHAPTER FIFTEEN

MARIAN

"O horror, horror, horror! Tongue nor heart cannot conceive nor name thee." —*Macbeth*, Act II, Scene III

*D*UFF had a hard time getting through her eulogy. As I watched her, shaking like a leaf as she stood in front of that ridiculously over the top Christmas tree, my heart went out to her, my annoyance and upset from before forgotten. She caught my eye, and I gave her a subtle wink, and she registered it with the smallest of smiles before she took a shaking breath and went on. By the time she was finished with her touching speech, everyone was crying.

Now it was my turn.

I hadn't wanted to speak today any more than I wanted to go on some stupid hike afterwards, but what could I do? Tell Quincy Banks' grieving, destroyed parents that I wouldn't speak at their only daughter's memorial service?

For the past two days I'd tried to write something resembling a speech, to think of any combination of words to celebrate my friend and bandmate, but I'd come up empty. No matter how many cups of coffee I'd drunk, I just couldn't make sense of it. I couldn't think of a single thing to say.

Luckily, there was something else I could do.

I sat there for a moment, gathering my strength, as Duff approached. She walked over to me, arms outstretched, the tears already rolling down her cheeks. She glanced to the right and Lawrence, who was sitting in the chair beside me, jumped up and made room for her to sit. Thank god he did; I couldn't have dealt with the tension between those two right now. Duff collapsed into the chair beside me and I rested my head briefly on her shoulder, the best semblance of comfort I could give. I was so shitty at making people feel better.

I looked at Lawrence over her head and gave him a quick nod. He leaned over and grabbed my acoustic guitar from the floor and handed it to me, blowing me a kiss with his other hand as I took it. I was so grateful for his presence. When he'd asked if he should come, I'd told him it was up to him, and that I'd understand if he didn't want to. So I'd been surprised when he'd sat down beside me, just before the service started, and leaned in to whisper in my ear, "Sorry I'm late. I had to get my suit pressed." He'd put an arm around me and pulled me into him, holding me like that throughout the entire service, until he'd vacated his seat for Duff.

On the other side, on my left, was Mama. Of course, she'd insisted on sitting with me, opening her purse and trying to pass a piece of Doublemint gum into my hand just before Duff had started speaking.

I'd shaken my head with an exasperated sigh and waved her away. I wasn't a kid anymore, and this wasn't Sunday School services. What the hell was she even playing at? She'd cried all throughout Duff's eulogy—everybody had, so I wasn't begrudging her that, but why did she have to be here at all? She'd barely known Quincy. Her little swallowed sobs and hiccups were distracting and over the top. She always did this.

TJ was tucked in the back, in the same row as The Hecks (why had *they* come?). I'd managed to find her and pull her aside before the service had started, and begged her to come with us up the mountain. Her eyes had filled with tears. "I can't, Marian," she'd said apologetically, dabbing at one eye with a tissue. "I've got to drive back to Emory right after the service. I have midterms tomorrow." I'd tried my best to hide my crushing disappointment, but considering the dozen or so "sorrys" she'd given me before dashing off to her seat, I hadn't done a very good job. Despite that, I still wished she was sitting beside me. Teresa-Jo always made me feel so supported.

As I stood up, holding my guitar and smoothing out my shirt, Mama put a hand on my arm. "You can do this," she said, smiling through her tears.

"I know," I said, a little more forcefully than I needed to, and felt my cheeks immediately turn red, hoping nobody else had heard me. I pasted on a smile, feeling my own eyes begin to fill, and croaked out, "Thanks."

I walked slowly to the makeshift podium and took my place in front of the Christmas tree. It was enormous and beyond gaudy, but even I had to admit, it was beautiful. The Banks' had decorated it with a weird combination of lights—gold, purple and blue, with lots of pink ornaments. I'd never seen such a color combination—most people either went with all-white or multicolored lights in these parts—and it was actually really pretty; sparkling and vibrant and quirky, very Quincy. I looped the guitar strap over my head and stepped up to the microphone, adjusting it to my height.

"I'm Mac—er, Marian. Quincy's bandmate, and her friend," I began, hating the way my voice wavered. It was something I was working on at home; being in the public eye with a weak, nervous voice was a kiss of death. I had to learn to project with confidence. I cleared my throat and tried again, stronger. "I have to admit that when I was asked to speak today, I had no idea what to say. I wasn't sure where to begin…what to say and not to say. There's no real way to sum up Quincy Banks, and what she meant to our band. What she meant to me."

I swallowed, feeling a lump in my throat, my eyes watering from hay fever thanks to the March pollen. But that didn't matter; everyone would assume it was tears. Duff's eyes caught mine, and she winked at me, the same way I'd done for her. I took a deep breath. "So I'm not going to try. Quincy Banks had a lot of love languages, and if I know her at all, she had different love languages for all the different people in her life. For her and Duff, it was bonding over TV shows. They barred me from watching *Sex and the City* with them after I told them Petrovsky was my favorite of Carrie's boyfriends." I looked at Duff, waiting for her to smile. "But for Quin and me, it was always, always about the music." I plucked a string on my guitar. "So I figured, what better way to say goodbye to my friend than with a song?"

Lawrence was staring at me from his seat, his eyes shining with tears. I stared at him for a moment, gathering up my strength. In the very back, The Hecks made imposing figures against the back of the wall, and I avoided making eye contact with them, forcing myself to keep Lawrence and TJ in my sights instead.

"Quincy tried to drag me to *The Nutcracker* every Christmas. Admittedly, it wasn't my thing. But there was one Christmas song we always bonded over. Bing and Bowie's 'Little Drummer Boy/Peace on Earth.'" And with that, I began to play.

It had taken me a few hours to work out how to translate the song, originally recorded in the 1970s, to acoustic guitar, but with Lawrence's help, I'd done it. I played slowly, singing Bowie's part, then Bing's, hoping my voice sounded okay, as cloaked as it was with tears and nerves. Once I got warmed up, I realized that despite the sad occasion, I *liked* singing. It felt good, playing and singing along, and my voice didn't sound half bad. To my surprise, when I got to the bridge, the part where Bowie and Bing sing together, I could hear Ross and Duff singing along from their seats. Pretty soon, everyone was. Lawrence was smiling as he wiped at his face, mouthing the words, and I smiled back at him as I strummed into the final verse, the one I'd written to fit in neatly at the end, just for Quincy.

My finest wish
Did come true
When you met me, and I met you
You changed our lives completely
Quin with the voice of an angel
We'll never forget you
As long as we have ears to hear.

I gulped nervously as I finished the last lines. I'd agonized over the lyrics, wanting to fit the tone of the original song but not wanting to seem too cheesy. To end it on a hopeful note, to celebrate Quincy, without devolving into religious sentiments that I didn't adhere to.

Looking at the wet eyes of the crowd, it appeared I'd managed it. Ross was wiping at her cheeks, Teresa-Jo stared at me proudly, her eyes shining, and Duff and Mama of all people were clutching each other, crying. I felt a pang of jealousy, watching them—for once, I wasn't the one consoling my crying mother.

A flash—Ian's sad eyes. Quincy, laying peacefully; asleep. I shook my head furiously, forcing the image away.

With a trembling, anxious breath, flooded with a strange combo of endorphins and grief, I gave an awkward little bow and rushed back to my seat, sandwiching myself between Duff and Mama.

Both Lawrence and Duff reached for me, but it was Mama who got me first, wrapping her arms around my neck and sobbing into my hair. "That was so beautiful, honey," she murmured, and I reluctantly put my arm around her, letting her hold me. She smelled like her signature White Diamonds, tempered with the bright, starchy smell of White Rain hairspray, her crispy hair tickling my face. Suddenly, I felt like a kid again, sitting on Mama's lap, singing my ABCs. I breathed in for a moment, clutching at her, squeezing her back, then caught myself. *No.* I let go of Mama and sat upright in my chair, forcing my tears—real ones this time and not allergies—back lest anyone see them.

"Are you okay?" Lawrence whispered, leaning over Duff to offer me his hand.

I took his hand in mine and gently removed it. "I'm fine," I said through clenched teeth. Duff gave me a searching look, then turned back toward the front.

CHAPTER SIXTEEN:

DUFF

"Even though everybody's lives are different, in general we're all human beings, and we go through the same things: disappointments, the pleasures of life, life and death." —Joan Jett

I didn't want to think about it.

And yet.

While Marian sang, Ross was holding my hand from behind, much in the way Quin used to before...yeah. My mind couldn't go there quite yet. We were at her fucking memorial service and I still expected Quincy to come through the door and plop next to me in one of these uncomfortable chairs, like that first high school lunch together.

"I'm womanspreading," she would joke, and honestly? We laughed every time. That was the power of Quincy Banks. She took up all the space available to her and then some, and you loved her for it.

Anyway, Ross was crying. I could hear her sobs. I was too, and I wished I could return to a state of comfortable numbness, just like the moments after my abortion. I was more concerned with making sure I took the second pill at the exact right time—I set at least two alarms—and having orange juice on hand. Normally I hated orange juice, but for some reason I *needed* it for my second pill. A craving? Possibly. I remembered thanking my mom a million times for coming with me until she finally shushed me, tears in her eyes—not because of the decision I'd made, she told me later, but because I had to make it at all.

Anyway, the feelings really hit me a few days later, when Michelle ate the last bag of Lays. They weren't even my chips; they were for everyone. But I screamed at her, and she cried, and then *I* cried, and then I went to my room and didn't come out for a month except to pee.

I wiped my runny nose with a tissue Ross held out, trying to stop blubbering by concentrating on details. My outfit. My speech, which apparently went well. And letting Ross hold my hand even though she was squeezing really hard.

I should have been more moved by Marian's beautiful music tribute. It's not that I didn't think she was genuine. I knew her so well and I knew when she was faking emotion, which happened quite a bit, honestly. Here, this was true. That little verse she added? All real. Mac was truly and deeply sad.

Why, then, was I starting to suspect something?

Mac and Larry M had been the last of us to see Quincy Banks alive. Now, Larry M, I didn't give a shit about. I'd been so Midwestern nice about calling him *Lawrence,* even, and no more. We'd never officially taken him on as our manager, but it was just kind of happening and honestly, Ross and I were too exhausted and grief-stricken to do much about it. It was sort of an unspoken agreement between us not to argue anymore. When we *had* argued, we'd had Quincy, and now we didn't anymore. What if we lost Mac too?

Maybe it was our fear of yet more loss that kept us from pressing Mac for details about that final night. About how Quin, who never ever touched alcohol, ended up overdosing in a shitty apartment. *Something* had clearly gone down.

And more and more, I was wondering if Mac knew something. If so, what did she know?

The sound of clapping jerked me out of my inner monologue. I hadn't been to many funerals, but seeing a standing ovation at a person's memorial was jarring, to say the least. All for Marian and her beautiful song.

At the front of the room, she was smiling.

She bowed.

"Duff!" Teresa-Jo fell in beside me, taking short and careful steps in her sky-high black heels with their red bottoms. Louboutins. Quin always wanted a pair.

The service was officially over, but people were hanging around. Maybe we all collectively realized that once we went back to our lives, Quin would officially be gone. And we would have to deal with that.

"Duff!" Teresa-Jo said again, and I snapped out of my reverie to look over at her. Instead of her usual warm smile, TJ's bright red-lipsticked mouth was set in a firm line. "Can you like, *not* with Mac right now?"

I took a step back, grateful I'd worn flats, so I didn't topple over. "Can I not what?"

TJ rolled her eyes, another uncharacteristic gesture. My hackles rose and I took a deep breath, mentally reminding myself that we were *all* on edge right now. "Mac says you and Ross are pressuring her to go on a hike or whatever." I could tell from the crease between TJ's eyebrows that she was struggling to be empathetic and Southern-polite. "Can the hike wait? Mac just lost her best friend, you know."

Actually, Quincy was my best friend, I wanted to spit back. Anyway, both TJ and I were a hell of a lot closer to Mac than Quincy had ever been. *I'm not pressuring Mac to do anything. And I don't know if Mac's as sad as she's letting on.*

That last thought surprised me, as did my next one: *Typical Mac, making everything, including a goddamn funeral for a friend, all about her.*

Where did *that* come from?

"Duffy Kate?" Granny touched my shoulder before I could formulate any kind of retort, and Teresa-Jo murmured a goodbye before clearing off, back to Emory and exams and traditional college/girlfriend life. I knew she wasn't mad at me—Teresa-Jo wasn't that kind of person—but still, her admonishment stung.

I didn't cry, but I swallowed hard—not just because of TJ's accusations, and my grief *and* mounting anger, but at Granny's simple gesture of kindness, the tangible reminder I was loved. Granny saw it in my eyes, because she was good like that, and pulled me in for a tight hug. "You poor sweet thing. All of you," she murmured in my ear. "She was too good to go so soon."

"No more nanner pudding," I said when we pulled away from one another.

Granny looked into my eyes. "*All* the nanner puddin'. We're gonna keep that girl's spirit alive for as long as we can, hear?"

I nodded. Of course, she was right.

I put my arm around my granny, who suddenly seemed so *little*. I knew how lucky I was to still have her around, making nanner puddin' and keeping my friend's spirit alive. Out of the corner of my eye, I saw Annie in a tight black dress, hair teased to the sky, chatting with a good-looking guy. I cocked my head in her direction. "Hope there's no vodka in her water bottle."

"Duffy Katherine Devereaux O'Brien." Uh-oh, Granny was full-naming. She ducked out from under my arm, put her manicured hands on her tiny hips, and lowered her voice. "Annie Shepherd is not a drunk, no matter what Marian says." Granny's mouth turned down. "Now I know that girl has been through a lot, but I can't believe you're still falling for that story about her mama. You take back those words this minute."

I wasn't sure Granny knew "that story," as she called it—I mean, addicts *lied*, right? Wasn't that their whole thing? But I also knew this wasn't the time to argue. "I'm sorry, ma'am."

"It's all right, baby. We've had a hard day. Anyway," Granny continued, "Quincy's mama and daddy want a word."

"Oh." I looked around. "With the band or—"

"Just you," Granny said. She followed my eyes to Marian, and her mouth made a thin line. Granny loved Annie, always would, but her contempt for Mac was getting less and less subtle by the year. And maybe, just maybe, I was coming around to Granny's train of thought.

But I didn't have time to stress about that now. Nodding at Granny,

I made my way toward Mr. and Mrs. Banks.

"Duffy," Mrs. Banks said as soon as I reached them. I'd never known them the way I did Annie. By the time Quincy started hanging out with us, she and her parents were barely speaking to one another, each choosing to grieve as separately as they could.

And now Quin's mom and dad would have to grieve all over again. My knees nearly buckled at the thought. *Later, Duff. This isn't about you right now.* "Uh, Granny said you wanted to talk?"

Quin's dad—a short, stocky guy whose remaining hair was the same shade of blond as his daughter's—blinked very hard behind his glasses. "Duff. We wanted to thank you for that lovely speech." He cleared his throat. "And for being such a good friend to Quincy. She thought the world of you."

My heart warmed, and like coming out of frostbite, it also hurt. "Oh, thank you. I thought the same of her." My voice broke. Shit, I couldn't cry again. Not in front of these people whose losses were so much larger than my own.

Mr. Banks cleared his throat and looked down at his polished shoes. Mrs. Banks took over. She was beautiful like Quincy, but a faded sort of beauty, like a porcelain doll left in the sun all year long. Her black suit was perfectly tailored, and I wondered whether she'd gotten it just for today or if it was the one she wore in court.

"As you know, we chose to have Quincy cremated." She talked fast, maybe to avoid a breakdown, just like I was at that moment. "But we—and I hope this isn't uncomfortable for you, Duff—her father and I wanted you to have some of her ashes."

"Oh." Quin's remains had been present at the service, given pride of place front and center, in a hot pink urn. I had no idea where one would find such an urn—Etsy?—but I knew my friend would have loved it.

I hadn't known, however, that wasn't all of her.

"Is it okay?" Quin's mom bent down, looking in my eyes, searching. "You can do whatever you like with them, but if it's too much, we can—"

"No!" I cut her off. "I…I'm honored. I could maybe spread them somewhere?" My dad's side was Catholic, and they weren't big on cremation, but I'd seen that done in movies. And the moment the words were out of my mouth, I realized I'd like to do that for Quincy. Instead of laying forever under some scary gravestone, she could be part of the earth. Or the water. Or wherever.

One last act of friendship.

I thought of the time we almost kissed. What if we'd gone ahead? Become girlfriends? Would we all be standing in front of a funeral home right now, Quin-less and bereft?

Mrs. Banks pressed a small bag into my hand, and my fingers closed around what used to be my best friend. My *real* best friend, if I was being truly honest. "Thank you, honey." She took a deep breath. "She loved you so much."

"I loved her too," I said, and hoping it wasn't too weird, hugged them both.

I really needed to talk to Mac.

CHAPTER SEVENTEEN

MARIAN

"Be bloody, bold, and resolute: laugh to scorn the power of man." —
Macbeth, Act IV, Scene 1

ON the car ride to Brasstown Bald, I desperately wished I had
Lawrence beside me, even though I'd sorta pushed him away at the
service. Or TJ; damn her for having to go back to Atlanta so soon.
Hell, I'd even have taken Mama at this point. Anyone to cover me, to
provide me with some semblance of security.

Crowe wasn't even joining us now. Evidently, me asking the girls to
wait a day had posed a scheduling conflict for their mom, Gwen, and
now it was just going to be the three of us at the mountain. I *did* feel
kinda bad about that.

No sooner than we'd fastened our seatbelts and turned out of the
Banks' driveway, Duff had turned around from the passenger seat and

peered at me. "Can we have a conversation?" she asked. "About the last time you saw Quin?"

I gulped. "Okay."

"I know it's hard…to remember," she said, her voice softening. "It's just that I can't make heads or tails of what fucking happened, and I need to know, Mac. I need to know everything. I can't move on until I understand."

"I'm not sure I'll be much help." My voice was hoarse, and I tried to clear my throat, pulling a tissue from my pocket to dab at my nose. "But I'll try."

"Whose idea was it to meet up?" Duff began.

"Hers," I said. "She said our fight upset her, and she wanted to talk it out." I didn't add that Quin had suggested meeting at Devereaux's for wings, and I'd suggested Rick's, a greasy local spot that was more bar than grill, instead. Duff wouldn't understand.

"What did she seem like?" Duff asked. "That night?"

I shrugged. "Fine. Seriously, she seemed normal. Well, at first." I swallowed. "We made up, said our sorrys about the fight… She told me she didn't begrudge us going forward with the band and with Lawrence as manager." A shadow passed over Duff's face, but was gone quickly. I tensed. "She said it in so many words… She said she'd come to understand our relationship, and why I trusted him so much. She said we were a family."

"That's not the same as inviting him to manage us," Ross said from the driver's seat.

"It was implied," I argued, rolling my eyes. "I've known Quin a long time. I know what she meant."

"Just tell us what else happened that night." Duff's face was pure misery. I went on, unable to stop my voice from wavering.

"So yeah, we made up…talked…then she put Joan Jett on the jukebox. She had a, um, a debate…with Lawrence about how 'I Love Rock 'n Roll' is a cover. He didn't know that, and she—we—had a little laugh at his expense. And we danced. For a long time, just the two of us. It was kind of wonderful. At one point, she got up on the bar and danced to the Charlie Daniels Band like she was in the movie *Coyote Ugly*. It was pretty funny."

"She did that sober?" Duff was smiling now, her eyes wet.

"Well," I said, not sure if I should divulge this detail, but deciding to do it, anyway. "Don't get mad at me, but Quincy did have a sip of my drink." I rushed to clarify. "Just a *sip,* mind you. Not enough to get drunk, but… Well, you know she was a lightweight. Had to have been—she didn't drink!"

Ross turned, momentarily taking her eyes off the road. Her eyes flashed. "Exactly. So why would you give her booze, Mac? That's fucked up!"

"I *didn't* give it to her," I spat back. "She picked my glass up off the table and took a gulp without even asking before I could stop her." I shrugged again, meeting Duff's eyes. "I swear. I don't know what got into her. She was drinking her Roy Rogers and she just like, got a wild hair and grabbed my glass. But it was just the one sip."

"What then?" Ross asked.

"At some point, I got her down off the bar. We hung out a little while longer, talking, then she said she was tired and ready to go home. Lawrence and I ordered an Uber for her. We stood with her outside the bar until they came."

"Did you notice anything weird about the driver? About her?"

"Nothing." I sighed.

"What about you and Larry—er, Lawrence?" Duff pressed. "Did you guys stay at the bar after?"

"We left around the same time as Quin."

"And she didn't call or text you to say she'd gotten home?"

"No." I shook my head. I knew why Duff was asking—the four of us *always* told each other to call or text when we got home safe. That was our girl code. It started around the time the band formed, since the three of us were making the drive from Athens to Hiawassee so often. Ian had insisted we be safe and look out for each other to check in regularly. "I guess I should have called her to check, but…"

"Something doesn't add up," Duff said, shaking her head. "Was there anyone else with you guys at the bar? Anyone watching her? Anyone she was talking to on her phone?"

I shook my head. "Not that I noticed."

"Something isn't adding up for me," she said again, her brows furrowed. "Quincy didn't drink. And she damn sure wouldn't have gone home and…did what she did. She wasn't suicidal, and she didn't do drugs. For god's sake, she wore her D.A.R.E. T-shirt from elementary school unironically!" Her eyes searched mine, her expression tense and a little angry. Was she mad at me? I couldn't think why. All I could do was look at her helplessly, wishing I was anywhere but in the backseat of Ross' car, getting ready to hike up a fucking mountain.

CHAPTER EIGHTEEN:

Duff

"Girls have to be allowed to be sexual too, because they are... It is wrong to say they can't be, that they can't own it." —Joan Jett

HOW *the fuck did I get here?* I thought as I felt Josh's hot breath on my neck and an equal warmth down my entire naked body as he entered me in the woods. Hard. The cries of the other two Hecks echoed around me, bouncing off the tall, tall trees.

And I came harder than I ever had.

I couldn't even say, "it started like a normal day," because what the fuck was even normal anymore? Within two months: our manager, gone. Our drummer, lead singer, and best friend: gone. Any iota of normalcy I possessed: gone. No one could blame me for what I was doing.

But I didn't want anyone to know.

I wanted the night to be mine.

Anyway. The woods.

I made it through the Devereaux-catered luncheon after the memorial, where I tied an apron over my black dress and dished out Granny's best local recipes alongside her. Once in a while, she'd put her hand on the small of my back. Granny knew anything else would send me over the edge.

Oddly, The Hecks showed up at Devereaux's, seemingly materializing just like they had at the memorial. They didn't make a weird scene: no prophecies or anything. Just filled their plates, said "thank you, ma'am" to Granny like good boys, expressed their condolences to Quin's parents. I was so fucking tired of being hugged, and yet when Josh's hand brushed my arm as he reached for the sweet potatoes, I was filled with longing.

Ross and I had just barely convinced Mac to pay tribute to Quin at Brasstown Bald, sans Larry. I was staying at Granny's for the next week just to clear my head and...not be in our shared house for a bit. I owed myself that much, I figured. She was going to drive me back into Athens after that.

We got through it. On the way there, Ross and I tried to have a conversation with Mac about Quincy's final hours.

I knew she wasn't telling me the whole truth. Maybe I should have been pushier. Asked questions that were more probing. Grilled her while I had her captive in an enclosed space. I could have shone my phone's flashlight in her eyes or something.

Truth was, I was tired. Tired of hugs I didn't want and tears soaking the shoulder of my cardigan. Tired of tossing and turning, knowing I'd never have a buddy to share sleepless *Sex and the City* nights with ever again. Tired of the endless game of what-if I was playing with myself, knowing I'd always be the loser.

It's hard to fully focus when you have your dead friend's remains in your pocket.

I'd told no one about my conversation with Mr. and Mrs. Banks. Not Ross, not Granny, especially not Mac. Just like I'd never told anyone about the almost-kiss just a few months ago. I wanted to keep one last thing between me and Quin.

So we got to the Bald. Marian was evasive. I was tired and frustrated, and Ross was Ross, Sad Girl Edition. No fire this time, we agreed; we'd probably dodged a bullet when we memorialized Ian. No speeches, either, as we were talked out from the memorial. Most importantly, no Larry. Marian had the sensitivity not to invite him along, thank god.

Our hike was quiet. Contemplative. Once we reached a little clearing Quincy had Instagrammed more than once, we stood in a circle. Had a moment of silence. And when I started Quincy's memorial song to Ian, Ross and Mac harmonized till the last note, which we held as long as we could, tears streaming down our faces before we moved in for a tight group hug. The remaining Scottish Play, us versus the world.

"I'm gonna stay," I told Mac and Ross when they started back down the mountain. "Y'all can find your way back to the car, right? I'll get an Uber from the general store or something."

Ross nodded but exchanged a worried glance with Marian. "You okay, Miss Duff?" Ross asked. "It's getting dark."

Mac looked back at me, and there must have been something in my expression, but she quickly said, "She'll be okay. Been coming here for years, right, Duff?" I smiled at her, grateful. I realized then that I hadn't smiled in…a while. Whatever suspicions I had, my heart brimmed with love for Mac, for her understanding. Maybe she wasn't being evasive earlier.

Maybe I just needed to give everyone a break.

But now? I needed to be alone with the trees. And the air. And the quiet.

And Quin.

I didn't want to linger too long. As Ross said, it *was* getting dark. But at the same time, I didn't want to rush.

I thought of HAIM's "Found It in Silence," which Quin and I had both loved. I hoped I could find…whatever it was, in this silence, with just the cricket chirps and gentle breeze around me. I made sure my hand was strong and steady before reaching into my jeans pocket for the little plastic bag.

"Um," I said to the air. "Hi." I looked up at the sun, glowing orange and beginning to sink. "I don't know if we ever talked about God or Heaven or whatever. I'm not sure what you believed." I swallowed hard before continuing. "Other than music. And *Sex and the City*. I hope you don't think it's stupid, that I talked about it at your memorial. But it just felt very you, Quin."

Could anyone hear me? I didn't know, and I didn't care. "I know we're going to have to move on. I guess, though, in these last moments, I want to say…thank you. For making The Scottish Play so amazing. For sitting with us that day at lunch. For always being so unapologetically you." My voice broke on that last syllable. "I'm gonna miss you so hard, bitch."

My voice echoed, then faded. Time to get down to business, and get the hell on with living. Whatever that might look like.

How exactly did one scatter ashes? I didn't want to touch them (sorry, Quin), so I took the plastic bag full of crumbling gray, knelt down, and emptied a small part of the bag into a small pile, brushing away a fly who'd landed right next to the ashes. Not exactly scattering, but I didn't want to venture too far into the woods because it was fully dark now.

I knew Quin, wherever she was, would understand.

I took what I thought would be my last lungful of fresh mountain air before heading back, when I heard a rustle.

Fuck.

Guess I wasn't alone after all.

I looked over my right shoulder and…there they were. The memorial and lunch were one thing, but this was quite goddamn another.

"Hecks." My voice came out smaller, quieter, the way it had since that awful morning when I got the call that Quincy's body had been found.

"Duff."

Josh's voice sent me hurtling back to the present. An odd feeling shot through my torso, right down to my groin.

"I'm not in the mood for y'all's shit today," I said, shouldering my backpack and tightening the straps. "Literally just had a moment with my friend's remains."

"We know." It was Zak, his hair newly flame-red. Like a tree in autumn. "We're so sorry." Then I remembered what he'd said the *last* time I'd run into them on the mountain, after Ian had died. *See you next time.* They had known. They had tried, in their weird way, to warn me.

I could have left. I *should* have left. Gone on with my hike and my grief and my life.

But something kept me and my brand-new boots rooted to the spot.

"What the *fuck*?" I said, turning to face them. They were almost part of the trees, set off from the path about ten feet away from where I stood. Had a fire going. How did I not see that before? "Is this what you meant by that stupid prophecy? That I wasn't *done with death* or whatever?" I don't know why I said *whatever* when those words, that encounter, played out in my dreams as vividly as Steve and Miranda's scene on the Brooklyn Bridge. *Sorry, Quin, I'm never watching the* Sex and the City *movies again.*

"We didn't," Pete said. His shadow, at least seven feet tall, loomed behind him. There were tiny purple flowers stuck in his ass-length dark brown hair, bound in a messy braid, making him look like a slightly goofy Dionysus. "We're so sorry. She shouldn't have gone like that."

"What the fuck happened?" Now I was yelling. I guess this was the anger stage of grief. "Why her? Why now? Why like *that*?"

"We don't have the answers," Josh answered softly.

"Great, so you can't help me at all. Typical." *Now* my feet seemed to be working. "Thanks for coming today, I guess."

I was less than ten steps away when I heard Josh say, "Duff."

Something in his voice...

I turned back. "Come here."

Those two words were all it took.

I turned on my heel. And walked—no, *floated*, practically—to the three weirdest guys in my high school class.

What happened next is still a continuous blur with very clear images that come in flashes when I think about it, late at night when the covers are pulled over my head. Flash: the four of us, adding wood to a completely illegal fire till it climbed so high, and the occasional passersby completely ignoring us and our pyromania, as if we weren't there at all. Flash: pulling my tank top over my head, stepping out of the stretched-to-hell jeans I'd had since tenth grade, before Tinder and Hiawassee when I was just a naive girl in Michigan. Making short work of my sports bra, my granny panties. Running my hands through my hair, which was getting so long, almost the length Quincy had when she passed by me on my first day at school, a golden flag. When she was still class president. Unattainable. Beautiful. Untouchable.

Flash: the four of us, Josh and Pete and Zak and me, dancing around the growing bonfire, not a stitch of clothing among us, scraps of fabric discarded on the forest floor, thrown up and dangling on the branches, bright flags and relics of the kids we once were.

Flash: our collective primal scream, up to the sky of bright stars. My hope that somehow, somewhere, Quincy heard us.

Flash: their beautiful, beautiful bodies. Muscles and hair and breath and skin. And most of all, their collective intake of breath as I stood before them completely naked. Like I was the answer to every spell they'd cast.

Flash: mouths and hands everywhere, all over one another, my senses overloading in the best possible way. Everyone knowing where to touch and how well.

Flash: our cries echoing through the empty woods. Ecstasy. Over and over and over again.

I woke to a glorious sunrise, mostly pink, like the highlights in Quin's golden hair.

"Hi, honey," I mumbled, still half-conscious. "You're right. Steve Brady is boyfriend goals."

Slowly, I sat up, first only to my elbows, then fully. I had the tired sense of a hangover, but no pain. Still naked, but a fuzzy blue blanket covered my body, soft as anything. I touched my hair, and a shower of purple flowers rained down on my lap. I looked around and realized I was resting on a bed of leaves.

Not another human in sight.

Three hours later, my phone rang with a number I didn't recognize. I don't even usually answer those. But I felt...strangely compelled.

It was Josh.

"You good, Duff O'Brien?"

I knew Granny wasn't in the house—she'd gone to open the restaurant—but I still looked over my shoulder. Like she'd *sense* my sins. Nothing, at least not Granny. But I couldn't shake the sense I wasn't alone.

I'd retrieved my clothes from the branches, pulled them on behind the nearest tree. My backpack was untouched near the blackened-out twigs. The only sign that what had happened wasn't a figment of my imagination. I double checked for the rest of Quin's ashes, which I'd stashed in the front pocket. Still there. As I made my way back onto the trail, I got a clear signal on my phone and even though Uber drivers did *not* like coming out this far, had a ride within seconds.

And what's more, I felt better than I had since I'd gotten that terrible call. Settled. Pleasantly sore and wrung out.

Beautiful.

I had no idea how Josh got my number. I didn't care.

I was grateful.

A slow smile spread over my face, taking over until my cheeks hurt. I took a deep, clear breath and answered Josh.

"I'm good."

CHAPTER NINETEEN

MARIAN

"Screw your courage to the sticking-place." —*Macbeth*, Act I, Scene VII

THE bath was so full I sloshed water onto the tile every time I moved, and it was scalding. My entire body, save for my head, was a shade of pinky-red that could only be called *neon,* but I didn't care. Every time it cooled, I'd turn the tap and add a little more hot, which was why it was so full. I liked my showers and baths hot enough to scald; always had. I'd read something once about how women like scalding showers because they satisfy some inner need to be hurt or something, but fuck it, who gave a shit? I'd been languishing in the bathtub for over an hour, my phone propped up on the counter above me, playing YouTube singing tutorials.

I squirted some of Quincy's vanilla body wash on my loofah and scrubbed absently at my arms as I watched. I'd already washed myself three times, but I had to do *something*. Besides, smelling her signature fragrance made me feel like she was still here. Duff's line of questioning in the car on the way to the mountain had left me feeling rattled.

There was a gentle knock, and Lawrence came into the bathroom, shutting the door gently behind him and sitting down on the closed toilet seat beside me. His long legs splayed out in front of him, and I glanced at his muscular calves and thighs, disappearing into the folds of his blue kilt. I didn't have that much experience with dating, and what little I had was with guys I'd been pretty dispassionate about—they were a way to pass the time, that was all.

Lawrence was different. I *craved* him. I wondered if that feeling ever went away, or if I was doomed to follow him around like a pheromone-starved puppy for the rest of my days. Every time we were together, I got what felt like a hit of the purest dopamine, and I didn't want that to stop.

Even when he was acting like an utter ass, I still wanted him. In fact, that was when I wanted him the most.

Fucked up, huh? Well, blame my mother. I'd spent my childhood watching her break up with her boyfriends just as things started to get good. It was like she was addicted to cutting herself off at the pass, to depriving herself of happiness right before she fully got it. And the ones that *didn't* make her happy, who treated her (and me) like shit and neglected her and fucked around on her…she kept *them* around long past their sell-by date. Always looking for Deddy in the face of every man who darkened our doorway.

Lawrence smiled, running a hand through his auburn waves, but his face was full of concern. "Bad cramps? From the endo?"

"No, I just felt like taking a bath. What's up?"

"Are you getting out soon?"

"Yeah, I guess. Why?" I leaned up to pause my video, sloshing water all over the floor.

Lawrence cursed and wiped water off his Doc Martens. "Ross is here. She and Duff are in the kitchen, and I thought it might be a good time to talk."

"Oh. Great." I splashed water on my arms, rinsing off the vanilla-scented bubbles. "You want to do it now? Not at like, the next practice?"

"That would be fine if you guys had anything scheduled, but I haven't heard you mention any upcoming practices," he said. "That's part of what we need to talk about. If I'm really going to be manager, we need to set a schedule going forward and get back into a routine." He leaned over and grabbed a handful of foam from the water and plopped it on my nose. "I'd talk to them alone, but god, you know those bitches hate me."

"Don't call them bitches," I said with a frown, gesturing for a towel.

"I didn't mean it like that," Lawrence said, handing me my favorite oversized black towel. "I like them a lot. You know I do. It's just...they scare me." He grinned.

"*They* scare you?" I said with a laugh, emerging from the water, my foot slipping on a puddle and almost sending me flying. Lawrence grabbed my elbow and steadied me as I hopped onto the bathmat. "Have you met *me?*"

"You're scary for sure," Lawrence said with a chuckle, still holding my arm steady as I dried myself off. With his free hand, he reached around and smacked my still-wet bottom. "But I know how to keep you in hand."

"Do you now?" I leaned up and pecked his stubbly, dimpled cheek, the cold air in the bathroom sending a chill up my damp back. "Are you sure?" From the way Lawrence shivered, I knew he felt the same chill.

I'd started a little bonfire in the backyard, using the firepit that Ian had built when it was still his primary residence. I could imagine him and Gwen and tiny Crowe clustered out here, tucked into their soft winter coats, listening to music or enjoying hot cider while warming themselves by the flames. They probably had parties, holiday get-togethers, acoustic shows out here, the whole nine. Ian was such a lover of life, such an extrovert, such a robust person... He hadn't ever done anything halfway.

Duff, Ross, and I stood here now, huddled in our coats, each of us lost in thoughts of our own. Duff's face was flushed as she stared straight into the flames, which cast a glow on her pale cheeks that seemed almost ethereal. Her lips were parted slightly, and her eyes sparkled. Whatever she was thinking about, I was certain it wasn't Ian or even Quincy. Weirdly, she looked happier than I'd seen her in months.

Ross, for her part, was sullen and quiet, her hands jammed into the pockets of her burgundy peacoat. She hadn't touched the cup of hot chocolate I gave her, and shook her head when I'd offered to pour a slug of Bailey's or Jameson in it. I shrugged and let it go. I was trying, and Ross wasn't. If she continued to be a problem, Lawrence and I would simply deal with it. Maybe Ian was right that day we'd fought at practice, when he suggested one of us might want to leave the band.

"This is nice," Ross said, feeling my eyes on her, trying for a smile as if she'd heard my inner thoughts. "We should come out here more."

"I agree," I said. "Maybe an outdoor show sometime soon?" I would gauge their reactions to see how to proceed. Everything—our future as a band—hinged on how the girls felt tonight. I knew that much from Lawrence's face. He was ready to move forward, though, and honestly? So was I.

We'd all lost enough. It was time to gain.

To my surprise and relief, Ross nodded. "I love that idea," she said. "What do you think, Duff?"

Duff didn't answer; she was still staring at the flames. I assumed she was mooning over her potential new boyfriend, Josh the Heck, whose appeal I still couldn't understand. I'd been trying to make the moniker "Heckin' Josh" stick for the past few days, but nobody seemed to find it funny but me. Apparently, *my* boyfriend was the only one who got a disrespectful nickname.

Josh was okay… I didn't dislike him any more than the other Hecks (for my money, Zak was the interesting one, even if he did give me the creeps). I just thought Duff could do better than some wannabe librarian from Hiawassee who made shitty prophecies with his crew in his spare time. Like some hot lead singer or a fellow bassist. Duff was corn-fed hot, and she was easygoing, too—the type of girl guys swooned over. Sue me; I thought she could do better than Josh.

Honestly, I always kinda thought Duff would end up with Quincy. I could never tell her that now, and honestly, I was kind of relieved it had never happened.

"Duff?" I said, waving my hand in front of her.

She started. "Oh! Sorry you guys, I was lost in thought. Um…yeah.

That sounds good." I wasn't even a hundred percent sure she knew what we were talking about, but I'd take it.

I turned to Larry, who was seated a ways behind me in one of the old lawn chairs we'd found in the garage. He was cold; his bare legs under his kilt were prickled with gooseflesh and I gestured for him to join me. I slid my arm through his and smiled at my friends. "Ladies, whenever—and I really mean *whenever,* there's no rush—when we're ready, I want to talk."

Ross gestured at me to continue, and I breathed a sigh of relief.

"I know we went over this already, and I heard you guys loud and clear, but like…Quin is *gone,* and if we're going to move forward, we have to reach a decision." I cleared my throat, my practiced speech going out the window as my words came out in a flood. "The Scottish Play needs a manager. And a drummer. That, or we have to break up. Maybe that's what's best after losing them, but *dammit,* I hate to see it all go up in flames."

My voice wavered. "I still think Lawrence is the obvious choice. He's qualified and he can step right in without us worrying ourselves over interviews, not to mention money. But if you guys have someone else in mind, well…go for it. And if you want to kick me out of the band…again, by all means. I'll go, if that's what you guys want. I'd rather you guys move on without me than be unhappy."

Duff cut in, her eyes wide. "You don't make us unhappy, Mac."

I shook my head. "No, I do. Sometimes. I know what I'm like." I managed a dry laugh. "But you guys, Lawrence has ideas. To move forward. With the band, right now. He's right here, ready to go. If you guys would just let him give you a pitch, if you'd just hear him out—"

Duff interrupted me. "Fine."

I waited for Ross to frown, to protest, to glare in our direction, but she didn't say anything at all. Relieved, I gestured at Lawrence to talk.

Lawrence swallowed. "Well...so first thing I'd like to say is obvious: Quincy Banks is irreplaceable. There'll never be another Quin. I know how much you all loved her." He paused and looked at me. "But if you all want to continue, you'll obviously need a percussionist. So, to that end, I've placed an ad on Craigslist and on the Facebook marketplace to vet for drummers here in town. I hope you don't mind—I figured even if you choose someone else to manage you, that was the least I could do."

His handsome face was more animated now that he'd gotten his bearings. "Second...well, if you girls think you'll be ready, you've had an offer to open for Punkin' Pi at Eddie's Attic in Atlanta. You've no doubt heard of it—it's a killer venue and if you play a good show there, you'll have a really good shot at making a name for yourself."

"When?" Ross asked.

"In about a month," Lawrence answered.

Ross looked at Duff, and the two locked eyes for a moment. Then Duff slowly nodded and Ross turned back to us. "Punkin' Pi is awesome, and they've got a cult following. We'd be stupid not to do it. Provided we've got a drummer by then who can learn songs quick."

"We'll need to fit in at least two practices," Duff agreed. I felt my heart rise with relief and gratitude. They were coming around. Finally.

I looked at Lawrence, my cheeks flushed from the warmth of the fire and the grin that was threatening to bust them wide open. "I'm getting the Jameson," I said, handing him my cup of hot chocolate. "We have to toast this."

Lawrence leaned over and placed a sloppy kiss on my cheek. His dimples popped out adorably as he grinned at Duff and Ross. He was so happy. My heart clenched as I watched him dancing in front of the fire, his eyes bright. He clearly wanted to make us happy, too. Why didn't they like him?

He turned to me, beaming, as I made my way toward the house, and called out, "You're headed for the big time now!"

I'd won.

"That went well," I said later, peeling off my thermal leggings and thick woolen socks. "I was so afraid they'd both run away screaming, or try and stab you or something."

Lawrence laughed. "I knew they'd come around. They're too smart *not* to take those opportunities."

"Just make sure you follow through," I cautioned. "They can change their mind at any time. So don't give them a reason to."

Lawrence watched as I pulled my black-and-white striped sweater over my head, only to reveal another long-sleeved shirt underneath. "Why do you dress like you're out in the tundra?" he asked, laughing as I almost fell over, trying to pull the too-tight collar over my head. "You're in Georgia where it snows once every five years and never gets below thirty degrees."

"I've always liked cold, dreary weather," I said with a giggle, reaching behind me to unclasp my bra. "I own so many scarves and mittens and earmuffs and coats...and I can't ever wear them. It's never cold enough. So sometimes I just feel like playing the part. Hand me my pajamas, will you?"

"I told you. It's not that cold." Lawrence folded his arms over his chest and gave me a mock glare. "Sleep naked."

"I never do that! What if there's a fire?"

"The only fire I see is the one in my loins, looking at you topless."

"Ugh. What a line," I said, but I slid my panties down anyway, staring at him head on. "I don't think I like you anymore."

"Liar," Lawrence said, his full lips in a smirk. "You love me, my little frontwoman. And just so you know, you may have an opportunity to wear those winter clothes you love so much again soon, if you play your cards right."

"What are you talking about?"

He crooked a finger and gestured for me to come to him. "Something to sweeten the pot for your friends, guaranteed to make me their favorite manager. A little trip, somewhere cold? We'll have to see. Depends on how good you are to me."

I reached him in two steps, and crouched down on my knees before him, pushing his kilt up to reveal his strong, pale thighs. I bent down over him, trailing kisses toward his groin, smiling as he groaned above me, his hands buried in my hair. A memory pricked at my consciousness as I ran my fingers up his tattoo, watching his skin erupt in gooseflesh; memories of a tattoo peeking out from beneath a kilt, me wondering how far up it went...

Lawrence had lots of tattoos: a full arm sleeve, back tattoos, one on his chest and another on his forearm. But it was the one on his thigh that had always captivated me: a tiny black spider, dangling from the bottom of a tattered but elaborate black web. Many of Lawrence's tats were Scots-themed, and this one was no exception, though you wouldn't realize it unless he told you.

When I'd first asked about it, he'd answered my question with a question. "Do you know the story of Robert the Bruce and the spider?" When I'd said no, he told me about how King Robert the Bruce of Scotland failed in battle so many times he was on the verge of giving up when, hiding out in a cave one dark and stormy night, he saw a spider struggling to make its web. The spider had failed and fallen six times, but was able to build the web successfully on the seventh try. It was then Robert the Bruce knew he'd win the seventh battle. He did, and Scotland won their independence from the English.

"It's a mantra for my life," Lawrence had said at the time. "To never give up."

A pretty cool mantra, I had to admit, but also, the spider just looked really *sick*.

"Keep going," Lawrence commanded now, and I did, shaking my head to clear my thoughts of spiders. I ran my finger over his tattoo one more time, and pinched the delicate flesh there, making him gasp before bending my head down. After a few moments of the most delicious noises, I looked up, meeting his eyes, loving the look of breathless pleasure on his face. I smiled, my hands caressing him, making him groan.

"You're so beautiful," he said, looking down at me, his hands still running through my hair. "Even more so now that you've got this beautiful hair, and you've taken that bull ring out of your face...so delicate and innocent. Like a classic painting."

I frowned, but he touched my chin with a finger, producing something shiny from his pocket. "Let me see your wrist."

From his pocket, he produced my charm bracelet, the one I always wore. I'd never even noticed it was missing, the rascal. I watched, wide-eyed, as Lawrence took my hand in his and slipped it back over my wrist, his fingers warm on my skin. "There. Now it's perfect."

I stared down at the bracelet, the new charm that hung there shining back at me, so bright it almost hurt my eyes. I looked up at Lawrence and, after a moment, smiled.

Maud Findley was tall and thin, and looked very much the fifties throwback in her slim pencil skirt, pressed shirt with the scalloped collar, and kitten heels. Her hair was pulled back in a bun, though she had thick, blunt bangs in front, and she wore red lipstick that I knew must be the original Revlon Red that went for a pretty penny on eBay these days. She looked like she'd stepped right out of Hollywood's Golden Era, at least until she spoke.

We were all a bit surprised when Maud sat right down at our kitchen table and started rambling off, in a sweet, slightly too-loud voice, all the names, ages and hometowns of the original Runaways. When she finished with the main five, she went on to name all the members who came and went after Cherie Currie and Sandy West.

"I'm impressed," I said with a laugh when I was able to get a word in. "You know your stuff!"

"I'm a veritable encyclopedia; my mom always says so," Maud answered with a self-effacing grin, though her eyes stayed stuck on the table. "'*Mama always said*'...that phrase has been popularized by many different things in pop culture, but perhaps its most famous usage was in the 1994 movie *Forrest Gump,* with Tom Hanks, America's Dad. I assume you all know that it was filmed in Savannah?"

"Of course!" Duff said, giggling. "The famous bus stop scene."

"I regret to inform you that the original bench is now gone," Maud said, nodding in thanks as I pushed a glass of wine toward her. "Thank you, Marian. I rarely indulge, but I'll have a sip."

"I love your dress," Ross said from her vantage point in the corner, where she was leaning up against the counter. "Is it vintage?"

"It is!" Maud answered, touching a finger to her collar. "About seventy-five percent of my wardrobe is vintage. I scour flea markets and thrift stores. I generally only choose items from the 1950s, though, so things are getting harder to come by."

"Why only vintage?" Duff asked, interested.

"Well, sometimes I become overwhelmed when trying to pick out clothing. It can be so hard to predict the weather, and what is comfortable now may not be later. Also, the possibilities with fashion are so endless and ever-changing. With vintage clothing, there are a finite amount of choices and possibilities because there are only so many pieces that still exist. So it's easier for me to choose," Maud answered with a shrug. "And they look good."

"You do look great," I said. And she did. I wished I could look half as sleek in such a classy old dress. I was barely getting used to the modern dresses I'd been ordering online, much less how naked I felt without my signature bright blush and heavy shadow in my beloved, blocky bright colors.

"I hope I'll fit in. I know my look, or aesthetic, is quite different from Quincy Banks." We all looked at her in surprise, and Maud's cheeks flushed. She pulled up something on her phone and pushed it across the table. The three of us leaned forward to look, and Duff made a choking sound. It was a video of us at the 40 Watt show, performing "Ray of Sunshine." The camera zoomed in on Quincy, bashing her drums hard, pink-and-blonde hair flying around her sweaty face, as she belted out the lead vocals in perfect tune. "I hope you don't mind that I looked Quincy up online. I wanted to see her perform, so I'd have some idea of what you were looking for. She was very talented. And beautiful."

"She was," Ross said quietly. I was surprised to see her eyes glisten with tears.

Duff and Maud were bonding over *Sex and the City*—she'd instantly endeared herself to Duff when she'd said she was a fan—when Lawrence walked in, holding a stack of papers under his arm. "Right," he said, nodding at Maud, who he'd met and interviewed the day before. "Important question: do you all have up-to-date passports?"

"No," I said with a snort. "I've never left the country."

"I do," Ross said, and Maud nodded, too. My cheeks burned with embarrassment. Why had I admitted that? I felt like a total bumpkin.

"I don't have one, either," Duff said, nudging me in the side, and I glanced at her gratefully.

Lawrence touched me on the arm. "We'll get them expedited," he said with a grin. "Not to worry, love." He plopped himself down at the table and looked at us all with a huge grin. "Now. Who here has heard of Glamis?"

"Like the castle?" Ross asked, and he nodded, opening his mouth to launch into an explanation, his face alight with excitement.

But Maud cut in. "Glamis Castle is located in County Angus, Scotland, and has existed since the 1000s, though the castle as we know it was built in 1372. It is most well-known as the site where Macbeth—he of the infamous Shakespeare play for which your band is named—murdered King Duncan, and it was also home to Robert the Bruce, first King of Scotland and assumed progenitor of House Stuart, of which the most famous member is arguably King James the First. Or Sixth, depending on which country you swear fealty to. You've all heard of the King James Bible, no doubt. Most recently, Glamis was home to the Queen Mother and her daughter Princess Margaret, and is—*naturally*—rumored to be haunted." Her eyes sparkled as she relayed this information, the entire weighty sentence coming out in one big barrage of words. "I can tell you about the alleged ghosts, if you like?"

A tiny look of irritation crossed Lawrence's face, and he let out a sigh. "Maybe later, Maud." I could tell she'd taken the wind out of his sails. Lawrence loved few things as much as he loved his Scottish culture, and he'd likely been planning to tell us all that himself.

I gave Maud a bright smile, then turned to Lawrence, hoping I could meet them both at the pass and turn this into a shared interest rather than a battle of wits. "You're looking at Robert the Bruce's number one fan and descendant here." I gave his arm a loving squeeze. "He even has a tattoo of—"

Lawrence laughed, a little too loudly, and cut me off. "No need to start detailing my ink, honey," he said, his cheeks flushed. Rather than making him feel better, I'd embarrassed him. He clapped the table excitedly, so hard it made me jump. "It'll bore everyone to tears. But yes, Maud, *that* Glamis Castle. I'm glad you've heard of it."

We stared at him expectantly, my friends obviously sensing that he'd been offended somehow, not sure what to do or say next. The whole thing had become uncomfortably awkward, and we *still* didn't know what the hell was going on.

Lawrence sat there for a moment, silent, and I had the sense that he was punishing Maud in a way, for speaking over him and stealing his thunder. I swallowed. No more tension, not now. I couldn't take any more. Especially now that Quincy's pretty face, streaming hair, and melodic voice were once again fresh in my mind.

After a moment that felt like years, Lawrence clapped the table again, his bright smile back, awkwardness forgotten.

"Well, ladies, dust off those passports, because we're headed to Scotland!"

CHAPTER TWENTY:

DUFF

"At a very young age, I decided I was not going to follow women's rules." —Joan Jett

I was not a fan of Larry M.

And it was getting harder and harder to camouflage my feelings.

I've never had a great poker face. In fact, my sister Michelle— weirdly an ace, to the point she wants to go to Las Vegas when she's legal and really play the tables—would always make fun of me. She says I have so many tells: "Duff, you wrinkle your nose. You clench your hand into a fist when you're not telling the truth. And your eye rolls are *so* obvious."

Anyway, Larry M. I appeased Mac by calling him Lawrence to his face, but in private he would *always* be Larry M. My small act of rebellion against a growing list of gripes.

He called us "ladies," which bugged me for some reason. Never mind that Granny had referred to us, as in my mom, my sisters and me, and then The Scottish Play, as "girls" forever, and would until the day she died. I'm a woman and proud of it. But anytime Larry drawled out "ladies," or worse, said it in that weird approximation of a Scottish accent, it was not only fucking patronizing, but also sounded like he was leering.

Speaking of.

Dude was obsessed with our bodies. Now, I wasn't naïve. We were public figures whose following was growing by the day, both online and IRL. And we were young women in a patriarchal society, meaning we'd face extra scrutiny on how we looked. No one criticized Keith Richards' appearance, and that guy looked at least a hundred years old as well as "rode hard and put away wet," to borrow my favorite Granny-ism. Plus, in this industry, it unfortunately went with the territory. I shuddered to think about what Kim Fowley said about the bodies of his underage Runaways. Gah.

After our last Atlanta show, however, Larry made a comment that had me reeling.

"He said I could stand to lose a few!" I ranted, sticking a cigarette in my mouth in the alley behind Eddie's Attic. I was trying to cut back on smoking, I really was, but nights like this it wasn't going well. "Who even words it that way anymore?"

"That is not subtle at all," Maud agreed, waving away the smoke even as I exhaled away from her. She hated smoking, but usually came out for moral support. "And I should know. *I'm* not subtle at all!" I laughed. Maud was an absolute gem, and a breath of fresh air for our still-grieving group. We'd immediately bonded over *Sex and the*

City—the rapid-fire dialogue, the cool fashion, and the strong female friendships—and she reminded me a lot of Carrie: introspective, sweet-voiced and with a style all her own. We also followed Sarah Jessica Parker and her shoe line obsessively, choosing what we'd buy if we had unlimited funds. (I favored bright-colored flats, while Maud liked tall heels.) Of course, Maud would never replace my beloved Quin, but it was nice to watch my favorite show with a friend again.

Not to mention her drumming skills rivaled Quincy's and her vintage-only style was fresh and unique. And she was so *herself*. I respected that.

I wondered if Larry did, though. Maud wasn't going to let him mold her as easily as Marian had.

"And your body is absolutely beautiful and you should know that," Maud said, jerking me back to the present. I knew she wasn't trying to hit on me, just telling the truth about what she felt. Maud Findley was incapable of lying.

"Aw, thank you!" I ashed with my opposite hand and gave her my first real smile of the night. But the seed was planted: I looked down at the fake leather leggings I'd been ecstatic to find online. Did they make my thighs look huge? And why was I letting one asshole's remark get to me? "I'm not gonna lie. That comment made me super self-conscious."

"Who's self-conscious?" Ross spoke up behind me, bringing out her own pack of smokes. She rarely indulged, but apparently tonight was the night for that.

"Lawrence criticized Duff's physical appearance," Maud said as I took another drag. "Which is completely inappropriate, if you ask me. Though I suppose it's par for the course, considering we have an onstage persona." She took a deep breath, about to launch into another

"Maud fact," as Ross and I liked to call them. "It's like he's never heard of Karen Carpenter, who was a phenomenal drummer *and* singer, but was only eating popcorn by the end and developed a case of anorexia nervosa that eventually killed her. All of that could have been avoided if it weren't for patriarchal standards for young women regarding their talent and their bodies."

"Uggggggh, right? Fuck that guy," Ross groaned, ripping the plastic off the soft pack and tapping one out. "Got a light, Duff? I'm such a bad smoker I forget most of the time."

"You're a *good* smoker," I corrected her. "You haven't made it a habit."

She grinned. "Give me time. And more of Larry correcting my fingering. He *did* make that word sound totally gross, in case you were wondering."

A look of confusion came over Maud's pretty face. "Does Lawrence even play rhythm guitar? Or any instrument?"

"No," Ross, who played several instruments, and I answered in unison as I tossed her my lighter. She nodded at me, grateful, and stuck the smoke in her mouth. We eschewed vapes. Not hardcore enough, and way too bro-y.

Ross seemed to be leaning more into her rock persona. She was growing her curly hair longer and wilder. She was going to quit her job, become a substitute teacher and tutor online and in person, just to have more flexible hours for gigs and rehearsals. And more than that, she was picking her battles with Marian.

The Scottish Play was ramping up, and I grudgingly had to credit Larry M. The guy had hustle, and he had connections, thanks to internships at recording studios and a PR firm. I had to hand it to him—we were everywhere now, not just the usual Athens clubs, but more and more venues in Atlanta. We'd gone to Nashville and Memphis a couple of times, even though they weren't really rock towns.

And best of all, we were recording more. With Ian, we had a few EPs, but nothing major, as he wanted us to keep developing as musicians. Now, though, I was grateful that we had recordings of The Scottish Play with Quincy. I knew her parents were, too.

Ian had an old-school sensibility with musicians; he was content to let us grow our sound, however long that took. Larry, however, was an incoming train, hurtling toward the final station, eager to make it on time or early if possible. We were gonna get there, wherever *there* was, and fast.

And now, thanks to him, we were going to Scotland. I couldn't lie. I was excited. I'd never traveled overseas before. Neither had Mac, and now we were both scrambling to get our passports. Ross and Maud had been out of the country, but only on educational trips with specific agendas and curricula. This was completely different. Also, I'd never even *seen* a castle in person, let alone played one. Sleeping Beauty's Castle at Disneyland did not count.

So yeah, Larry was getting us seen and heard by the right people. He'd even hired a social media person, who along with Larry and Marian, was constantly talking about "branding", a word Ian *never* used. Which is probably why he made that comment about my weight.

Ass.

"This where the cool kids hang out?" And there she was, leaning against the brick wall like she was posing for an album cover. Marian "Mac" Shepherd, always posturing these days. Her tight pants hugged her small curves and her cinched belt made her waist look even tinier.

A burgundy leather jacket that cost more than my share of the rent topped everything off. Mac had always been petite, but now she was little and fierce thanks to her new ensembles.

Larry had hired a stylist for her; just Marian, mind you. He cited budgetary reasons for this, but we all knew it was bullshit and he wanted his girlfriend to stand out among the rest of us. Not to mention that she was our newly minted lead singer since Quincy had...done what she did.

I didn't feel shoved to the back, exactly. Unlike Marian, stardom was never in my sights. Nothing wrong with wanting to be on top, but I would have been fine if The Scottish Play never made it beyond garage-band status, playing our friends' parties (we were doing Teresa-Jo's wedding reception in a couple of months) and buying instruments secondhand. I also knew I wasn't the most gifted bass player. I was serviceable, but not musically inclined like the rest of my bandmates.

I *was* writing more songs. Not that Larry wanted to look at them. "When we make it even bigger, we'll have people doing that *for* us," he said when I offered him my notebooks, including the one Quin and Ross gave me at Waffle House.

I'd had to bite back, "it's me, hi, I'm people '' and turn away so he couldn't see my massive eye roll.

"Good show tonight, huh?" Marian asked us, pulling out a long silver vape pen. She held it out. Maud shook her head. Ross held up her own cig, and I stomped mine out, grinding it beneath my favorite secondhand Doc Martens.

"Duff, your vocals were getting a little overwhelming," Marian said after taking a hit and exhaling vanilla-scented smoke. Who did that remind me of?

"Oh, so now *you're* giving me notes?"

Maud and Ross glanced at me sharply, eyes wide. Okay, that came out snippier than intended.

Marian took another drag, then switched off the vape and slid it in her jacket pocket. "Okay, out with it." Her eyes, with that ever present subtle black liner, were unreadable. Some days, I missed her crazy fuchsia makeup. It felt more like *her*.

I crossed my arms over my Runaways tank. Larry could pry this off my cold, dead, three-pounds-too-heavy-according-to-him body for all I cared. "Out with what, Mac?"

She gestured with her pen elegantly, like she was conducting an orchestra of one. "Whatever issues you have with Lawrence. Who, may I remind you, is doing more for us than Ian ever did."

"Excuse you." Now Ross was standing next to me. She'd taught teenagers for the past five years and, as a result, didn't suffer fools kindly. "I'd watch how you speak of the dead, Marian."

Now Quincy was among the dead. I bit my lip, willing myself not to cry as Ross continued. "And if I'm remembering correctly, Marian, you are *here* because Ian saw a video of you playing a high school party and took a chance on someone with no formal music training, no band name, and no real sense of self."

Ouch.

"Larry M is doing a lot for us, I'll give him that," Ross continued, and I could tell from the way her shoulders tensed, just like they did before a particularly big show, that she was just warming up. "And I'm grateful—hell, I'm going to be able to quit my job so we can tour, which is something I never thought I'd be able to do." She smiled a little bit, deservedly proud of her talent, before her face got serious again. "But we're worried. You're in love with him, and that's great and everything, but we want you to remember who *you* are."

"Who I *was* before *Lawrence*," Marian said pointedly, "was *nothing*." She looked at me. "This is about the weight comment, isn't it?"

"Body positivity and acceptance still have a long way to go," Maud murmured tentatively. She shifted in her red heels, clearly uncomfortable as the newest member of the band. I turned my head just slightly to give her a half-smile of gratitude.

"It was creepy," Ross stated. "Duff, and me, and Maud, all look just fine how we are. And we play like a dream together, which is something I didn't know if I could say after…" She trailed off, and even Marian's mouth turned down at the corners.

"Anyway," Ross said, regaining her composure, "if Larry's so concerned about our overall look, why did he hire a stylist for just *you*?"

"Because I'm the lead singer now!" Marian snapped. Bringing the pen to her lips, she inhaled hard, but her jaw was still clenched when she exhaled. "Because I am the face of The Scottish Play." Her face softened just slightly. "And I know we all miss Quincy. I do too. But we have a chance to really go places. Not just Georgia and Scotland, but like, stadium tours. Number one on iTunes. The whole nine. Larry is getting us there, and way faster than Ian ever would."

Maud stared down at her shoes, fiddling with the hem of her petticoat, folding it over and over with her fingers before letting it go and starting again. I knew by now she was stimming because it was all becoming too much. I took a step closer to her, not touching, but just so she knew I understood.

Ross was shaking her head now, chaotic curls going back and forth.

"Marian, I want you to listen to yourself. I love this band. You know I do. I love you and Duff and I'm so glad we found you, Maud." She turned back and smiled at Maud, who smiled back, still fooling with her underskirt. "But he's controlling you, and he's trying to control the rest of us."

Her cigarette had ash a mile long, and she looked down right before it would have burned her fingers. "Yikes." Ross stepped on the almost nonexistent butt, offered a sheepish smile to Mac. "I'm sorry if this upset you. I don't like to cause drama, but I did think it was important you knew how I felt."

She looked at me and Maud. "See y'all tomorrow?" We nodded, and Ross disappeared down the alley, slinging her backpack over her shoulder.

"Guess she's not gonna help us load out," Marian muttered, rolling her eyes.

I turned back to her. "Really? *That's* your takeaway?"

She said nothing. Now I was the one who needed to leave.

"Help me pack up, Maud?" I asked. She nodded, lips pressed tight. I looked at Marian. "Let me know if you're coming home tonight."

"Whatever." Mac shrugged and leaned against the wall, putting her pen to her lips. We were going to be a moody little brat tonight, apparently.

"Your phone's buzzing," Maud pointed out as we made our way back into the rapidly emptying club.

I pulled it out of my pocket. Josh.

I felt the smile growing on my face before I even read the text. He'd had to work tonight, shelving books at the UGA library, but sent his well wishes before we'd gone on. And before I could think too hard about it, I'd texted back, inviting him to Scotland.

Now, his reply: *I'd love to, but work and money and stuff probably aren't going to let me. Make it up to you when you get back? :)*

Well, good thing our performance had kicked ass, because otherwise, tonight fucking blew.

CHAPTER TWENTY-ONE:

MARIAN

"Lechery, sir, it provokes, and unprovokes; it provokes the desire, but it takes away the performance." —*Macbeth,* Act II Scene III

IT irked me to no end that I had to go through my mother's boyfriend to get my damn passport. Of all the people to rely on when things were *finally* going so well, it had to be Mama, of all people, and her piece of the month. And there had been a lot of pieces over a lot of months—more than I'd ever want to count, some of whom I hoped to never think of again.

Annie Shepherd's latest boyfriend was a balding, overweight man in his mid-fifties who went by Ace, even though his name was actually Kevin. He worked part time at the library to supplement his income, since his day job as a mechanic didn't quite cover his mortgage, at least according to Mama. Ace was a single father to two young daughters, his wife having died of cancer several years before.

I'd been trying my best not to pay attention to Mama's latest romance, feeling bright-green with envy at how much she seemed to dote on the two little girls who were not her blood relations and likely wouldn't even be her stepdaughters, since Mama always ended relationships before she had to fully commit. She had been trying for a solid month to get me to meet them. I'd been invited to movies, to cookouts, even to church. "Bring your fella," she'd say. "We need to meet each other's beaus."

Since when did Mama talk like a debutante? Besides, she'd already met Lawrence once, at the 40 Watt show. I'd tried to ignore the memory of her snaking over to his table and pulling him into a hug, the two of them giggling like schoolgirls and looking up at me, snapping pictures on their phones as I'd tried to concentrate on playing my solo in "Alabaster."

"That didn't count," Mama had said when I pointed it out. "We barely got a chance to talk." Never mind that I didn't *want* to meet her beau and didn't want her getting to know mine. My feelings didn't matter.

But she wouldn't stop trying. When she'd overheard me on the phone to Lawrence, griping about how to expedite my passport, she enlisted Ace/Kevin's services without even asking me, much to my irritation. And then Lawrence insisted I take him up on the offer, and even called Mama to *thank* her for being so helpful, irritating me further.

But I couldn't tell Lawrence that. I couldn't let my own shitty, toxic relationship with my mother possibly compromise the band. To everyone else, it looked like she'd done something nice for me out of the goodness of her heart.

Only I seemed to see the truth: people don't do anything without an ulterior motive.

Duff never understood why I hated my mother. We both knew how much her granny loved Mama, and if the sainted Granny Devereaux was a fan, you were *in*. The fact that the woman's approval had never extended to me, Annie Shepherd's *daughter,* had never seemed to matter to anyone, except for maybe TJ. Not to mention that whenever Duff was around, Mama was her best self: smiling, funny, letting us drink or smoke pot, "so long as you stay here at the house." Duff was the only friend I'd brought home recently, and Annie had thrown herself into playing the *cool mom* when she was around. So gross.

Ian hadn't ever understood my bitterness toward my mother, nor had Quincy. They'd both liked Mama, too, though I'd keep them away from her more often than not.

None of them could understand the feelings I'd never vocalized— to like Mama meant they didn't really love *me*.

Oh, Annie was easy to like on the surface. She was friendly, pretty, charming—she'd been a cheerleader and prom queen, and guys from her school days still stopped her in town to joke with her about how they were aging like milk and she still looked like dynamite. It was true. With her normally dishwater blond hair, dyed platinum in recent years but still hairsprayed to oblivion like a true throwback (even though she'd come of age in the '90s, Hiawassee had been decidedly behind the times), and her wide mocha-brown eyes and button nose, she looked like a sparklier, bubblier version of me.

She was nice to everybody, full of Southern manners and just the right amount of flirtation to make folks think they had a shot. Most

GRITS (girls raised in the South) claimed this skill as a birthright, but that part of Mama had never stuck on me. The only part of her I came by honestly was the bitterness, still spilling out of me years after Deddy had left us both.

I wouldn't tell Lawrence all of that. Oh, I could, and he'd probably understand—his own parents were shitasses, to use his term—but it had very little to do with the band, and besides, I couldn't stand pity from anyone. Better to minimize my feelings and keep Mama at a distance while pretending that everything was peaches. Lawrence would find out eventually, but it didn't have to be *now.* Not when the band took precedence.

So I'd gone to the damn library and let Ace/Kevin guide me through the paperwork and take my photo and listened to his bad jokes and him detailing how he got his nickname (as if I couldn't have guessed he was a KISS fan), and smiled politely when he'd shown me pictures of Ivy and Maple, his twin daughters, and nodded and thanked him for working whatever magic he was working to expedite the application. I suspected he'd paid a little extra, or maybe Lawrence had, but nobody asked *me* for the cash, so I guessed it didn't matter.

But now Mama had something to hold over my head. To try and force me into some dumbass relationship with her new "daughters" and our *beaus.* Barf.

"Ace says your passport should arrive within the week, unless the postal service has delays," Mama said now, tipping back her glass of Sprite as she sat across from me on the couch. I eyed her warily, irritated that she was passing on this information. Ace could have just texted me. "I hope you thanked him properly for helping you with that, Marian."

"Thanked him properly?" I repeated, noting the nasty tone that crept into my voice. I couldn't help it. Ever since Duff had said Mama called her, I'd been polishing my stone of anger to a shine. How dare she go behind my back and try to press my friends for info? I was a grown-ass woman. She had no right. "How, exactly? With the company you keep, I'm a little afraid of what's expected of me."

"Marian!" Mama's face instantly fell, her gasp full of hurt. "That's uncalled for, and really unfair. You need to apologize."

I shrugged, saying nothing, and went back to my tablet, where I was doing some online shopping. Lawrence had suggested I might want to pick out a few pieces for the upcoming tour, so I was selecting some items, which I'd then send on to the stylist. She'd pair them with matching accessories and help me purchase them. So far, I hadn't been asked to pay for anything.

When I pressed the issue with Lawrence, he just smiled and told me not to worry about it. I was so surprised and pleased when he hired her for me. My one-off comment I'd made about being a fashion novice with no skills who needed some help—made when I was half-asleep and nestled in Lawrence's shoulder—must have stuck with him.

For the first time, I had a boyfriend who spoiled me, who let me know how much he loved me. Duff, Ross, and Maud could fuck off into the sun. I wouldn't give Lawrence up for anyone, or anything, no matter how many times they cornered me in back alleys to try and convince me otherwise.

I had no idea where he was getting the money, though. Lawrence's waiter's salary was pitiful, even with the choice tips from Grit regulars, and he hadn't worked a shift in weeks. What little cash he made from our shows was even less than us bandmates. But I didn't ask, not wanting to look a gift horse in the mouth.

As for my stupid bandmates, Duff, Ross, and Maud, they were being nothing but shits to him. Nitpicking every single word out of his mouth, gossiping about him behind his back and contradicting everything he said. Lawrence *did* occasionally put his foot in it—I'd experienced that myself, and I knew it could sting when he made the odd insensitive comment—but he wasn't doing it on purpose, and it irritated me that the girls were so quick to excuse Maud's occasional faux pas, but couldn't do the same for Lawrence. They were determined to hate him, using everything he said to back up their own confirmation bias. Lawrence had grown up looking after his brothers, and he naturally fell into a routine of caring for people. He didn't mean any harm when he suggested things or took charge. But there was no point in trying to explain that to Duff. She—and the others—were determined to hate "Larry M."

"...identity," Mama was saying.

I snapped back to reality, hitting "save" on a little black dress with a flouncy hemline, the lace at the collar threaded with a pretty dark red. It would look fantastic with my red Chucks. I frowned. Lawrence had told me my wearing those on stage felt a bit like Joan Jett cosplay. Well, maybe just this once. I looked at Mama. "What did you say?"

She sighed, looking down at her glass. "I said I want you to be careful. What you said about the men I used to date... Well, you know what to look for. Just because they seem like they're taking care of you—doing all these things to make you feel loved and cared for—a lot of the time that's just grooming. They're controlling you and making it look like they're taking care of you, and you lose your identity." Her face went pale. "And then once you realize what's happened, you're in so deep you can't get out. I read about it in a book and it really hit home since I've lived that experience."

I snorted; of course she had read about it somewhere. She wouldn't have thought of that psychobabble on her own. Mama took no notice of my reaction and went on. "I just want you to keep your eyes open." She stared at her glass a moment longer, then set it down on the table, seeming to come to a decision. "I know you spent a long time watching me mourn your father and deal with all that trauma. I haven't set the best example. But I know you're far too smart to make the same mistakes as me. That's all."

"Thanks for the advice," I said, rolling my eyes.

Her expression was sad. "You're welcome. I just hope you take it."

Mama was right about one thing—I was far too smart and I'd seen far, far too much. Too much to let anyone, even her or the rest of the band, divert me from my dreams. And those dreams included Lawrence MacLaren, whether anybody liked it or not.

"I'm still waiting on that apology, Marian."

I looked Mama dead in the eye. She stared right back. Finally, I looked away. "Fine. I'm sorry."

"Are you, though?" she asked in a quiet voice.

"Yes," I said, and she smiled, getting up to put her glass in the sink, patting me on the head as she passed. I looked at her retreating back and mouthed *No.*

I grabbed Lawrence's Coke Zero from the middle console of the car and flipped open the lid, pouring the entire mini bottle of peanut butter whiskey in it. I handed it to Lawrence, who took the cup and positioned it between his legs as he drove, his face twisting into a grimace. "I'm Scottish, woman. Why do you force me to drink shite?"

"Because you wouldn't let me buy the House of Stuart bourbon that was fifteen dollars a bottle, so this is as good as it's gonna get," I said with a laugh, upending two mini bottles in my own full-sugar Coke. For a health nut, I couldn't understand why Lawrence drank diet drinks—I'd always understood that artificial sweeteners were way worse for you than regular sugar, but what did I know? I took a long gulp and grinned. "Down the hatch, MacLaren. It's not bad. It tastes like Butterfinger Pie."

"I've never had Butterfinger Pie," he said, still grimacing, but he dutifully took another small sip through his straw.

"What? And you call yourself Southern!" I gulped some more. "Well, Granny Devereaux would probably never lower herself to make it, but Butterfinger Pie is basically a white trash delicacy. It's pretty much just whipped cream, peanut butter, cream cheese, and crushed butterfingers, all mushed together and shoveled in your face."

"That sounds disgusting," Lawrence said, turning onto Highway 77. "And so is this drink. Seriously, Marian, you couldn't have just bought some Jack Daniels?"

"I could never insult his Scottish Highness's royal taste buds with such a thing!" I giggled, draining my cup. "Are we almost there?" We'd already been in the car for forty-five minutes. It was a hike from Athens to Elberton.

No sooner than I'd said the words, the GPS sounded through Lawrence's phone, telling us to turn left in one point two miles. I grinned and reached over to caress Lawrence's knee. He was wearing jeans today, and I found myself a little sad not to see his muscular, tattooed legs beneath his kilt. I'd become so used to seeing him in it that he almost seemed like a different person when he dressed normally.

Lawrence turned to me and smiled. "I still love you, even though your taste in booze is absolutely horrific."

"And I love you," I said, winking at him and squeezing his thigh harder. "Even though the jeans you're wearing are veering into dad territory."

"Och!" Lawrence made a distinctly Scottish noise and put his hand over his heart, affronted.

"Look! There it is!" We were passing by several hilly, vacant fields, pale green grass and the odd tree muted against the darkening blue light of the sky. It would be dark in less than an hour. Off to our left, I could see the faint outline of a granite structure off behind the trees. My palms began to tingle.

"It's smaller than I thought it would be," Lawrence mused as we turned onto the road.

"But beautiful," I said as he parked the car. For a moment, we sat there and stared. I opened another mini bottle of peanut butter whiskey and downed it, gesturing for Lawrence to finish his own drink. I'd decided before coming that we should have a nice buzz first to give us a little liquid courage.

The Georgia Guidestones loomed above our heads, the late-evening sun shining off the five main pillars and the capstone, making them look pocked, shadows casting over the ground like dark pillars. I'd been here a couple of times before as a kid, and they'd always scared me a little. They weren't that old—they'd only been erected in 1980, but somehow, they had an ancient, timeless feel to them. Of course, part of it was that they reminded you of Stonehenge, though far smaller and less grand.

The way the stones stood out in the middle of the elements, the sun casting down upon them, marking the time, and the inscriptions in eight different languages, gave its own version of the Ten Commandments, advising humanity on how best to coincide with nature and live responsibly. It was a unique little landmark in the middle of nowhere in Elbert County, Georgia, but something about it had always felt…weird. Almost as if it called to me. In a way, I wasn't sure if I wanted to answer.

And it had been calling to me for days.

When I'd suggested to Lawrence that we visit the Guidestones to say a little prayer for our safe travels, he'd looked at me oddly. "You're not religious," he'd said, and I laughed.

"No, I'm not. Like, at all," I reassured him. "But that place has always felt…big…to me. I don't know how to explain it. I think I should go. Just to like, breathe in the air. Hold space or something."

"Did those stupid Hecks put you up to this?" Lawrence asked, his face scrunching up.

"They did not." I knew The Hecks *didn't* like the Guidestones, a fact that perplexed me. I'd heard Zak talking about it once when we were still in high school; something about how it was rumored to be tied to a dozen different political and spiritual groups, half of which were completely kookypants, to say nothing of the mysterious wealthy benefactor who had ordered the monument's construction and maintenance. Now, the place was just a tourist zone for dumb hipsters who liked to pose for Instagram pictures, who had no real connection with nature or the occult. I wasn't sure how much of Zak's information was accurate, but I still remembered his admonishment: "I'd sooner go see the horses in the pasture next door before I'd go see those dumbass stones."

As we got out of the car, I pulled my jacket tight around myself and smiled. The horses in the pasture just behind the structure *were* really pretty.

But we had bigger things to do.

The three peanut butter whiskeys I'd had were kicking in now. My legs felt wobbly as we walked to the stones, and I held out my hand to let my fingers graze the granite, feeling very much like Claire in *Outlander,* secretly hoping Lawrence would reach out and pull me back, crushing me to his chest at the last moment like Jamie Fraser. Instead, he stepped ahead of me and reached the stones first, running a finger over the engraving in English, murmuring.

"Population control... Personal rights and social duties... Fitness and diversity... Petty laws and useless officials..." Lawrence turned to me and laughed. "Well, I think I have some idea of the folks behind this thing."

"Don't make fun," I cautioned, chills suddenly going up my back. The sky was a lot darker now; it was going to get dark quicker than I'd anticipated. "Look up at the capstone. See that gap there? The sun shines through it, and that little point of light... It'll tell you what time it is."

"Or I can just look at my Apple Watch."

"Stop!" I glared at Lawrence, wishing he'd take this seriously. "Don't you feel it? The energy here? It feels like..."

"Like what?" Lawrence's eyes narrowed a little. He looked around, as though he might see someone else, but we were alone.

"Like it wants you to take it seriously."

"Fine. I'm sorry." Lawrence pulled me to him, and I settled happily into his chest, breathing in his cologne, enjoying the feel of his scratchy jeans against my legs, even if they were ugly. "It is rather quaint, in its own way. Nothing compared to Stonehenge, of course, but I see why people find it interesting."

"Do you feel the energy?"

"I do, a bit," Lawrence said. "Well…I feel *something*, anyway. Though I'm not entirely sure I like the feeling." He swallowed. "Or perhaps it doesn't quite like me."

A car slowed down, then passed us. One star had appeared in the sky. I wrapped my jacket even tighter around myself and pressed myself closer to Lawrence, the chill suddenly feeling ominous.

"We should go," he said, squeezing me tight. "You're cold."

"Not yet," I said. "We have something to do first. Come on."

I grabbed him by the arm and pulled him away from the Guidestones, down the little hill, and into the expanse of grass below, just far enough down the slope so that passers-by wouldn't see us. The horses and lone donkey watched us, curious. I crouched in the grass and pulled Lawrence down with me, taking the little bag from my jacket pocket and opening the drawstring.

"What's that?" Lawrence asked, his eyes flashing with curiosity and a touch of fear.

"My little bag of charms," I said, and his eyes flickered to my bracelet. "Not those charms. These are magic charms."

"I thought you said this had nothing to do with the Hecks—"

I cut him off. "It *doesn't*. Those stupid boys don't know everything there is to know. Maybe *I* know a little something." I poured the bag out onto the ground, letting the stones scatter, and picked up the little purple candle. I rummaged in my pocket for a lighter, then lit the wick. The brand-new candle caught immediately, the spark on the wick surging into a large, orange flame. I grabbed a twig, pressed it to the flame, and let it burn, followed by a handful of grass.

The truth was, I wasn't entirely sure that this would work, though I'd read a little bit about charms and spells, just enough to get started. "We're going to pray for our safe travels… For success as a band…and for us. You and me, Lawrence. For our future. We're going to set it in stone."

Lawrence had gone totally silent. I'd expected some excitement, or at the very least, a smile. But Mr. Make It Happen only sat there in the grass, watching me warily, his eyes wide and his face pale. I could sense his fear—he was really freaked out—but rather than guilt, I felt emboldened by it.

Powerful.

I let the candle burn for a few minutes, dripping rivulets of purple wax on the grass and the stones, running my fingers through the dirt to mingle them. "I pray for our travels. For our band and its continued success. For my friends. For Lawrence MacLaren. And for myself, Marian Shepherd." I let the candle burn for a few more moments, running the flame over my skin, not hot enough to singe, but just enough to feel the delicious tickle of heat. Then I blew out the candle. The smoke trailed off into the sky, a ghost-like gray wisp, and then it was gone.

It was full dark now. Lawrence shivered and rubbed his arms, moving to get up. "We should crack on," he said, offering me his arm. I could see the goosebumps on his skin, even in the dark. "We've got a long drive back."

"Not so fast." I pulled him back down to the ground and kissed him, hard. When I pulled away, he was panting—from lust or fear, I didn't know, and didn't care. "I wish you hadn't worn those jeans. It's going to be harder to get them off you." I reached for his belt and he stared at me with wide eyes. I kissed him again, rougher this time, and climbed right into his lap, running my hands through his auburn hair and making my intentions clear. After a moment, he began to kiss me back, his own hands running under my shirt, up my back and to my bra strap, which he unhooked with trembling fingers. Our tongues touched and our panting breath mingled, and he groaned against my lips.

We lay down in the cool grass, the stones beneath my back as Lawrence fumbled with his pants, pulling off his belt with some difficulty and easing them down over his hips. I watched silently as he struggled to pull the jeans free from around his ankles, discarding them in a heap by the pile of stones, and coming to lie down on top of me, propping himself up on his elbows. He kissed my neck, behind my earlobe, my chin, then made his way back to my mouth, groaning softly. "There's no time," I whispered hot in his ear, and grabbed him, hard, pushing him into me.

The noise he made was not unlike a screech, and he thrust into me, his hands clawing at the grass beneath my head, guttural sounds coming from deep within his chest, sounds I'd never heard before. I screeched back at him like a wild animal, clawing my fingernails down his back, feeling myself draw blood. I bit him on the neck and he pulled back, momentarily stunned. His face changed from shock to pain to anger to determination, all in a flash.

Then, with one sudden, violent thrust, we came together.

We lay there for a moment, side by side, panting. I could see Lawrence's hands as they lay curled on his stomach, still trembling. Then he began to laugh.

Lawrence sat up, grabbed for his grass-stained jeans, and pulled them on, his chest heaving. "Maybe I like peanut butter whiskey after all."

We stared at each other a moment, breathless. Then, suddenly, we became aware of headlights appearing over the crest of the hill. "Shit, we've got visitors." I said.

"Marian, that's a *cop.*"

"Oh, fuck. Oh, fuck." I scrambled to pull down my skirt, and quickly gathered my stones and threw them back in my bag. "There's no time, shit." Once I grabbed what I could, we scrambled back up the hill, trying to calm our breathing. There was grass in my hair and I did my best to shake it out. Lawrence pulled his phone out of his pocket and acted like he'd been taking a picture as the deputy from the Elbert County Police Department approached us, his flashlight shining in our faces.

"Out for a romantic stroll?" the police officer asked, his Southern drawl dripping with bemused disdain, and Lawrence grinned sheepishly, squinting at the bright light.

"I wish. No, my girlfriend just had to pee, and she was afraid a coyote was going to get her. She thought she saw one out in that pasture. I told her she was crazy, that a coyote wouldn't run up on a bunch of horses and donkeys, but she swore she saw it. I was standing guard so she could go." He flashed his best *bitches be crazy* look and to my surprise, the cop laughed.

"Ha. Well, alright then. Y'all better get on now. It's getting dark. I dunno about no coyotes, but you *will* see a bunch of deer out on these roads. Hate to see you hit one and destroy that beaut of a vintage car you got there."

Lawrence nodded at his Stingray and grinned. "You got that right, sir. I spent years restoring that thing."

"Y'all have a nice night, now."

"Thank you, officer," I said, giving him a grateful smile of my own. He hadn't noticed as I'd dropped the half-burned candle at the foot of the Guidestones. I kicked a little grass over it as Lawrence and I walked back toward the car. As we buckled up, the deputy got in his own car and drove away. I let out a sigh of relief.

Lawrence started the car. He looked at me. "You didn't say 'safe.'"

"Huh?"

"Back there, that spell you did... You said, 'I pray for our travels...' But you didn't say 'safe.'" His face had gone white again in the dark of the car. "Do you think that's bad?"

"Of course not," I said, but the look of worry settled between Lawrence's brows and took up residence there, never leaving his face as we drove back to Athens in total silence, my body thrumming with a feeling that was warm, intoxicating, and utterly terrifying all at once.

CHAPTER TWENTY-TWO:

DUFF

"Rock and roll by its nature is sexual." —Joan Jett

I made a noise that, thankfully, my granny was nowhere around to hear.

Josh raised his head from between my legs, wet lips grinning. I was grateful my thigh-grip didn't kill him. And for the mind-blowing orgasm he and his magic tongue just gave me.

This was hedonism, pure and simple. I truly felt like a rock star, spread-eagled on his black sheets smack in the middle of a king-sized bed in the mid-afternoon, having just been serviced by one of the hottest guys I'd ever seen, let alone slept with (along with two of his friends). My arms were thrown over my head, I was pleasantly sore in all the right places, and I hadn't thought about Mac and Larry M in... shit.

"Where'd you go there?" Josh was now lying beside me, pulling the sheet over us so I wouldn't get cold like I always did after sex. He was thoughtful like that.

"Never mind," I said, kissing him hard and tasting myself. I'd been with my share of flings since we moved to Athens, but so many of them performed oral like they were brushing their teeth—a necessary task, not an enjoyable one, and always done by rote. When I'd shared this with Josh the first time we were together—just the two of us—he said, "fools, all of them" and proceeded to show me what I'd been missing. Over and over again.

But even in my post-coital haze, I couldn't get Annie's phone call out of my mind.

Pulling up to Josh's place for a little prearranged afternoon delight, I was surprised to see her name pop up on my phone's display. I'd had Annie's number programmed in since high school, but she hadn't ever just called me that I could remember. I put the car in park and hit accept.

"Hey Annie, what's up?" I hoped it was nothing to do with Granny—she showed no signs of slowing down, but I knew that our bodies could break down without warning. And ever since I'd gotten the call about Quincy, I worried even more. However, I had to ask. "Is my granny okay?"

"Oh darlin', she's just fine!" Annie's breathy words rushed through the connection and the butterflies in my stomach stilled. "Ornery as anything, as usual. I didn't mean to worry you."

Josh appeared at the doorway of the small house he shared with Pete and Zak, who I knew were both working this afternoon. He waved; I grinned and held up one finger. He then held up two fingers and flicked his tongue between them, and I snorted. "Sorry about that, Annie. And no worries, I know you didn't mean to scare me. What's going on?"

"It's Marian." Oh. "How is she doing, honey?"

I hadn't seen much of Mac since Larry made the announcement about Scotland, outside of rehearsals and gigs, of course. I was still smarting from Larry's weird comments about my body and Mac's lack of reaction, and these days I preferred the company of Ross and Maud, and increasingly, Josh. Hence our afternoon delight.

Wait. Was Josh taking off his shirt in the doorway? Guess I wasn't the only horny one in the vicinity.

"She seems, uh, fine to me," I said, trying like hell to tear my eyes away from Josh's eight-pack and failing miserably. "Honestly, we've been really busy getting ready for Scotland and all. That's exciting, huh?" I rolled my eyes a little at Josh and gestured with my hand that wasn't holding the phone, opening and closing it like *talk-talk*.

I knew I shouldn't disrespect Annie, but…really? She was concerned about her daughter *now*? What about when we were in high school and Annie was buying us alcohol and getting sloshed herself behind closed doors? At least that's what Marian always said. Even though I'd never witnessed the latter.

"It *is* exciting," Annie said quietly, then hesitated. "I just…I'm worried, Duff. I'm worried this Lawrence isn't the best influence on her. I don't want her doing anything she'll regret."

I thought of Mac and Larry M's little trip to the Guidestones. I'd overheard The Hecks talking about it in high school, how that place was bad magic you didn't touch with a ten-foot pole. I'd scoffed and rolled my eyes at the time, but for some reason, the "bad magic" part stayed with me. I was afraid to even *visit*, let alone…do what Mac and Larry M had. Peanut butter whisky, magic charms, post-spell fuck and all.

Should I tell Annie? Wait, what am I saying? I do not want to get into Marian's sex life with her mother.

Josh shut the door. Tease. Also, now it was getting uncomfortably hot in this car.

"I'll keep an eye on her," I replied. She had me at Lawrence. Annie Shepherd and I didn't have much in common, except loving my granny and now, side-eyeing the problematic dude in Mac's life. "I promise. I gotta go now, though, okay? Text me if you need anything else."

"Okay," Annie said. There was a pause, like she wanted to say something else, but then she just signed off with, "Bye, hon. Have a safe trip."

I couldn't get to the door, and get Josh's mouth on mine, fast enough.

"She's a mom," Josh said, propping himself on one elbow after I told him about the call. "Moms worry. You should hear mine when she sees McDonald's wrappers in my car."

I rolled on my back. "Not Annie Shepherd. She kind of let Marian fend for herself all those years. And *now* she's concerned? It's just weird."

"Hm." He traced my bare shoulder with one finger, making me shiver in the best possible way. "I guess I have Annie Shepherd to thank, though."

"How's that?"

He kept tracing, avoiding my eyes. "This is probably the most open you've ever been with me."

I pulled the sheet a little higher. "Excuse me, were you not there when I banged you *and* your two closest friends? Outside? By a giant illegal bonfire y'all somehow got away with more than once?"

Speaking of, hanging out with one guy after you've had group sex with his friends? Not as weird as you'd think. The Hecks were chill, and in turn, so was I. We all kind of understood without saying that our little sojourn was a one night only deal.

Josh rolled onto his back so we were both staring at the ceiling. "Not like that." He swatted an errant fly. "Just...we've been hanging out since then. And it's fun. And the guys really like you, not like *that*, just in the way they always have. You're a cool customer, Duff O'Brien." Josh slid his arm behind me, and pulled me close. "You just don't talk about yourself that much, you know?"

So much warm, bare skin. I couldn't resist twining one leg around his. He moaned a little, but didn't take the bait. I was tempted to slide down, take him in my mouth, and avoid this conversation. But I knew we'd get back to it. I also knew that, much as I hated to admit it, Josh had a point.

Since that night at the Bald, we'd texted every day—not obsessive lovey-dovey shit, but funny memes and observations from our respective work and rehearsals. I'd written a song about that magic sexual encounter—"Ride Me by the Fire"—and shared a phone recording with him before I'd brought it to the band, who loved it, though I didn't tell them its origins. (Even Lawrence was a reluctant fan.) Josh came around to our place sometimes, and I to his. We fit in each other's friend groups with ease on the rare occasions we weren't banging it out in our beds.

I just hesitated to make this, whatever, anything more than it was. Maybe Marian and Larry's insta-relationship had left me a bit hesitant. I didn't want to lose myself like Mac had. And The Scottish Play was my everything. I wanted to keep it all mine. Who knew if pillow talk was the gateway for discarding one's entire identity? Certainly not me. I was relatively inexperienced in the world of dating.

If that's what we were even doing. Yes, I'd invited him to Scotland, and I was bummed when he couldn't come, but I invited him just so I could fuck on foreign soil, right? Right?

Josh and me, we...clicked. And that scared me. Like so many things did these days.

"I don't want to push you," he said gently. "I know you've been through a lot. Like a *lot* a lot, with Ian and Quincy so close together. I just..." He trailed off, taking a breath. "I worry about you, Duff. Me and Zak and Pete, we all do."

I felt a little *ping* in my heart.

"That's nice," I said.

Josh pulled me even closer. "What is?"

I smiled into his chest. "You. And your boys. Someone other than my granny actually worrying about *me* for once." I debated whether to go on, then decided what the hell. In for a penny, like stupid Larry always said, but I liked that saying too. I lifted my head so he could hear me. "My life's been tied up with Mac's for so long now, you know? And we're on the verge of breaking out as a band. I think about her constantly—not in a romantic way or anything, but how these losses are affecting her, how her whirlwind relationship could have long-term consequences for everyone, even why she's suddenly become Miss Glamour Queen when I can tell it wasn't really her idea in the first place."

Now I had the courage to meet his eyes, which were soft. I could tell he was really listening. "Mac, Mac, Mac and band, band, band. I'm afraid to lose focus on any of it. I mean, I lost sight of Quincy for one fucking night and…"

I swallowed hard, burying my face in the curve of his neck, the part I'd always loved most on a man. So soft and vulnerable, but at the same time strong. Josh murmured, not even words but sounds of comfort, and the knot in my stomach slowly loosened, bit by bit.

I didn't cry, though. After that night in the Bald, I was all cried out.

"Sorry," I said, coming up for air.

Josh shrugged, and I felt his shoulders go *up, down*, a release. "Hey, it's been forever since a woman bared her soul *and* ass in my bed."

With my free arm, I reached for a pillow and bopped him on the head. Josh sat up, his mouth dropping open, and it was on.

I was grateful. To this big silly boy, not only for making me come and sending me the best *Drag Race* gifs, but also for *not* saying Quincy's death wasn't my fault. And for engaging in a pillow fight when I was finished being vulnerable with him. For the moment, anyway.

It's why after a few minutes of shenanigans, I slid down between the sheets and lay there with my face between his legs, using my mouth and hands to properly thank him for being so good, until he pulled me up, put on a condom, and plopped me down on his cock and I rode the waves into another set of unforgettable orgasms. While I was on top, I heard the other two guys come in and for the first time since the Bald, I was utterly unself-conscious of how my pleasure sounded.

They'd heard similar out of me before.

I pray for our travels, I thought, my head thrown back in ecstasy.

I pray for my friends.

"Someone's glowing," Ross observed an hour later as I sailed into band practice wearing disheveled clothes and the biggest smile I'd had in ages. She fist-bumped me as I reached for my bass. "I'm thinking a Duff O'Brien fuck-jam is coming our way, ladies."

Maud giggled, bringing one white-gloved hand to her red lips. Larry, sitting on the green couch, rolled his eyes to the ceiling.

And Mac, my Mac, who felt further and further away each day, didn't even acknowledge I was in the room.

"By the way," I said directly to her, strapping up, "your mom called."

CHAPTER TWENTY-THREE

MARIAN

"I have supp'd full with horrors; direness, familiar to my slaughterous thoughts cannot once start me." — *Macbeth*, Act V, Scene V

OUR trip to Scotland marked the first time I'd ever been on a plane. And the first time I'd ever left the country. As the plane descended, Lawrence handed me a piece of gum, advising me to hold my nose and gently blow if I felt my ears start to pop, and I felt a wave of gratitude and love. Not toward just him, but my friends, too.

I'd been at odds with all of them for weeks. I hadn't spoken to any of them much, even Duff, aside from when I had to at practice. But looking out at the patchwork quilt of the Scottish landscape, capped with craggy mountains and lush green, I felt some of my bitterness fading. Here we were, touching down in beautiful Scotland, ready to take our band—how serendipitous that we were literally named *The*

Scottish Play—out into the world, to make our mark! I resolved to stop being so moody and let myself enjoy it. After all, the spell couldn't work if I wasn't open to letting it.

I was jet lagged as all get out, we all were, but nothing could dim my happiness as we grabbed our bags, Ubered to the bed-and-breakfast that Larry had booked for us, with me staring out the window at the ethereal green landscape all the while. I was seconds away from hanging my head out the window like a dog and panting with contentment, even though watching Duff beaming at her phone, which she'd started tapping on the minute we'd exited the plane, filled me with an irritation I couldn't quite explain. Here we were in paradise, following our dreams, and she couldn't stop talking to that *Heck*.

The bed-and-breakfast was in Angus, only a couple of miles away from Glamis Castle, which was partly visible from the road as we arrived in the village, its ancient spires dark and beautifully gloomy against the bright blue sky. I couldn't wipe the grin from my face, leering like the Cheshire Cat even as I fell asleep later in our room, Larry insisting that we should nap before getting ready for our first show at Rory's Pub later that evening.

Scotland!

My heart was still in my throat hours later as I pulled on the black and red dress and my Chucks (Lawrence had acquiesced on that one, much to my joy—the ensemble looked incredible) and checked to make sure I had all my equipment in my guitar bag. Lawrence had gone ahead of us to make sure everything was ready at the pub.

There was a knock at the door and Duff entered, her face all smiles too.

"Just wanted to check that you're ready," she said, staring at me.

"You look really beautiful."

"So do you," I said honestly. Duff was wearing a black overall dress over a hot pink tiny tee, with Airwalks and knee-high black plaid socks. "You look like you stepped right out of 1996. Where did you get the kicks?"

"They were my mom's!" Duff laughed, kicking up a leg. "I stole them off her before I moved and she's never getting them back."

"They're awesome," I said, deciding to extend an olive branch. "Look, I'm sorry about what Larry said. About your weight. He can be kind of tactless sometimes. I'll talk to him about it."

"I appreciate that, Mac," Duff said awkwardly.

"And I'm sorry about…being distant. Or whatever." I shrugged. "Shit's been…a lot lately."

Duff stood there for a moment, deliberating, then rushed forward. She gave me a tight squeeze, which I returned. "I can't believe we're in Scotland, Mac!"

"I know!" I exclaimed, and when she pulled away, we were both giggling with excitement. We'd giggled just like this in Teresa-Jo's tiny bathroom after playing that house party. Years ago, now, and yet it felt exactly the same. Mac and Duff, two peas in a pod. Times like this I could feel all the terrible things that had happened to us and between us, all the tension, all the bad vibes, melting away, and it was just Mac and Duff, the way it should be.

"I'm glad we're here together," I said, and I meant it.

"Me, too." She cuffed me on the shoulder. "Your boytoy did us a solid, Mac."

I knew Duff was only being generous, extending an olive branch of her own so that the show went well, but it still made me smile.

"Thanks."

"Well, I'm going to go finish my makeup." Duff walked to the door, then turned with a wry smile. "Break a leg, Mac."

I winked at her. "You break one, too, Duff."

"Tomorrow."

"Tomorrow."

Rory's Pub was a smaller place, dark with an intimate, cozy atmosphere, and we *killed* it. Our audience was a mix of locals and young people who had traveled to see us, and they'd all been cheering as we'd finished our last song: the cover of "I Love Rock 'n Roll" that still left me a little choked up, thinking of Quincy. But tonight, it sounded better than it ever had before. Almost as if she was with us.

Lawrence came up to our table as the four of us were having a celebratory drink, grinning ear to ear. "Well, ladies, you've done it," he said, exhilarated. "Not only did you play your best set yet, but you sold almost every single piece of merch we brought with us."

"You're kidding!" Ross exclaimed, her face breaking out into a smile. "Even the trucker hats?"

"Especially the trucker hats." Lawrence nodded. "It's a good thing I have a backup stash of shirts and buttons for the Glamis show. It's all gone!"

"That's amazing." I leaned forward and placed a sloppy, wet kiss on his pretty lips.

When I pulled back, Lawrence laughed. "I'm so proud of you all. And you most especially, Marian." He pulled me in for another kiss. "You sounded amazing. And looked so beautiful. I've never been so chuffed in my life."

"Me, too," I murmured against his mouth, ignoring the mock groans of my friends as we kissed. "We couldn't have done it without you."

He pulled away again and looked at me with a serious expression. "I love you."

"I love you, too," I said, meaning it. I moved in for another kiss, but he stopped me, putting a gentle finger to my lips and flashing a coy look. "I want to run something by you."

"Oh yeah? What's that?"

"Why don't we get married?"

I barely heard the gasps of my friends, or the crowd of people around us, or the next band on the stage. All I heard, loud and clear, was the roaring of my heart in my throat as I threw my arms around Lawrence's neck, pulling him close, and exclaimed, "Yes! Of course; yes!"

Never in a million years had I thought that I, Marian "Mac" Shepherd, she of the "bad end" of Hiawassee, Georgia, would get married in a beautiful, traditional handfasting ceremony under the stars in Angus, Scotland, to a gorgeous and sexy auburn-haired Adonis with thighs like tree trunks and eyes like sapphires. And yet, here we were.

Lawrence had spoken to a local priest before he'd even asked me. Evidently, he'd been planning this; his seemingly impromptu proposal was actually weeks in the making. He'd thought of everything: had arranged for the small garden area outside the pub to be opened up for us, with a flower-covered archway perfect to conduct the ceremony. He even smuggled a dress in for me—a lacy little black and red frock that ended just above the knee, tight in all the right places, but gauzy and ethereal enough to make me feel like a princess.

We'd make everything all legal and official at the courthouse in Athens once we got back, but for now, this was absolutely *perfect*. Paperwork was for accountants and lawyers; what we had was beyond all that.

My soon-to-be husband was wearing a sleek, fitted black blazer and his dressy black kilt, and had his hair slicked back, making his blue eyes pop. He looked very much like he had the night of the 40 Watt show—handsome and a little dangerous. A small, dark red rosebud was pinned to his lapel like a perfect bead of blood. He really had thought of everything.

I wondered what he would have done if I'd said no.

There were benches outside the pub for people to enjoy their drinks in the summer months, and our friends joined us there, along with a few random people from the pub who had caught on to a wedding and decided to check it out. So it was there, out under the bright, twinkling stars, the night a little cold, me in my black and red dress and red Chucks, that I was joined with Lawrence MacLaren, handfast and vowing to be his wife, in sickness and in health, until death did us part.

Duff had called me "Mac" ever since the day we'd met. And now, as Marian MacLaren, I really and truly *was* Mac.

It was meant to be.

Duff, if she'd had any reservations, kept them to herself. She'd hugged me with tears in her eyes, wishing me genuine congratulations. She'd clung a little tightly during that hug, but when she'd pulled away, her smile was real. "Mac, I hate to ask, and feel free to tell me to fuck off, but don't you think you should call your mama? She's going to be *devastated* to miss your wedding..."

"Annie doesn't need to be here," I said firmly. "Can you imagine her shitfaced and flirting with locals at the pub? It'd be too embarrassing for words—besides, she can't afford to fly out." I brightened, remembering. "She'll understand. She and my deddy got married spur-of-the-moment, too."

"Gotcha," Duff said, biting her lip. "But you will call her and tell her at least? After all, you've gotta ask her for that coconut cake recipe, now that you're gonna be an old married lady."

I blinked for a second. Duff really never forgot a damn thing you told her. "Sure, I'll call her," I lied, glad that Maud and Ross had come up at that moment with their own congratulations before she had a chance to bring up TJ, who I knew would be devastated to miss my wedding, and make me feel even guiltier. *I'll invite Mama and TJ to the ceremony at the courthouse,* I told myself.

It was all I could hope for. The ones who mattered most were *here,* and they loved me. Everything else would work out in time. I was getting married! To my soulmate. And now that he was well and truly *family,* I hoped they'd warm to him.

It was all a happy blur—the handfasting, making out with Lawrence under the stars, a firepit crackling cozily nearby, keeping us all warm, my bandmates joining the other band to play an impromptu acoustic rendition of "Long, Long, Long" by the Beatles, a George Harrison-penned piece that Duff knew I loved. That was all her, and I teared up as I swayed in Lawrence's arms, knowing my best friend had organized it for me on the fly, despite her misgivings. Then, after a few glasses of champagne and some more hugs, Lawrence had whisked me off to our room at the B&B, where he'd lit what seemed like fifty candles, and slowly undressed me by candlelight.

His kisses were hot against my skin, and I committed each one to memory, running my fingers through his auburn hair, moaning against him as he finally entered me. It was the total opposite of our night out by the Guidestones. Rather than being rushed and frenzied, it was slow and sweet. Every touch was exquisite. We stayed up all night making out, making love, and making plans.

That was Lawrence and me—together, we made things. Beautiful things.

It was a night to remember. Absolutely perfect in every way.

If only it could have lasted.

CHAPTER TWENTY-FOUR:

DUFF

"If you really believe in yourself, you cannot listen to other people."
—Joan Jett

I dropped pieces of her wherever I went.

Just outside the Edinburgh airport; there was so much gray that no one noticed a little extra.

In the gravel outside of the B&B. Outside of every place we rehearsed, shopped, had tea, played gigs. Buildings hundreds of years old and ones that were brand spanking new. Everyone always had their faces upturned in awe, so they didn't notice me dropping a little crushed-up bone.

I did not drop them at Mac and Larry's handfasting.

The first place I scattered Quincy Banks's ashes was in Brasstown Bald, right before The Hecks caught me in the act and Josh and I kickstarted our…whatever was going on. I liked to think she had some responsibility for that, maybe not anything as generic as divine intervention, but a power that was uniquely Quin's. Because wherever and whoever she was now, I refused to believe she was only contained in her ashes.

And everywhere I scattered them, a flash of memory would come to me, clear as lightning.

Senior year, just after the news broke of the meth lab explosion and the couple whose remains were found inside. Everyone knew it was our class president's aunt and uncle. And then our class president wasn't that anymore. In her place was a girl with a raggedy bob, silver jewelry, and an exquisite cat eye. It's not like she radiated anger wherever she went— that was Marian Shepherd, my new best friend. But Quincy Banks was different. And who could blame her?

I was cutting through the halls to make it to physics on time when I heard it through an open door.

The mournful lines of "In the Waiting Line," an old song I'd always loved and most people my age hadn't heard of unless they'd watched movies or shows from the early aughts. The voice was ethereal, yet a little bit pissed off.

And very familiar, from all those school assemblies we skipped out on, but not before she sang the national anthem because she was just that fucking good.

Before I knew what I was doing, I'd stopped in my tracks.

"Is that Zero 7?"

Inside the music room, Quincy Banks screamed. She was sitting at the piano, though she hadn't been playing. For a moment we looked at one another, her expression not unlike a trapped animal's.

"I'm so sorry!" I held up my hands. "I just love that one. My older sister, she went through a Garden State phase and had the soundtrack playing constantly for about six months while she tried to write poetry. Then she came out as a lesbian."

What the fuck, Duff? Why the psychotic babble? And don't you have class like, now?

Quincy Banks snorted. One corner of her dark-pink painted mouth curled up just a bit.

She beckoned to me. I looked behind my shoulder just to make sure I wasn't mistaken. Then I stepped inside, still hovering in the doorway but a few paces further.

"My aunt fucking loved that shitty movie," she said. Her speaking voice was also transformed, lower than before. "I did not. But I have to admit, the songs are incredible."

She smiled the slightest bit bigger. I smiled back. This was the longest conversation I'd ever had with our class golden girl.

"I'm sorry I scared you," I said. "I shouldn't have been eavesdropping like a creeper."

Quincy Banks shrugged. "Whatever. At least you're not making the face."

"The face?" I stepped in a little closer.

"This one." She made a comical frown and tilted her head so far to the side it was practically on her shoulder. "Accompanied by a 'how are yeeeeew?' And possibly an offer of pie."

"Oh, so I shouldn't leave some Devereaux shoofly in your locker?"

"I'm way more partial to your granny's nanner puddin'." She hit middle C to punctuate her statement. "I don't know what she puts in it, but that shit is insane."

"I'll let her know you like it." Or maybe I wouldn't... I knew Granny had sent some food the Banks's way, as was her way, but one compliment from Quincy Banks and she might just become their in-house chef. Without charging or asking first.

But there was something I could ask.

"You should sit with us," I said before I lost my nerve. Quincy Banks might not be class president or the school's golden girl any longer, but she still felt... untouchable. "Me and Marian Shepherd. At lunch. It's a very exclusive invitation," I tacked on, feeling like a dork as soon as the words left my mouth. What exactly was I trying to prove?

Then again, I'd seen her sitting alone while her former friends giggled away at the next table. And it hurt my heart. I didn't like seeing anyone excluded.

Quincy's smile faded, and she looked down. "I dunno. Mac seems to want your company, and yours only. I'm no fifth wheel." Those last words hardened, and I immediately felt bad for making her feel like a charity case.

Still.

"No, seriously," I said. "We're kinda the self-proclaimed misfits of the senior class, unless you count The Hecks, and they're just weird. We just talk music and bullshit."

"Music and bullshit," Quin repeated. She'd been looking at her lap, and now her eyes met mine. "I could vibe with that."

Just then, Jeff Floyd, the biggest jock and biggest asshole in our class, who I'd disliked from my first day when he offered to show my tits around Hiawassee, passed by. Humming very loudly. The song he was humming? "Feelin' Good."

A great song, but also the theme to Breaking Bad. *Quin's new nickname among our less-sensitive peers. And there were a lot of them.*

"You better get to class," Quincy Banks said quietly. So she'd heard it too. Her shoulders were slumped, and she looked about twelve years old.

What was wrong with people?

I didn't protest, just drifted away and out to the courtyard. I didn't want to go to physics, anyway.

While I was staring off into space, I saw it—Jeff Floyd's obnoxious monster truck. On huge tires raised a foot higher than necessary, Punisher skull and Confederate flag decals on the back window, and disgusting "truck nuts" hanging from the back. "Short-dick trucks," Mac and I liked to call them, because only a dude with something lacking downstairs would drive such a planet-killing eyesore.

And I remembered what my older sister Liz—she of the Garden State *obsession—had enlisted me to help with when someone not unlike Jeff Floyd called her a bull dyke.*

When the bell rang for next period, and Jeff Floyd went out to smoke, you could hear his scream throughout the school. His right front tire was flatter than a pancake.

Quincy Banks sat with us that day.

Later, Mac let Quincy think she'd *let the air out. I never corrected anyone. Who cared? Quin was one of us now.*

Now it was the end.

I stood at the cliffs, fingering what was left of her bony ashes in their plastic bag. I'd never tell anyone, but last night I'd sprinkled the tiniest bit into my beer, when no one was looking. They felt gritty going down, and it made me feel metal as fuck. Practically, I knew I'd pass them at some point, but the woo-woo part of me hoped she'd be inside me forever.

And I'd saved the best for last.

It was mid-afternoon—teatime. Everyone was enjoying their little afternoon ritual, taking a breath and having a conversation over a snack and a bevvie. Americans didn't know how to relax, but the Scottish definitely did. Moreover, it gave me this one last time alone. We were doing a special high tea at Glamis, but that wasn't until later, so no one would wonder where I was.

"I don't know what to say," I told the brisk, gray air, the gentle lap of the waves sounding below. "You weren't the praying type and neither am I. Plus, I did your eulogy. I hope you liked it, by the way."

I squatted on the grass and emptied the little bag, making a tiny, neat pile of ash and bone. "You made it to Scotland too, Quin. You're still part of this band. And I wanted pieces of you to stay here always."

I then sang a little incantation Josh had taught me to acknowledge a spirit, thank it, and set it free.

For a moment after, I focused on the horizon, where the sky met the sea. No more tears. Just a grave sense of memory.

And fear.

Should I tell her?

Oh, what the hell. I was alone, after all—might as well get it out. I glanced over my shoulder just to make sure.

Nothing. Just bristly trees and rough-hewn heather. Like one of those PBS adaptations of the Brontës. I knew Quin's aunt had loved those, too. I wish I could have met her. Before.

"I'm scared, Quin." I took a deep breath, my thighs beginning to burn, still focusing on the horizon. Though I was alone, I kept my voice quiet. Just in case. "I'm really scared, and I'm not quite sure why. I mean, we're *doing* this. You'd like Maud, I know you would, and my songs have gotten even better, even if Larry's still kind of a dick about it. We have actual fans now, and we can pay our rent with our music. And Scotland loves us. It's everything we dreamed of in high school and way more."

I stood up, brushing my jeans with hands growing numb with the late afternoon chill. "So why does it feel so scary? Why am I constantly looking over my shoulder? It's not just because I don't want to make a big thing of spreading your ashes." I made myself inhale, exhale, again. "And speaking of big things, they got *married*, Quin. Mac's as good as family to me, so that means now Larry's family too, and it also means we're never going to get rid of him. And okay, if he were just an asshole, whatever, but what if he's actually dangerous?" I hesitated. "What if *they're* dangerous together?"

Rustle.

My head snapped over my shoulder. I knew I hadn't imagined that. It was a clear rustling of brush behind us.

Was someone watching? Spying? Listening?

Oh god. What if this got back to Marian and Larry?

What if…?

I couldn't entertain that possibility.

I stayed still. Listened as hard as I possibly could. If someone was hiding, they'd make another sound, right?

Nothing. No movement. No noise.

I don't know if I was there, head wrenched over my shoulder to the point I'd feel a crick in my neck for the next thirty-six hours, for five minutes or thirty.

Either way, eventually I made my way back down the trail, my Airwalks and their shitty tread crunching over gravel, poking my feet.

Teatime was over in Angus. People were milling in the streets again, shouting greetings to one another in their cheerful burrs, like the beginning of *Beauty and the Beast,* only Scottish. I should have taken comfort in the humanity around me.

Instead, I didn't fully breathe again until I was back in my room, the door double locked.

And I couldn't get Quincy's last night out of my mind. I hadn't thought about it in the rush to memorialize her, try to move on, and get my ass to Scotland. Who knows, maybe I'd blocked it out, the way I heard people did with traumatic events.

Now, as I lay on my bed, it rushed back.

I knew she'd met Marian for drinks. I'd turned in early for no real reason, burrowing under the covers and running *Sex and the City* on my laptop until I drifted off to the sounds of a cheerful girl-brunch and debate of whether babies should be allowed in fine establishments. I don't even remember when my eyes closed.

Then I had the dream.

I was walking to Jittery Joe's for a coffee. The air was mild; the sun shining. I had my hands in the pockets of my favorite leather jacket when my phone buzzed.

It was a text from Quincy.

If anything happens, look within. And then, an emoji of a fly.

When the phone rang very early the next morning, I could barely understand Marian's words through the hysterical crying on her end.

But I knew.

I never told anyone about the dream, not even Josh. Dreams don't have to mean anything, right?

Or maybe I was afraid to tell Josh. Afraid of what he'd say.

Laying on my bed in the B&B before high tea at Glamis, I squeezed my eyes shut and tried not to think of the dream text.

The direction to look within.

CHAPTER TWENTY-FIVE

MARIAN

"This castle hath a pleasant seat; the air nimbly and sweetly recommends itself unto our gentle senses." —*Macbeth,* Act I, Scene VI

I ran my hands over my arms to stop the goosebumps as I stared up at the entrance of Glamis Castle, feeling an odd sense of déjà vu. It felt just as it had that night years ago, staring up at Teresa-Jo's house, just before I'd gone inside to play the house party that had sealed my fate. This, while on a *much* larger scale, had that same vibe: something in my life was about to change irreversibly, and this beautiful, ancient old castle was bearing witness to it.

It was an imposing thing, Glamis. It was *alive,* the sheer size and magnitude—to say nothing of its age and historical significance—of the place so large and grand that I could barely comprehend it. The gray stones, each one set upon the other in an intricate pattern, were cold to the touch as I reached out to caress them. The magnificent green gardens that surrounded it, the blue sky above, and the sheer *aura* of the place...it was a little overwhelming.

In many ways, the mountains of North Georgia and the highlands of Scotland were exactly the same. According to Maud, who had talked all our ears off on the plane about it, they were actually the *same* mountain range and during Pangea, the Scottish Highlands and the Appalachian Mountains were connected, which was why so many Scots immigrants had flocked to Appalachia during Colonial times, because they felt in their bones that it was home. But the truth I'd never say out loud was that Scotland was a little more beautiful. I loved my mountain home, but something about the backdrop of bright blue sky, the greenest of grass over craggy rocks, the mountains looming tall and strong and silent, against the cold slate of a castle turret, filled me with a kind of emotion I rarely allowed myself to feel. It was equal parts majestic and imposing; so full of history and memory that the land itself felt like a story.

I could see why Lawrence loved the place. I could easily love it, too. Deep down though, I wondered how long someone like me would last among this much majesty: the grandiosity, the sense of identity, the pride in heritage and culture... While it was certainly nice for the short-term, that kind of depth of feeling wasn't something I was used to, and didn't really want a part of. It was too much pressure, that kind of belonging. It made me claustrophobic.

I'd rather look out for myself.

"Alright?" Lawrence offered me his arm, and I smiled, slipping my arm in his, attempting to shake off the weird feeling I'd had since I woke up.

Lawrence and I had finally drifted off to sleep sometime between three and four—the witching hour—and I'd woken up shortly thereafter in a cold sweat. In my dream, I was standing atop Brasstown Bald, in the same spot we'd always hiked with Ian, and later had visited with the girls to memorialize both him and dear Quincy, but this time I was alone. So alone; the thick fog surrounding me so I couldn't see, the only bit of light a small purple pinprick off in the distance. I'd walked toward it, getting closer and closer, the light shining brighter and brighter, until I'd realized it was an eye.

A figure, in fact, with *two* glowing purple eyes.

The Hecks. Two of them stood with their backs to me—I recognized Pete's long, dark hair, and Zak's ever-changing curly mop, standing straight and still. And Josh, facing me, just stared, his eyes glowing purple, the same purple of my now-burnt candle, his expression one of deep, deep sadness.

And then I woke up. I thought about telling Lawrence about the dream, but what was there to say? "I had a weird dream where this guy I sorta know that my friend is fucking had purple eyes and flies for eyelashes?"

I still felt a little wonky from the dream—it just felt so *real*—but I had more important things to think of right now, so I shook off my feelings of unease. Inside, the castle was surprisingly warm and vibrant. I had expected something cold, aloof. But there was a fire roaring in the main room, and a liveried employee led us to the kitchen, where we were immediately given refreshments and offered a tour. After finishing our hot cider and ale, we were led to the crypt, where there was another elaborate set-up, and invited to sit down for high tea. Whether this was something offered to all guests, or something Lawrence had arranged just for us, I didn't know, but I tried to let myself enjoy it.

As the staff set down trays of cucumber and scallion sandwiches, scones studded with sugar, clotted cream and jam, along with fancy porcelain pots of steaming hot tea, I leaned over to Duff. "What color are Josh's eyes?" I asked.

She glanced at me, confused, and shrugged. "Brown. Why?"

"I just couldn't remember."

Duff raised her eyebrows as I put a scone on my plate. "You're weird."

I busied myself pouring tea for both Duff and Larry, happy to have a task to focus on. Ross ordered a "whisky and co-cola" and the server's eyebrows rose into his hairline at her Southern pronunciation, sending us all into a fit of giggles. We were surrounded by ornate antiques and beautiful paintings. There was opulence everywhere we looked.

The room was very cluttered but cluttered *by design;* everything had its spot. Antique chairs and tables were carefully placed all around, and combined with the sloped, ancient ceiling above us, it gave the entire room the feeling of being inside a miniature, as if we'd all shrunk down a la *Alice in Wonderland,* or were all medieval Polly Pocket versions of ourselves. Even the dishes and silverware on our table were a carefully selected mishmash of pieces designed to be just so. I felt my dour mood begin to lift as I raised a delicate sandwich to my mouth, delicious in its simplicity.

Everyone ate quietly as Maud regaled us with the history of Glamis, starting with the infamous Banquo, who had been wrongly assumed to be the father of the Stuart line for generations. If Lawrence was irritated at Maud's monopolizing of the conversation yet again, he wasn't going to say so. I offered him a bite of my cucumber sandwich and he waved it away, but he was smiling, dimples present and accounted for. He reached for my hand under the table and I grabbed it eagerly, his warm fingers threading through mine.

After the tea and sandwiches were gone, the staff brought out a bottle of expensive wine. Lawrence moved, his kilt momentarily catching on the chair, and I pulled it free for him as he winked at me and stood. He raised his crystal glass in the air and said, "To The Scottish Play."

Everyone raised their wine glasses—Maud raising her glass of blackcurrant juice, and Ross, her whisky and Coke—and murmured back, "To The Scottish Play." The girls were smiling, and Duff was absolutely *beaming*. A tender feeling pierced my heart.

Lawrence placed a gentle hand on my shoulder and looked down at me, his blue eyes bright. Either from the warm glow of the torchlights or tears, I couldn't be sure. "And to Marian Shepherd MacLaren," he said, his voice catching a little as he stared down at me. "My wife."

"To Marian," everyone parroted, and I looked down at my plate, equal parts embarrassed and touched.

I felt tears come to my eyes as I drank, the wine rich and delicious, and beat them back, not wanting anyone to see. Lawrence took his seat, his warm hand finding mine and clenching it. Duff was smiling at me across the table, and I gave her a genuine smile in return. The fire in the fireplace was roaring, and as I felt the delicious wine course through me, my entire body was filled with contentment. Finally, everything was as it should be.

For the first time in as long as I could remember, I was *happy*.

We enjoyed talking, eating, and drinking so much we overstayed our welcome and soon found ourselves without remaining staff to serve us, save for one liveried server who was failing in his effort to hide his irritation. With one slightly raised eyebrow—which may have been more of a reaction to the sight of Duff and me with our wine glasses in one hand, cups of tea in the other, alternating sips—he bent down at the waist in a polite sort of bow, and said, "Ladies…and sir? The dining portion of your tour has now finished and the castle must lock up for the evening. If you'll please finish your drinks, then make your way out of the dining area and towards the exit." He gestured toward the entryway, then added as an afterthought, "Thank you."

As I stared at the archway, with its dark, uneven stones—it was as though I could *feel* their cold roughness all the way from where I sat—it seemed like the walls were closing in, the ceiling lowering. My breath felt tight in my chest.

"I paid a bloody fortune for this tour. The least they could do is let us finish our scones," Lawrence muttered beside me. "We've barely touched the jam and clotted cream." I wondered if anyone else noticed the pointed glance at Maud, who was spreading a generous amount of butter on her scone, oblivious.

"It's fine," I reassured Lawrence, handing over my cup of tea. "Finish my tea? I've still got this whole glass of wine."

He gestured for me to hand him my other glass and gave me a wink, which, in the dim candlelight of the room, seemed briefly sinister. "Let's switch. You've had more than your share of wine, Mrs. MacLaren."

I scrunched up my nose, but handed it over, taking the cup of tea and downing it in a gulp, wondering if I'd ever get used to *Mrs. MacLaren*. We scooted our chairs back and stood up, all of us clumsy on our feet, the server respectfully backing up as we made our departure.

I turned to look as we left and saw him swatting away a fly as he began to clear our plates.

We milled through the narrow, ancient halls of the castle, my friends stopping to gawk at paintings and armor along the way through their wine goggles. But the wine had made my sense of claustrophobia worse; the sloped, curving ceiling that had seemed exquisite now felt like it was closing in on me, the ornate furniture so strategically and carefully placed now like barriers to hinder us from leaving. I looped one arm through Lawrence's and the other through Duff's as we slunk drunkenly through the winding halls, turning toward the main hall that led to the kitchen, and beyond that, the foyer.

The hall was dim, with only torchlight to guide us. It was atmospheric, and at another time I might've loved the decidedly goth aesthetic, but now I felt a chill go through me. The warm, cozy vibe from earlier was gone, and quite suddenly, I was *very* ready to get out of what was beginning to feel like a dungeon.

Duff felt it, too. It was evident in her tense shoulders and loud, labored breathing. I let her lead the way. She was practically sprinting through the corridor, her breath fast and heavy. And then suddenly, abruptly, she stopped. She gasped. I crashed into her shoulder, Lawrence crashing into mine.

"What is it?" I asked stupidly. But I didn't need to ask. I saw what she saw.

Lawrence's voice was barely a whisper behind me. "What the... *fuck?*" He saw it, too.

I blinked and reached out for the wall to steady myself, my limbs shaking with fear. *This isn't real.* I *had* drunk an awful lot. I closed my eyes, counted to five, then opened them again, sure that the blurry vision I'd just seen was nothing more than a drunken hallucination.

I stared, gaping, my stomach rolling over and over. It was no hallucination. *She* was no hallucination.

"Jesus. No," Duff wailed miserably, clutching at her heart. From somewhere behind me, I heard a tiny shriek, either from Maud or Ross, but I was too afraid to turn around and look. I was stuck to the spot, unable to do anything but stare ahead, slow-blinking in horror.

Standing before us in the doorway, one bony, pale finger beckoning, her face as beautiful and innocent as ever—but the eyes, the eyes, dark and wild and full of rage—was Quincy Banks.

CHAPTER TWENTY-SIX

DUFF

"I'll be working 'til I die." —Joan Jett

SHE looked so beautiful.

What a strange thought, seeing the ghost of your dead best friend, right? Yet here we were. And here was Quincy.

"Jesus. No," is what came out of my mouth. Because I hadn't been seeing things earlier, and Quin clearly wasn't human anymore. And my heart, it hurt. I wondered if I hadn't been a little bit in love with her after all.

Why else would I feel like I was dying?

I'd let go of Marian's arm. She reached for it again.

"No!" I jerked away, stepping further toward Quin. The ghost of Quin. Whoever she was, with her hair looking perfectly blonde and pink, just the way she used to wear it. I searched her arms for track or needle marks, or blood, or... I guess I didn't know what I was looking for, anything that signified the horrible way she'd gone.

Even in the moment, I wondered why I wasn't exactly scared. I was more sad and nostalgic than anything else. I had the strangest urge to invite Quin to my hotel room for a *Sex and the City* marathon before our next show. She could watch from the audience, or maybe Maud would tag her in. Or she could take over from Marian, be our lead singer again.

"Duff?" Ross's voice broke through the static in my head. Just then I realized I was taking steps, slow but steady, my Airwalks moving toward the specter of Quincy Banks.

I was drawn to her, this ghostly spirit with the perfect hair and pure white babydoll lace dress and the knee-high lace-up Docs, her favorite pair for performances because she could move around and work the pedals of her drum set, and because they were what she felt sexiest in, she'd confided in me. She'd bought them secondhand, with the money we'd made from the first gig Ian found for us, at Dynamite, one of our fave vintage stores in Athens. It was like they were meant for her, she'd said. So many years ago. And now she was *here* at Glamis Castle, looking like a cross between Hole-era Courtney Love and Disney's Sleeping Beauty with a cool-ass haircut.

Had I conjured Quincy Banks from her own ashes?

I didn't give a shit. I just wanted to talk to her.

"Hi," I said softly, and Quin-ghost smiled. She hadn't smiled at Mac and Larry. "Are you okay, honey? I've been so worried."

"How fucking wrecked is *she?*" I heard Larry murmur. I wasn't sure if he meant me or Quin. Ross and Maud loudly shushed him—guess they could see what I saw. Maud had never even met Quin in real life, and the thought crossed my mind that I should introduce them. Was this some kind of collective hallucination? *Were* we feeling all that wine? Had Scotland done a number on us all?

Or were we really in the presence of a ghost?

"Can you talk?" I asked Quincy. I was now a foot away from her, rooted to the spot. She seemed…real. I could smell her—the strawberry-vanilla body lotion she'd always favored and just underneath, the unmistakable sweet hint of rot.

She shook her head.

"Are…" I trailed off, swallowed hard. What the fuck was I even doing? "Are you okay, Quin?"

It was then I really looked into her eyes. No longer that old-fashioned color aptly named Alice Blue after Teddy Roosevelt's wild child of a daughter. Coal black. Empty as holes.

A breeze passed through the hall and I shivered from head to toe.

"I miss you," I whispered so only she could hear.

She smiled, pink lips pressed together. So odd how she wasn't transparent, didn't have a halo of light around her or anything you saw in movies. She looked as real as I felt. The best imitation of herself.

Only her blank, Coraline eyes and stony silence gave her away.

Quin looked right at me and I had to resist looking away from the emptiness in her skull. She pointed one purple-manicured finger at Lawrence, her expression unreadable. Then she pointed at Mac.

Then the ghost of Quincy Banks opened her mouth and the rotting stench, only discernible before, intensified as a host of flies swarmed out.

"Oh my god!" That was Ross, her voice about five octaves higher than normal. I turned around and she and Maud were clutching one another, ducking as the cloud of black buzzing insects flew over their heads.

I looked back at Quin. She closed her mouth, nodded like she used to when we got a song just right in practice. *That's done.* Like the class president she once was.

Then she turned her head, and I saw him.

"Ian," I whispered.

Our former manager hovered at the dark expanse at the end of the hall. His T-shirt was tight, his kilt (the traditional sky-blue and emerald green Duncan tartan, which I'd never seen him wear in life) pleated over muscular calves. He wasn't wearing the necklace Crowe gave him, but he looked complete.

Ian's ghost caught my eye and…grinned. No flies. No empty eyes. Ian, unlike Quincy, was positively radiant.

He reached out his hand to Quin, and she ran toward him in her Docs. Silent. Her feet literally never touched the ground.

They didn't fade. Instead, the hallway went pitch-dark, like a blackout, before the lights fully blared back on. We all looked at each other, at a complete loss. Like the spirits before us, no one uttered a word.

"What'd Larry M have to say about that?" Josh asked.

I pressed the warming phone to my cheek—my room seemed colder than usual tonight. Wasn't it supposed to chill when there were spirits present? I jerked my head around so fast I felt a sudden pain in my neck that would undoubtedly get worse before it got better.

Nothing. No one. Just my duffel bag, yawning open.

"Oh, exactly what you'd expect," I told him, grateful for the surprisingly excellent reception in this bed-and-breakfast that, like everything else in Angus, probably used to be a castle or at the very least a prestigious hall of government. Needless to say, I had to tell someone about what I'd just seen: the boots, the flies, the whole nine. "Asshole has an answer for everything."

A trick of the light, Larry M had scoffed once we'd hauled ass outside. I immediately lit a cigarette and Ross reached out her hand so I would break out the pack. I gladly obliged, not in the least, because smokes were way cheaper here. Maud was bouncing from foot to foot, a feat considering her teetery vintage heels, her eyes huge. And Marian stepped a few feet away from us. I couldn't see her face at all.

"But then Mac agreed with him," I said to Josh. "Like always. Now that they're married, she doesn't have a brain cell of her own anymore. They said we're all drunk, still jet lagged, need some sleep, blah blah blah."

I think Marian and Larry expected the rest of us to argue, as we'd been doing more and more lately. But Ross and Maud and I were tired. Completely certain of what we'd witnessed, but freaked out and exhausted. I didn't have to ask the other two about any of this. Their faces said everything.

I plopped down on my creaky mattress. Not that it mattered, because my knees were still shaking. "Thanks for listening. Although..."

"Yeah?"

I debated for a second whether to bring this up. What the hell, I decided. "You don't sound surprised. Or skeptical. Or anything. I'm telling you we saw the ghosts of our dead band manager and bandmate, after I spread that same bandmate's ashes while chanting an incantation that very possibly could have *literally* raised the dead, and you're acting like I'm describing the scones I had at high tea."

"Look." I heard a deep breath on the other side of the phone. A flick of a lighter. I could still taste my previous cig and now I wanted another.

More than that, I wanted Josh the Heck. The strange guy from high school who'd put a literal *curse* on me and my friends before I had sex in the woods with him and his friends. The one who'd called the day after and I'd been texting or calling or in some form of communication with every day since.

I waited. He exhaled.

"Why don't we talk about this in person?"

Whatever I was expecting, it wasn't that. "What do you mean, Josh?"

"I meeeeeean…" he drawled. "I may have hit up Pete and Zak for a loan. Begged for time off work. Told my boys and my supervisor how there's this bass player I can't stop thinking about…"

He wasn't serious. "You're coming to Scotland?"

Josh laughed, low and rough, the warmest sound I'd heard all night. "Surprise."

CHAPTER TWENTY-SEVEN:

MARIAN

"That which hath made them drunk hath made me bold: What hath quenched them hath given me fire." —*Macbeth*, Act II, Scene II

I raised a hand to knock on Duff's door, letting my closed fist linger there in the air for a few moments, unsure. I heard Duff laughing on the other side; she was either on the phone or had company. She likely didn't want to see me, anyway. I let my hand hang in the air for another minute, pressing my fingers up against the cool, rough wood, then walked back down the hall.

I couldn't stop thinking about the way she'd looked at me out in the courtyard of the castle. The accusation in her eyes, the hurt, the wild, crazed fear. But most of all, the anger. Anger at my betrayal. Once again, I hadn't had her back.

Yes, it *had* looked very much like the ghost of Quincy Banks standing in front of us, but hadn't the castle's tour guide also been blond and cute? Wasn't it true that torchlight could cast weird shadows on the cool stone of the castle walls? Wasn't it true that all of us were piss-drunk on Scottish wine with an alcohol content we weren't used to? That we were already freaked out before we ever saw—or thought we saw—anything?

One thing was most definitely true: I was terrified. Because whatever we had—or hadn't—seen had pointed their bony finger right at me.

I was so rattled by the spectral form I'd come back to my room and downed several bottles of booze from the minibar, despite already being drunk as piss. Then, as soon as we'd hit eleven this morning, I'd downed several more in lieu of lunch.

"Penny for your thoughts." I stumbled and turned, halfway back to my own room, to see Maud standing in the hall. She was dressed in a sleek pair of tapered black capris with her signature kitten heels and a white cardigan with a strand of classy pearls around her neck, looking every bit the Jackie O.

"You're the only woman my age who can wear pearls and not look like an absolute TWASP," I said with a laugh.

"Twasp?" Maud's bright-red lips curled into a smile, but her brow furrowed in confusion. "I don't think I am familiar with the term. Can you enlighten me?"

"It's a combo of WASP and twat," I said, suppressing a hiccup. "We had this English teacher in eleventh grade—me, Duff, and Quincy—who was from New England. She was this privileged white Karen who tried so hard to be 'one of us,' you know the type? She wore these blazers and skirts that aged her up. She always wore pearls, and all she could talk about was her WASPy family. She was just, like, insufferable." I shrugged. "So we coined the term. It stands for 'Twat with a Stupid Pantsuit.'"

Maud giggled, eyes wide like she was slightly scandalized. "I see. You all have such wonderful memories with each other."

I shrugged again. The square pattern on the hall carpet was making me dizzy. "We thought we were funny back in the day." Then, to my horror, I burst into tears.

"Oh. Um," Maud said. She reached out awkwardly and patted my shoulder, her touch feather light. "I, um, I'm not great with emotions, Marian. Would you like a hug?"

"No, I'm not a hugger," I said, furiously wiping at my face. "Thanks for asking. Most people don't."

"I'm not a hugger, either," Maud said, looking visibly relieved. She swallowed. "Are you upset about the castle? The apparition?"

"I would've thought you of all people would realize what we saw— or didn't see, rather," I said, still wiping my eyes. "I mean, we were all so drunk. Are *still* so drunk." Or maybe that was only me.

"I only had a sip from the glass that was handed to me," Maud said softly, brushing her blunt bangs from her face. It was a nervous affectation, I could tell, because none of the hairs on her head were ever mussed. "I didn't even drink during the toast. I was decidedly not intoxicated. And I saw... Well, I saw something."

"What did it look like?"

Maud paused, took a breath. "I couldn't see so well, but…it looked like Quincy Banks."

A shudder went through me.

Maud hadn't known Quin. She barely even knew what she looked like.

She could be mistaken.

As if she'd read my thoughts, Maud reminded me, "I looked up those performances of hers... I'll never forget her face. She was so striking." She looked thoughtful, then added, "She still is, I suppose."

Another shudder tried to roll through my shoulders. *What a weird thing to say,* I almost responded, but was it? This was starting to feel like our new normal. "And you're sure that's what you saw. *Her.*"

"Maybe..." Maud trailed off, lost in thought. "A shadow...possibly a figure in the shadow? But I'd swear it was Quincy Banks. It was blurry, and at first I thought it was just a trick of the light, or even some kind of production the castle was putting on for us—they do light shows, and retellings of *Macbeth,* and things like that, you know—I read about it in the tourist guide—but then...the flies." She shivered. "And the *smell.* " She blinked nervously: *blink, blink, blink.*

"Lawrence and I thought that the flies were probably just coming from the dining area," I offered. "Having high tea in an old crypt is bound to draw in some critters."

"Perhaps," Maud said. "But then again, the Queen Mother was born at the castle. The revenue it brings from tourists every year... Can you imagine the budget they must have for pest control?"

"It's a centuries-old building and pests have no regard for royalty. Or tourists," I argued.

"Perhaps," Maud said again. Then she cocked her head. "But did you see it—her—pointing? The specter?"

I stared at her. "No. I didn't."

She stared back for a beat, then said, "We'll be needing to check in for our show soon... I really should go and get ready."

"You're already ready," I observed, forcing a laugh. "Perfectly so, as always. Are you just trying to end an awkward conversation?"

"Perhaps." Maud's eyes twinkled a little that time.

"*Perhaps, perhaps, perhaps.*" I sang the Cake song after her as she walked toward her room, feeling a little more cheerful despite Maud's observations of the night before. At least she didn't hate me. Like I suspected, Duff was starting to. Like Ross already did.

Joke's on them, because nobody hates me as much as I do.

Lawrence was just emerging from the shower as I came in, a cloud of steam billowing out of the bathroom as he dried himself in front of the mirror. I opened my mouth to say something naughty, considered sauntering over and snatching the towel clear off his still-damp body, but the look on his face stopped me. "We're going to be late," he whined, giving me a pointed look to remind me that I hadn't yet dressed. "And I still have to tune your guitar."

"I'll do that," I said easily, careful to keep my tone light and breezy. Lawrence had already put the ghost topic to bed, and I knew I was not welcome to raise it again. He'd been a glowering, irritable pile of nerves all morning long. I was trying to be as careful as possible not to set him off, but everything I did, from the bagel I'd ordered from room service to the scent of my deodorant, seemed to bother him. "I need to do things like that for myself. Get used to the process, you know?"

"You don't know a G string from an E string," he said in a sullen tone, running a comb through his auburn curls. "And you've been drinking."

"I know what a G-string is," I said saucily, coming over and putting my hands on his chest, resting my head on his back. "I'm wearing one right now."

He shrugged me off him and I stepped back, hurt. He noticed my face fall in the mirror and sighed. "Please, Mac. Go get dressed, okay? Jesus Christ."

The pub where we were playing our second show didn't even have an official name, at least not that I could gather. It was just "the pub 'round the corner" according to the two locals I'd asked, and boy, were those locals *rowdy*. We were only into our second song—one of Duff's better tunes, "Bald as Brass," a punk-folk ballad that reminded me of The Dropkick Murphys. I made a mental note to ask Lawrence how we might get a guest musician to throw a bagpipe in there—but the crowd barely paid us any attention. Between the very drunk crowd's raucous laughter and conversation, and the rugby game they had on the other side of the bar, each try resulting in loud cheers and screams, we were all but drowned out. We'd all (except Maud) had several drinks before, starting just to calm our nerves, the rowdiness of the crowd making us feel rattled and play off-kilter.

I probably should've been grateful for the mayhem. I'd tuned my guitar carefully, using an app on my phone that boasted five-star reviews, but I could hear as clear as day that I was out of tune. The band could too, judging from the wince on Duff's face every time I hit a note, and the furious glower of Lawrence, who stood right in front of the stage, his arms crossed over his chest, his mouth pursed into the tightest of grimaces. I'd insisted on tuning it myself, and I'd cocked it up.

Fuck.

Our second show and we'd bombed. No, *I'd* bombed. The rest of the band played fantastic. It was all me.

"Sorry, guys," I said as we took our gear off the stage toward the truck Lawrence had rented for equipment. "I must have tuned my guitar wrong, and I totally missed that cue on your song, Duff."

"Yeah, well, I doubt anybody in the pub noticed," Duff reassured me, shooting me a conciliatory look over her shoulder as she carried one of Maud's drums. "It wasn't that bad."

"We all have off nights," Ross said, and her out-of-character expression of empathy rankled me.

"*You* never do," I said, and Ross shrugged. She wasn't going to argue; she knew how good she was. And that rankled me even more.

"I'm sure this was just an off night," Maud agreed as we walked back to the pub to get the last few chords and pedals. "I didn't play my best either, and the crowd didn't help. I couldn't even hear you well enough to keep time with. Sometimes an audience is just not ideal. The show tomorrow at Glamis will go much better, I'm sure of it."

"I'm not so sure, myself." I turned to see Lawrence standing there, his arms still crossed over his chest. "A word, Marian, please?"

"You can speak to her in front of us," Maud said, and I shot her a grateful look. "We all played badly, not just Mac."

"With all due respect, Maud, Marian is my partner, both in business and in marriage, and I would like to speak to her alone," Lawrence said. "I didn't ask for your input."

Maud took a step back and blinked hard. I wondered if she was trying not to cry. Duff immediately rose to her defense. "Don't talk to Maud like that, Larry. We're all tense. It was a shitty show. We just don't want you going after Mac like it's all her fault. The crowd was awful, and she's been having issues with her guitar..."

"The only issue with her guitar is that she's too lazy—or too stupid, or too drunk, I don't know which—to tune it properly. I've tried to teach her, but she insists she's got it, even though she decidedly does *not*." Lawrence's eyes flashed, and I felt myself turn bright red. I wanted to sink into the floor. His critical eye—and tongue—were no secret to the band, but he'd *never* talked to me like this. I was humiliated. "And my name is not Larry. For the hundredth time."

"You're an asshole, *Larry*," Ross said, stepping forward and staring him straight in the eye. "It's no wonder Mac's messing up with you breathing down her neck like that. It's not that deep, dude, it was just one show." I looked at her in surprise. I hadn't expected Ross Smith, of all people, to defend me.

"One show that I moved mountains to get for you ungrateful lot!" Lawrence spat, but I could see that his resolve was starting to weaken. Good, let him feel as embarrassed as I did. All these people standing around, right in the middle of the pub, yelling at me like I was his employee, or worse, his servant.

"We're grateful for the show…Lawrence," Duff said evenly. "And for all you've done for us. But we will not tolerate disrespect. We're a team, and as you are well aware, team members can be replaced." She raised her chin slightly and added, "And after what we all saw last night… Well, it's no wonder we sounded like shit."

"Not this again…" Lawrence sighed.

"We all saw it, Larry," Ross said, her tone defiant. "I don't want to believe it either, but I have eyes. Are you going to keep denying it?"

Lawrence's tone was placating, not unlike the one Ross used when she was in teacher mode. "Look, we're all just upset. You're right, tomorrow will be better. Let's all just… I don't know, let's all just go back to the B&B and get some food and rest. We'll all feel better in the morning." He wasn't ever going to acknowledge what we'd all seen, but he did at least hold out an arm to me, his face softening, his eyes saying the *I'm sorry* he didn't vocalize. "Alright, Marian?"

I stared at his extended arm for a moment, hearing Ross mutter behind me, "Fuck this. I'm getting another fucking drink." I considered staying, to hang out with my friends sans Lawrence, having another much-needed drink (well, probably *not* needed, considering my two-day binge, but my buzz was now gone) and a vent session.

But I took Lawrence's arm anyway, pasting on another fake-ass smile, and turned to my friends. "Sorry I fucked it all up tonight. Tomorrow?"

"Tomorrow," they said in unison, but Duff looked down at the floor, her face sad and angry, not meeting my eyes.

Lawrence had been on his phone ever since we'd gotten back to the room.

I picked at my chef salad, starving and wishing it was a bowl of Granny Devereaux's famous macaroni and cheese, which I was suddenly feeling a wave of nostalgia for—anything but the limp bowl of nothing in my lap. Lawrence had rubbed off on me, and now all I could think about was how many calories and carbs I was consuming. Never mind that he'd ordered a full-size fish and chips and had eaten every bite.

As I'd pushed cucumbers around on my plate, Lawrence's face was stuck in front of his phone. He hadn't even looked at me the entire time we'd been back. He was finished griping, but now I was getting the silent treatment. I supposed it was what I deserved after playing such a garbage show.

I stared at his profile, unable to stop looking at him even for a moment. I wanted him to look at me back, to acknowledge me, to smile and take me in his arms. I hated being ignored. Everything had been so perfect; why was he ruining it? Why couldn't we just go back to being happy?

Larry's phone lit up, and he smiled, then tapped out a response. He was still grinning at his screen two minutes later when I set my still-full salad bowl on the nightstand and reached over to touch his arm.

His smile immediately fell. "What is it?"

"Lawrence," I said gently, caressing his biceps. "I know you're mad at me, but can we stop this?"

"Stop what?" he answered, eyes flicking back to his phone. "I'm not doing anything but answering emails."

"You're angry."

"No," he said. "I was disappointed, but I'm not angry. There's no point."

"Can we talk about it?" I asked. "The show? Or whatever's bothering you?"

"There's no point," he said again with a sigh. "You'll just turn it around so I'm the bad guy. I'm always the bad guy, the mean guy. The one who can't do anything right."

"No," I said. "I'll listen. I promise."

"Fine." He put the phone face down on his chest and looked at me. "I'm upset at how you played tonight, how you wouldn't let me tune your guitar even though I *knew* you didn't know how to do it. I'm upset at how much you've been drinking. It seems with as much as you complain about your mother's drinking problems that you'd take care not to repeat…" He trailed off, shaking his head. "I'm just upset at how you girls are letting this whole thing become some kind of like... paranormal shit show. It's ruining everything."

I looked at him, confused. "What are you even talking about?"

"Even before we left the States, it was prophecy this, prophecy that. You dragged me to those creepy stones and..." His face flushed, remembering. "Duff keeps citing those idiot guys and that dumb fortune telling or whatever it was...like we're supposed to take some greasy stoners seriously. Fucking losers, that's all they are."

"They aren't losers—" I began, then cut myself off. Why was I defending The Hecks, of all people?

Lawrence sighed. "It's like...you all brought that damned curse with us. I've done so much to make the tour perfect, paying out of pocket, networking for you, working my bloody *bollocks* off, and you're all determined to ruin it one way or another. If it's not a curse, it's seeing a ghost in the castle. Maud, who never seems to stop showing off with her useless information. Or you, not tuning your fucking guitar." Lawrence's face was red. "Why are you sabotaging everything?"

"I think you're overreacting," I said, trying to stay calm. "Duff has only mentioned The Hecks like one time in the past few weeks and that's only because she's dating Josh now...or whatever it is they're doing. Maud's just excited—she likes to share information; that's how she communicates. And the ghost thing, well, I agree that was fucked up, but it's behind us now." I'd bristled when talking to Maud about the ghost earlier, but now, I couldn't stand to admit to Lawrence that I shared his dread. "As for the guitar, I've already apologized..."

"You let your friends disrespect me. You know they hate me and you just allow it. In fact, you bait them."

"I do not. They're grown women—"

"I think you enjoy being caught in the middle," he said, his eyes flashing. "As if you don't get enough of everyone's undivided attention."

"How dare you!" I gasped. "That's beyond the pale!"

"Is it, Marian? I'm certainly not paying for a stylist for Ross. I didn't make Duff frontwoman, even though she sings as well as you do. No, instead I've done everything you asked of me and more. So you can chase your dream. And maybe even catch it."

He shook his head angrily. "I even married you, Marian. I tied my life to yours for better or worse…because that's how much you mean to me. I've got Teresa-Jo on speed dial, helping me pick out gowns and loaning me money to reserve the pub, and for what—"

"You WHAT?" My face went numb. Lawrence and Teresa-Jo had only met twice in person! She'd been tucked away at Emory living her perfect college life, visiting her boyfriend on weekends pretty much the entire time Lawrence and I had been dating. Why were they talking?

Teresa-Jo had known about my wedding even before *I* did? The thought made my blood boil. My voice came out cold and barely above a whisper. "How dare you!"

"My brother gave me Brian's number and I reached out. So your friend helped me plan the wedding. Big bloody deal." Lawrence shook his head. "She's a sweet person, a kind person, and she loves you. Just like I do. We wanted you to have the best day ever."

"Yeah, well, a sweet, kind person doesn't gallivant behind her friend's back with her fiancé, no matter the reason," I spat. "Teresa-Jo has always been obsessed with me, wanted to be part of every single thing I'm involved in, but this takes the fucking cake."

Lawrence looked at me in surprise. "Listen to yourself, Marian. Angry someone did something nice for you. You're so distracted by ghosts and magic and *Hecks* that you can't see the wonderful things around you. Including me." He shook his head. "Everything I've tried to do…and all I've got to show for it is a band that hates me and thinks I'm playing favorites, because I *am*. And you can't even…"

"Can't even what?" Anger flooded through me. "I married *you* too, you know. I'm right here. Doing everything you ask of me, and believe me, you ask a *lot*."

"You ask a hell of a lot more than I do," he threw back. "Do I need to remind you just how much you've asked of me?"

"You were only too happy." I raised my chin and stared at him. "To help."

"To do what was necessary," he spat. "To give you the life you want."

"I thought you wanted it, too."

"The only thing I ever truly wanted was you, Marian." Lawrence sighed. "But it's all for bloody naught, isn't it?" The more upset he got, the weirder his pseudo-British accent sounded.

The more I listened, the angrier *I* was getting. "It seems to me like *you're* the one who is sabotaging this!"

"You always do this, say you want to talk and then when I try to express my feelings, you cut me off, make excuses and tit-for-tat. See what I mean? No point." Lawrence sighed, leaning over to turn off his bedside light, placing his phone beside him. "I'm going to sleep. I suggest you do the same. Big day tomorrow. I'd like this one to go well." He lay down, his back to me, and pulled the pillow over his face.

I sat there for a moment, staring at his still form, wondering where I'd let it go wrong. I swallowed the boulder in my throat and turned off the light, laying down without even brushing my teeth, not wanting to disturb Lawrence's temporary peace.

I jerked awake to a bright light in the room. Lawrence's phone had lit up with a message. I could hear the vibration against the night table.

Lawrence was sound asleep, the pillow still pulled over his face, his strong arms holding it tightly as though it were a teddy bear. I looked at him, a tender feeling going through me. He hadn't meant what he'd said. He was under a lot of pressure, I knew that. The Scottish Play, with our strong personalities, didn't make things easy for him. I was sure he'd apologize in the morning, and we could move on.

I settled back against the pillows, drifting back to sleep, when the phone vibrated again, the light filling the dark room. I groaned and sat up, pushing at Lawrence's shoulder. "Your phone," I said. He didn't answer. A light snore emitted from somewhere under the vicinity of the pillow.

Vibrate. Light. Vibrate. Light.

I threw off the covers and padded around to his side of the bed, grabbing the phone, meaning to put it on silent and face-down so it wouldn't wake me again. Lawrence was right, I needed my sleep. As I flicked my thumb over to the silent button, a slew of texts became visible, and despite myself, I read them.

Can't wait to see you tomorrow. Can't wait to get my arms around you and 'hug yer neck'!

I swallowed the bile in my throat and scrolled down, reading the next message.

I've missed you too much. I know things have been rough for you just lately, but you've done it. Sooooo proud of you babe, you've worked so hard xx

And the kicker.

*Think you'll be able to get away for a quick drink, one on one? Catch up on old times? *winky face* Literally so excited to take you in my arms*
xx xx

They were all from the same woman. And it wasn't Teresa-Jo. It was a curly-haired, gorgeous vixen, saved in my new husband's phone as, simply, "Becs."

JOSH YANG

I wasn't supposed to have my phone on.

And yet, when the flight attendant came on over the PA, saying, *Ladies and gentlemen, we are experiencing some turbulence, nothing to worry about,* blah blah blah, I was glad I'd broken that rule.

Ignoring the glares of the old white lady next to me, and after swatting away a fly that had somehow made it a million feet in the air, I shot a quick text to Zak and Pete:

Plane going down. Hold space.

Two thumbs up, one from each, right away. As if they were waiting for my text.

Which they probably were.

I could hear it in the flight attendant's voice: the calm, sweet tone with the faintest edge of panic. It's likely there were engine problems earlier, if her strained smile when she handed over my 7-Up was an indication. Or maybe she was banging the pilot or the other flight attendant or both and they'd just broken up with her. I'm intuitive, but I don't know everything.

About my intuition...

I don't call it "the gift" or any of that bullshit. If anything, it's more of a pain in the ass. Sure, I leaned into the weirdo label in high school, pooling cash from my McDonalds job with Zak and Pete to buy that stupid van we painted in bright colors, growing my hair long and scruffy, wearing secondhand clothes even though my mom and dad *hated* it and felt the need to keep reminding me that they could afford to buy me anything I wanted. (Generational wealth is real and old money is weird.)

Now I just keep my head down. I love my boys, my Hecks—the nickname everyone gave us in school that stuck, even among us. Our quarterly camping trips are my favorite, and yes, it's very convenient we can conjure invisibility so no one notices that we're pitching a tent (a real one...uh, except for that one night with Duff) where it is one hundred percent illegal to do so. We're not doing anything wrong. We just like the open space, the inner peace, the way it quiets the voices in all of our heads.

Pete and Zak and I, we're not Wiccan, no matter what anyone in Hiawassee would tell you. Nothing that formal. But we do believe in their "do no harm"-type tenets. Despite the bullshit rumors in high school, we've never sacrificed animals or hurt any living thing. Pete's been an on-and-off vegan since he was twelve, for fuck's sake. So to further clear things up, we are definitely not devil worshippers.

What we are is intuitive. Four syllables, so much fucking baggage, especially when you're young and fucked up. It's easier to travel in a pack.

I was in private school in Duluth before we moved to Hiawassee. I'd never *not* been able to predict things before they actually happened. What I could predict, however, was unpredictable. I've sharpened my skills since I've gotten older—practice makes perfect—but it isn't a science.

In sixth grade, I made the mistake of telling my friends that our teacher was a closet homo—our gym teacher, who was an aggro asshole to those of us not built like mini-Brett Favres, to complete the entire cliche. I wasn't homophobic, I just thought it was ironic in my immature eleven-year-old way that he was paying rentboys when he wasn't screaming at us to do more pushups or singling me out with anti-Asian stereotypes. (He used the word "sushi" a lot, which, considering I'm Chinese-Korean and I was born at Grady Hospital, didn't even make sense. Asshole.) I felt cool even knowing what a rentboy *was*, though I'd never seen one in real life.

Because this was a conservative Southern private institution, and because one of my classmates had a big fucking mouth, Mr. Davidson was fired.

Two days later, he hung himself.

And I wanted to hang *my*self, and told my dad, who got me the fuck out of that school and into Hiawassee, where I transferred in seventh grade, way late in the year. Something Duff and I have in common, matriculating midstream.

My dad didn't know that I knew about Mr. Davidson, that I'd told my friends because I genuinely thought it was funny, that even though Mr. Davidson was a racist bully, I still blamed myself for his suicide. Dad didn't know about my intuitions. He's just a good father who saw his kid suffering and did something about it. And when I got tight with Zak and Pete pretty much right away, finding them instinctively the way weirdos do, Mom and Dad didn't love that, but they also saw I was happy. And the boys, being Southern, were always polite and friendly.

The Hecks were drawn to each other from day one.

As for us being freaky in high school, I mean, who *didn't* lean into whatever label was foisted upon them? Pete was an athlete, so he broke the mold a bit, but he was way more comfortable learning tarot with me and Zak and driving down to Athens with us on weekends to visit occult stores than doing keg stands with his teammates or whatever the fuck those jackholes did to get themselves off. We also liked intimidating people, if I'm being honest. We were kids.

Only toward the end of high school did the three of us get serious. We knew we were bonded for life, but we also knew we needed to grow up. Zak started working, Pete and I went to college at different schools. He played on scholarship, while I worked at the university library. But we could never get The Scottish Play, that band of girls we'd been in English and pre-calc with, who we knew were on the verge of something big before any of them played together, out of our collective mind.

For some reason, most of our major prophecies have centered around this band.

No, we were not drunk or high the night of Teresa-Jo's party. If anything, we were more on edge because of the fight that broke out right before we decided to calm things down, distract people with a fortune. We were *planning* to say something stupid, bullshit everyone, sort of revenge for how many of these people had treated us all through high school.

That didn't happen. Our vision of a man ruining them for good was real. As was what we told Duff years later, that she wasn't done with death. Poor Quincy—she was always kind to us, if a little bit wary. It's horrible what happened to her aunt and uncle, and like everyone else in Hiawassee, we didn't see any of those drug deaths coming. We've tried to summon Quincy, or at least some kind of personal memory of what really happened that night. I don't think she overdosed on her own. That girl would have been a force for good in this sick, sad world.

If I'm being honest... I've had a thing for Duff since the first time I saw her in the hallway senior year, talking to Marian Shepherd by their lockers. I was passing by when they first met, trying like everyone to get a glimpse of the gorgeous new girl from a faraway land called Michigan.

Something about her struck me right away. Not just that she was pretty, tall, and kind of gangly in a way that suggested she still had some growing to do, with that dirty-blonde hair she later bleached almost white. Those big blue-gray eyes, so expressive when they met mine. She often rolled them at me and looked away, but I *was* staring so fair enough.

I intuited she'd been through some shit, and that shit involved an older guy and an abortion. But beyond my intuition, I could see it in her face. A sadness. A sweetness, too. It's why she's such a good performer—she puts all that out there. Marian tends to have a facade. Duff is genuinely, well, *Duff.*

She fascinates me, but I was always too chickenshit to even say hello, let alone ask her out.

I'm bi and have known that since my teens. I also practice polyamory, or ethical non-monogamy, which means I often have multiple partners, but I make sure everyone knows what's up and is cool with it. Running with witch and nerd types, all those circles overlap quite a bit. Aside from the occasional asshole—usually a cishet white dude with an eye for the youngest and most naïve women in the bunch—the whole scene is way less dramatic than you'd think. A lot of board game nights and wrestling watch parties.

Duff O'Brien is the first person who's got me thinking that, even though of course I'll always be queer and part of me will always be poly in spirit, I could settle down with just one person. Her.

Even before that encounter in the woods, one of my top-five sexual experiences and I know Zak and Pete would say the same, I've felt drawn to her. I've tried to keep our burgeoning relationship casual and not overwhelming, because I know I can be a lot and if she doesn't feel the same way, that's just fine.

No, my bullshit "gift" does not extend to knowing whether Duff O'Brien is in love with me.

She sounded so excited when I told her I was coming to Scotland.

What if I don't make it?

While I've been lost in this reverie, the turbulence has grown stronger. My stomach is dropping. Babies are starting to scream and that's bad because they're naturally intuitive, all instinct before their brains fully develop and the natural cynicism that comes with living in this world sets in. The flight attendant has come over the PA again, giving us instructions and repeating one word: *Brace. Brace. Brace.*

I don't know if I will live or die.

I close my eyes, tell myself to breathe, and summon my Hecks.

And brace.

CHAPTER TWENTY-EIGHT:

MARIAN

"Let fall thy blade on vulnerable crests; I bear a charmed life, which must not yield to one of woman born." —*Macbeth*, Act V, Scene VIII

I dreamed about a plane crash the week before 9/11.

I still think about that sometimes, when September rolls around and everybody starts trotting out their memories—Americans love their collective trauma porn—and the documentaries and tributes are all over TV. I'll think back to that weird dream, one of the first dreams I could recall, in fact one of my first real tangible memories in general, and I get the heebie jeebies all over again.

I'd only been a toddler when 9/11 happened, but like most people, it felt like a wound that would not heal, invisible under the skin.

In the dream, I was standing with my mother in a parking lot, probably our local Walmart, clutching her hand tightly as a huge plane, its belly white and fat like the underside of a whale, floated like a bloated blimp above us. "Mama," I said in my still-baby voice as I watched it overhead, drifting down almost in slow motion. "Is a plane supposed to go that slow? Or be that *close?*"

"No, honey, it isn't," Mama said, her voice eerily calm, her hand cold in mine. She turned to me, her eyes puffy, as always, from crying. "It's going to crash." But we didn't move, only stood there, watching the oddly bloated plane slowly descend above us, until it disappeared from view, the loud *boom* and explosion of fire that followed loud enough to wake the dead.

Then I woke up, screaming in panic in my baby bed. It took ten solid minutes of screaming to wake up her and my father, who was still around in those days. They said it was only a nightmare, and not to worry. *Go back to sleep, Marian.*

According to my mother, when the planes hit the Twin Towers a week later, I'd been sitting in my highchair, enjoying oatmeal—and by enjoying, I mean squishing it with my grubby hands—*The Today Show* playing in the background as Mama folded laundry. When the second plane struck, Katie Couric said, "Oh my..." and I screamed bloody murder and shot up in my highchair, tumbling headfirst out of it and onto the floor.

Mama came running, cradling me in her arms, demanding to know why I'd jumped out of my chair, and all I could do was point. "Plane, plane!" I screamed, pointing. "Dream! Dream!"

That was the first time I dreamed about the future. It wasn't the last.

"All right, Marian?" I shook my head, startled from my memories, and turned to Lawrence. He stood at the foot of the bed, two steaming cups of coffee in his hands, reaching one out to me. I took it and muttered my thanks. He looked chagrined, his face pale and sad and guilty.

"I'm so sorry," he said as I took a sip of the coffee, willing my face to stay impassive, not wanting him to know what his apology meant to me. "I was being such a shit last night. There's no excuse for it—all that stuff I said. It was so unfair and just...I'm really sorry."

"It's fine."

"No, it's not fine," he said, sitting down across from me on the bed. He put a hand on my knee. "I've been trying so hard to do everything perfectly that I've become a fucking nightmare. I'm like a parody of all the worst managers in rock."

He chuckled, but his face was serious. "I've been wanting a music career for so long that I guess I let my dreams get out of hand. It was easy to blame you for everything. But the way I've been acting...to the rest of the girls, but especially to you, Marian, is unacceptable. I tossed and turned all night, thinking about it. I can't go on like this, not with so much bad blood in the band."

"Are you quitting us?" I asked in surprise.

He hesitated. "I don't want to. But if you guys do...then I'll bow out. *You're* the most important thing to me, Marian. Not the band, not my career. *You.* You're my wife now." His voice caught. "I meant one thing I said last night, that all I *really* want is you. And you're what's important to me. Making sure you're happy, that we're happy."

"I am happy," I said, but we could both hear the reluctance in my voice.

"I don't think that's true, Marian," he said, his voice gentle.

"Well...in that case," I said, then took a deep breath. "Who's Becs?"

Lawrence's brow furrowed in surprise, seemingly at a loss for words for a moment. "Becs... How do you know that name?"

"I saw it in your phone," I said. "She was blowing it up last night with messages and it kept waking me up."

"You went in my phone?" Lawrence looked surprised, and to my irritation, a little offended.

"No. I just saw the lock screen," I said defensively. "I'm not a snoop."

"Well, it doesn't matter," Lawrence said after a pause. "Because you're my wife, like I said. Becs is... She's an old friend. I met her back in Athens, years ago. We interned at the same recording studio. She was a student at UGA at the time."

"And now she's here in the UK?" I asked. "That's convenient." My tone was pissier than I meant it to be.

"Yes, she is," Lawrence answered. "She's from Ireland and now lives in London. She's been there for a few years now. Took this cool job as a music journalist and reviewer with one of the big UK music mags."

"I imagine that made you jealous," I said, not sure why I was deliberately trying to poke at him.

"It did," Lawrence admitted with a grin. "Still does. But she deserves it. Becs is a lovely person, and she's an amazing writer. Plus, she knows her music."

"So why is she late-night texting you?" I asked. "Talking about the rough go you've had of it lately and 'taking you in her arms'?"

Lawrence laughed, but his eyes were troubled. "That's just how she talks. Trust me, there's nothing between us, Marian."

"Are you sure about that?"

"Yes, I'm sure," he said, giving my knee a squeeze. "Because I tried, years ago, and she shot me down."

If he said that to make me feel better, it had the opposite effect. Now I knew that Lawrence had had feelings for this woman, who I knew from her avatar was drop dead gorgeous. And successful and talented. And she wanted to take my husband into her arms. "I see."

"Kinda weird that you're jealous," Lawrence said, cocking his head at me, "Considering you've been chatting to someone yourself."

"I have not!"

"No? What's the guy's name? Jeff? The one you met at the 40 Watt show?" Lawrence scratched his chin thoughtfully. "We weren't exclusive then, so I guess I can't really be mad, but…"

"You mean Jack? From Rope 'Em?" I shook my head defiantly. "He followed me on Instagram after the show, but we've *never* talked." I swallowed. "I mean, other than just networking stuff—"

Lawrence cut me off. "Okay, Marian. If you say the two of you have never flirted, I'll believe you." I stared at him. He'd managed to turn it all around and rendered me momentarily speechless.

"Trust me, Marian, there's nothing for you to worry about with Becs," Lawrence said again, his face relaxing. "In fact, you owe her a debt of gratitude. She's the one who helped me book the Scottish tour. She's the reason you guys are playing Glamis."

I didn't feel grateful. It made me feel cornered, trapped. Besides, her favor was more for Lawrence than for The Scottish Play, and the last thing I wanted was to feel indebted to some woman my husband once wanted to bone.

Lawrence stood up and walked over to his suitcase, pulling out a black T-shirt and his worn black denim jacket. He unfolded his kilt from the bedside table. "Becs knew Ian Duncan, by the way."

I gaped at him from the bed. "What? She did?"

He nodded. "That was another reason she was so happy to help you guys out. She worked with him briefly—like one summer, I think?—at his management company, before she and I met. I knew who he was because she'd mentioned him a few times back when we worked together..."

"Why the hell didn't you tell me about this earlier?"

Lawrence's face was contrite. "Honestly? Because I wanted to take the credit. I wanted you to think I came through for you. I guess that's shitty, huh?" He sighed.

I waved him away. "It freaks me out that she knew Ian," I said. "That this random woman did all of this for us—for you—and I didn't even know she existed until last night." The same way it bothered me that he'd been chatting with Teresa-Jo without telling me. She was supposed to be *my* friend. But I didn't say that part.

"Why?" he asked, looking at me curiously. "Because..."

I frowned. "Because nothing," I said finally. "I'm just in a mood." As poignant as it was, Ian Duncan was still helping us from beyond the grave, and how believable it was that this Becs woman had known and loved him—everyone who knew Ian Duncan had loved him—uneasiness rolled around in my stomach. Too much serendipity, too many people and things tied together in multiple ways, making everything feel like pre-destiny, like fate.

Like a trap.

And that made me think of The Hecks.

Which reminded me of another memory—one that nobody, not even Duff knew about—the time that Zak had leaned up against my locker one random afternoon in tenth grade and asked, super casual,

"So, Marian, how long have you had the sight?"

I'd looked at him, momentarily shocked, then glowered at him and told him to fuck off, that I had no idea what he was talking about.

"Yes, you do," he insisted. "Haven't you read *The Shining?* You shine bright, Marian."

"So does your greasy-ass forehead," I said.

He chuckled, running a hand through his hair, bright green that day. "Sure, okay, Marian," he said easily, sauntering off. Then he turned his head and said over his shoulder, "But you might need it one day. You might need *us.*" As Zak walked down the hall, he called out, "We could help you."

Fat chance. As if I'd ever, *ever* join that group of degenerates, those weird little punks. I stomped off down the hall and promptly forgot all about Zak and his stupid sight or shine or whatever the hell he wanted to call it. Or so I pretended.

Lawrence was staring at me. "Do you believe me, Marian?" he asked quietly, shaking me from my memories. "About Becs? We have to have trust if we're going to do this thing for real."

I swallowed another sip of coffee and stood up. "Sure. I believe you," I said, grabbing a towel and ignoring his hurt expression. "I'm going to take a shower. Gotta get ready for the show."

"Good call," Lawrence said, his face still a little sad. As I headed into the bathroom, he called "I love you," and gave me a bright, sunny smile with his signature dimples.

"I love you, too," I said automatically, but as I shut the door behind me, I was already lost in thought again, my mind back to the dream I'd had the night before, the one that had woken me up in a cold, damp sweat, my heart racing.

I'd had the plane dream again.

I took one last look at myself in my compact. I was sitting in the back of my Uber, ready to go in and meet the band. From the looks of it, things were already going off without a hitch, the stage fully set up near the gardens, techs and maintenance workers milling around, getting things in place. I'd needed an extra few minutes to apply my makeup and do my hair and run through my vocal exercises—or so I'd told everyone.

The truth was that I'd needed to get my face on. Not just a face of makeup, but my *public* face. My nerves had been shot ever since I'd woken up from the nightmare and, for the first time since starting the band, I wondered if all this was a bad idea.

I kept having flashbacks of the dream: holding Mama's hand tightly in mine, the fear that seized my throat and made it close up, the smooth, fat underbelly of the plane as it seemed to float down from the sky, sailing slowly but determinedly toward the earth like a whale being dropped from a skyscraper, waiting for the inevitable *boom* and the orange fire that would overtake my vision as the plane crashed and all its occupants perished in fiery, indescribable pain.

It had been *exactly* like the dream from my childhood in every way except one.

This dream had The Hecks.

Well, two of them.

Pete and Zak stood with me on my left side, since Mama was on my right, all of us silent as we stared up at the giant plane falling through space. They were full-grown men, but I was still a child. I'd looked over at them, noting the tear stains on their faces, and had asked, "Where's Josh?"

Neither had answered, but Zak had pointed one pale finger upwards, his eyes big and sad.

At the plane.

The plane's lights blinked. Blink, blink, blink, reminding me of the stim, Maud's tic when she was nervous. Blink, blink. No longer blue and red, the plane's lights—its eyes—were blinking purple. Like the purple Christmas lights on Quincy's last Christmas tree. Like my purple candle.

Like the purple of a certain person's aura.

Josh.

I began to cry.

Pete looked at me and said in a gentle, sad voice, "It's going down. He's going down."

A man will bring you down.

A flash. Ian's soft, sad brown eyes. Quincy, in repose.

Before I could reply, *boom.* The plane crashed, and my world turned orange with flames. I'd woken up drenched in sweat, my heart pounding so fast I thought I might have a heart attack.

I swallowed now, shoving my compact back into my purse and paying the Uber driver, who responded with a flat, "Thanks luv," that made it very clear he'd like me to get out of his car. I scrambled out and ran toward the stage, nervously pulling at my bangs, hoping Lawrence wasn't irritated at me for being late.

But Lawrence was all smiles as I reached the cluster of chairs where he sat, a clipboard balanced on his leg. I glanced down and smiled, seeing that he was writing out a schedule for recording time. So he wasn't going to quit after all.

"Hey, honey," he said, his face erupting in a bright smile when he saw me. "You look absolutely gorgeous."

"Do I?" I asked self-consciously, looking down at my ensemble. For the Glamis show, I'd chosen a black turtleneck with puff sleeves, slightly reminiscent of a royal dress from the Elizabethan era, with its big, poofy shoulders, also similar to something Joan Jett had worn in one of her cheesy eighties videos. With it, I paired black skinny jeans— another nod to Jett—which I'd cuffed at the shins, and black flats with little skulls on them. Easy to jump around in, but dressy enough for a show. A bright blue scarf completed the ensemble. My makeup was understated, a neutral shadow with only my eyeliner pronounced and bold, but I'd gone for a sassy red lip that I worried was too much like my old style.

"Gorgeous," he repeated, gesturing for me to come closer. He placed a gentle kiss on my lips, then checked to make sure he hadn't messed up my lipstick. "I can't wait to get you alone tonight." His blue eyes worked me over, pleading with me for forgiveness, saying the things he didn't say out loud; another *I'm sorry.*

"Me either," I said, beaming, letting him see that he was forgiven. "I guess I'll go find the girls and warm up."

"They're behind the stage," Lawrence said, turning back to his clipboard. I saw his phone light up on his lap and tried to ignore it. "They've got an area set up for you guys. Break a leg, Mac!"

Lawrence's eyes were wide and happy and proud as he blew me a kiss. I smiled back at him and gave a little wave, kicking out one leg, making him laugh. Then I ventured backstage, willing the butterflies in my belly to go away, wondering if he'd picked up his phone to check for messages from *her* the moment I was out of sight.

"...Ladles and Germs, *The Scottish Play!*"

As soon as I stepped onto the stage, the crowd started to scream and clap, and a huge, beaming grin broke out on my face. As I looked over at Duff, I could see that she was grinning ear to ear. So was Ross, and a quick glance back at Maud showed that she was over the moon, holding her drumsticks high over her head, her red mouth brimming with a huge smile.

Duff, ethereally beautiful in a gauzy white dress and purple velvet boots, nodded at me and I launched into the intro to "Alabaster," one of the first songs Quincy had ever written, which contained not only a nasty guitar riff, but a delicious bass lick. It was one of our favorite songs to play, not just because it reminded us of our friend, but because it sounded damn good. And I realized as I watched her that Duff was holding her *old* bass, the one I'd bought her years ago, before we'd ever even talked about forming a band. My grin was wide enough to split my face open.

So much had happened, but Duff was still mine.

To my excitement, the crowd immediately began to dance and mosh around, and I could see Lawrence in the front row, be-bopping along, his auburn curls bouncing as he danced right along with us, his combat boots stomping the ground, his kilt flying around his knees. His own grin stretched from ear to ear. Jesus, he looked *hot.* And happy. And proud. My eyes met his, and I could feel his gaze scorching me all the way onstage.

As I launched into the second verse, feeling great about my vocals,

Lawrence's smile got even bigger. But I felt my own face fall as a tall, statuesque Black woman with striking features approached him, her graceful, long arms extended in front of her for a hug. Lawrence's already elated face lit up as he saw her. The woman did an excited little wiggle as she practically leapt into his arms, her long, curling black hair falling gracefully down her back as he squeezed her tight, lifting her up off the ground.

Becs.

I concentrated on my vocals, determined not to let it get to me, but Lawrence wasn't even watching us now. He was fully enmeshed in conversation with the stunning woman, who had to be six feet tall, model-gorgeous, and from the way I could see her eyes flash all the way from the stage, adored my husband.

He'd said they were only friends.

But what friends hugged like that? What friends looked at each other like that?

As the last notes of the song faded away, the crowd clapped and cheered and Duff looked over at me, exhilarated and grinning. We'd killed it.

But I couldn't enjoy it. Because Becs Webster had put one delicate, manicured hand on my husband's bicep. She'd given it a squeeze. And to my fury, he'd reached his own hand over and placed it atop hers, squeezing it back in a gesture so familiar and natural that I knew he'd lied. His smile was genuine and pure and open, reaching all the way to his eyes, and Bec's body leaned into him, mirroring his body language, the way that only a lover can do.

The fire from my dream had felt like it was inside my head... When I woke, I could feel the heat on my cheeks, the hotness of my tongue against the roof of my mouth, the roaring of the flames in my ears. I felt consumed, like I might spontaneously combust like in those old stories I'd read about as a kid. Even though I knew it was not real, I still felt its heat, the scorch of the flame against my skin.

Ian's soft brown eyes. Quincy, asleep.

As I watched Lawrence laugh with Becs, her hand still resting lightly on his arm, I felt the flames again inside my chest, growing higher and higher until they threatened to burn me to ash.

CHAPTER TWENTY-NINE:

DUFF

"I don't wait 'til stage to use my sexuality. My zipper's down right now."
—Joan Jett

EVERYONE loves "Cherry Bomb."

They love it even more when you and your bandmates wear corsets.

I can't blame them in the slightest. The song's a fucking banger, full of the usual rock innuendo but sung by young women, which gives it an unexpected edge. Mac always made fun of me for being a cliché, but it's the first Runaways song I ever loved. The first song I learned a bass part for. And the one I always pushed to play, even when Mac and Quincy and later Ross rolled their eyes and groaned.

I maintained that "Cherry Bomb" was part of our set at that high school party, the video Ian saw that led to him subsequently signing us, so it was good luck as well. Later, it became a remembrance, a memorial to Ian. And not much later than that, to Quin. We even had a YouTube video of her wailing it out. No one could argue with that.

Tonight was different. Ross and Mac not only acquiesced to playing it for our encore, they'd agreed enthusiastically. Maud then regaled us with trivia about *The Runaways* movie, as was her way. None of us minded, as was *our* way.

A little over a week in, I felt like Scotland was changing us all for the better. Marian seemed happier, more content since the handfasting. I still didn't get why a commitment ceremony was necessary, but The Scottish Play had done everything in our power to make it a memorable evening for her and Larry, from raiding each other's suitcases for our best handfasting outfits, to picking out the perfect song to perform, to reminding each other not to roll our eyes and just drink our feelings away. At the end of the day, Marian was one of us.

Ross was waking up at the asscrack even after the latest of shows, jogging around the village and befriending the shopkeepers, pub owners, and school kids, learning new card games which she'd then teach to us.

She'd officially finished out the school year and quit her teaching position before we flew out, and gabbed every teatime about how she'd miss "her" kids but she wouldn't miss teaching to the test, paying for beakers and Bunsen burners out of her own pocket, dealing with a principal who still couldn't wrap his old Southern head around a pretty young woman teaching bio and chemistry, and most of all, being perpetually broke.

And Maud had her eye on someone: a roadie Larry'd found through a social media post named Shirley, who was a gorgeous genderqueer hottie with triceps and quads to die for. The two of them were constantly together when Maud wasn't rehearsing or having tea time with us. I'd never seen that girl blush before now.

Even Larry was...mysteriously less annoying, or else he just didn't bother me as much anymore. He *had* done a lot for us, and whatever I thought of the guy's personality, he continued to deliver, and he made my best friend happy. He even helped us source real corsets, not the fake kind made of plastic boning and flammable fabric. Who knew how he'd done it? I didn't ask anymore, just gasped in happiness as I took the delicate garment out of the ivory tissue paper.

Except for the last show, when he maligned Mac in front of us all and basically erased most of the goodwill he'd earned in Scotland. Asshole.

And me? Well. Josh was coming tonight. Hopefully *I'd* be coming later, again and again. He'd gotten a later flight so I wouldn't see him until after the show was done, but I was looking forward to reliving that wild night in the woods, with just us two. Let's just say I was beginning to understand what Heart's song "Magic Man" really meant.

And dammit, I'd *missed* him. I'd had my share of flings, but up until now, missing a dude was beyond me.

Josh was one of the reasons I wanted to wear a corset during the encore; doing a quick change out of my white dress during that really fake part of the show when *everyone* knows the band is going to do an encore but we all pretend otherwise and then the audience goes apeshit when we come out again and start rocking our asses off. One of my favorite charades. And that night, I wanted to go from ethereal beauty to straight-up sexpot, just like Cherie Currie.

Maud and Ross weren't on board with this idea.

"Despite my well-documented affinity for retro fashion and period clothing, I find the boning on a true corset much too constricting," Maud had explained earnestly when I first broached the topic. She took a delicate sip of her green tea, a special locally sourced blend I knew she was hoarding to take back to the States. "Most 1950s clothes have a more form-fitting silhouette, but corsets just push me over the edge, sensory-wise."

Ross nodded. "Agreed. Well, not the sensory stuff," she clarified. "It's just...not me, y'know?"

Marian and I looked at each other. We knew. We were on the same page for the first time in what felt like forever.

"Of course," Marian said. "Y'all can stay in your show outfits or change into whatever you feel your best in. Rocker chicks have been pressured to look heteronormatively sexy for way too long." I grinned at her—she was even sounding like her old, Hiawassee-based self.

Tomorrow, I mouthed to her as the other two got into a debate about which kind of finger sandwiches were the best, the kind of delightful exchange you can only have when you're away from the pressures of home. No, we weren't saying goodbye, but for Marian and me, those three syllables spoke volumes. Our secret language from the old days.

She winked at me and whispered, "Tomorrow."

Now it *was* tomorrow, and Marian and I were sing-shouting those unforgettable bad-girl lyrics, trussed up with our boobs pushed up to our chins, feeling fine as fuck. I knew something was bothering her, but it's not like I could stop the show for a heart to heart. Besides, these things really *were* constricting.

I turned my whole body to her, and she did the same almost simultaneously, as if we'd choreographed it. I teetered over to her mic in the high heels I absolutely was not used to wearing and leaned in, praying I wouldn't go ass over teakettle, bass and all. My old bass, the one we'd found together. Mac would never admit it, but I saw her eyes well up just slightly when she saw I was using it.

We did the final refrain together, looking in each other's heavily lined eyes and getting each other's spittle all over our faces. I could smell the tipperary cakes she'd sampled pre-show on her breath as we sang, then screamed. All that rage and angst and happiness you can only comprehend if you've grown up female.

It was magic.

For a second, we were just Mac and Duff, little mountain girls with big dreams, who loved hiking and movies from the 1980s, and most of all, making music even when it sucked. *Especially* when it sucked, because it was all love. In the middle of my laced-to-the-hilt corset, white edged in black just like Cherie's—Marian's was blood-red, even though Joanie had never been a corset gal—my heart grew three sizes. I hadn't exactly been the Grinch lately, but maybe I'd forgotten what this was all about: the music. My best friend. Making music *with* my best friend.

It was the last time we'd ever sing together.

"Hey, have you seen Josh?"

I was still yelling because being literally surrounded with very loud instruments and microphones and cheering crowds really fucks with your hearing, even with earplugs. We'd all dutifully worn them for every single show after Ian had drilled it into our heads, but it didn't matter because I was yelling this at Marian. I was also riding that after-show wave where you feel like you're made of pure adrenaline and will say just about anything, because you're so grateful you got through it all and kicked ass besides. Nothing like it.

"About that…" Marian took me by the elbow and we made our way through the throng of people, some of whom were *also* yelling in our faces, to a quieter spot about twenty feet away, where I could actually hear myself think. She took a deep breath, and I could see the fear in her eyes. Was she about to break up with Larry? *Don't cross your fingers, don't cross your fingers…*

"I had a dream," Marian said. Her voice was softer now, and much more urgent.

"Oh." I knew about Marian's dreams. She'd told me about the 9/11 one during our first sleepover, when I'd only been in Georgia a matter of days. I also knew she didn't take them very seriously. Or at least, that's what she'd pretended, and I went along with it while also realizing she shared her dreams for a reason.

But it was late, and I was horny and I wanted to see the guy who'd flown here to see me. "Mac, honey, I don't want to be rude, but I really do want to make sure Josh found the place okay."

"Josh was in it."

Before I could reply, Larry yelled Mac's name. Her full name, of course. When he did call her Mac, it was never in front of a crowd. Her onstage persona was *Marian,* pure and simple.

And as always, Marian sprang to attention.

"I gotta go," she said, scampering off as fast as her Doc Martens would take her, corset-cleavage on full display. All he had to do was snap his fingers. Nothing had changed.

I would *never* let Josh—or anyone—treat me like that.

As I made my way back into the crowd, now after-partying like it was their job, someone handed me a glass of champagne. Someone else, not Shirley but another local roadie, handed me a shortie robe, dark blue silk, and my ringing phone.

"Hello?" I picked it up without even looking at the screen.

"Duffy Kate!"

"Blanche!" I cried at the sound of my granny's voice. She sounded like home. "God, I miss you. What time is it there?"

"Oh, 'bout seven a.m. I'm up with the roosters like always."

"Granny, you don't even have roosters." Even as a wide smile overtook my face, practically cracking my thick foundation, a pang of guilt poked me right in the gut. Back in Athens, or even when we were touring, I'd made it a point to drive to Hiawassee once a week for "Sundee" dinner—like most Southern biddies, the word "dinner" actually meant lunch at Granny's—with Granny and a hike just with myself. I'd bought her the nicest version of a smartphone with the first real money we made and taught her how to text, so she'd never be far away.

But since we'd touched down in Scotland—and if I were being honest, the escalating drama with Larry and Marian, which thankfully seemed to be dissipating—I'd been slacking on my communication. A lot of missed calls from her, unanswered texts. And mounting guilt on my end.

I wanted to hear every Granny word, so I made my way to a little patch of pure white flowers I'd just learned were called snowdrops. They were so delicate and pretty, and apparently there was a festival for them every year. I made a mental note to tell Josh about them when he got here, *and* to take photos to send Granny, who loved any and all blooms.

"Anyway," I said, swallowing hard, "what's going on in the 'Wass? Mr. Floyd still coming in everyday for shoofly pie?"

"Oh darlin', you have no idea." Granny groaned. "I'm not lookin' for a trophy husband, especially one who never learned to wash his own underwear! I knew his late wife to see, and that woman talked about *everythang*."

I was still laughing when my phone buzzed. "Hey Granny, can you hold on a sec?" Maybe he was here. I pulled the phone away from my ear to look at the screen.

Not Josh, but Pete. *Can you call me ASAP?*

That was strange. Taking the last gulp of my champagne, I set the plastic flute on the ground and reminded myself to pick it up later. I then looked around quickly, just in case Josh was lurking around, waiting to surprise me.

And I saw Marian and Larry. Arguing. Marian was gesturing wildly, the way she only did when she was really upset.

My gut flared.

Just then, Granny's voice echoed through the phone. "Honey, is Marian okay?"

Holy shit. Was Granny here too, waiting to surprise me among the snowdrops? Could she see what I saw?

"Um." Whatever was going on with Mac and Larry was clearly escalating because now *he* was gesticulating too, and I'd never seen him do that. Marian was the hand-talker in that relationship. "Why do you ask?"

There was a pause. "Annie's been picking up some shifts lately, and she's just...concerned. About the way Marian acted before y'all left. And about her, uh, relationship."

Well, Annie's gonna hate *that they're kinda married, Granny. Plus, she called me before we left and I brushed her off. And maybe I shouldn't have.*

But I didn't say any of that. I took a deep breath, and figured Marian's issues were her own, at least regarding her and Larry. "You tell Annie that Marian is doing just fine here. I think she really likes Scotland, and we played amazing tonight."

"Well, of course you did, baby." Her voice was so warm I nearly cried right then and there, and not just because I was relieved my lie seemed to be effective. "That band is lucky. You're their damn heart and soul."

"Aw, Granny. Thank you!" I kicked off my heels, figuring they'd tortured me enough for one evening, and picked them up with the hand that wasn't gripping my warm phone. Out of one corner of my eye, I saw Ross making out with a tall Black guy in a purple kilt. Not far away, Maud and Shirley were chatting and giggling. Padding on the grass, trying not to trample the snowdrops and ignoring the well-wishers, I made my way closer to Marian, who was now screaming.

All I could make out was "other woman."

Shit.

Before I could run interference, my phone buzzed again. This time, Zak.

Duff pls call me or Pete soon as you get this thx.

"Granny?" I said. "I'm sorry, but I gotta go. Talk soon." We said a quick "tomorrow" and "I love you" and disconnected.

I should have warned Granny when I had the chance.

I should have done a lot of things.

I scrolled back to Pete's name and tapped on the contact. He picked up before it even rang. "Duff."

"Hey." I squeezed my shoes between my thumb and forefinger. It was getting harder to breathe in this corset. "Do you know if Josh—"

"He's missing, Duff."

I dropped my shoes. The grass was still under my feet, soft as it had been a second ago, before I hit Call. The midnight starry sky was above the ground below.

But everything was upside down.

Pete didn't wait for me to respond. "His plane. It went off the grid. No one knows what happened, if they're alive, where it is, even." He stopped to take a breath. "He texted just before it went down."

Why didn't he text me? I wondered. I knew how petty that was. But still.

Why was this corset so goddamn *tight*? And how did it work again? Undo the front hooks or the back laces? I was going to figure it out and soon because now my lungs were constricting.

"We're writing a spell right now," Pete said. "But of course, we wanted to tell you. He was so excited to see you, Duff." He paused, took another breath. A rough one this time, but I envied his ability to inhale and exhale because I now couldn't.

Pete's next words came out garbled. "I can't sense Josh. I've always been able to ever since I first met him. And now..."

That's when I collapsed in the snowdrops.

CHAPTER THIRTY:

MARIAN

"Out, Damned Spot; out, I say!" —*Macbeth*, Act V, Scene I

LAWRENCE was on his third denial when I saw Duff hit the ground right in a patch of snowdrops.

I was standing there in my ridiculous corset, too tight and leaving me gasping for air, arms crossed over my chest (or as far as I could get them, anyway) as I listened to my husband once again explain his relationship with Becs, the woman who had been brazenly caressing his bicep less than twenty minutes ago. Who had, wisely, disappeared into the crowd when she'd seen me coming. I felt like an idiot because I'd thought Lawrence was different.

"I told you, Marian. She and I were friends back in Athens. We worked at the studio together. That's it. Tonight was the first time I'd seen her in person in at least five years."

"Do you Facetime?" I asked, gulping in air. "Slide into each other's DMs? Talk on the phone, old-school style?"

He'd laughed, infuriating me. "I don't talk to anyone on the phone, and neither do you. Nobody does these days."

"You didn't answer my question." I shifted my weight to one foot, looking at him expectantly. "Did you sleep with her? Back then?"

His eyes flicked ever-so-slightly to the right, then they were back on me, sincere and open. "No. I never slept with Becs."

"But you've done other things."

"We kissed. Once," Lawrence admitted with a sigh. "I made the first move. She pushed me away and gave me the friend talk. That's the one and only time anything ever happened between us."

"She certainly wasn't touching you and fawning all over you like friends do just before," I countered, and he blushed. Actually *blushed*. Lawrence always flushed like that when things were getting sexy… He flushed just *talking* about that night at the Guidestones. And he had flushed in much the same manner the first time we kissed, after Porchfest, in my front yard.

"She's a flirtatious person," he said after a pause. "Not gonna lie, Marian. I did have a crush on her once. But that's all over and has been since before she left the States. She's engaged, I think. And besides, I'm happily married. You're the only one I want."

"Uh-huh." I rolled my eyes. I knew he was about to launch into how great she was for getting us this show, and even though it was true, it was the last thing I wanted to hear.

And then I looked over and saw Duff, standing a ways from the castle, in front of the beautiful bed of silky-white flowers, holding her phone. She turned pale, clutched a hand to her chest, pitched forward, and hit the ground. As if on instinct, Lawrence and I were both running to her, fight and Becs forgotten.

We reached her at the same time as Maud and Ross as Duff scrambled to her feet, clutching her phone, staring at the blank screen, shaking it like it was a Magic 8-Ball. I gently took the phone from her hand and she looked at me dumbly.

"What's wrong?" I asked, putting an arm on her shoulder. "Are you okay?"

But it was Ross who she reached for, tears running down her face, as she grabbed the phone back and shook it again, her hand raised toward the sky like she was yelling at God. "He's missing! His plane! They think it went down!"

"Whose plane, honey?" Ross asked, her face lit up in alarm.

"Josh!" Duff screeched, her knees starting to buckle again. Ross held her fast, and I reached out to grab at her, to reinforce her. But she shrugged me off, the second time in as many minutes.

"Josh was on the way here," I explained, hiding how stung I felt by Duff's rejection. "Duff, what makes you think his plane went down?" But I was already thinking back to the dream I'd had, the same one that had haunted me since childhood. The crashing plane.

And I knew what she was going to say before she said it.

"The Hec—the Hec—" Duff was nearly hyperventilating. "The Hecks."

She finally got the words out, and Lawrence's face turned. I watched as it fell, his brows going slack, his mouth pursing into a hard line, the hue of his skin darkening right on cue. Without a single word, he turned on his heel and stalked off in the direction of the parking lot, kilt flying against his knees.

"Lawrence! Where are you going?" I called after him. "Where is he going?" I asked my friends stupidly.

"Who knows? And who fucking cares?" Ross's voice was dispassionate as she looked at me. "Seriously, Mac. *Who. The. Fuck. Cares.*" Maud's arm had gone around Duff, all three of us clutching at her, holding her up. But the icy look in Ross and Maud's eyes as they stared at me made it very clear that I wasn't welcome any longer.

"I'm sure Lawrence has gone to see what he can find out for you," I said to Duff, but she didn't meet my eyes. She was still staring at her phone. "I'll go see if I can help. Then I'll be right back, okay?"

"Bye, Mac," Maud said in a sad, soft voice, but her face was as blank as Ross's

voice had been.

With one last desperate glance at Duff's crumbling face, I ran off in the direction of the parking lot, after Lawrence, passing the upside-down snowdrops, which, not fully bloomed, looked more like tears.

I banged on the door to our room for a solid two minutes before Lawrence finally pulled it open. I glared at him. "I forgot my key!" I shouted as he stared at me dully. "What the fuck is going on? Why did you just bail? Right when Duff needed you?"

"She didn't need me. She needed *you*," he said, and I blanched, because it was true. And I'd left her.

"Yeah, well, I had to leave and follow you, because you went running out like a crazed maniac. What the hell is going *on?*"

Then I noticed the packed bag on his shoulder.

He saw me looking and sighed. "I'm not leaving you or anything...

I don't think… I just need…some time."

"Are you fucking *kidding me?* You're going to abandon me in Scotland?!" I shouted, poking him in the chest with a finger.

"Marian, please." Lawrence's voice was pained as he held up his hands in a gesture of surrender. "I don't have the bandwidth for any more fighting right now. I just can't."

I forced down the sarcastic retort that was trying to bubble out of me. The *bandwidth?* Which Instagram therapist had taught him that nonsense? I swallowed my hateful laughter. Maybe if I could be calm, be nice, he wouldn't leave. When I spoke next, my voice was even. "Where are you going?"

Another sigh. "I don't know. I assumed I'd figure it out when I got there."

"Why?" I demanded, tears prickling at my eyelids, once again losing my composure. "Are you going to Becs?"

"Oh, Jesus Christ, Marian." Lawrence pushed past me and flew out into the hall. He turned back to me angrily. "There is nothing between me and Becs. I've told you a million times, and I've had a gutsful! No more! You're so worried about *her* that you can't see the *actual* problem!!"

"What actual problem?" I demanded, following him as he headed toward the elevator.

"Oh, I don't know. Prophecies and fortunes and ghosts and curses, maybe?" Lawrence whirled on me, his face red. "And those ever-present yokels you call The Hecks constantly showing up and wreaking havoc. Did you not listen to a single word I said last night?"

"I'm sure Josh is okay…" I started, and he threw up a hand to stop me.

"You just don't get it." His face was a thundercloud. So much for not having the bandwidth.

"We've been through…things, before," I said softly, putting a hand on his arm to calm him. "We'll get through this too."

"Oh, we got through it alright," Lawrence said, his voice iced over with sarcasm. "You and me especially."

"Lawrence—" My eyes widened, and I squeezed his arm tightly to make him stop. Not here, not now. But he threw off my grip and stalked toward the elevators, leaving me staring after him dumbly.

"There's nobody here but us, and still you can't stand to say it," he accused, his eyes flashing as he hit the elevator button, jabbing it hard with his thumb. "You still can't face what we did to them. Can you?"

"Stop," I begged, moving toward him, but he put up a hand to stop me.

"They're dead, Marian," he said, his voice so low and desolate it was practically a wail. "Ian and Quincy are dead. Their deaths are a stain you and I will never, ever be able to get rid of. Don't you get that?"

"No," I said, putting my hands over my ears, not wanting to listen. "No."

"You know it's *us*, Mac," Lawrence said sadly as the doors whooshed open and he stepped into the elevator. He turned to look at me, all the anger gone out of him. His shoulders sagged. "The curse. It was us all along."

I shouldn't have followed him.

He hadn't explicitly said so, but I knew Lawrence wanted to be alone. Who better understood that need for space, for silence, for privacy to work through things, than me? I'd spent my entire childhood and most of my teen years self-isolating, trying to be invisible.

But I followed him anyway. From the lobby, I'd watched him get in an Uber, then I'd hailed one of my own, ducking in and telling the driver to follow. Despite the undeniable tension I felt, it was a little exhilarating. It felt like I was on a high-speed chase, like in the movies.

Did he know I was following him? Probably. He wasn't stupid. Or blind.

Who did he think he was, running from me? I was his *wife*! He couldn't just abandon me in a foreign country because things got tricky. He couldn't abandon me at all.

The drive took about twelve minutes, the roadside turning rocky, the smell of salt permeating the air. I did mental math to make sure I had enough money in my bank account to cover the fare back, on the off chance I had to make the journey alone.

Finally, after forever, the Uber in front of us stopped, and Lawrence got out. He stumbled out of the car, almost forgetting his duffel bag, running back to get it. The look on his face was frenzied and confused. Were there tears in his eyes?

Maybe I'd pushed him too far with the Becs stuff. Maybe he'd been telling the truth.

Maybe he was right. Maybe it *was* us.

I got out and followed him as he walked down a little trail toward what I now knew was the sea. Maud had told us when we'd arrived in Angus that we were only a few short miles from the coast. I could hear seagulls and the gentle roar of waves against rock as I stumbled a few paces behind Lawrence. He walked with purpose, like someone who had been here many times before, though I knew he hadn't. The sky was gray, and so were the large, sharp rocks beneath us, and so was the water that frothed and foamed back and forth, carrying stones and debris out to sea. The slight breeze that whipped around us was cold and damp. Everything was gray, which was apt, because that's how things were beginning to feel.

Gray as the stones of Glamis Castle. Gray as the granite of the Georgia Guidestones.

The path opened up into a little clearing of beach. Lawrence threw his bag down in the sand without even looking, walking straight out to the rocks ahead without even bothering to take off his Doc Martens. I winced as the expensive leather shuffled through the grainy sand and into the salt water, but he didn't so much as flinch, not even when the foamy spray of the tide hit his legs, drenching his kilt up to the thigh.

I stood there, watching, as Lawrence knelt down on a rock and began to wash his hands.

He scooped up the salty water into one hand, splashing it onto his forearm and then doing the same with the other hand, lathering up his fingers and palms, running his hands over each other again and again, then dunking them in the water to rinse them. As I watched, he did this again, and again, and again, his movements becoming increasingly jerky and frenzied as he scrubbed furiously at his palms.

Then I heard his muffled sobs.

I found my legs and ran to him, as fast as I could travel in the damned corset, carefully stepping out onto the rocks, which were more slippery than I'd anticipated. Gingerly, I made my way over to Lawrence and reached down to put a hand on his shoulder. It was damp with sea spray and cold.

He looked up at me for a brief moment, his eyes red-rimmed, tears pouring down his cheeks. Then he turned his head back down to the water as if he hadn't even seen me and resumed washing his hands.

"Lawrence," I said gently, giving his shoulder a small squeeze. "Honey. What are you doing?"

"I can't get it off," he answered, his voice a whine, still scrubbing at his fingers. I could see the delicate skin of his palms was turning red, but still, he scrubbed. "It won't come off! Marian, help."

"Help with what?" I asked. "You can't get what off?"

"The blood," he replied, sounding very Scottish. *Bludd.* "Help me get the blood off."

"What blood? Lawrence, there's nothing there!" His hands were empty; clean and reddened and chafed. "Stop that. You're hurting yourself!"

"I have to get it off. Fuck, why won't it come off? Get out! GET OUT!" Lawrence scratched at his hands with his short nails, over and over again, raking the tender flesh of his palms until finally, blood *did* appear—his own. He held one bleeding palm out to me as if to say, *see?*

"Fuck, Lawrence, have you lost your mind?" I was starting to get angry now. This was the last fucking thing we needed. The very last thing. "Stop it. Get the fuck up, now! Let's go back to the room and we'll—

"Marian, the blood! So much blood. Help me get the blood out." He looked at me, eyes pleading, begging, still scrubbing at his hands, perching frog-like on the slick rock, losing his balance, slipping, and almost falling into the sea.

"No," I whispered, shaking my head. Tears threatened to fall, but I beat them back, blinking like Maud, forcing them to stop. "No."

"Help me, Mac!"

He never called me Mac. His eyes were wild and terrified.

"No," I said furiously, stepping back off the rock. Back into the sand, back on solid ground.

"Mac!"

"No," I said again, the wind taking my words and pulling them away, away, away.

Lawrence watched me retreat, his wet face drained of color, my name dying on his lips as he clutched his own bloody hands. He stared at me, solemnly, silently, tears pooling in his eyes, for one more moment as I backed away, then fell back to his knees and resumed scrubbing.

CHAPTER THIRTY-ONE:

DUFF

"I'm concentrating on...trying to understand the universe, where science and the spiritual meet." —Joan Jett

I couldn't let go of my phone. The same phone that kept me close to Josh these past weeks as the band and I toured the South and then flew half a world away. If I scrolled through, I could see our endless text thread, everything from salacious stuff like the color of my thong to the most innocuous memes about cats and Carrie Bradshaw.

If I held on, maybe he'd sense *that* and call me. Wherever he was. I couldn't entertain the alternative—that Josh *wasn't* anywhere on this earthly realm—and at the same time, I knew I might have to.

I'd just hung up with Pete and Zak. They'd completed their spell. Kept me on FaceTime for it. I watched as they took stuff and boiled it all in a soup pot on their stove, and as they told me, they'd later bury something else under the moonlight, accompanied by other incantations.

Before we left Glamis, Ross pulled up CNN on her phone, and the awful news was true. The very plane Josh was on had gone off grid over the Atlantic. The powers that be were trying to pull up black box info, but no one knew anything at this point. Once Ross read it aloud, she and Maud got me into an Uber back to our B&B, unlacing my corset the whole way.

Now Maud and Ross sat on either side of me on the bed I'd hoped to be sharing with Josh by now, buttressing me as we squinted at my phone and chanted together, call and repeat style. I didn't know how much they believed all of this stuff. Hell, all these years later, I wasn't sure how much *I* believed.

But I believed Josh when he'd told me about his intuition, how that bonded him to Zak and Pete. I believed Pete when he said he could no longer sense Josh anywhere. And that was enough for my bandmates. My friends.

Most of them.

"He'll be okay, Duff," Maud whispered, touching my face. Like Mac, she wasn't big on affection, so even in this pitch-dark moment, I loved that she was going beyond her comfort zone to comfort *me*. "Things like this happen. But Josh is strong. And he's special."

Meanwhile, Ross pressed something into my hand that wasn't gripping the phone. I hadn't even noticed she'd left and come back. "Bourbon and branch. Well, more bourbon than branch." She smiled shakily. "My granddad was a huge *Dallas* fan, the original series."

The pads of my fingers brushed the moisture on the cloudy hotel tumbler. I took a tiny sip, then a larger gulp. It burned all the way down and I welcomed this sensation, the first I'd felt since I came to after passing out in the field. "How the hell did you find bourbon in *Scotland*?"

Ross laughed. "Glamis gift shop." She pulled out a small packet with a silver marijuana leaf on the front. "I'm also really good at getting shit past airport security. Gummy? Hid 'em in the toe of my sock. Not super strong, but might help you sleep." Her eyes were soft, hair a wild mess of natural curls. She looked like an angel, and for a moment, she reminded me of Quin. "Fear-based adrenaline's a bitch."

I glanced at Maud to see how she felt about all these substances. She shrugged. "I don't judge anyone who possesses self-control *and* is in the midst of a major crisis."

I knew Ross didn't mean anything by it, and I'd certainly enjoyed a gummy or six in the past, but right now that little silver pot leaf, its forbidden nature, reminded me of Quin. Someone else I never saw again.

"Maybe later," I choked out. And then it happened—I started sobbing. I always reacted this way when bad things happened: I'd keep it together, insisting I was fine (even when my body suggested otherwise by shutting down, as had literally just happened). I could talk to people, even smile at their kind words, and return their hugs. And then, the tiniest thing like the offer of a damn weed gummy would set me right off.

I buried my face in my lap and sensed Maud and Ross looking at each other in alarm before murmuring comforting syllables, smoothing my hair, rubbing my back through the terry cloth hotel robe. (My corset was long gone and I didn't give a shit where. I never wanted to see that stupid choke-inducing thing again. No wonder Joanie wasn't a fan.) Not even Mac had seen me like this, or at least not in a very long time.

Mac.

"Do you—" I raised my head, gulping in a shit ton of air.

"Breathe, honey," Ross said. Maud raced to the desk and fetched a box of tissues, which she brought back, handing me two.

"Do you think we're being too hard on Marian?" I asked.

Maud bit her perfect red bottom lip. "Duff, please take care of *you* right now. Something scary is happening to your...uh..."

"Boyfriend," Ross said.

"I don't know if he's my boyfriend!" I wailed, sounding for all the world like the spoken bridge to a 1960s girl group song. Lesley Gore would be proud.

I looked at Maud on my right side, Ross on my left, and the three of us started giggling, then laughing uncontrollably. Tears were running down my face, my neck, and into my cleavage. I mopped them up with the tissues Maud had provided, and she pulled more out of the box neatly, one by one.

"If he's coming to Scotland to see you, he is definitely your boyfriend," Ross said. "And don't argue with me. I taught hormonal teenagers and I *know* what young love looks like."

"I'm not young and you're like five years older, so if I'm young, so are you," I retorted, blowing my nose.

Ross rolled her eyes. "That doesn't even make sense, but I'll let it go under the circumstances." Her face grew serious. "But we have to believe Josh is okay, Duff. At least until we hear otherwise. Okay?"

I nodded. She was right. No matter how superstitious I got, thinking the worst wasn't going to bring Josh back. Might as well be optimistic until I no longer could.

"Do you want me to look up plane disappearance statistics?" Maud asked. "Or would that trigger you?"

I sniffled loudly, hoping I didn't suck too much snot back up. "I'm okay, Maud. Thank you though." Information was Maud Findley's love language, and I knew exactly how kind this gesture was.

Ross placed the packet of gummies in the bedside drawer, right on top of the thick Bible. "For later, just in case," she clarified, gently closing the drawer. "Why the fuck are you worried about Marian right now? Considering she didn't stick around to help you."

"Following Larry like always," Maud said, her sweet voice edged with poison.

"I know," I said, lying back and staring at the ceiling. Again, something I thought I'd be doing with Josh right now. The girls lay back with me. "But...I'm worried about her. I have been for a while, and her mom is too, and now Granny's worried, and she doesn't even *like* Mac." I took a deep breath, not wanting to voice my concern for fear speaking the words aloud would make them real.

What the hell. If I couldn't tell my bandmates, who could I tell? "I think Larry's getting dangerous. Like, really dangerous."

"More than just a toxic shitbag?" Ross asked.

"How so?" Maud said at the same time.

I addressed the ceiling. It was easier to get out what had been haunting me for weeks if I didn't have to look anyone in the eye. "I mean, for a long time, we thought he was just super controlling, right?"

"Right," they replied in unison. I glanced over at my friends. Ross was lying next to me, hair fanned out on the pillow. Maud was sitting up, looking down at me like my mom used to do when I had a bad dream in the middle of the night. Such dears, the both of them. Just then, I noticed a snowdrop petal on my robe. I left it there as I continued.

"I really hoped Marian would see the light way before now. But now they're married, and even if it's not legal yet, it's clearly real to them. I do think he's genuinely into her, as unhealthy as their relationship is. But…" I glanced at Ross, then at Maud. I knew my makeup was smeared to hell, but both of their faces were still perfectly in place. I couldn't believe just an hour ago, we were still onstage, rocking our hearts out, sucking up that adrenaline that only came from performing, certain the good vibes would never end.

I picked up the petal, rolling it around my fingers. "Her charm bracelet. I got a glimpse during our first pub gig. She's worn it since high school, so I never really look at it anymore unless she has a new charm she wants to show me. It's basically a part of Marian. And um…" I couldn't believe I was about to voice this, this personal ghost, but I pressed on.

Things couldn't get any worse, right?

I gave Maud the briefest of rundowns of our history with Ian and what Crowe, and the necklace, had meant to him, before running out of breath. I gulped another mouthful of air. "I hadn't thought about the necklace in a while, especially since we've also lost Quin since then, and I took that really, really hard, especially considering how she…" I trailed off, and Ross made a beeline for the bed, lifted me up gently, and leaned her head onto my shoulder. I could tell from how her body had suddenly tensed up that she was trying her best to keep it together. She'd loved Quincy too.

"But you guys," I said, trying to get the words out. They needed to know this. Even if I didn't want to say it aloud, for fear of making it true. "Marian's bracelet. I think she has the charm from Ian's necklace."

If Ross had been tense before, she was absolutely stiff now. She took my hand, and I could see her eyebrows knit together. My bandmate was *pissed*. "That's…" I could tell she was trying not to scream. "Are you *sure*, Duff?"

I shook my head, wishing I could wash the image away: Marian, pushing her hair behind her ear. That wink of tarnished silver. Her sleepy, almost smug grin when she caught my eye, almost as if she'd *wanted* me to spot it. But she just looked like that sometimes. Right? "I'm not, that's the thing. I mean, the first day here was hell because we were all so jet-lagged, but we had to press on so our bodies could adjust, right?" Maud and Ross nodded. Their eyes were boring holes into me. Ross was now breathing deeply. Maud was sucking on her lips.

I looked down at my hands, which were rubbing the petal together. One over another, again and again. Now that beautiful little snowdrop was nothing but sticky dust in my hands. I needed to wash them immediately.

Maud and Ross exchanged another glance.

"I just…" My voice broke and this time I wasn't thinking about Josh. Much. "I think she might be in really deep. That something's going on beyond the textbook unhealthy relationship she and Larry M have going."

And just then, my brain shut down and my body took over.

First, the bathroom. I don't even remember getting in there, but suddenly I *was* staring at my mirror image: the smeared remains of cat-eye, robe akimbo to the point where it was practically a wardrobe malfunction, lipstick a faint memory. My hair was a mess, the roots an inch long now. I scrubbed my hands raw and rid of that stupid petal until the tiny but solid bar of free soap was but a sliver.

I realized for the first time that I was topless under the robe, only wearing fishnets and booty shorts. Hands stinging, I strode over to my closet and grabbed the first clothes I could find: skinny jeans, my favorite shoes, a hoodie, and a T-shirt with the face of poor Mia Zapata, gone way before her time because some shitbag stalker thought he was entitled to her body, her life. The musician the police didn't care about because hey, she was a riot grrl walking alone late at night. She may as well have asked for it.

But her friends cared. Joan Jett and Mia's former bandmates from The Gits, plus Dave Grohl and everyone else. They finished her recordings and did benefit shows to raise money for the investigation.

They didn't give up on their girl.

And neither would I.

"Um, where are you going?" Maud asked tentatively, still sitting on the bed with Ross.

I'd set my phone on the bed so I could dress and now I grabbed it to call an Uber. "I'll be fine," I said over my shoulder, shutting the hotel room door before they could protest and pull me back into the room for more bourbon and gummies and Kleenex. Before I could let them.

I had to find her.

LAWRENCE MACLAREN

"LARRY M"

I'VE only been in love twice.

I'm not old—still three years from thirty—but I was forced to grow up way too fast. At fifteen, I started taking care of myself and my younger brothers when my mother shacked up with her fifth and current husband, who took her away from our house and into the life of a Holy Roller. Forced to start working under the table to feed my brothers Nate and James, I had no choice but to grow all the way up quick.

Even before Mom left, she wasn't really there, always worried about her latest relationship, forever just beginning or just ending. Always holed up at some dude's house, leaving us alone for weeks at a time. She worked and provided for us, technically, but she was absent in every way it counted.

Jessica MacLaren (this was how I still thought of her, despite her surname changing three more times) wasn't there when I needed her, but she did manage to teach me two very important things.

The first was how to use medicine. From the tender age of seven, I knew which over-the-counter meds were best for a cough, which one for a fever, and what to take if you had a stomachache. Mom taught me about pharmaceuticals and holistic remedies in equal measure. Brought up by genuine hippies in the sixties, she'd grown up unvaccinated and relying on things like white willow bark and camphor to get her through flu season, then, after obtaining her pharmacy degree, quickly acclimated to dispensing prescriptions all day. She believed in a balance of the two, and she taught me the same. "Trends change in medicine," she'd told me once, "But ignore them. Don't be afraid of science, but don't ignore nature and your intuition, either. They're meant to work in tandem."

Mom had carefully shown me how to dry herbs and make tinctures and solutions, and gave me her dog-eared copy of *The Pill Book*, a tome with detailed descriptions of every single medication under the sun and what they were used for. I read it for fun when I was barely eleven. In fact, I still carry it around with me and use it for reference from time to time, a fact that might've proved dangerous if Ross Smith paid better attention.

Once, as Ross helped me carry boxes of flyers out to my car, she'd noticed it sitting on the passenger seat and asked me why I had a pharmaceutical book. I made up a story about my mom leaving it there, and she seemed to buy it. At least she hadn't asked more questions.

In a way, that weird encounter was a blessing, because it stopped a course of action I wasn't sure I'd wanted to ever start.

Mom also taught me about the bad drugs: which to take in

moderation, and which ones to *never* take. The ones that would kill you "deader than shit"—her words. A lesson that had proved useful in more ways than one.

As to the second thing my mother taught me. That love—finding someone to love you—was the most important thing of all.

My first love was Rebecca "Becs" Webster—well, if you can call it love. Looking back, it was just a crush, an infatuation. I'd somehow finagled my way into an internship at the local recording studio fresh out of high school. No idea how I'd managed to charm the studio into hiring me, with no experience and job history whatsoever. They must have just liked my gumption and excitement (and the fact that I'd happily scurry out to get them all lattes from Jittery Joe's when they asked).

The moment Becs had waltzed in and sat at the desk across mine, looking like a curly-haired Naomi Campbell, I'd been smitten. She was five years older than me, born in Dublin, and had lived all over. She'd had plans to move to London when she finished at UGA. Nervous and stupid, I made a joke about her being Phil Lynott from Thin Lizzy's illegitimate daughter, given that she was Black, Irish, and obsessed with rock music. I worried I'd gone too far, but to my delight, she'd thrown back her beautiful head and laughed. I worshipped the ground she walked on.

And, predictably, she'd broken my heart.

The time I'd gotten up the guts to kiss her, Becs gently pushed at my shoulders and smiled, her breath close enough to smell, sweet like peppermint as she delivered her kiss off: "Our friendship means too much to mess it up," her red lips parting into a conciliatory smile.

It wasn't easy, but I let her go, and gained a great friendship out of the deal. I had to believe I'd find eventually someone else—someone who shared my love of music and the music business, and who had the same tenacity and drive that I had. Someone who was beautiful and dark-haired—I did have a type, after all—and mysterious. Someone *perfect*. The Great Love my mother had taught me to look for.

I'm not a monk. I've gotten lucky plenty. But I never was the type of guy who could be happy playing the field and keeping things casual. Every woman I ever took to bed, I was scoping her out, wondering if she was *the one*. Disappointment rose every time I sent her home, realizing she wasn't. After a while, I stopped even trying to date. I was so sick of playing games. I wanted to get serious with a girl, to give her my whole heart.

And then, I found her. Or rather, she found me. My Great Love.

My everything.

Marian Elizabeth Shepherd.

I met her years ago, but she doesn't remember me. I think Duff does, but we've never spoken about it... Not sure why, though it's not a secret.

One weekend, my brother Nate called and invited me to a party in Hiawassee. One of his buddies from work, Brian, was dating this girl Teresa-Jo, the daughter of this bigwig and known for her house parties. Getting an invite to a Garcia party was a big deal. The place was huge: gated, with a sloping green lawn, pool and jacuzzi and tennis court, the whole nine, and everybody loved Teresa-Jo, who was sweet as the day was long. Nate thought it'd be a good networking opportunity for me; he'd heard there was going to be live music. I made the drive up to the mountains in the rain, figuring nothing would come of it, but hoping I'd maybe see a cool band or meet a pretty girl.

I just barely missed the band, but I *did* meet the pretty girl.

Stumbling out the door right as I got there, three sheets to the wind, was Marian Shepherd, a gorgeous, dark-haired slip of a girl with so much *attitude*. Hanging off her shoulder was a badass guitar, just dangling there collecting rain, as if she'd forgotten it. That's how cool she was. Marian looked at me with those dark eyes, her drenched, shaggy dark hair falling over her smooth forehead, and that was it for me. I didn't even *need* to hear her band. I was a goner.

Then her friends spirited her away. I thought I'd never see her again.

But fate has a funny way of looking out. Five years later, on her twenty-second birthday, Marian Shepherd stepped into The Grit. I served her a Golden Bowl, and my heart stopped when I saw those dark eyes again. I knew immediately this was *the girl*. From the party.

I decided right there and then I'd ask her out. Only she asked *me* out first. I was definitely not cool in my rush to say yes, not believing my luck. I'd watched her from the bar, opening yet another magnificent guitar, sharing peanut butter chocolate cake with her friends, just shaking my head and thinking to myself, *I'll do literally anything to be with that woman. Just to be in her orbit.*

The only problem was Ian Duncan, who was overseeing both the cool band *and* the pretty girl. *My* girl. Ian Duncan's reputation preceded him. He was even more of a bigwig than the Garcia guy, though he didn't act like it. He'd managed all kinds of semi-famous bands in the South, had a side-venture in the vinyl business, and he was rich as hell. Marian Shepherd didn't need me to make her happy; with the help of Ian Duncan and her band, she could make that happen for herself.

I'd been trying to get a job working for Ian Duncan for years, but when Marian Shepherd came into my life, he stopped being the goal and became the competition.

It's like I spent the last six months of my life falling down the rabbit hole, and no amount of potions or spells could ever put me back to rights. It's all a game to her, and I'm the bird who ends up as the croquet mallet.

My brain is split into two segments: *Before Marian. After Marian.* Never the twain shall meet. I am split apart.

It wasn't personal. The truth was, I had no problem with Ian Duncan. I admired him. If there's anyone whose career I'd like to emulate, it's Duncan's. I wanted to *be* the guy. I never wanted to hurt him.

And Quincy Banks was the beautiful, innocent, amazing girl I *should* have ended up with, in another life maybe, where I was a better person and girls like her looked at guys like me twice. I never wanted to hurt her, either.

I never wanted to hurt anybody.

But when you've got a raven-haired angel (devil?) in your arms, one who can sing like a siren, pulling and drawing you into those eyes, offering you your every dream on a silver platter... Well, you'll do more than you ever could imagine to keep it. You'll move mountains for the Great Love.

You'll kill for it.

The water is cold; far colder than I'd imagine the North Sea would be this time of year. The salty spray dries on my shins and ankles, making me itch beneath my woolen socks and thick black boots. For once, I wish I was wearing jeans instead of my kilt.

Of the things I'm proudest of, naturally the first is my wife, Marian Shepherd MacLaren. My muse, my heart, my soul, my every desire. The second is my career, what little I've made of it. The third is my Scottish heritage.

Mom didn't teach me that. It was my dad, Lawrence "Larry" MacLaren Sr., who has been in prison since I was a pre-teen, who boasts the Scots ancestry. He didn't come around when I was a kid, but I knew he had red hair and participated in Highlander games when he was young. I traced my ancestry when I was old enough and found out he was from the Highlands, like for real; my grandparents had come over to the States in the '50s. And to my delight, I discovered that there was a real, genuine link between the Scottish Highlands and the Appalachian Mountains (Maud isn't the only one who knows things, despite what she might think). Growing up in Tallulah Falls, right near the gorge with its craggy, steep rocks, rich green fields and powerful, magnificent waterfalls, it felt fated that my ancestry was what it was. It became an integral part of my identity, growing up largely on my own.

It didn't hurt that the class divide in Tallulah Falls was as deep as the gorge itself. You can imagine what side I grew up on.

The girls in the band make fun of me. They joke about my affectations (they think I don't know) and Maud likes to lord her knowledge over me. I let them. It's easier than trying to explain.

I know they think the kilt is weird. I don't care. I'm Scottish; it's who I *am,* and for many years, hungry and alone, wondering where my next meal would be, wondering where on earth my stupid mother was tonight, fretting over whether or not my brothers were passing their classes and hadn't outgrown their hand-me-downs, studying my

Scottish ancestry was all I had. For many years, Scotland and music were literally the only things I had to comfort me to be proud of. To call my own.

I carved out an identity for myself; I scraped it up with my bare fingers from nothing. I'll be damned if anyone tries to take it from me.

And here I am, crouching on the rocks on the Scottish coast, the North Sea lapping at my ankles, my authentic tartan whipping around my legs... Here, finally here. I've come home to claim my birthright.

So why do I feel like I'm dying?

And why do I keep seeing Ian Duncan, a pale-gray apparition, standing yards away on the surface of the water like Jesus himself, wearing a kilt not unlike mine? I try to be brave, to meet his—its— eyes, but every time I tremble and look away, because Ian Duncan is silently weeping.

The poet Robert Burns, himself a Scot, once wrote, "The best laid plans o'mice an' men oft gang agley." It's no excuse, but my plans—*our* plans—went awry, Ian, and I was powerless to stop them. I didn't want to hurt you. But once you were gone, we found it was so easy to just... do it again.

Marian told me sacrifices were required for greatness.

I'm so sorry. I'm so sorry for what I did to you and Quin.

The blood won't come out of my hands. I've scrubbed and scrubbed, and it won't go. The stains have seeped into the pale flesh of my palms and stayed; they are a part of me now. I'm stained forever; tainted. My heart is as stained as my hands.

The damned spots will not come out, and I know I have betrayed everything I ever was. All for a love that I can feel slipping away.

Marian is gone.

The lives of innocents—people who had loved her as much as I do, if not more—sacrificed at the altar of Marian. And for what? Her love has turned to barely disguised disdain. She doesn't trust me. She doesn't *like* me. And she's realizing she doesn't need me, either, which is the worst of all.

I live for her.

But it's no life at all.

I'm still scrubbing, but the blood won't stop, will never stop. What can I do? I reach a raw, aching hand down and dip it in the ice-cold sea, swirling it around and around, until it goes numb, the water around me turning pale pink. But the blood remains.

And then, from the corner of my eye, I see her.

Marian. I look up, feeling the dried tearstains on my cheeks, my legs numb and covered with dried salt. She stands there in the sand, a vision in a soaked red corset, her dark hair whipping around her face, flying against her pink cheeks. She is so beautiful it causes me pain. The expression on her face is hard to read from so far away, but I think maybe she's sad? Or perhaps not; I can't tell. So often she seems... empty. The essence of her, the thing that makes her Marian, stays gone for longer and longer now. A sob catches in my throat. I call to her, pleading with my eyes, begging. "Marian! Mac!"

She stares at me; her shoulders heave. She turns slightly, and her profile is visible. She beckons with a finger. *Follow me.*

So I follow. I would follow her anywhere, even now.

At the cliffs, the wind is stronger. It blows my hair into my face, whipping my kilt straight up. But nobody is here to see my nakedness, and it doesn't matter. Marian stands at the foot of the cliff, staring down. "Come back!" I call. She'll fall if she's not careful in her ridiculous shoes. Nothing is more important to me than Marian, even now. What a poor show I've made of it, though. No wonder everyone she loves hates me.

I reach Marian, reach out an arm to grasp her, to pull her back to safety. I'm surprised when she immediately sinks into my arms, smelling of sea water and her usual powder-and-roses fragrance, and under that, the smell of vetiver and cedar—my smell. She is mine and I am hers. I weep with relief that she came to save me. My Maid Marian.

She presses her sweet lips to mine and pulls me down to the grass, where we kiss and she presses my bloodied palms to her lips and washes away my wounds, takes away the stain of death, of betrayal. My hands sting, but I welcome the touch, because it's her.

I press her into the soft ground and push up her skirt, then my kilt, entering her quickly and roughly, Marian moaning beneath my mouth as I thrust into her, rushed and frenzied. Our legs are damp with cold sea water and we slide against each other. It feels like we're racing against time, trying to push back a clock that has already started ticking. Marian writhes beneath me, her teeth grazing my neck, her fingers scratching down my back, ripping the supple leather of my coat. A flash of the Georgia Guidestones fills my mind, remembering the lust, the terror I'd felt as Marian writhed beneath me. We're both panting now, just as we were that night, and my bloodied fingers clutch at the grass as we both come together, our moans carried away by the wind.

I sigh, pressing my face into her neck, breathing her familiar scent, calmed. I nuzzle into her, whispering a soft word into her ear. "All these lies… All the hurt we've caused… We could set it right, you know." I graze my lips against her ear. "We could come clean. Tell the truth." Marian turns, looks at me in surprise, then, to my relief, smiles. Nods.

All will be well again. We took a little turn, cracked under the pressure, but it will be okay now. As long as we're together, nothing—and no one else—matters.

Marian told me that, when we first started dating. *We're destined for greatness, you and I,* she had said. *As long as we're together, nothing and no one else matters. Just us.*

I took her words to heart. I'd have done anything to make her dreams a reality. I would lie. Cheat. Steal. Kill.

And I have done all four. For her.

Marian laughs softly, the sound tickling my ears, and she places a gentle kiss in my hair. I rise and stand, my legs still shaky beneath me, and offer her my arm. She takes it, rising on her platform shoes—*How on earth did she get up the trail in those*, I wonder absently, admiring the muscular length of her graceful legs—and wrapping one arm around my shoulder. I lean over, still sweaty and out of breath, and kiss her.

I raise a hand to caress her soft cheek, to touch a finger to her smiling mouth, and stop. The ragged, torn flesh of my palms is still stinging, the blood pooled and coagulating there, and I've left a dark red stain on Marian's pale neck. The blood, the blood.

It won't ever come out.

Oh no, it's happening again. The darkness is overtaking me. I begin to shake.

Marian's eyes burn black as I stare at her. And then her arm around my neck is gone, my still-shaking legs have given way, and I'm slipping, falling, falling, falling.

And she's watching me fall, her eyes as black as coal.

And I'm hitting the jagged rocks, every limb, every muscle alight with pain as I crash into the slick rocks, the salty North Sea washing away every stain, every memory in an instant, as if I never existed at all.

My last thought: *Marian, I love you.*

The spot is finally out.

CHAPTER THIRTY-TWO

DUFF

"I think I was born strong-willed. That's not something you can learn."
—Joan Jett

MARIAN looked at me. I nodded.

Without another word, we headed away from the cliffs, walking and walking until Marian could get a phone signal to call an Uber.

"We could just hoof it back to the B&B." That was the first thing she'd said since I found her and...him.

"Okay." That was the first thing *I'd* said.

So we did. Marian mentioned she was hungry and even though this is a town that rolls up its shutters at nine p.m., we managed to find a pub that made us meat pies. Meat in a pie—not something I'd experienced in Michigan, or Georgia, other than the occasional chicken pot pie, usually from a box, but here, rich meat and other savories tucked in a neat pastry crust was as normal as a ham biscuit back home. I'd miss them when we left.

I expected Marian to kick up a fuss or just order fries, being a vegetarian and all, but she gobbled hers down and had a glass of whisky, but just one before she asked for a bottle of water. She seemed sober and now well-fed. Just quiet. For a while, there were no other sounds but the scrapes of silverware on rapidly emptying white china plates that were probably older than we were. It was Mac who broke the silence first.

"I love that shirt," she said, nodding at Mia's beautiful, angry face, frozen mid-note forever. "I hate how she was taken from us. She could have been the next big thing."

No irony in those words, by the way. She didn't seem bothered at all.

And I was bothered at how not bothered *I* was.

I'd just witnessed a murder. Maybe. Or a suicide. Either way, sane people didn't jump off cliffs, or push others. And why was I even thinking *murder* or *suicide*? Technically, I wasn't sure Larry M was dead, and I hadn't exactly stuck around to check.

It scared me how little I cared. How much I was thinking about what Marian would be like *without* Larry M's influence, control, and possibly abuse. How strangely optimistic I was feeling, now that I knew he was really gone.

Because instead of freaking the fuck out, here I was, shoveling meat pie in my mouth between swigs of thick beer, thinking I'd never tasted anything better in my life and wondering if Granny could recreate the recipe if I described it well enough.

"I'll bet she could," Marian said, and I realized I'd spoken that last part out loud. "Granny can make just about anything you'd want."

And then I noticed: her Georgia twang was back with a vengeance.

Around the time she started dressing differently, Mac started talking differently, too. Kind of like an old movie star, but less affected. Definitely enunciating more and saying "ing" instead of "'in" at the ends of words, even a Britishism now and then. As with everything else, the rest of the band and I suspected Larry M.

Larry M. Who was now probably dead, and if not, well, I certainly hadn't helped matters by leaving with his wife. Without calling for help or even checking to see if he needed it. Without asking any questions of Mac, who was right there when...whatever happened, happened.

What I did feel was the tiniest flame of gratitude. This was the most time I'd spent with my best friend in a long while. Just the two of us. The way it used to be before Quincy came on the scene, and sometimes during, when Marian couldn't stop complimenting me: my hair, my "cool" accent, my evolving style, until I begged her to stop because it embarrassed me. Back then, we'd hardly have to talk at all to completely understand one another.

Even so, that was a long time ago. Now we should probably at least get our stories straight. And maybe then I could figure out why, aside from my full tum, I felt strangely outside my body.

"Hey, Mac?" I said.

"Yeah?" She looked up from her plate, practically licked clean. She'd *really* chowed down on that almost-rare meat. Mac's dark red lipstick from the show was completely rubbed off and there was a little streak of grease on the corner of her mouth. Or was it blood?

She looked happy.

She looked happy and so I chickened out.

I tried a smile. "Feel like heading back?"

Once we reached the hotel, we were greeted by Ross, Maud, and all four of their arms, which they threw around both of us in fierce hugs. Apparently, Maud and Mac were foregoing their "no touching" rules. I could smell shampoo and sweat and a tinge of weed and bourbon on Ross and I never, ever wanted to let go.

"Are you guys okay?" Maud asked. "We were so, so worried!"

Ross didn't say anything. "Ross *cried*," Maud told us breathlessly.

"*Maud!*" Ross snapped, but now that I looked, I could see her red eyes. I'd never seen Ross even close to the point of tears, save for Quincy's memorial.

"Well, I'm sorry!" Maud said. "I didn't know that was a secret."

"Aw, Ross," Mac kidded, the four of us still in a tight clinch, not caring that it was whatever o'clock in the morning and the front desk person was *definitely* glaring. "I didn't know you felt that way about me."

"Just..." Ross looked away for a moment and I could tell she was trying to keep from breaking down. I raised my eyebrow at the other two like, *no more teasing.* She smacked Mac on the arm. "Don't scare us like that!" And then she smacked me. "You too! You'd think when your boyfriend's been found safe, you'd..."

Wait.

"Who's safe?" Marian asked at the same time I shrieked, "*Josh?*"

"Thought it was a fuckbuddy thing?" Marian muttered. Later, I'd wonder why she didn't look more surprised. Then I realized she knew he was missing and just didn't care.

"Duff," Maud said gently. She gave the other girls a look and led me to the couch in the corner of the lobby. Ross and Mac followed. "Have you not been checking your phone?"

Well, Maud, I was kind of occupied with whether or not to save our asshole manager's life, then getting my best friend the hell out of there before anyone could see us, so...no?

"Look at it now," Maud said gently, and I pried my phone out of the back pocket of the jeans I'd put on what felt like a lifetime ago.

Texts upon texts upon texts. I didn't know where to start.

Ross must have sensed that, and she reached over Marian to put a hand on my arm. "Josh is okay, Duff. The plane was able to land safely in a field. A few injuries, but no fatalities."

"They're calling it a miracle," Maud chimed in, eyes wide behind her cat-eye glasses.

Mac and I exchanged a glance. "Hecks?" she murmured, and I gave the tiniest of shrugs. But I knew it had to be. That boiling pot on the stove, the bespoke incantation.

"We were worried when Mac disappeared and then you ran away," Ross said, her soft hand still on my bare forearm. "We thought maybe we'd never see either of you again..." She trailed off, her voice catching.

Marian put her arm around Ross, who leaned into her, all previous beefs forgotten. "Just, come on," Ross said. "After we lost Quincy like that, you can't blame me for jumping to conclusions."

"Hey," Marian said. "How about we head up to our rooms and let Duff call her..." She glanced at me. "Boyfriend?"

I nodded, realizing just then that a giant and probably dopey grin had taken over my entire face.

Marian rolled her eyes, but she was also grinning. "Okay, whatever."

So we aren't gonna talk about the body on the rocks. He's your husband, Mac—or was*—so I guess it's your call.*

We'd barely stood up from the couch, which was quite a squeeze for four people, when a...police officer or whatever they were called in Scotland burst into the lobby. I'd have giggled at how very out of an old school British movie he looked, all round belly and dark blue uniform with a funny hat, if it hadn't been for the horrified expression on his face.

And then he looked directly at us.

"Marian Shepherd?" he asked. "Do you lasses know a Marian Shepherd?"

Fuck. Fuckfuckfuck.

I was this close to putting my hands up (did people do that in Scotland? Did they do that in the States even, or had I just watched too much *Dateline*?), when Mac said, "I'm Marian Shepherd, sir." Her voice was clear as a bell, that Georgia twang on full vocal display. I noticed she didn't use the last name *MacLaren.*

The police officer nodded at the clerk and lumbered toward us, head down. Mac found my hand. I laced my fingers through hers and squeezed for my life.

I'd go down with her.

"These ya friends?" asked the officer.

"My band," Marian said calmly, as if she was back in the pub, chowing on a meat pie and shooting the shit with a stranger.

"Why don't ye all sit?" the officer suggested gently, and the four of us sank back down on the couch. I snuck a glance at my other bandmates. Ross's face was white, and Maud was chewing the red polish off her right pinky nail.

"Ms. Shepherd," the officer said quietly, haltingly. I squeezed my eyes shut and braced myself for *you're under arrest.*

"They've found a body on the beach, and they think it's your husband."

"Oh, my god!" Ross blurted out, and the clerk, who had clearly been eavesdropping the whole time, leaned over their desk so far, I was surprised they didn't fall over. Maud put a hand on Marian's shoulder.

Meanwhile, the bones in my hand were almost a pulp, Marian was squeezing so hard.

All she said was, "Oh."

"Officer," Ross said, still rattled, but now in "I've been trained in active shooter drills so I am great in a crisis" teacher mode, "can I go get her some water? Or something stronger? I think she's in shock—I've known her for five years and I can tell."

Either Marian really *was* in shock, or she was doing a good enough job to fool Ross, who never missed a trick. Or Ross was just that loyal to her bandmate.

Whatever her motivation, I wasn't saying shit.

The officer nodded, and Ross crossed the lobby in two strides to confer with the clerk, who immediately pulled out a bottle of Macallan from under the desk. "No glasses," Ross said to Mac when she got back. "Don't gulp, okay?"

Marian nodded, taking the tiniest of sips.

"I assume ye lassies have been online tonight?" the officer asked. God, he sounded like a Scottish person from a movie. I hadn't heard so many *lassies* and *lasses* our whole time here. Not that I was going to comment on it now.

"No. We've been, um…" Maud trailed off, and I tried my best not to change my facial expression, the position of my hands, anything. Shit. I likely had *guilty* written all over my body by now. Or at least *she knows something.*

"Exhausted," Maud finished. "We're here on tour and there was a big show earlier, the biggest of our career to date, and we are all quite exhausted." No more nail-chewing, and her voice was steady and calm. I noticed she hadn't said anything that would put me or Mac outside the hotel. Or about Josh, when I'd barely processed that news myself. "We're also still suffering from jet lag."

Even at our most turbulent, The Scottish Play looked out for one another.

"Ma'am," the officer said, now looking straight at Marian. "There's a video of ye husband that is, eh, *disturbing,* to say the least. There's also a woman posting on social media, asking for information." He reached for his phone, pulled something up, and handed the device to Marian. The four of us crowded around the tiny screen.

Larry M. Lurching around in ankle-deep water, his kilt flapping in the strong wind. Screaming about blood. Scrubbing his hands in the sea, over and over and over again.

Probably just before I got there.

It would almost be funny if he weren't so clearly unhinged.

"Wow," Marian murmured, beautiful face unreadable, and I steeled myself not to scream at her: *Did you see this? Did you film it? Share it? What the fuck is going on?*

About Larry M himself, though? I did my best to conjure up sympathy in that moment, taking into account not only what I'd witnessed at the cliffs and how I'd reacted, but also that my missing, presumed dead boyfriend had been located very much alive, and that for the first time since I was sixteen, I was using the word "boyfriend" in reference to my own relationship.

I still felt nothing.

CHAPTER THIRTY-THREE:

MARIAN

"Look like the innocent flower, But be the serpent under it." —
Macbeth, Act I, Scene V

I'VE always been a cold person. Standoffish, slow to warm up to people, even slower to trust them. My face is the epitome of the RBF. It's why people like Duff's Granny don't like me (to little old Southern ladies, warmth is a fucking birthright); it's why I didn't date much throughout high school—we were all self-proclaimed dorks, but they always pulled guys easier than I did. I'm not approachable. I don't like hugs—a fact that everyone knows and yet they're all constantly hugging me and touching me, as if saying "I know you aren't a hugger" before and after is enough to make trampling my boundaries okay). I'm not a big fan of flowery displays of love and affection, and most people's love languages seem fake to me.

Most *people* seem fake to me. A therapist would probably call that "projection."

I was like that even as a baby. Mama has always said I didn't have much need of her. I wasn't one of those babies who cried all night until she'd pad over to my crib with bleary eyes and spirit me off to her bed for co-sleep. I took care of my own needs, from my earliest memory of sitting alone in my crib, staring at the ugly pattern on our trailer's wallpaper, counting blue roses.

Sometimes Mama would tell me this as a point of pride, but most of the time she was leveling it at me like an accusation, when she'd throw some half-hearted attempt at support my way and I'd brush it off. "You were always so cold, since you were a baby," she'd say with a distasteful expression, and I'd usually counter with a reminder that she was a terrible mother. I'd recently read an article talking about that very thing: babies who are calm and fail to bond with their caregivers learn in very early infancy that they can't rely on the caregiver to give them what they need, so they just sort of...stop expecting it.

Imagine being such a shit parent that your *newborn* has no expectations.

I've always been happy to cultivate the "cold as ice" image for people. They're going to think whatever they think of me, anyway. After so many times, you get tired of meeting basic ass vanilla bitches who look at you from beneath their perfectly shaped eyebrows and say things like, "I thought you were a bitch when I first met you. You just looked so *mean*." You lose interest in reassuring someone who can say something so rude—and *I'm* supposed to be the standoffish one?—and you start just leaning into it. Maybe I *am* a fucking bitch, Becky. Maybe I just am.

I tried to change for Lawrence MacLaren. For the first and only time in my life, I really tried to become something different, better. And I *wanted* to. For him.

I took off all my armor, the septum piercing and the ear cuffs and the bright neon face paint I used to make myself look harsh and wild and abstract. I softened my hair style. I feminized my clothes, putting away all the leather and ripped denim and the scuffed, masculine shoes. I made myself pretty, sweet.

Duff, Ross, and Quincy thought I was acquiescing to some swinging dick's controlling idea of what a woman should be, but the truth is, the idea was all mine. Lawrence held me accountable to it, because that's the type of person *he* was: used to getting things done, to being responsible for those weaker than him. He happily fell into the role, and I just let him. Encouraged it. In the bedroom, I demanded it. For the first time, I felt comfortable, safe. Taken care of by someone who cared how many calories were in my goddamn bagel, who cared that I was a sugar addict. Who wanted to see the beautiful, delicate face beneath the layers of blush and thick, black crayon eyeliner.

Lawrence wanted to see the *real* me. The me only Mama knows; the real reason she holes up in her bedroom crying, wishing Deddy would come back and save her; the real reason she avoided me so much as a child. The me who scares her.

Lawrence wanted the real me. So I gave it to him.

Unfortunately, he didn't know what he was asking for.

I can't tell you how long I stood there in the sand, my shoes pinching my feet, the grains of sand impossibly wedging their way through the leather and laces, down into my socks. As I watched Lawrence on the rocks, I wiggled my toes up and down, trying to dislodge the sharp grains.

My husband was clearly having a nervous breakdown, but what was I supposed to do? I'd tried to reassure him and it hadn't worked. I was helpless to assist. What else did he want from me? A fucking hug?

For months now, I'd been in his arms every night, achieving a physical closeness I'd never felt with anyone else. We'd gotten handfasted! I'd hired him as my manager! I was his, wholly his, he had *me,* so why was he falling apart? It was hard not to take it personally. How now, at zero hour, right as we were finally getting everything we'd ever dreamed of, after all we'd sacrificed, he was crapping out at the finish line.

How dare he!

After watching Lawrence for a time, I became aware of someone else on the beach a few yards down from me. Just some random man walking his dog; a beagle, from the looks of it. The man's pants were rolled up messily to the shins, and he was bald. The famous T.S. Eliot poem immediately came to mind, something about, "I grow old, I grow old, I shall wear the bottom of my trousers rolled...my hair is growing thin!" I giggled despite myself, and the man looked up sharply, noticing me standing there. I gave him a little wave, hoping he'd move on down the beach to dumbly collect his shells or whatever he was doing—but then he'd noticed Lawrence.

I watched him as he watched Lawrence, his face turning from placid to curious, his brows furrowing in confusion as he saw what I saw. A kilted man, kneeling on a slippery rock, washing his bloody hands over and over in the salty spray, keening like a fucking baby. And me standing there, giggling like a loon.

I forgot to mention that part, didn't I? I wasn't *trying* to laugh; nothing about it was particularly funny, even. It just...came out.

I knew what the old man was going to do before he did it. I was not at all surprised when he reached into his jacket pocket and pulled out his smartphone. I was not at all surprised when he started recording.

Part of me was *glad*. Good, let Lawrence be embarrassed when it went viral, and he looked like a fucking idiot, losing his goddamn marbles right in the North Sea. Let that be a lesson to him that any man of mine, to quote Queen Shania, had better have a strong fucking spine.

Now, there's a lyric. I made a mental note to write that down when I got home.

It was only after the old man stopped recording and sprinted down the beach, the phone now held up to his ear, that I realized I probably should have stopped him. Thought of the repercussions of what he'd just documented and where it might end up. Thought of who he might be calling.

Like a lot of things, I realized just a little too late.

Lawrence finally came off the rocks. I did what I could to get him away from them, to make sure he didn't go back, lest someone come looking for him. I led him up the trail to the cliffs to show him the gorgeous view. The coast of Scotland, his ancestral homeland, the place he'd been wanting to go since he was a little boy. All his dreams realized.

After a moment, he smiled. He let go of the breath he'd been holding. I put an arm around my suddenly fragile husband, my handsome auburn-haired darling with ice-blue eyes and the killer smile. And I whispered that I forgave him for everything. And I meant it.

"I hope you forgive me, too," I'd whispered as I pulled him down onto the damp Scottish ground.

"Nothing to forgive you for," he said back in such a painfully sweet voice that I almost cried, and he'd thrust into me then and we'd made love right there on the edge of a cliff, like it was the edge of the world. The sky above us going from light to dark, dusk deepening as we clung to each other, our sweat mingling, our moans carried away by the wind.

For that brief moment, it was *us* again.

I lay beneath him, enjoying his warmth in the dreary coldness. Sighed as he closed his lips over my earlobe, speaking in hushed tones, his voice nearly carried away by the wind. But I heard him loud and clear. I turned to him and nodded.

Ever the gentleman, he'd helped me to my feet after, noting my pinching, horrible shoes, and offered me his arm. I took it, remembering the dozens of times I'd taken it before, how good and right it felt to be here, how much I loved his old-school romantic notions, no matter how Ross Smith might sneer at it. We smiled at each other, the first hint of stars beginning to twinkle over our heads. It felt like things might be okay.

That's when I saw them.

The sight frightened me so badly, I almost pitched forward and fell right over the edge of the cliff, clinging to Lawrence's arm so hard I'm surprised he didn't wince. I stared, sputtering, unable to speak.

Ian and Quincy, standing there. Both still as statues, shrouded in the darkness, their eyes the only thing that burned in their pale faces.

Devoid of any kind of feeling.

Watching me. Bearing witness.

Lawrence didn't see them. He was too busy smiling at me, his face tender now, the madness from before forgotten. He reached out to touch a finger to my face, and I reared back, feeling a slick wetness on my cheek. He looked at me, then his hand, with surprise. A wound on his palm had reopened, and he had marked me.

Marked me with his—their—blood.

They still stood there, silently watching, and in the quiet darkness of the night, the only other sound the wind whipping Lawrence's kilt, I began to hear the buzzing. The buzzing of a hundred—no, a thousand—flies.

Quincy's once pink-and-blonde hair was dark; every single beautiful strand crawling with flies. They ran over her face; one crawled up her nose, another into her mouth, but still she did not move. I stifled a scream.

Ian Duncan's hand reached out and beckoned, outstretched, the same way I'd beckoned at Lawrence just before. Ian's eyes burned red in the darkness, his lips pursed in an expression of fury I'd never seen on his gentle face in life, his once-tan arm pale. His hand shook in the air, furious, demanding. In my head I could hear his voice, crackling with fire and a hatred I didn't recognize.

You took a life. You must give one back.

Lawrence looked at me, his eyes soft and imploring. His neck, beneath my hand, pulsed with vitality, his pulse quickened and strong and steady.

You took a life. You must give one back.

Yeah, well, love you Ian, but it won't be mine. Not when it's finally starting.

Someone would be here soon. They'd find… Well, it was no matter now, it couldn't be helped. I should hurry.

Lawrence's eyes searched mine, always searching. All he ever wanted was love, that guy. He wanted the storybook romance, the HEA, the kind of sweeping, romantic story with soulmates and fate and bright-hot fire that fades into best friendships, the kind of love that lasts decades, with grandkids and front porches and saccharine memories framed on the wall.

He wanted to know the real me, and to love her.

There's only one problem.

The real me is not loveable.

And Larry M found that out too late.

As I stared down at the broken body on the rocks, another snippet of the poem came to me. "Till human voices wake us, and we drown."

I felt a tear roll down my cheek and wiped it away, staring at the teardrop on my finger, slightly tinged pink with the blood from Lawrence's last caress. I smiled, touching the teardrop to my mouth, tasting the salt, and blew Lawrence MacLaren one last kiss. *Thank you.* In my own way, I meant it.

I craned my neck slowly, gingerly, afraid of seeing them, those ghosts—afraid of Ian's beckoning hand and Quincy's mouth full of flies. But as I finally swung my eyes over to that damned spot, all I saw was the lush dark grass, the sky full of stars. The wind flew around me, gentle on my skin, and beneath me, I heard Duff panting as she ran up the trail to join me at the cliff, frantic, and I heard the crash of the waves on the rocks, lapping in time, a melody as steady and heavy as the beat of a rock n' roll song.

CHAPTER THIRTY-FOUR

DUFF

"Partly, I like a bad reputation. But I also want the reputation of being a good person."—Joan Jett

MARIAN'S lips were on mine; what the fuck?

Rewind:

After the police officer departed, taking Marian's number and promising to call with updates, Ross and Maud had gone back up to their rooms. Marian and I were following them through the lobby, toward the ancient European elevator I secretly always worried would kill us all, but we were on the eighth floor so what could you do, when suddenly, she *ran*.

Yup. Just started running, clear out of the tiny B&B lobby and into the Scottish night.

I knew where she'd gone.

And I knew I had to follow her for the second time. Even though it was almost tomorrow.

Problem was, the girl ran damn fast. Mac always had, so much so that Pete tried to recruit her for track senior year—he ran in addition to playing soccer—when we were already deep in plans for The as-yet-unnamed Scottish Play. Maybe if Zak had asked her, she might have considered it (as if I didn't know about her monster-sized crush on him, despite claiming she hated him—Mac, thou doth protest too much). Marian, Quincy, and I had snorted and rolled our eyes at Pete and his earnest request. We could be such bitches.

Dammit, Mac. I hate running, and yet here I go. Following you once again.

As I ran, I pulled up my phone with so many unread messages. God, in the craziness of it all, I'd forgotten to text *my own boyfriend*. I didn't even know if he was reachable at this point or getting checked out in a hospital or whatever, but I figured I should text just in case.

So glad you're okay. I have to take care of something, but please call when you can. <3

Maybe I was a terrible girlfriend, but as soon as I sent the text, I forgot about it. I swiped out of WhatsApp and immediately pulled up Uber.

We hadn't been best friends for five-plus years for nothing.

Sure enough, when I got to the cliffs ready to pull off my own hoodie in case she was cold, I saw Mac. Hoodie pulled up over her new highlights, rocking the baggy jeans she was wearing the first day I met her and looking, from the back at least, just like her mom, only with dark hair. For a moment, I'd thought of hiding myself in the branches and leaves around me, approaching her on the sly and taking her by surprise so she wouldn't be able to avoid me. But there it was: that best friend intuition. She knew I was there. I took a deep breath.

"Mac."

"Duff," she replied without turning around.

"What's up?" My voice, as casually as I tried to make it sound, shook.

"The sky." Now she turned around and I swear her eyes looked completely black. Involuntarily, I took a step back and stumbled on an errant rock.

Marian rushed over to me, and suddenly she was Mac from high school, Mac from Athens, my best friend Mac all over again. "Oh my god, are you okay?"

"Yeah," I said, straightening up and smiling slightly. A wave of relief rushed through me because she sounded normal again, but something else was creeping in as well. Looking back, I think it was adrenaline.

And fear.

"You didn't answer my question," I said, now that we were face to face. "What's going on, honey? You just got some crushing news, and I wanted to check on you." I tried to make my voice as gentle as possible, but my growing realizations about the woman I'd called my best friend for five years were leaving me more and more scared.

I now knew what Marian Shepherd was capable of.

And I was wondering, more and more, exactly how much Larry M had to do with it.

"You followed me?" The hard edge was back and now *she* retreated from me. No tripping this time.

"We're all worried," I said, trying not to match that edge. She was going through a major loss, after all. I hadn't seen what had happened between them, but the end result was that Larry M was dead. I couldn't think of my reaction, how I could have saved him. No matter what kind of a person she was, I had to help my friend. "Me and Ross and Maud. We care about you."

"You care about me now that Larry's gone," Mac replied flatly. "And *you* aren't innocent in all this."

I shut my eyes. She was right. I opened them again, and she was in front of me, close enough to kiss.

And that's just what she did.

"What the fuck!" I screamed as I ran toward the cliff, the sea rushing below me. I knew it wasn't the wisest move, but whatever I was expecting? It wasn't *that*.

"Duff." Now she was talking down to me, and I knew if she weren't so short, she'd be looking down her delicate little nose. Her eyes were still black as the night. "We all know you're in love with me." She slid her hands in her back pockets and jutted one hip to the side, striking a pose. I could practically hear my own adrenaline at this point, rushing through my ears like the waves below. "Might as well make it official now that I'm single, right?"

And I couldn't help it. I laughed.

"That is such bullshit," I said levelly, just loud enough for her to hear. "I have never *ever* been in love with you, Marian. If I was in love with anyone in our band, it would have been Quin. Maybe that's why I took her death as hard as I did. Speaking of, *you* got over that pretty quickly."

I had no idea I felt that way until those words came out of my mouth, but then I realized how true it was. I kept on. "You and your boy toy were pushing for a replacement when Quin, *our best friend*, was barely in the ground and Ross and I were still in shock from losing her *and* Ian. I know people grieve differently, but I also know our friend's overdose didn't seem to affect you, like, at all."

And then it occurred to me. No. No. No. It couldn't be true, and yet my mouth seemed to know what my brain—and heart—were still processing.

Yet in some way, I'd been aware all along.

"You knew, didn't you?" She could push me off right over the edge now and I'd meet the same fate as poor Larry and I'd never see Josh or Maud or Ross or Granny again. I was completely aware of this. And yet here I was, pointing the finger at Marian Shepherd.

She snorted, rolled her eyes. But I wasn't the sister of a master poker player for nothing. I knew Marian Shepherd's tells.

"You knew," I repeated, nodding. *Now* I was feeling something, or rather all the things: a reprise of my Quin grief, a healthy dose of anger, and that creeping fear. Still, I had to know what really happened. I owed it to that beautiful, vibrant blonde who had probably been my true best friend all along. "Quin's overdose wasn't an accident, was it?"

"It was him!" Mac strode over to me and I immediately stepped out of pushing distance. But instead, Marian pointed down at the rocks, like she was issuing a proclamation. Was it just me, or were the waves getting louder? "*He's* the one who got the Rohypnol, the heroin."

"And you didn't stop him," I countered. Mac's face squinched up, trying to conjure tears, and now it was my turn to roll my eyes. "Don't do that shit. Not with me." Her face un-squinched just as quickly. "Not only did you not stop him, you encouraged it," I said, my certainty growing with every syllable that came out of my mouth. "You wanted to be frontwoman, and Quin was everything you weren't. Not only that, but she was at the end of her rope with *Larry*" —I spat out his bastardized name, expecting Marian's hackles to rise, but she just stared at me, cool as a cucumber— "and you know what, Mac? I don't care how you dress yourself up or scream into the microphone. Quin was a better frontwoman than you ever will be. She fucking had *heart*. And you have none."

Marian said nothing to this, only looked at me quizzically for a moment, before cocking her head and asking, "Did Ross tell you?"

My mouth dropped open. "*What?*"

And then I saw it in the moonlight, dangling from Marian's ever-present bracelet.

The charm from Ian Duncan's necklace. So it wasn't jet lag after all.

Marian saw where I was looking and *smirked*.

"Why?" is all I could muster. "Ian was our friend. He was *family*. He was helping us."

"Not fast enough," she said coolly. "He kept putting us off when Lawrence and I tried to talk to him. We planned on breaking in to scare him, that's all. Maybe dust things up some, intimidate him enough so he'd skip town. I don't know."

She looked down at her bracelet again, shaking all the charms. The guitar from Annie. The little macaroni noodle from my granny. The half of the Best Friends heart *I'd* given her in a fit of old-school nostalgia, that we'd giggled about for most of my eighteenth birthday. All sharing space with the ill-gotten talisman of one of the kindest people I'd ever known.

Was anything about our friendship real? Was anything about

Marian Shepherd even real? And was I next?

If I was going to die right here, right now, I at least had to know the truth.

"So what happened?" I struggled to breathe. In, out. Like my mom and I had done at that abortion clinic so long ago, before I ever knew the name Marian Shepherd.

Marian shrugged, looked down at her shoes. For all her posturing, I could tell what she was about to say still ate at her. "It really was a heart attack. No drugs or violence or anything. Unexpected."

"But Larry still set it off," I said. "He literally scared Ian Duncan to death." I swallowed hard.

"No." Now she sank down on one of the rocks, looking like a moonlit painting of the saddest girl alive. "It wasn't seeing Lawrence that set off Ian's heart attack. It was seeing *me.*"

My blood ran to ice. Marian had been there. I managed to whisper, "You took a father away from his child."

"I'm sorry," Marian said, her voice flat and soulless.

"Not sorry enough not to fuck with Quincy," I muttered. Of course Mac heard me, and her eyes narrowed, devoid of all color once again. Still, I had to press on. "Why, Mac? Was she asking too many questions?"

Mac laughed, dry and cold. "You watch too much *Dateline,* Duff. No, she wasn't 'asking too many questions.' Lawrence wanted me to be the lead singer, the face of the band. It was his idea."

"Sooooo, instead of kicking her out of the band or going solo like a non-psychotic person, y'all drugged her to death while she was still in mourning," I finished. "Broke her parents' hearts, knowing full well their family history. Just to twist the metaphorical knife."

"What can I say?" She laughed again. "Larry always was a poetic soul."

Larry. She called him Larry.

I was frozen to the spot. Why *wasn't* I running? She wasn't advancing on me, or brandishing a weapon, or being particularly threatening in any way. And yet, I could see the truth in front of me.

Marian Shepherd was dangerous. Always had been. Always would be.

And even if it killed me, I wanted her to know that *I* knew that.

"Mac," I said slowly, knowing that if I got out of here alive, these might be the last words I ever spoke to her, the girl who'd brought me here, the girl who since senior year of high school, had been everything to me. "Even if killing Quin was Lawrence's idea"—I didn't want to further incite her by calling him *Larry,* even though now she was, apparently—" you could have at least warned her. Even fucking *school shooters* do that. You could have told him not to get the drugs. He *listened* to you. And you know as well as I do, she would have been fine just drumming."

She never craved the spotlight like you did, Marian. Not enough to kill for it.

But I knew by now what not to say out loud.

I didn't know if I believed her, really. If Larry really had just intended to scare Ian, to intimidate him. Worse, if the plan to eliminate Quincy *had* been all Larry's idea. I remembered senior English class, our unit on the "unreliable narrator."

Could never have predicted I'd have one so close to me.

Wait, was Annie Shepherd even an alcoholic? Or was that a lie, too?

And it was then that Mac lunged at me.

Like a tiger, a tiny predator in baggy denim, fueled by ambition and moonlight and a body rotting on the rocks below. That fast. That lethal.

"No one of woman born can stop me!" she screamed.

Was she *serious?* I would have laughed if I hadn't completely lost my breath from sheer terror.

I still don't know what exactly got me out of there. I'm slow by nature. A plodding walker who doesn't pick up her feet or wear shoes that travel well. Someone who almost failed the mile in gym until—you guessed it—fast-ass Marian Elizabeth Shepherd slowed the fuck down to run with me until I was finished.

But that night in Angus, me and Quincy's knee-high Doc Marten boots (and I like to think, her spirit) got the fuck away, scrambling down the moonlit path before any more bodies could be counted.

However, I couldn't resist yelling over my shoulder, "I was a C-section baby, bitch!"

When I finally, mercifully, reached town—looking over my shoulder the whole way—I found the pub that had served us meat pies just a while earlier. It was last call: they were sweeping the floors and wiping counters, the smell of old beer permeating the air. The proprietress, a stout woman whose kind face reminded me of Granny's, took pity and let me stay inside with her and the servers until my Uber safely arrived to spirit me back to the B&B, where I went straight to my room and didn't come out until a few hours later, when it was time to return to the airport.

Mac wasn't there.

Ross and Maud noticed my pale face and rumpled clothes from the night before and my hastily packed luggage. I hadn't texted them, only Josh—now waiting for a flight back to Georgia—to say we were leaving and I'd see him soon and I loved him (eep), but I knew *they* knew, at least on some level. They said nothing, just stayed on either side of me, like they had the night before that now seemed like a hundred years ago. They also didn't comment on the absence of our bandmate as we left behind a foreign land and a whole world of questions.

We were in line to board when I got a text.

Tomorrow

The sign-off we'd had since high school.

Before promptly blocking Marian "Mac" Shepherd from every possible way she could contact me, I texted back one final time.

Goodbye.

ROSS SMITH

ANTIFREEZE.

That's how she was gonna do me in.

I never trusted Mac Shepherd.

Maybe everyone's saying that now, the way they do when a person is outed as a rapist or a general bad person, and then someone says they never liked them, and then everyone else chimes in with "well, that's neither here nor there," and this is why I hate social media. But really.

From day one when I met Marian Shepherd, then a little eighteen-year-old fresh out of the mountains, I worried she'd kill somebody one day. Or multiple somebodies. Just something in her eyes, the way they never quite lit up, just stayed blank. I'd seen that same expression in certain kids I taught. The ones I knew I'd never reach.

So why did I join The Scottish Play, you ask? Simple: they were good. Like, *really* good. When Ian told me about three girls who wanted to move to Athens and break into the music scene big time, I shrugged and said I'd meet them. The ink was barely dry on my degree and I was feeling open-minded, but I also knew they were five years younger and hadn't been playing very long and Ian Duncan was, as usual, doing a favor for an old friend. I figured I'd have some face time with these kids and then I'd go back to prepping for my new teaching job and playing open mics when I could before fully settling down into domestic life with James. (Ha.)

But when we played together, it was *magic.*

I didn't even know about The Hecks and the party prophecy until way later, when Josh and Duff became a thing. After we lost Ian and Quincy, I *did* wonder whether these girls were into some sort of witchcraft; they played that fucking well. With me, they played even better than fucking well. I've played multiple instruments since I was little, and I'd never gelled with a group like this.

And from the beginning, Quincy and Duff radiated this positive energy and light. They were badasses onstage and so sweet off. I got drunk with them once—well, Duff, of course Quincy just had Cokes—and decided I wanted to protect them.

Protect us all.

I can be harsh, I know. Part of it's from working with teenagers—you can't show one iota of weakness—and part of it is how I've always been. I don't talk much about my family, not even to the band who I was spending more and more of my time with outside of school, but I had to look out for number one from *day* one when my mama gave me bottles of Mountain Dew instead of formula.

My mama who I don't really talk to anymore…

She's a drunk. Like an *actual* drunk. That whole side of my family are drunks, to the point where if it weren't for my biological dad (who had another family) paying for private high school and then college, not to mention all the music lessons I wanted, I wouldn't have gotten anywhere in life. I sure as hell wouldn't have left Dahlonega.

Being around drunks my whole life means I can spot one a mile away. I only met Annie Shepherd in passing at gigs, but from those brief encounters, Annie Shepherd did *not* seem like a drunk to me. Just a sweet, lost soul who loved her daughter way more than her daughter loved her.

Why would Mac lie about that? I always wondered. Sure, everyone's experience is different. Poor Quincy's aunt and uncle had their own horrible downward spiral. But I've been to enough Alanon-type support groups over the years, in addition to my own experiences witnessing debauchery and downfall and promising to stop and then never really stopping, to know that there are patterns to alcoholism. And nothing Marian said ever sounded quite right.

The biggest sign of all, though? When you're descended from drunks, you don't talk about it. In meetings with like-minded people or with a therapist, sure. In my case, sometimes when I myself was drunk. (I'd learned long ago I didn't have the *need* my mama did, so I could indulge or not, though I was still careful not to reach for a bottle when I was sad or one too many kids mouthed off to me that day.) It's not casual conversation, ever.

Mac's stories about Annie, the supposed lifelong alcoholic, sounded more like someone who wanted sympathy and excuses for her own shitty actions, and who wanted to blame her mother for her own psychopathy.

That's right. I'm no doctor, but that bitch is a straight-up psychopath, and I'd wager she always has been.

I knew how Duff saw her, not just as a best friend, but a poor girl without many advantages, who Duff had to protect. Save. The way Duff perceived matters, Mac fell under the spell of big bad Larry M and once he was gone, because he would be, we'd all go back to normal.

This is what I mean by *nice*. With Duff's niceness comes naivete. Poor Quin always preferred Duff, that was obvious, but she'd known Marian the longest and history forgives all kinds of sins. Later, lovely Maud didn't know Mac, or any of us, well enough to point fingers.

And that's where I come in.

"I'm onto you," I said to Mac as she drove us home from the Bald, the night we laid Quin to rest as a band. After Duff stayed behind, Mac, seeing my shaking hands and anxious demeanor, had offered me a ride. I didn't love *that* idea, but in my keyed-up state, I knew it was for the best. There was no way I could navigate my way down the winding, bumpy mountain road in the pitch-black dark *and* have the conversation I needed to have.

I meant what I said as a joke. Or at least I wanted *her* to think that.

From behind the wheel, Mac looked over at me with one eyebrow raised. Cocky. "You're onto what, exactly?"

I smiled. I wasn't scared of her. Well, I *was* a bit, but I knew I had to tread carefully—working with teens also means you have to deal with powder kegs. Diffuse. Deescalate. But still make your point.

"Your whole deal," I said to her lightly. "With Larry M." Before she could divert me, I corrected myself. "*Lawrence*. He's trying to make you the star, and honestly, whatever. I'm not in this to be a frontwoman."

By this point, I knew she was watching me, even though we were still on the winding mountain road, and I prayed she wouldn't just drive us over the edge. I stared out the window and gave my best nonchalant shrug. "I love our band more than life, but I just don't trust you, Marian. Either of you. And you should know that."

She snorted a little. "So you know."

Here it came.

"Look, it was the best thing for Quincy," Marian said.

Wait. *What?*

My mind raced. I'd just been trying to give Mac a warning that I was keeping an eye on her and her idiot boyfriend so they wouldn't screw us over. What the hell did our lost bandmate have to do with anything?

"Quincy," I repeated, trying like hell to buy time as my mind raced.

"It's so sad." Now Mac's eyes were on the road, as we wound down, down, down, back to the real world. "You know, about her aunt and uncle. She hadn't been the same since senior year when we first started hanging out. Lawrence and I agreed that fame would have literally killed her. And then Ian died, and she was devastated all over again. Who *wouldn't* get into drugs after that?" She let out a little sigh, *and so it is.* "It was a kindness, Ross. We made sure she didn't have to deal anymore."

You know the phrase "my blood ran cold"? I'd always written that off as an AP English cliché. But my teeth started chattering.

I was trapped. And Mac knew it. Or did she? Yes, she had her eyes on the road, thank god. But the dreamy quality to her voice… She was in her own little world. I don't know if she even remembered I was still in the car. Why on earth had I allowed her to drive?

I stayed quiet, concentrated on the winding roads out the window. Reminded myself to take deep breaths. Didn't move a muscle.

Deescalate.

"As for Ian," Mac went on, taking a hairpin curve a little too fast for my taste. I gripped the armrest. "We just wanted to talk to him. We tried to crash his dinner with Crowe, but he wouldn't let us in. Said it was family time." She bit her lip. "I thought I *was* his family, and when you have a partner, they get absorbed into the family, right? Guess not."

This was reminding me of the James Bond movies my ex loved, where the villain strokes a white cat and recites all of his evildoings while Bond is restrained. I would have laughed if I weren't so fucking paralyzed with fear.

"We broke in later," Mac said. "Just to *talk*, you know? Lawrence said if we took him by surprise, it would be easier. We didn't mean for him to have a heart attack."

Now we were going even faster. I white-knuckled the door handle, praying to a god I didn't believe in that I would quit drinking, call my mama weekly, send even more money when I could, never let an unhinged bitch drive me around again...if I could just get off this goddamn mountain intact.

And Marian, bless her heart, kept going. "Ian was Lawrence's idea. Quincy, though, that was mine. Out of everyone, I've known her the longest."

If I get home alive, I will forget this conversation ever happened. I will say nothing. I promise. I couldn't even talk by this point, but I hoped against hope Marian would pick up on my silent plea.

"You get it, right, Ross?" We were on the highway now, and instead of going fast, she was at a perfectly normal speed, a little under the limit even. Cool as a cucumber, like those hairpin curves hadn't happened at all, *lalala.* "You and I, we're the same in a lot of ways. Probably why we butt heads." She laughed, and I forced myself to join in. A short, barked *ha!* I was still in a moving vehicle with her, after all. "We do what needs to be done."

What did I do about *this*? Call the police? Tell Duff?

But who would believe me? Marian was a hundred pounds soaking wet, and Lawrence liked to think he was Super Physically Intimidating Man, but he was more wiry than bulky. I mean, I could take him. No one would look at those two and say, "yeah, total serial killers." If the coroners couldn't find anything suspicious on Ian or Quincy the first time around, would they really change the autopsies because I'd had a *conversation?*

Plus…I knew, I just *knew*, if I said a word about any of this to anyone, I would pay the price.

I might already be paying.

"Ross."

We were in front of my house, the one I'd bought with James and he'd moved out of. The one where I now lived. All alone.

Because Marian knew where I lived.

"Ross, come on," Mac said, her face pale and bloodless. "I was just kidding."

I stared at her dumbly. I blinked. "Kidding?"

"Gallows humor, and all that." She smiled. I could swear her eyes were black.

"See you day after tomorrow at practice?" she asked cheerfully, like we'd been talking about the weather, or Jett vs. Currie for the thousandth time.

"Uh, yeah," I said, opening the door slowly instead of throwing it off its hinges, running up my sidewalk and locking myself inside forever, which is what I really wanted to do. But I couldn't let Marian Shepherd see me sweat. "Bright and early."

I gave that bitch a *hug*. To this day, I hate myself for that. For assuring her with the squeeze of my body that her awful secrets were "safe" with me. And I'm well aware of the "fawn" trauma response. I was grateful she hadn't killed me in the car, because she very well could have, and she didn't, and she wanted me to know that.

I hugged Marian Shepherd. Then I watched her leave, waving goodbye until her taillights disappeared around the corner.

I didn't sleep at all that night.

The next morning, I realized my phone was missing. I may hate social media, but like everyone nowadays, I always had my screens within reach. When I tell you I tore apart the house, that's not an exaggeration.

I realized I'd never see it again.

I did *not* record Marian's confession. I was too scared to move, and honestly, the thought didn't even occur to me. You'd think I'd never seen *20/20* when really, I watch every week. But apparently, she wasn't taking any chances. To this day, I don't know if it fell out of my pocket or if she used some weird sleight of hand. Besides, she said she was *kidding*. So how would her confession hold up, anyway?

When I got a new phone, all my previous data was erased. And at the next practice, Marian gave me this look like, *I know you'll never tell, bitch.*

Again, why didn't I leave? Why didn't I say something? I know people wonder, even when they don't ask.

Scotland. Increased visibility. I got to quit my job—and don't get me wrong; I adored teaching, but not all the bureaucracy bullshit that failed faculty and students alike that came with it. Truth be told, I became a teacher in a STEM field because it was stable, the opposite of what I'd had growing up with Mama. But music was my passion ever since I found a toy keyboard at my bio-dad's house when I was three years old and plunked out "Mary Had a Little Lamb" without even thinking about it, my body and the notes taking over.

The other reason was my bandmates, the ones who were still alive. If something happened to Duff or Maud? I'd never forgive myself.

Plus, there was always a possibility Marian *was* joking. That was the bitch of not having proof.

That didn't mean I wasn't on high alert. Probably why I found that scrap of paper in the hallway of our bed-and-breakfast that I might have stepped on otherwise. It bore the scribbly handwriting I recognized as Mac's.

Antifreeze.

Can't find in Angus.

And then, my name. Underlined.

I got real, *real* lucky.

Now, I *do* remember this from *20/20*. Antifreeze is easy to get, especially in places with a lot of agriculture, and it's sweet. To the point where if you put it into a sweet drink, the drinker won't taste it. And I'm a Southern gal who *loves* her sweet tea and co-cola. Sure, I watch when my alcoholic drinks get poured, because I'm a woman living in a world of Rohypnol, but not the refreshments we might pass around at practice.

Anyone born and raised in the South knows that you never let your pets wander into certain yards. We'd all lost a dog or three to antifreeze set out in a nice, inviting bowl by some asshole who hates animals. And people can also fall prey.

Antifreeze will fuck you up, but good. Even if you survive a poisoning, which most do not, it destroys your organs. We're talking brain damage. Permanent disabilities.

Mac Shepherd hated me that much. Along with anyone else who got in her way.

First Ian. Then Quincy. Then, as it happened, Lawrence—whose drug manual I saw one day and side-eyed, who I'd tread carefully around ever since, who I still didn't feel sorry for despite the way he died. Toxic is toxic.

And then? To paraphrase the Backstreet Boys, it was gonna be me. The Woman Who Knew Too Much.

After Marian disappeared, I decided not to tell anyone. What was the point?

When we got back to the States, though, I put my house on the market. Found a good deal on a condo in downtown Athens, surrounded by humanity. Five floors up, with a front deskperson on duty 24/7. Security cameras and multiple strong locks.

Just in case.

CHAPTER THIRTY-FIVE

MARIAN

"Fair is foul, and foul is fair
Hover through the fog and filthy air." —*Macbeth*, Act I, Scene I

I had to toss my phone in the sea. I'd carefully extracted the SIM card first and smashed it on the rocks under the heel of my boot. I listened to enough true crime podcasts to know to do that. Then it was bye-bye, iPhone.

Before tossing it, I logged into Twitter one last time and entered Lawrence's name into the search bar. To my horror, what I'd feared had come true: not only was the old man's video from the beach trending, but Becs Fucking Webster was using her professional work account (with her 350k followers and stupid fucking blue check) to basically live-tweet Lawrence's death. She definitely wasn't going to be writing up our killer show at Glamis, that was for sure. I had scrolled hastily through her account, seething all the way. Even her bio was cringeworthy. *Becs Webster. London, UK. Music Journalist, Producer, Promoter, and all-around Melody Maker. BLM. She/Her.*

Her bio might be cringe, but Becs' Twitter feed was no joke. Each Tweet in the thread, which so far contained over thirty Tweets, had dozens of replies each. All of them talking about Lawrence.

And talking about me.

"My dear friend, Lawrence MacLaren, who is visiting Angus with his wife and her band The Scottish Play, which he manages, has gone missing. Lawrence has been suffering from some mental health issues of late, and I'm concerned. If anyone has seen Lawrence MacLaren near the Angus area, please DM me."

What the fuck did *she* know about Lawrence's mental health? And she called him one of her "dear friends"; barf. She was vowing she wouldn't leave Angus to go back to London until he was found. Funny how they were soooo close, but he'd never mentioned her until Scotland. That was the least of it, though.

Becs had retweeted the video of Lawrence scrubbing his hands in the North Sea, the one taken by the old man, with the caption, *"Dear God. This is him. It was taken only hours ago. Someone please, please help. Has anyone seen my darling Lawrence? Please be okay, please be okay. XX"*

Personally, I thought she was laying it on a bit thick.

But those were nothing compared to the tweet after Lawrence's body was discovered.

"Thank you, everyone, for the support, help, and well wishes. I am devastated to report that my friend Lawrence MacLaren has been found deceased. Police are investigating and we ask for everyone's prayers at this time. I am gutted. I will likely be offline for some time."

So much for that. Becs was tweeting again less than two hours later. *"I'm hearing police suspect foul play. Marian Shepherd, Lawrence's wife, is also missing. Police would like to further question her about Lawrence's death. If anyone has seen her, please contact Scotland Yard or DM me directly and I will notify police."*

That one had a picture of me. Not my best, honestly. It was an old one, with the septum piercing and heavy eyeliner, and I looked drunk as hell. I bet Becs did that on purpose. And now I knew how Scotland Yard had known Lawrence was my husband.

The final tweet before I logged out: *"If someone hurt Lawrence MacLaren, we must help bring them to justice. PLEASE help us find Marian Shepherd. Only she knows what happened out on the rocks last night."*

That's when I destroyed and tossed the phone. Not so much out of self-preservation, but of sheer rage.

The audacity of that bitch.

I found what was probably the only working payphone in the entirety of Scotland, maybe the world. We certainly didn't have them back home anymore. What did they call them here? A callbox? Likely something stupid and overly twee. I was so sick of Scotland. So ready to get out.

My hands shook as I dialed the number, including the international codes I'd carefully written out on a slip of napkin before tossing the old brick.

Mama answered on the first weird ring. "Marian?" How did she know?

I didn't bother with greetings or formalities. "I need help getting out of here," I said, pressing the plastic phone receiver tightly into my cheek. My hands were curled into fists, my nails scratching rivets into my palms, mirroring the wounds on my husband's hands.

My *dead* husband.

"Out of Scotland?" she asked. Dumb. So dumb.

"Of course," I said, an edge in my voice. "Where else? I need money. A ticket. I need you to find a way to get me out of here. Maybe like...a train to England first, or maybe Ireland? Then a first-class flight?"

"Marian." Mama's voice was sad. "I've been waiting for your call. I'll help you get back, but...honey, there are conditions."

I almost hung up right there and then. But I was too desperate. And she knew it, damn her. "And what are those?"

"The folks on the news are saying you might have had something to do with that boy's death," she said, and I felt a chill go up my back. The news had reached the States? Fuck.

This was all down to Becs Webster and her meddling ass. So much for her and Lawrence being "just friends." I knew the fervor of a girl obsessed. I bet they *did* fuck.

He was *my* goddamn husband and here she was, acting like she was the caretaker of his memory, trying to play the grieving widow.

"*Did* you do something?" Mama asked. "Marian?"

I should have just let Becs have him before it all came to this. He'd been useless at the end, anyway.

I'd mocked Quincy so many times for how pathetic she was, simping over Ian Duncan. And I'd gone and let Lawrence MacLaren ruin everything. He'd been so confident, right up until the end, when he'd fucking cracked and ruined my life. It was his own stupid fault he was dead.

Mama was still talking. "I'll fly out, Marian. On one condition: that you'll turn yourself in. Ace and Teresa-Jo have both offered to pay for a good lawyer. You'll tell the police everything you know. We'll fix this. And we'll come home and start over."

I said nothing, gripping the receiver so tight it should have splintered. Of course Teresa-Jo had offered. Of course, she was knee-deep in with everyone who had ever fucked me over when she was supposed to be *my* friend.

"And Marian, when you get home...I want you to go into therapy. We both will. It'll be a new start for both of us." Mama's voice broke. "I hold myself responsible. I should have been there more when you were little. I looked past the signs. I just kept hoping..." She cleared her throat. Suddenly my mama was self-aware? Hell had apparently frozen over. "Together, we'll make it right. So, what do you say?"

I found my voice. "You want me to turn myself in. Meaning, you think I'm guilty."

Mama didn't answer this, only said, "It's for the best, Marian. We'll hire the best lawyer, and—"

I slammed the phone down in its cradle.

I stood there for a moment, my split hand aching, my head racing, and thought.

I wouldn't call Teresa-Jo. I knew she'd help me in a heartbeat, but Brian was good friends with Nate, Lawrence's brother, and she'd already been in contact with Mama. More than that, though, I knew Teresa-Jo would be expecting my call. Assuming I'd come to her first. She was such a good friend that honestly, she'd probably help me and keep it from Brian if I asked her to. She'd do anything I asked of her, anything.

But no. She'd crossed a boundary, violated my trust. And now she was talking to Mama, too. Let Teresa-Jo sit and wait for a call that would never come. TJ was dead to me.

I sighed and picked up the phone, dialing the other number scribbled on the napkin. I swallowed down my nausea as it rang, remembering high school when he'd leaned against my locker and told me so confidently that I might need him one day. I hated that he was right.

It rang eight times, and I was just getting ready to hang up when a familiar voice finally answered. "Hello?"

"Zak," I said, making my voice sound unbothered. "Hey, it's Mac. I need your help."

"I knew you would call," he said, his own voice calm and clear. I smiled. I always knew those boys liked me. Well, except for Heckin' Josh, who had always had eyes for Duff, and vice versa, something I'd never understood.

"I need your help," I repeated, twirling the cord around my finger. "With what?"

"I need to get out of here. But things are tricky. Work your magic or something...figure out a way to get me out without being seen." Zak was silent on the other end of the line, and my voice took on a desperate lilt as I pleaded with him. "They're trying to pin Lawrence's death on me... You know I could *never* do something like that, Zak. You *know* me."

"Interesting," he said, and I frowned. When he spoke again, his voice was apologetic. "Sorry, Marian. No can do. We've decided to stop all this...our practice. It brings us nothing but trouble. It hurts the people we love, and one of the tenets of our beliefs is 'do no harm,' you dig? Josh is over it, and honestly, Pete and I are, too. What you did to that guy, to the rest of them, just own up to it."

"I told you, I *didn't*—"

"Mac," he said in a sad voice. "Don't you know we've seen it all?"

I gripped the phone so tight it could have splintered in my hands.

"All," he repeated, his voice low and sensual in my ear. He was practically purring; I felt a thrumming in my belly against my will. "Even Ross."

"What about Ross?"

"We know you were planning to hurt her." Zak's calm, measured voice was like a knife in my ear. "Like you did the others."

"I don't know what you're talking about," I muttered.

"What's that joke? Denial isn't just a river in Egypt? God, Marian, I wish you would have joined up with us in high school. We saw what you were back then. We could have helped you fine-tune your gifts. We could have saved you from yourself." Zak's voice was sad. "The last fortune I can give you, Marian, the last piece of advice, which I hope you'll take this time, is to face the music. You'll feel better when you do."

"What the fuck kind of Dr. Phil shit is that?" I yelled into the phone. "You three little assholes have been torturing us since high school—you're the ones who told me all about the man who would bring everybody down, and now that he's dead and it's all crumbling at my feet you just say 'sorry, my bad'?"

"You misunderstood, Marian," Zak said quietly. "When we said *a man will bring you down,* we didn't mean the band. We meant *you.*" My heart leapt into my throat as he spoke. "Larry M's death will finally expose you for who you truly are. It's too late to stop it. You can run, but you can't hide. One way or another, today, tomorrow…it's over, Mac. Larry M *will* bring you down."

I slammed the phone down for the second time and punched the wall of the phone booth, tearing open the knuckles on my already injured hand.

Turn yourself in. Face the music, they said. No way in hell was I doing that.

I could never go home again.

And I sure as fuck couldn't stay here.

Not with the band turning on me—if they hadn't already, they would once they knew the truth. Not with Becs Webster spewing bullshit online. Not with the video circulating of Larry losing the plot and me standing in the background, laughing. The police might not have seen that video when they'd talked to me earlier, but now they knew I'd been there when Larry had died. They suspected *foul play.*

I began to giggle. Not a damn thing was funny, but I kept thinking of that stupid line in that stupid fucking play Lawrence had made me re-read. Bloody *Macbeth.*

Fair is foul and foul is fair.

Soon enough, everybody would know everything. Well, I damn sure wasn't going to stick around and wait for fair to catch up with foul.

The police would likely track the calls from the payphone, knowing I'd been nearby. I pulled up the hood of my black jacket so it covered my hair, wrapped my aching hand in the napkin with the scribbled numbers that had proved so useless, and rushed down the street as fast as my legs could carry me.

When it was safe, I'd acquire a burner or use another public phone. I had one more number to call. This one I hadn't had to write down—

I'd had it memorized since I was seven. Just in case I needed it one day. Just in case I had the courage to finally dial the damn number.

It was funny. For a deadbeat, Deddy hadn't moved in almost twenty years. Mama and I used to drive past his house from time to time, her hands gripping the steering wheel, head down, peering out from the bottom of the window as though she could will herself to him. Inside, always just inside.

Deddy's number was still the same, too. He'd never changed it. As though, for all these years, he'd *wanted* me to reach out to him.

One more call, then I'd disappear into the night forever.

They'd all better *hope* it was forever.

EPILOGUE

two months later

"What's done cannot be undone." —*Macbeth*, Act V, Scene I
"I feel like it's my job to carry the torch." —Joan Jett

"Y'ALL ready to rock?" I asked, practically licking the mic.

The crowd went apeshit; as apeshit as a country club wedding reception crowd can, anyway. Teresa-Jo, resplendent in a poofy white dress, twirled around like a cupcake in the very front, just like she did at our very first show way back when, when this band looked a whole lot different.

I was the sole survivor of the original Scottish Play.

I tried not to dwell on that.

TJ and I had gotten a lot closer since I'd returned to Athens and found a new place, as Crowe rented out the old house and all of its memories. I'd even surprised myself by helping with the wedding:

writing thank-you notes, confirming flower delivery and that kind of thing. I hadn't known TJ too well in high school and after, and now we were both realizing that was Marian's doing, like so many things. What my therapist called "triangulation:" a manipulation tactic of a recently departed probable narcissist. TJ also confessed to me that she always worried Marian only liked her for her money, her connections. I didn't have the heart to lie and reassure her otherwise.

But here we were at the wedding, TJ in her gorgeous gown, her now-husband Brian in a fitted tux, and me up on stage in a deconstructed red lace dress, in honor of the blessed day. Both survivors of Hurricane Mac. Both exactly where we needed to be.

"That's what we like to hear," Ross yelled from next to me, and the band immediately launched into Nanci Griffith's "Going Back to Georgia," which we'd prepared specifically at TJ's request for this show, our first of many (hopefully) back in Hiawassee. Okay, so I hadn't grown up here, but as far as I was concerned, I was a full-fledged Southern lady now, honey-tinged drawl with nerves of steel underneath, happy to make a pie *and* bury a body, or seven. Just like my granny, who was working in the back, making sure all the dishes were ready to go and everyone would leave with a full belly and a warm heart. TJ's dad had had to wrangle the country club chefs, but the proprietress of Devereaux BBQ made the best food. And we respected our elders 'round these parts.

Ross was in her element right now, acoustic guitar slung over her sequined evening gown. She loved Nanci's duet of this old fave with Counting Crows' Adam Duritz, one of Ross's personal heroes. After last weekend's gig at UGA, our new lead guitarist had shyly asked me if she could sing Adam's part. Of course, I said yes.

Everything was so much easier without Mac.

Two months later, I was still coming to terms with the hold she had on me all these years. And working, with the help of Dr. Jules, to shake it. And to *not* feel guilty for not feeling guilty.

Not so very long ago, even that simple cover of a Southern song—a gift to those who'd supported us from the beginning—would have been a battle of wills, of wits, uphill both ways in the deep snow, as the old people used to say in Grosse Pointe. For one thing, Ross had never even asked to sing a lead part. I never questioned it, figuring she was more comfortable kicking ass on rhythm guitar and keys, a steady presence whenever we needed her. Just like how I didn't speak up for Maud as much as I should have when Larry M rolled his eyes as she shared her bottomless wealth of knowledge: the way she showed people she cared. Just like how when Marian said plaid flannel shirts were her thing, I stopped wearing them altogether.

Now, my Black Watch plaid flannel shirt was rolled up at the wrists over my dress, exposing my sinewy forearms, so the cuffs wouldn't get caught in the strings of my bass. The shirt was Josh's. As Ross's and my voices blended in harmony, I spotted him in the crowd, Zak and Pete on either side, all bopping along and looking somehow *lighter* than they ever had since they put away the tarot cards and spell books. He winked. I blew him a quick kiss as I went into the instrumental.

Ever since I'd run into the Atlanta airport and into Josh's waiting arms, we'd been joined at the hip, except for when he had work and I had band practice, of course. He'd just gotten a promotion at the UGA library and was thinking about getting his advanced degree in Information Science. He was a hit with the band, and naturally, he and Maud got along like gangbusters, trying to outdo each other with the most random factoids while the rest of us just shook our heads and laughed. (Plus, Zak and Ross had hooked up more than once. They acted like the rest of us didn't know.)

Me? When I wasn't jamming with my girls, learning piano from Ross or rushing to a gig, I was sitting at Jittery Joe's or in what used to be Marian's room, writing new songs. Shortly before he died, Ian had mentioned a friend of his who was looking for new talent, *and* that songwriting could be pretty damn lucrative. I, and my trusty notebooks, were then brushed off by Larry and then... everything else happened. Once we landed back in Atlanta, safe and unharmed but nearly destroyed by what had happened around us, I decided to bite the damn bullet and give Academy Award-nominated songwriter-turned-producer Tina Marceline a call.

You only live once.

Turns out Larry M was wrong, and I *was* good after all. "Raw, but good," Tina said after I played a few originals for her. She'd gotten me a gig right away, penning for a new pop group out of Atlanta. I had to say, I loved songwriting so much. Almost as much as our new band name.

"Thank y'all so much for coming out tonight," I said after we finished the song and the applause went down. "We are—"

"Southern Ladies Under Turbulent Stress!" Ross, Maud, and I yelled in unison. (We usually preceded that with "SLUTS!" but out of respect for Teresa-Jo's 90-year-old abuela, decided to abstain this once.)

"And shout-out to our manager, the fabulous Crowe Germaine, for stepping up these past two months," I continued, pointing at Emory's newest first-year, who somehow booked us all over North Georgia while maintaining straight As on a full course load, after taking a semester off to mourn the dad they were resembling more and more every day. They were renting a room in TJ and Brian's house while scouting around for a place of their own. We'd be recording a brand-new album in Atlanta next month, and Crowe was also juggling offers of national tours and TV spots and about everything else—including messages from music journalist extraordinaire, Becs Webster, who wanted to pitch *Rolling Stone* a feature about our journey.

The three of us SLUTS, however, wanted to take it slow. Maud, Ross, and I were a little nervous about this sudden notoriety, of being the "cursed band" as the Internet denizens had dubbed us, of capitalizing too much on the wrong thing altogether. Hence, gigs at our favorite venues, shows for our oldest and biggest fans (complete with all the biscuits and nanner pudding you could eat), and figuring it all out from there. Oh, and a name that wasn't The Scottish Play.

Onstage, I continued. "No pressure, but there's merch in the back, including our new EP *Curse Free Since '23*, featuring the singles 'I Don't Know If You're My Boyfriend' and…" I had to stop and take a deep breath before I said the title. "'Ian and Quincy.'" The crowd hushed, an organic moment of silence. "Thank you. A portion of the proceeds will be donated to the newly formed Banks Foundation, which will work with rehab centers, nonprofits, and other organizations in North Georgia to provide better and more accessible resources to those struggling with addiction."

Blinking back tears, I smiled over at Quin's mom and dad, standing in the back with Granny and my parents and sisters, who were visiting for the weekend and who TJ also invited because "the more people who see me in this ten-thousand-dollar dress, the better!" Even Annie Shepherd had come with her fiancé, Ace, much to my surprise and delight, and I didn't fail to notice that she was drinking plain old Coca-Cola.

Out of the corner of my eye, I saw a tall man in a leather jacket, with curling auburn hair and bright blue eyes, and the hairs on my arms and the back of my neck went to immediate attention. *Larry M.* But another quick look proved me wrong: it was only Larry's brother Nate, who was a close friend of Brian's, and a nice guy. He nodded at me almost imperceptibly, looking away quickly, and I shook off the momentary panic.

I also hadn't failed to notice the fly buzzing around the groom's cake—devil's food, with a cherry glaze that reminded me a little too much of coagulated blood. But I'd shrugged that off, too, and told myself to stop seeing danger everywhere. Sometimes a fly was just a fly. And that cake had been damned delicious.

I still struggled sometimes. Still looked over my shoulder for impending danger. I think we all did, really, with that much loss in that little time. We didn't talk about it, but I knew processing our feelings with the help of professionals, individually, made us stronger as a collective. A three-piece band of fierce bitches with kind souls.

SLUTS forever.

I dreamed about Mac at least once a week. Not just the Mac who bum-rushed me on the cliff in Angus, eyes black after I finally challenged her. But the Mac who introduced herself my first day senior year, whose name I could see in lights, who helped me learn to play bass and bleach my hair and sing in harmony. Who'd helped make me the woman I was right now, grinning into the mic at a Georgia country club, and who, in my most vulnerable moments, I wished was still around.

Marian Shepherd, who wanted so badly to be Joan Jett and ended up more like Sid Vicious before disappearing off the face of the Earth.

The set kicked ass as we knew it would. After, I hopped off the stage, pulling Teresa-Jo into a gentle embrace until she practically strangled me in a hug. I shook hands with her dad and Brian, who resembled a teddy bear more and more each day. Then I felt a tap on my shoulder and turned around.

Josh.

"Hello, you," is all I could get out before his mouth was on mine. What could I say? We were still in the tongue-wrestling honeymoon stage. I hoped it would never end.

"Y'all!"

I reluctantly disentangled myself at the sound of a now naturally dark-haired Zak's voice, even thinner and higher than usual. He and Pete were standing next to us now, faces pale.

And I knew.

"Ross! Maud!" I called, and the two of them elbowed their way through the crowd, faces dropping from adrenaline-fueled, post-show face-popping smiles to expressions that were serious, scared. Like they knew, too. We formed a huddle with The Hecks, waiting for the ticking time bomb to emerge.

"Bouquet toss!" Teresa-Jo called, but suddenly her voice sounded very far away.

Zak turned his phone so we could all see, and for me at least, the happy burble of background noise quieted to a dull roar, then a frantic whine. Josh's arms were still around my waist, but they tightened, like he was holding on for dear life.

On Zak's home screen, there was a text. We didn't recognize the number, but the sender's identity was as clear as the starry night outside the country club.

Marian Shepherd.

Miss me yet?

The flowers, blood-red roses, soared above us.

ACKNOWLEDGEMENTS

LILLAH:

First and foremost, my deepest thanks to my co-author, Lauren Emily Whalen. For well over a decade now we've been gabbing about everything from *The Nutcracker* and *Sex and the City* to true crime, trash-talking bad TV, sharing fudge and frosting recipes, and pictures of our favorite outfits. Over the years you've become one of my favorite people, a true friend, and I'm so glad we decided to embark on this journey together. Catch you in the voice chat!

I'd also like to thank my dear friend and "constant reader" Elizabeth "Beth" Tankard, who is always willing to volunteer as a sounding board, beta reader and promotional cheerleader, and whose heart is half-spooky, half-rainbows, just like mine. I'm so grateful for you and your support!

Thanks to Jennia Herold D'Lima, who is also mentioned below, but deserves a special shout-out for always advocating for me and my work. Jennia, to date, has edited all of my novels save one, and a better editor and friend I could not ask for. Plus, she loves goth and grunge nostalgia as much as I do!

To Jessica Johnson ("Marge"), Amelia Ross, and Ellen Burke, the best coven of besties a woman could ever ask for: thank you for your friendship. Thanks to Jennifer Babineau, Jordan Rothacker, Jennifer Fisher, Alyssa Palombo, Emily J. Edwards, Daryn Cash, Tracy Adkins, Nicole Hensley, Jessica Brooks, Aleta Mendenhall-Turner, Rae Standridge, Avid Bookshop, and the Athens-Clarke County, Watkinsville and Madison County Libraries. I'd also like to thank my parents, John and Teresa Lawson-Drake, who fostered my love of music (especially my love of St. Joan) at a *very* early age, my aunt Kelley Lawson and Nonna Anita Licata Lawson, and finally, to my husband Blake and son Cal, who fill the house with their music all hours of the day.

LAUREN:

Lillah, we fucking did it! Thank you for rambling voice memos about everything from fictional band names to *And Just Like That*, podcast recommendations about troubled souls, and a thousand years' worth of moral support. I've never cowritten with anyone before, and with you I'll do it all over again (hint, hint)!

Sword & Silk team, thank you so much for welcoming me into your ranks with open arms—and for my first Publishers Marketplace blurb, which I may just frame and hang on my wall.

My groups of fellow scribes—Binders Full of Romance Writers, The Struggle Bus, and now, The Metawhores. Thank you for feedback and gigs and silly texts just when I need them. We'll always have Connecticut/New York/Paris/the World Wide Web!

Every friend who has supported, encouraged and listened, especially Beth Mamolella, Hannah Mary Simpson, and May Howard. Chicago Aerial Arts, thank you for providing a safe space for me to get out of my own head and make my Instagram a whole lot cooler.

My beautiful family of Whalens, Davises, Clancys and Botos, who added a special little person last year! Thank you for always cheering the loudest. Also, I'm totally the person who thanks her cat: Rosaline, my sweet void, I love you endlessly.

And finally, Rob Cameron, who gets his own paragraph this time. Thank you for twenty-three years of road trips, plus-ones, dogs and cats and TV shows, Pride parades and unending belief in me and my writing.

FROM US BOTH:

We would like to thank Mary Beth Dalto and Laynie Bynum for taking a chance on this dark, sexy little book, along with Jennia Herold D'Lima, Kristin Jacques, Celin Chen and the rest of the fantastic team at Sword & Silk Books! We couldn't have done this without you. Thank you to our friend Emily J. Edwards (and the Fuckbois of Lit podcast), and Katrina Escudero for believing in us and our stories.

Special thanks to The Grit (we still can't talk about it!), Tommy Valentine, Cate Short and the rest of the team at Historic Athens Porchfest, Timi Conley and the folks at The Wild Rumpus, The 40 Watt, Nuci's Space, Wuxtry Records, Shadebeast, Ann Woodruff and the team at Canopy Studio, Jittery Joe's, Hendershot's and SIPS (where

Lillah wrote much of her chapters while guzzling caffeine), the now-defunct Georgia Guidestones in Elberton (destroyed mere weeks after we wrote about it), the "awful waffle" aka Waffle House, and so many other Athens and North Georgia landmarks, organizations and businesses that inspired us and nurtured our characters. Thanks to Scotland, for y'know, being Scotland, and especially Glamis Castle (can you thank a castle?), home to queens, noblemen, and ghosties galore since the 1300s and before.

Our deepest gratitude to Willy Shakes: "This above all; to thine own self be true." Thanks to The Runaways, Jack White, and all the endlessly talented musicians who kept our momentum going; and last but not least, to our muse and shero, Joan Jett. May you continue to inspire girls to be their most badass selves for years to come.

ABOUT
LILLAH LAWSON

Lillah Lawson is the author of novels Monarchs Under the Sassafras Tree (2019); The Dead Rockstar Trilogy, including Dead Rockstar (2020) and The Wolfden (2021), with the final in the series, Driftwood Dreary forthcoming (January 2024); and upcoming novels So Long, Bobby (February 2023) and Tomorrow & Tomorrow with Lauren Emily Whalen (October 2023). Lillah enjoys writing across genres, including southern gothic, historical fiction, and horror, and her work is often set in her home state of Georgia. Lillah was a recipient of the UGA Willson Center/Flagpole Magazine's Micro-Fellowship for her short story Shoofly (2020). Her horror short The Lady and the Tall Man was published in the Shiver Anthology, edited by Nico Bell in 2021. Her story Burn the Witch appeared in Chromophobia, edited by Sara Tantlinger in 2022. Another story, Oblong Objects in the Mirror was published in the Aseptic and Faintly Sadistic Anthology by Cosmic Horror Monthly in May 2023. In addition to writing, Lillah is a genealogist pursuing her BA in History and English Literature, and proudly serves as secretary on her local library's Board of Trustees.

OTHER BOOKS BY LILLAH LAWSON:

Monarchs under the Sassafras Tree

So Long, Bobby

Dead Rockstar

The Wolfden

ABOUT
LAUREN EMILY WHALEN

Lauren Emily Whalen is the author of the novels TOMORROW AND TOMORROW (co-written with Lillah Lawson), TAKE HER DOWN, TWO WINTERS, and SATELLITE, and the nonfiction book DEALING WITH DRAMA. Her short stories appear in the anthologies LINK BY LINK, BEST WOMEN'S EROTICA VOL. 5 and BETWEEN THE COVERS. She has also written several books for Hachette's Running Press imprint, including I HEART JENNIFER COOLIDGE, QUEER EYE: YOU ARE FABULOUS, and SCREAMING GOAT HOLIDAY. Lauren is a regular contributor to GO Magazine, Q. Digital and BookPage, and has been published in Playboy, BUST and SELF magazines. She is a professional performer and very amateur aerialist who lives in Chicago with her black cat, Rosaline, and an apartment full of books. Learn more at laurenemilywrites.com.

OTHER BOOKS BY LILLAH LAWSON:

Take Her Down

Two Winters

Dealing With Drama

Satellite

You Are Fabulous: A Fill-In Book